The

Terrorist's

Grasp

By David Landt

Cover art by Cil Cheung

Cover art by Cil Cheung
Cover design by Shayne Lawrence, Catch This! Design

ISBN 978-0-6151-8773-0

This book is dedicated to my good friend, Lisa

Whose help and insight have been a part of this saga since its inception

Thank you

Preface to the third book in the series

For readers unfamiliar with Nicky Pops, as well as those who enjoyed the first two books of the *Terrorist's Saga*, this brief recap provides a summary of events leading up to the third book, a glimpse into the world of the September Alliance, and an introduction to its colorful cast of characters.

Nicholas 'Nicky' Papadopoulos belongs to an organization named "The September Alliance", a group similar to the real life Weather Underground. Their self-proclaimed mission is to end the influence and power of corporations in the empire of which North America is a part. To counter their activity, the empire deploys an elite police force, The Drummer Boys, commanded by Truman Hess. Nicky and other characters routinely refer to their agents as "The Specials".

Nicky's tale begins in *The Terrorist's Gambit,* which tells the story of his recruitment by Julie van Kessel, a.k.a Pixie. Julie, whose own story is told in the novella, *The Terrorist's Girl,* seduces a questionably stable Nicky into joining the September Alliance to serve under "Malcolm" and "Turk". After several missions, the Specials smash the cell and apprehend Malcolm and Julie. Nicky proceeds to rally the survivors behind a plan to force Julie's release by murderous extortion, making good on a promise to kill Specials every day until she is freed. One attempt ends in the death of Kathy Hess, Truman's wife.

As Nicky's attacks become more desperate, the other members of his squad, Boomer, Di, and Freddie, are neutralized in turn. Another, "Ice" turns traitor, betraying Nicky to nervous mobsters from whom the cell purchased explosives. One mobster is particularly ruthless, Donny Paglia.

In the end, Nicky sees on television that Julie has hung herself in her cell. His gambit has failed. Nicky is also faced with revelations that Julie had been far from faithful during their time together. Shortly thereafter, he flees to Greece with another terrorist, Cat, who becomes Nicky's romantic interest.

In *The Terrorist's Gamble,* Nicky and Cat return, this time to Los Angeles where they have a twofold mission. They take part in a September Alliance assault on Val-Mart, a megalithic retail giant. Simultaneously, they work to discover a traitor in the cell.

The Val-Mart mission is a spectacular success, thanks to Nicky and his new comrades, Deuce, Pyro, Maya, Gonzo, Zero, and Zsa Zsa. Deuce and Nicky wrongly conclude that Zero is the traitor but botch an attempt to kill him. Zsa Zsa sacrifices her life to save Nicky during a shootout with the Specials and Cat discovers, to her chagrin, that Piper, Zero's thirteen year old stepdaughter, is the real traitor. Piper exposes Cat to the Specials. Cat is surrounded, badly wounded, and captured. Nicky's daring plan to rescue Cat from her hospital room is successful. She goes underground to recover and Nicky flees Los Angeles with a new comrade, Lucky, a former prostitute who stands out because of thick knife scars on her face and arms.

It is at this point that Nicky's story begins anew, speeding across the Nevada Desert on a motorcycle after having received orders from his seldom seen superior, "Mitchell". With the saga background complete, the author proudly welcomes the reader to Nicky's third adventure, *The Terrorist's Grasp.*

Prelude

The business of revolution is never clean and I don't just mean that in a physical sense. The manual tasks of arson, bomb construction, and assassination might require you get your hands dirty, but the emotional and mental strain of taking life after human life also tarnishes.

For every bomb that explodes, you leave broken bodies in your wake. The lives taken leave behind widows, children, parents, and friends. Each bullet that finds its mark leaves a hundred unfinished stories in life. One death, but a dozen friends, girlfriends, boyfriends, co-workers, wives, husbands, daughters, cousins, and other relationships defined by a hundred names all end in mid tale, in an instant, never to finish. The picnic next week won't have the potato salad your victim planned to bring. An argument with a husband will never finish. The spat with a brother will never be reconciled. A child's life changes forever.

Everything in that stolen life stops in mid stride. Society doesn't feel the pain, but individuals do. We don't want to kill. Change is our goal, not death. To cause change, we cause fear.

Terrorism is a weapon that has changed society for the better. Before, when a CEO cooked the books, he could open his maw for more and laugh. Now, he might open his maw for more, but inside, he wonders if he might find men in ski masks waiting for him at home, or if the next limo the September Alliance blows up will be his. Before, justice was a joke, now it's a deadly possibility, and that means fear.

Will a CEO still lay off a thousand workers and give himself a raise larger than all their salaries combined while knowing the September Alliance is out there? Maybe he will, but then again, maybe not. Inch by inch we're gaining power through fear. Corporations can ignore a blogger's rant, but they can't ignore an ultimatum from the September Alliance, not anymore, not after Val-Mart.

As a member of the September Alliance I am the striking arm of justice in a corporate dominated world. Through my actions, violent as they might be, I make the world a better place. I am the enemy of Greed in its every guise. I am the vengeance of powerless people everywhere. I have killed hundreds of men and women, and I will kill more, because this revolution isn't about how or how many people will die, it's about how people will *live*.

I sacrificed a piece of my soul for the greater good of mankind, and it takes its toll. No matter how much grief I cause, I must be deaf. No matter how gruesome my work, I must be blind. I fight for a higher purpose than life. If I shrink from my tasks, evil will seize the world. I can't afford to cringe, and I can't afford illusions or delusions about who or what I am, what I do, or what still needs to be done, or my sacrifice will have been in vain.

Ladies and gentlemen, you know me by my *nom de guerre,* Nicky Pops.

I'm a terrorist.

The Terrorist's Grasp

Only a terrorist sleeps with one ear tuned to the ground, alert for sounds and tremors no civilian listens for, like too many feet coming too quickly up the steps, heavy boots trying to move silently. When you're a terrorist, you've lost the right to ignore that kind of thing, so when you hear those sounds, you snap awake and reach for your pistols.

Get up!" I told Julie with an elbow in her ribs for emphasis. "Something's wrong!"

Even in the dark I felt Julie's eyes open instantly under blonde bangs as adrenaline pushed into Julie's system before her cheek even left the pillow.

"Shit," she exclaimed, shock in her voice as she bolted upright in bed, going to her knees and clawing for a shirt.

I rolled out of bed wearing nothing but briefs, a crucifix, and a pistol in each hand. With a guarded step I crept to our bedroom door and poked my head into the front room, spying only our familiar worn sofa and wobbly coffee table. Behind me, Julie crawled to the edge of the bed on all fours and donned yesterday's mock rugby shirt. I heard her light feet hit the ground as the air took on the hostile scent of law enforcement. My muscles tensed in the curious mix of fear and elation only felt in the open defiance of authority.

In the quiet night, no light should bubble at the edges of drawn curtains, let alone have the rainbow tint of swirling color. My eyes narrowed as I waved with the barrel for Julie to be ready at the escape hatch, a bookshelf that hid a hole in the wall that opened into what had once been a service corridor, back when our converted apartment had been a hotel. Behind me, Julie's petite form tensed, tiny hands gripping the bookshelf, pretty bare legs ready to push it forwards with all her might. Her fiercely intelligent eyes waited for my signal.

The trembling on the old floor under my bare feet gave the attackers away before they rushed, but not by much. The old floorboards winced under the weight of too many heavy men in a small area moving too fast. The unavoidable tremors bought me just enough time to get the pistols up and pointed at the apartment door before a mighty crash splintered the portal into a million pieces, as if caved in by the bullet-like SWAT helmets emerging to the hoarse shouts of "Police! Police!"

"Go!" I shouted to Julie as light from the hall flooded the dim apartment. Three shiny helmets tried to push their way through the door as Julie's bookshelf crashed onto the floor.

With combat skills I didn't even have back then, my pistols barked before the stormtroopers could get a bead on me. They'd expected to take us by surprise, but instinct had intervened. One of the three helmets sprouted a hole, then collapsed. A shadow attached to another helmet cried something painful, but the third swung my way, rifle at the shoulder, a mounted halogen light and red laser beam cutting into our home.

On bare feet that got me out of the way just in time, I ducked, spotting Julie's bare bottom disappearing on all fours through the escape hatch just as bullets tore through the space I'd vacated and into our walls. Julie would get away if I could buy her ten seconds. She would flee down the service hatch, through the utility room, race three addresses along the common basement to an alley exit and then on to a safehouse. She needed ten seconds, then I could follow.

I rounded the corner fast enough to fire both guns at the doorway where more armored SWAT members emerged over the prone bodies of their comrades. Let them taste their own medicine for a change. They ducked for cover and wildly returned fire as I tried to spin away from the door.

A lucky shot from an assault rifle caught my right shoulder just before I cleared the cover of the doorjamb and my ballerina spin to the escape hatch turned into a wounded whirl that ended with me slumped against the wall. Stunned for a moment, I heard boots in the hall closing in and got the pistols up to cover the bedroom door, knowing even then that something was wrong, my right arm didn't respond right, floating instead of staying steady.

Red laser lances poked through the bedroom door, clearly visible in the floating gunsmoke and drywall dust. I grimaced and pretended I was a cop counting to three before aiming at the vacant doorway and thinking 'If it was me, I would rush... Now.' I fired, catching a black uniformed SWAT member just as he emerged. He staggered, then slumped. Something rolled from his hand. The cops shouted and dove for cover before a loud bang and flash filled the other room. A grenade had exploded in my family room, an explosive prelude to the end of my life.

"Ah shit," I cursed, trying to move.

Police curses accompanied mine as they regrouped. Figures tensed around the doorway. The pistol in my left hand came up, but the one in my right only floated aimlessly in the general direction of the door.

With a groan, I pushed halfway to my feet, using the wall to brace my back and coil for a lunge that never had time to materialize. In rushed the cops, four at once, firing blind. Glass and plaster exploded all around. The pistols went off in my hand as fast as I could pull the triggers but this time it wasn't enough. One cop spun away but the crisscross of lasers zigzagged, focused, then fired, bright muzzle flashes lighting the room like strobe lights. Bullets thudded painlessly into my chest and drove me back against the wall, making my knees buckle into a slump. From far away, I heard victorious cries of "Got him!" and "He's down!"

I'd bought Julie her ten seconds. I knew it even as I felt the world turn red, and defiantly lifted the pistols one last time before it turned dead black.

Only a sliver of light creased the darkness, a slim reminder that what I'd just half dreamed and half fantasized hadn't occurred at all. I lay awake on a motel bed on the outskirts of Salt Lake City, my heart beating hard, very much alive.

When the police came for Julie, I wasn't home. I'd gone to put my grandmother in a nursing home, then been waylaid by the local mafia to talk shop. All the while, police cars had surrounded our apartment. Julie might have resisted, or she might have been caught by surprise. I never knew what happened inside, but from a distance, arriving much too late to help, I'd seen the police escorting a handcuffed Julie away.

Memories of Julie crept back into my consciousness, maybe because Lucky, the naked woman on the bed beside me, looked so much like her, but more likely because I no longer had Cat to lean on. Cat had confined the ugly world of nightmares and grief to the periphery of my consciousness like shadows dancing outside the glow of a campfire.

Cat saved me from myself after Julie committed suicide and she now lay recovering from gunshot wounds in an unknown safehouse. I'd nearly lost her, but gambled on a one-man hospital raid and won. Others found the feat awe-inspiring, bravery bordering on lunacy. If they knew the demons Cat kept away, they would understand, yet there I lay in my underwear, wide awake next to a naked woman named Lucky, ironically sent by Cat.

If Cat thought Lucky's physical resemblance to Julie would banish my demons, then she'd gambled and lost. Lucky, though outwardly similar to Julie, was a completely different animal. Where Julie had been petite and cute, with soft good looks and a focused, compelling charisma, Lucky was a ferocious scarred beauty, as sinewy and tough as razor wire, fully able to use her body's well-honed appeal as a weapon. Julie could have hardened into Lucky, but Lucky could never soften into Julie.

With a sigh, I rolled from the bed and cracked the curtain. The dream had unsettled me, and I'd already been unsettled. The taste of old cigarettes in my mouth matched the sour press of my mood. I needed some old-fashioned comfort.

Without making a sound, I drew on my jeans and found the checkered flannel shirt I'd left on the floor. Putting my long hair up under a ball cap, I thought I had a decent chance of fitting into the general fashion trends of the Mountain Dominion. Salt Lake City seemed equally divided between bearded Mormons and casual rednecks. Since I wouldn't be passing for a Mormon, I imitated the latter.

I slipped out the door and strolled across the motel's gravel parking lot to a pay phone. Opening the sealed plastic binder, I thumbed through the yellow pages for the restaurant section, then located a short, very short, list of Greek restaurants. The biggest ad touted The Parthenon, located on a thoroughfare named Jameson Raids.

A short cruise on the motorcycle that had brought Lucky and me from Reno delivered me to The Parthenon, which, at two in the afternoon, was nearly deserted. A teenaged girl with a hunched back, limp, and hair in a bun identified herself as Lena then showed me to a table. Without thinking or looking at the menu, I ordered Athenian chicken and *loukaniko,* in Greek.

That kind of mistake can be costly in the revolution. It makes you stick out in people's minds. How many residents of isolated Salt Lake City would be able to order Greek food in Greek without so much as a glance at the menu? Back home in River Valley, no sweat, but in Salt Lake, three miles from Timbuktu, it would make Lena remember my face.

Lena, who looked Greek enough to have stepped off the boat yesterday, didn't seem to notice, merely asked in a very soft voice, in English, if I would need anything else before camel-walking back to the kitchen. The shy girl didn't seem to take any more notice when she set down half a loaf of sesame-crusted bread, a small plate of feta and olives, and a beaker of olive oil.

I settled in to wait, but after a moment of silence decided to pick up one of the free local newspapers at the front door. I selected the one that looked like it had the fewest ads for lawyers on the front and turned back to my seat when something caught my eye. There, pinned to a bulletin board, hung the weekly missalette for the Church of Saint Demetrios, a Greek name if ever I'd heard one. With a glance over my shoulder, I took the missalette down and tucked it into my pocket, then returned to the table.

The Pathenon's food turned out to be so-so. I could have done better, but the taste of lemon and oregano provided some of the comfort I needed. I ate every scrap, paid in cash, and bid Lena a good day just as a few customers came through the door.

I didn't need to look hard to find St. Demetrios. It turned out to be right in the neighborhood and I spied its rounded roof and sturdy Greek crosses over the bungalow rooftops. When I parked out front and walked up the steps, I took a moment to read, all in English, nothing in Greek, that Father Christakos shepherded his flock inside and offered services at regular intervals seven days a week but never in the afternoon.

Trying the door, I found it solid but unlocked, so stepped inside, basking in the altered light of stained glass and candles flickering from the vestibules. My nose caught the sharp aroma of spent incense. I'd never been religious, but after all I'd been through over the last two years, it felt good to bathe in the spiritual. My memories of Julie weren't a temporal issue. I needed a spiritual answer.

Taking a seat in the pews, surrounded by painted icons and relatively new gold paint and polished wood, I closed my eyes and purged my mind of the revolution. With each breath, I let the faces of the men and women I had murdered seep out into the holy air of the church, our closest representation of God's Kingdom on Earth. I let go the ghosts and guilt and found my head clear for the first time since Julie's suicide.

War had been with us through the ages. The ancients had fought the Persians and Turks to defend their lands. No one demonized them. In fact, they demonized those who had *not* fought. Thousands had fought and died for one political cause or another as lately as the time of the colonels. No one consigned their souls to Hell. Why should they judge me differently? Were the bombs I laid any different than the artillery they used? Did lack of a uniform make me any bit less of a soldier?

With both eyes turned up at the altar, I asked God if He would condemn me. I asked if He would call me wicked on Judgment Day.

To the best of my knowledge, I had taken the lives of nearly two hundred men and women in less than two years. By sitting in Saint Demetrios, symbolically before Him, I presented myself for judgment, for some sign that if I sinned, He could speak and I would listen. Of course I received no sign, but I thought, just for a moment, that I received a touch of His warmth.

When I rose from the pew, cleansed but still uncertain, I walked to the vestibule and made the sign of the cross before the glittering sea of votive candles. I'd purged myself of guilt, but not of Julie.

Taking a taper, I lit it from the thick candle, then touched it to one of the myriad tea lights, hoping that somehow, the tiny flame would carry my thoughts of her to wherever she rested.

In the quiet of the vestibule, I whispered, "Wherever you are, I want you to know that I forgive you for your betrayal as I forgive you your lies. Wherever you are, whatever you think, whatever you did, you are still loved."

With that, I extinguished the taper, and the memories of Julie. The business of the revolution was at hand. And bloody business it would be.

The following syndicated news article appeared worldwide one month before Nicky passed through Salt Lake City.

SEPTEMBER ALLIANCE CEASES FIRE

Once again shocking the world, the September Alliance has declared a ceasefire even before the ashes of their latest victim, Val-Mart, have cooled. With this move, the terrorist alliance has sent the experts, who had been predicting a bold expansion of Alliance activity, scrambling for explanations.

"It doesn't make sense," stated Professor Michael Howard of Oxford University. "Val-Mart was a huge win for the September Alliance. They should be capitalizing on this victory, using it to keep their momentum. Val-Mart did a lot of things the public didn't know about and it all came to light once the bombs started going off. A quarter of the population agreed with the September Alliance. We figured they would be after big pharma, big oil, or big agra next."

Indeed, companies throughout the empire have been taken by surprise. No one knows what went on in post Val-Mart boardrooms, but what had to hide in each and every mind was that if it could happen to Val-Mart, it could happen to them.

News of the ceasefire was warmly welcomed by Herman Sonnenblume, who, as a manager, was particularly relieved. His company, No-Tox Pharmaceuticals, had laid off its IT division, then rehired them as independent contractors without benefits. Said Sonnenblume, "This is the modern manager's nightmare, not a prolonged strike, but your company deciding to engage in exactly the kind of activity that gets September Alliance attention. You pray every night they don't do this kind of thing and then they do."

On the opposite end of the spectrum, Senior Chief Special Agent Truman Hess, head of the elite Ministry of Special Investigations' Anti-Terrorist Group known as the Drummer Boys, expressed no fear. "This ceasefire is an illusion," he informed the press today. "To have a ceasefire, both sides have to cease and we certainly won't curtail our investigations even if the terrorists decide to slow down or stop their bombing campaign. These are very dangerous people. They need to be tracked down. We're certain that by the end of next year, the September Alliance will be, as they say, kaput.*"*

Few companies will take solace in Hess' promises, citing the well-known fact that to date, very few terrorists have been apprehended, though many more have been killed. Val-Mart armed itself with state of the art security and received extensive protection from law enforcement yet suffered crippling damage all the same. If even such a rich, well protected company as Val-Mart could not prove intransigent in the face of September Alliance attacks, very few others could.

Why the September Alliance would cease fire at what is thought to be the peak of their power remains a mystery. Perhaps the empire is being given a chance to reform itself, or perhaps the organization has suffered more and deeper casualties than previously believed and needs time to regroup. No one knows for sure, but one thing we do know, is that the public has not heard the last of the September Alliance.

With the ceasefire, most of the men and women of the revolution went back underground faster than a coin into a bum's pocket. But as in any army, a ceasefire didn't mean all business ceased. For Lucky and myself, the revolution continued behind the scenes. We had orders from Mitchell, our superior.

We had a relatively simple task at first glance, find out who had been carrying out terror attacks against corporations using our symbols to mark their work. Our orders said to identify the perpetrators and make contact.

Lucky and I reviewed the attacks before we left Salt Lake City, and they all seemed well justified, well planned attacks against medium sized or peripheral targets.

Simple should not be confused with easy. The attacks took place in the two dominions where the revolution had the fewest resources, the Rocky Mountain and Great Plains Dominions. In total, we had just seven people divided into two squads for an area covering a third of the continent but with populations so small they usually listed as demographic footnotes. To make things even more difficult, only Denver had more than one comrade and it only had two, meaning we could expect only sporadic help at best and none of the attacks had taken place even close to Denver.

We had no names, no clues, nothing except a starting point named Larry Scheuer.

"He's a scumbag from what Mitchell implied," started Lucky at a rest area twenty clicks south of Great Falls. We'd taken a break from the highway to eat turkey sandwiches at a picnic table. "Scheuer is supposed to have been right up there with the supremos, was around when they founded the revolution. Just at some point he decided to quit. She thinks he'll help us anyway given the right incentive."

That explained a lot about our mission. The scars on Lucky's face normally twitched as she chewed, but this time they danced with her made up eyebrows. She didn't treasure her role in the incentive.

"Scheuer decided to be a blogger instead," she scoffed, "And ended up a drunk." Without asking, Lucky took my can of Dundalo Orange Soda and took a swig. Her red nails gleamed against the orange can. I wondered what the red signified. I knew by now she wore purple when she wanted me to see her as cute, and green for when she felt depressed or upset, but I hadn't seen her wear red.

Almost to herself, Lucky hummed bitter lyrics from a song I'd never heard. *He was a dirty old man and a horny old goat, He had a greasy right hand, wore a dirty overcoat.*

"Who's that by?" I asked, trying to keep my tone one of idle curiosity and not red flag alarm. To aid in that end I concentrated more on brushing classroom glue onto my fingers and palms, letting it harden into a fingerprint proof layer. Lucky was, by far, the most troubled soldier of the revolution I'd met to date and that included the ones who had committed suicide. It could be hard to put your life in the hands of someone like that.

"The Screaming Pervs," she answered, obviously thinking I would know them when I didn't.

Lucky seemed oblivious to the way I stared. Either that or she'd simply taken the look for lust and ignored it as a fact of life. The tight red t-shirt, jeans and red bandana in her hair were intentionally chosen to provoke a male reaction, but it didn't mean Lucky enjoyed watching it work. She polished off the last of her sandwich. I took a swig of orange soda and told myself Lucky amounted to more than a whore.

The key to understanding Lucky lay in her scars. With a thick lazy S on one cheek and an awkward lightning bolt on the other, you could almost forget the scars that laced her forearms, like she'd held them up to try and protect herself from some knife-wielding attacker. She had more scars, some even thicker. They laced her abdomen, ass, back, and thighs. Only her calves seemed to have been spared. Not now, but soon, I would ask Lucky about how she'd gotten those scars, and after she casually lied, when she told me the truth, I would understand her.

"Well let's hope Larry Scheuer lives up, or down, to our expectations," I told her in a patient tone. "So we can get on with our real mission."

The following APB went out over the airwaves in New Orleans just as Nicky passed through Great Falls. Obviously, it referred to a false sighting.

All units, all stations. Be advised to be on the lookout for September Alliance suspect Nicholas Papadopoulos last seen leaving Hefty's restaurant on Royale Avenue five hours ago. Suspect stands five feet ten inches tall, with brown hair to his shoulders, brown eyes, and is wearing a yellow sweatshirt with attached hood, red shorts and tennis shoes. Any officer sighting the suspect should call for backup as Papadopoulos is known to be armed at all times and has a history of violently resisting arrest. Use of deadly force is authorized upon sighting any weapon in the suspect's possession. Repeat. All units, all stations, be on the lookout for September Alliance suspect Nicholas…

L arry Scheuer lived in one of those houses you see getting towed around the freeway at a snail's pace with the 'wide load' sign on the back. You know the prefabricated houses they plop down onto a section of ground and then attach all the piping and connections to prepared fittings in the rear. Scheuer lived in one of those and had never painted over the factory finish or put out a welcome mat.

The glorified trailer sat in a clearing full of overgrown grass with just a trace of rusty barbed wire fence to mark the perimeter. Residing easily forty clicks from his nearest neighbor, Larry Scheuer intended to withdraw from the world, and he'd picked a good place. The heavy scrub and wild growth of bush and tree looked ready to devour his clearing the minute he so much as stepped out for milk.

Not even a dog greeted us as we tooled into what passed for Scheuer's front yard. The responsibility of caring for an animal would be too much for the owner of the portable hovel. An old wind chime clinked wearily in the afternoon breeze, the only decoration on the exterior besides a brittle Christmas wreath. I figured Scheuer had put it up the year before since most people didn't hang Halloween decorations in October. Strange to think he'd hung a Christmas wreath as I duked it out with the cops back in River Valley.

"Jesus Christ," murmured Lucky as I brought the bike to a halt. She slid off the back seat and lifted her sunglasses from her pert little nose. "We have come to the ends of the Earth."

"I think you're right," I nodded, noting the encroaching vegetable army laying siege to Scheuer's home. "Who would live here?"

"A better man than you," squawked a voice from behind us.

We turned to find ourselves looking at Larry Scheuer, just as he'd been described. He had light brown hair streaked with liberal amounts of grey that evaded a comb for weeks on end. Even covered by a faded, tilted ball cap his hair looked wild as a lion's mane. The unkempt hair and a long jaw made him look like a half breed dog, and only the round lenses of his wire-rimmed specs gave him the look of underused intelligence we'd been warned about.

To add to the impression of a renegade intellectual gone to seed and weed, Scheuer wore an oversized Hawaiian shirt that had seen better days. It draped over khaki shorts and he wore black nylon socks in red gym shoes. In short, he looked like the biggest slob I'd ever seen, and without the shotgun held at the ready, I would have been tempted to dunk his head in the toilet for a good flush.

"And who do you think we are?" I asked as if Scheuer might be the kind of guy that wouldn't know. It didn't take a genius to know that two strangers don't roar into your nest in the woods without some kind of reason. Unknown visitors would be presumed hostile because a man with no real friends doesn't get social calls. Larry Scheuer had severed most of his business with the outside world a long time ago. That left him expecting the mail, thieves and old business. Neither Lucky nor I looked like we'd deliver his mail.

"Like you don't know," spat the gnarled old man.

"Look at me, I'm stupid," I quipped back.

"More like too smart for your own good," he retorted without missing a beat. "But not smart enough to come on your own accord. Who sent you? Tess? Logan?" He waited a second for a reply, but then his face scrunched up, like he realized we might not know for certain just who *had* sent us. He leveled the shotgun, business end towards my chest. "Or do you even know?"

"Watch where you're pointing that thing," scolded Lucky, shying away from the gaping black muzzle. "Do you think if we'd been sent to kill you we'd come in broad daylight and drive up to your front door?"

Scheuer seemed to mull that idea around in his head like popcorn in the kettle before lowering the barrel slightly and fessing up, "No, probably not." He lifted the shotgun back and sighted down the barrel. "Even so, I have precious little reason to trust you."

"Well you at least know who we are," I gave up in return, not really caring that he'd guessed what we would have told him anyway. "And we're here to talk to you, nothing more."

Scheuer grunted like a pig. His wrinkled nose and curled lip clearly marked his disbelief. Somewhere underneath it all, below the ravages of anger and disgust, lurked the ghost of the professor he'd once been, but when he spoke, not a trace of that intellect tempered his voice. "Might as well come in then," he mumbled unhappily, then barked "But first you give up your hardware!"

With a shrug that tried to convey the act as meaningless, I drew open my coat and took the pistol from my belt, holding it by the barrel before setting it on an upside down flower pot. Lucky followed suit, though we still had to suffer the ignominy of a police level frisk. Lucky's suffered greater ignominy than me. She yiked loud, with a scowl on her face that told me when Scheuer frisked Lucky he'd probed a little more intimately than with me. Nevertheless, Scheuer didn't play games. Certain we were unarmed, he led us into his home.

Even over the short distance to the front door, Scheuer couldn't walk a straight line. He walked with a tired stoop, and his shoulders sagged with the cumulative fatigue of whiskey and sleepless nights, the reward of every bitter alcoholic. The pale flesh of his legs seemed slightly off color, like a yellow disease gnawed at his liver.

The inside of Larry Scheuer's house resembled a petrie dish more than a home, but instead of fungus it sprouted litter. Piles of clothes and newspapers grew like patches of mold in random piles. About the only thing that seemed to be neatly kept was a server rack and computer. Those two things would have looked at home in an office or a geek's home but Scheuer had discarded any care for his living arrangements. He'd long ago made the leap from ceramic dishes to paper plates and used them to decorate horizontal space. Empty liquor bottles told the rest of his story.

Scheuer ignored his own mess, even if Lucky wrinkled her nose.

"This place could use a woman's touch," she offered meekly.

"That it could," replied Scheuer with a cackle, sloughing onto a reclining chair next to the computer with the shotgun resting across his knees. He reached to one side for an open bag of potato chips. Without taking his eyes from us, he tilted his head back and shook chips into his gaping mouth. Chewing loudly, he set the bag back down on the floor as carefully as a surgeon lays out his scalpel. Scheuer's piggishly cunning eyes sized us up.

After a second, he muttered as he fixed on me, "Looks like you're about twenty-five give or take three years. You got brown hair and eyes, stand about average height." He half turned to the computer and jiggled the mouse without letting his hand stray too far from the shotgun trigger. Abruptly, the screen saver disappeared.

Scheuer clicked an icon, a program loaded, and he navigated through a few screens, then tapped keys with one hand while glancing at me every other second. A moment later, an unknown face outwardly similar to mine appeared on the screen.

"Look," I threw out as if for casual conversation, "I don't want to rush and get down to business or anything, but..."

"But you're taking up my time so we'll use it how I see fit." He clicked quickly through a parade of individual photos, all of vaguely similar young men, some in mugshots, some in graduation gowns, and some in various other settings. "That's what I used to tell my students when they came to my office. I used to tell them that they were taking up my time, so we would use it as I saw fit." He partly turned to Lucky. "Especially the pretty ones," he half scoffed and half sneered.

As quickly as my eyes could focus on faces on the screen, Scheuer clicked past. For a moment, I thought I recognized Boomer's face from back in River Valley, but before I could be certain, my own face appeared.

"Oh," Scheuer squinted at the type on the computer screen, sounding truly surprised. "They sent *you*."

Sometimes my reputation precedes me. My face covered half the screen with a data chart to the right and full paragraphs with a scroll bar beneath. With a click, Scheuer brought my face to full screen with superimposed text rolling top to bottom.

"Nicky Pops." Scheuer said with finality, but also an air of awe. "The psycho from River Valley…" He shook his head, then glanced at Lucky. "Let's see who you are, pretty lady."

I started to say something but Lucky shot me a look, and we waited in silence as Scheuer keyed in a few items of info with periodic and appreciative glances at Lucky, then started clicking through photos. Julie's face came up first and Scheuer paused, idly tracing the pointer of the mouse over her lips. I could sense the pervert's thoughts.

"I met her once," Scheuer mused. "Martin Cobb's girl." He scrolled down the superimposed data, eyes scanning as he read. "And your gal too," he conceded. "Quite the sharp cookie that one was. If the revolution had more like her I might have stayed in."

"She recruited me."

"I know," the momentarily sober old man droned with half his attention on the text. "Says it right here in fact." He scrolled lower. "How did such a bright girl manage to do something as dumb as that?"

I almost choked.

"What do you mean by that?" I asked, feeling a very unprofessional flare of temper that I couldn't quite keep out of my voice.

26

Scheuer looked back at me with wry distaste, apparently unconcerned.

"Didn't they bother to tell you why I quit the revolution?" he asked as if it were relevant.

"No," Lucky replied, taking a seat on the edge of a battered kitchen chair that had been left in the old man's sitting room. Something in the way she said it made me think she wanted to reply before I could. "Why don't you tell us?"

The former revolutionary turned to us. "I left because of people like you," he said, with a nod in my direction. "I left because there was a decision taken to let the revolution leave the hands of those who understood it and place it in the hands of people who didn't."

I blinked, in part at his gall, and in part because he genuinely seemed to know what he was talking about.

"After three years of using violence as a political tool, we realized it wasn't quite working," he explained. "We weren't making a big enough impact because we had a lot of thinkers and not enough truly violent people, too many generals and not enough soldiers. So we went recruiting.

"I was the only one who objected to that strategy," continued Scheuer, obviously suppressing pent up rage. "I argued that the only way to win the game was to stay true to our principles, even if it meant a longer war with a harder learning curve. We just weren't cut out to be terrorists, you know. Most of us worked in administration or education. Students formed our rank and file. Only a handful of us came from outside backgrounds. We didn't have the skills to be an effective guerrilla force.

"So we went recruiting, and we started with common criminals with a streak of Robin Hood, like your friend Turk. That helped us organize, but didn't solve the problem. We needed people who could really strike terror into the boardrooms, so we went recruiting again. This time, we went for people who could kill. One of the first people to be recruited was your old friend Ice. You know how well that worked out. We got more than we bargained for because just like we didn't have the combat skills to take on the companies, the people who did have those skills almost immediately started to rise in the ranks over those who had political sense. Look no further than your last two squads."

"How the Hell did you find all this out?" I asked Scheuer, kind of amazed. He had it all dead on. D Squad couldn't get more than two hits off per year before they recruited me. Julie even said so herself, they brought me on to make things happen faster. Malcolm, a.k.a Martin Cobb, really did try and keep the rest of us down. He tried to keep his students in control, but fought a losing battle. Violence had begun to yield results, and the people who could effectively produce results began to wield power inch by inch.

"I was *there*," stressed Scheuer. "I was there telling them not to go down this road. I mean recruiting guys like you has destroyed the revolution. Ever since you psychos started running the squads, and most of the squads are now run by people like you, like that little shrew of a Quebecois out in LA…"

"Deuce," I supplied.

"Yeah, Deuce," he agreed. "She took over out there and immediately people started dying. That's not the way this business needs to operate. It's about social change in a controlled and directed fashion, not a goddamned pyrotechnic joyride. All you guys do is kill people, and you're multiplying like fucking rabbits. People like Cobb are dwindling and that means the ideals of the revolution go to shit."

"Martin Cobb," I interjected forcefully, keeping righteous anger in check, "Betrayed his comrades to the Specials."

"So what?" came the unexpected response with a dismissive wave of his hand. "I knew Martin Cobb. He was a good man, a sharp and insightful leader. I'd trade a dozen of you for one of him. What matters is how he led, not how he behaved under torture."

I didn't bother to tell Scheuer that Malcolm, um Martin Cobb, had also betrayed people intellectually in tune with the revolution. He betrayed Di, Boomer, Cat, and Freddie just as quickly as he betrayed those of us Scheuer scorned. I let him rant rather than listen to another slight.

"There's fewer than two dozen people left in the revolution who have their heads pointed in the right direction. At the current rate, half will be dead or in jail within a year, and the other half the year after that. What happens next? The students don't take over from their professors. The hired guns take over. They can't recruit new students because they don't know what they're fighting for, so they take on criminals. Game over. Revolution over. Finished. Without the ideals of the teacher-student alliance you're just another criminal empire, run by the strongest."

"You really think that little of me?" I asked, wondering if it were true. In the name of the revolution I'd had a fingernail pulled from my finger. I'd been beaten until my ribs cracked. I'd lost loved ones. I'd frozen, sweated, hidden, grieved, and battled my way through almost two years of the Alliance gauntlet. Hearing it all reduced to so much stupidity didn't sit well and I needed to keep a rising tide of anger in check.

"Of course," Scheuer responded with disdain, turning to face me, quite serious in his righteousness. Lucky fidgeted and glanced nervously at me, like I might do something rash.

"Tell me," Scheuer teased like the playground bully, "What does Corporate Capitalism have in common with Mercantilism?"

I stared at him. I had no clue.

"OK then," he continued knowing I wouldn't know, "Tell me, where and how did Corporate Capitalism and Social Democracy diverge?"

Again, I had to stay silent, and felt my face flush with embarrassment.

"See what I mean?" Scheuer lifted his feet off the floor and spun back to the computer. With a couple stabs to the keyboard, he pulled up my picture, then scrolled down. "The Specials at least think you're rising in the ranks and they're probably right. If they weren't, you wouldn't be sitting in my living room."

"Enough already," pleaded Lucky. "This is going nowhere."

I disagreed. As much as I disliked hearing what Scheuer had to say, I thought it might benefit me to hear him out. By the same token, Lucky had a point as well. We had the business of the revolution at hand and we couldn't spend all afternoon listening to a yellow-skinned drunk rant about what should have been.

"All right then, pretty lady," spun Scheuer onto my junior comrade. "Since you seem to think there is something more important to discuss, and you you're not in the database, just what is the September Alliance offering me and for what?"

Lucky's voice dropped a husky octave. "You know exactly what we offer. And you have a good idea what we want in return."

If Lucky ever used that tone of voice on me, I would go limp. From her purse, she pulled a large, solid brick of pressed marijuana that had made the trip from Vegas in her backpack. She held enough grass to keep Scheuer stoned for a year, enough that Lucky handled it with two hands.

"Know anything about copycats?" she asked, sotto voce, one hand on her hip.

"The attacks around here?" Scheuer asked in a knowing tone, one eye on the brick of grass, the other eye focused on her. Lucky nodded.

"I knew it," the cranky old man huffed. "Those were way too precise for the crew that operates out this way, and too many in too short of a time for them to pull off unless they brought a pro in." He cast a disparaging glance my way. "So that's why they sent you," he grunted. "And here I thought you might whack me for being a security risk."

"Sorry to disappoint," I consoled sarcastically.

"Well, I don't know how much help I can be." He put his hand to his stubbled chin, got up, shuffled to an open cabinet in as much disarray as the rest of his place and took out a whiskey bottle. He took a sip, then a drink, and finally a gulp.

"I guess," he started, shotgun not forgotten, "these attacks all used C5. That's military grade, and the papers say it has a chemical signature inventoried in a local military base, which means they have a local source, and…" he paused. "there's only one local source for all practical purposes."

"Keep talking, I'll keep listening," I replied.

"The bikers," he added, taking another swig of the whiskey and eyeing Lucky. "A group called the Mongols are the one percenters out here. You know the saying that only one percent of bikers are outlaws, right?" I nodded. "Well it's really more like ten or twelve percent, but that aside, there's one group that dominates the illegal trade in weed and contraband. That's the Mongols."

"Any idea how we find them?"

Scheuer shook his head. "Finding them isn't the problem, meeting them is. They're not exactly a friendly group. Outsiders might find themselves in a little bit of trouble."

Lucky and I both groaned. Lucky stood up, reaching for the bag of weed.

"I told you he couldn't help," she lied in false exasperation.

"Wait!" called Scheuer in panic, his prize slipping away. "I don't know, but I know someone who probably does."

I lifted an eyebrow and gestured for Lucky to hang back.

"Goes by the name of Whirly, sometimes Whirly Bird," Scheuer explained. "He's like a sympathizer, but he's a Mongol. He deals me weed, always asks how many subscribers the blog is up to, asks what I'm writing, adds some comment of his own which half the time is senseless and half the time pretty insightful, but he likes coming to visit. You tell him I sent you, and you might find him willing to make a few introductions."

We spent the next few minutes nailing down a few hard specific facts about Whirly, and also got some information on the activities and breakdown of the Mongols. If we had to make contact, it might pay to know a few basic facts.

"OK then," I said, rising and motioning to Lucky, who passed Scheuer the bag of pot. Turning to her, I said, "I'll pick you up in the morning."

"See you then," she replied, and Scheuer grinned like a dirty old man. Clearly impatient to get his hands on Lucky, he wiped them free of chip oil on the front of his Hawaiian shirt.

"Wish I could say it was nice meeting you," I said to Scheuer in farewell before kicking though his trash littered floor on my way to the front door.

"Just don't slip in the bathtub," he cackled like he wished I would.

I shook my head and slipped out the door, retrieved our pistols, got onto the bike without looking back and kick started. Two minutes and three clicks away, I found an old logging road to turn into the forest and wait. Only then did I start to smoke, waiting for full dark.

A glance at my watch told me I had some time to kill, so kill it I did, swatting blackflies and by thinking on the words of Larry Scheuer.

I didn't have a Who's Who of the revolution. In fact, I scarcely knew anyone. The cell structure prevented that kind of familiarity, but I did sometimes see killed or captured comrades on TV, and thinking of it, a lot more of them had the feel of Malcolm or Boomer than had the feel of myself or Deuce or Ice, true shooters. Even in California, where I'd helped lead a cell, we'd watched four of the old guard, one 'professor' and three 'students' die if you counted the ones who bought it before I arrived. The ones who had taken their place were basically criminals converted to the cause. No one in Los Angeles currently had a strong background in the revolutionary ideals. Scheuer had a valid point. Gradually, the violence thinned out the people who knew the aims of the revolution.

That thought sobered me more than I liked. Julie always held back from me not because she thought I was a coward but because I didn't quite grasp the full essence of the revolution. I'd just done whatever she told said. Cat found that frustrating about me as well, though she was less forthright in letting me know and less likely to make it a central issue in our relationship.

I wondered how many true leaders the revolution had. Twelve? Twenty? In our cell structure, we had no way of knowing.

I dwelt on that thought for two hours, well past dark, smoking intermittently and checking my watch. By the time I brought the bike back to life and headed back to Scheuer's in low gear, I'd decided the time had come to take personal responsibility for the revolution, starting with my personal role. I wouldn't wait to finish the business at hand to start learning. No more fumbling through like a blind man. From then on, I would personify the revolution.

That thought burned in my brain as I approached Scheuer's ramshackle abode and cut the engine, coasting then pushing it into his driveway silent as a ghost. Moving like a cat, I slid up to his door, finding it unlocked, just as we'd suspected.

Scheuer had probably pounced on Lucky the moment I'd left. Poor gal. I wouldn't wish a tumble in the hay with Larry Scheuer on my worst enemy. As I inched the door open and slipped into the dark living room, I paused, nose wrinkling at the all too familiar smell of whatever wrapped in whatever. In the silent house, lit only by the computer screensaver and silent save for the hum of the electric fan, I could faintly hear the sounds of sex coming to an end. I drew the pistol from my belt and flipped off the safety.

We didn't have any signal other than that Lucky would ask Scheuer for something to drink. We couldn't do a green for go, red for no in the dark and besides, it would be a go no matter what. Scheuer wasn't smart enough to put the whole scene together or even lock his front door. Whatever revolutionary perch he'd occupied, he'd long since fallen, even if he preserved a few fading shreds of genius.

I waited. And I waited. I waited until I heard the faint sound of Lucky's voice, followed by shuffling footsteps. With the utter clarity only possible in a deathly silent home, I heard the bedroom door click open and slide along the carpet. Light spilled from the crack. I stepped into the hallway just as Scheuer's hand found the switch.

"What?" he gaped as the lights came on. He saw me there, pistol raised. His eyes registered shock in the split second before I fired, shooting him twice in the chest. The bullets pushed him back into the wall as he stared in disbelief, a low groan barely making it past his lips as his fingers splayed across his chest, blood seeping between them. Slowly, his legs dying beneath him, Scheuer sank into a slouch against the wall.

Lucky stepped into the hall, stark naked. Her perfectly kept body cast a shadow over Scheuer's dying form as she blotted out the bedroom light. She set her hands on her hips and gave his shoulder a nudge with one toe, making him slouch to one side. Whatever life remained in the failed revolutionary went out.

If Lucky cared about the life of Larry Scheuer, it didn't show on her face. Instead, she looked down on him with hands on her hips and spoke without looking up.

"Creeps like this always want anal sex," she half spat in a tone that dripped disgust. She sighed before heading back into the bedroom, walking in a way that left no doubt that anal sex was exactly what she'd submitted to, leaving me stunned, jaw slack in disbelief.

How, or why, did Lucky let him do that to her? She didn't have to. We could have carried out the execution without her doing that. Why did she submit to it? Something kicked in the pit of my stomach and I felt pity for Lucky. Didn't she have *any* self-respect?

The sounds of Lucky dressing in the other room sounded distinctly in the quiet house.

"Almost done?" I asked, in a voice that seemed to break a holy silence.

"Almost," Lucky answered with a grunt, probably trying to fit back into those tight jeans.

Why would Lucky let a guy like Scheuer sodomize her? He looked like…

I squinted down on Scheuer, trying to come up with adjectives. Nothing came to mind, but as I searched, his eyes opened in death but somehow looked very much alive, and focused on my face. It felt creepy, like he intentionally took one last look at me. His expression, no doubt entirely a figment of my imagination, dripped disgust.

I took a deep breath and turned my eyes away. Personal responsibility seemed more important than ever.

I let the breath out in a long even sigh as Lucky's voice snapped me out of my thoughts. She gave Scheuer one last rub of her toe to push his body over on its side.

"Mission accomplished," she said. "Let's go."

Professor Lawrence Scheuer had begun working on the article below. He intended for it to be a 30-page excoriation of Tory policies on personal freedom. Obviously, he never finished.

Nested deep inside the pending Patriotic Anti-Terrorism and Sedition Initiative (PATSI) approved by the Lords this week, lie provisions for state authority not seen in the dominions since the Eternal Charter bound our diverse citizens into one coherent realm.

If this act passes through the parliaments of fourteen dominions, as required to amend the Eternal Charter, then we shall see become law in all these lands provisions for state authority each of us would have deemed impossible just seven years ago.

To summarize some of the most important, though not by any means all, of the provisions contained in this act:

1. *Provision for arbitrary detention based solely on the discretion of law enforcement agents, not subject to judicial review and without oversight by any other agency or instrument of government*

2. *The monitoring of communications inside the dominions, again without court supervision or oversight.*

3. *In certain circumstances, warrantless searches of personal property. In other circumstances,* ex post facto *warrants issued after the collection of evidence.*

4. *"No Knock" warrants, whereby law enforcement personnel may simply break down the door of any citizen's home and enter of their own volition. Requirements for just cause are minimal. No recourse is allowed to the citizen whose privacy is thus invaded.*

5. *The right to an attorney will be stripped from any person deemed a possible terrorist by an unelected and, once again, un-judicially supervised tribunal.*

6. *Military tribunals for those accused who are apprehended outside the territory of the dominions, either in the colonies or abroad.*

7. *Warrantless examination of personal financial records, patents, medical records, library records, even dental records.*

8. *Trial in absentiae, not just of terrorism suspects, but of any suspect person whose actions could potentially aid terrorism, for example drug dealers. Trial in absentiae is also possible through military tribunal.*

Taken together, these so-called patriotic measures are designed to reign in the movement known as the September Alliance, whose terrorist agenda has claimed some five thousand lives in six years, over half in the last two. Law enforcement officials of every rank and stripe have made the September Alliance their top priority, so it comes as a shock to find out that neither law enforcement nor imperial prosecutors are pushing for these amendments.

The logical question that follows is, if not law enforcement, then who? A look at the act's sponsors proves revealing.

First, we have Member of Imperial Parliament (MIP) Bernardo Luis Obrajon-Cabraldo from the Argentine Dominion, more commonly known as "Big Agra's Man in London", with the agricultural chair. Second, chairing the Health and Medicine committee, is MIP Donovan Culpepper, representative of the eight companies commonly known as Big Pharma. Now for a shocker! We have the parliament's energy czar, MIP Justin Jones of the Texas Dominion, so long beholden to Big Oil that his nickname in Houston boardrooms is 'Ole JJ'. Last but not least comes a man shared by both England and the chemical industry, MIP Bart Sweeney.

There are more co-sponsors, but those four give away the game. Big business is pushing to get this act through parliament and no one really knows how much they have spent, or will spend, doing so. No one knows, because they don't have to tell, having successfully lobbied last year against transparent disclosure due to possible terrorist threats.

Already, their legislation has cleared the Imperial Parliament and it remains to be ratified by two thirds of the dominions before becoming a founding principal of the law of the lands. A free way of life will disappear so that a handful of corporate officers can sleep at night.

What are the chances of passage at this point? If the votes were taken today, experts assume that the act would pass through twelve dominion parliaments and fail in six with the English Dominion leading the ayes and the New England Dominion leading the nays.

That means that the pro-Act camp needs to rally support in the two undecided regions, namely, the fiercely independent Rocky Mountain and Great Plains Dominions. Although close for the moment, these two sparsely populated dominions appear to be drifting towards the rejectionist camp. Good news for the people, bad news for corporate fat cats.

What does business do when it gets bad news? It opens its purse strings, and then proceeds to...

Professor Scheuer's article, intended for his own blog, never left his personal computer. After his death and in accordance with his wishes, his computer and all other worldly possessions were donated to a primary school on the Crow Indian Reservation.

When you serve the revolution, there are times you take orders without asking questions.

We accepted the execution of Larry Scheuer as one of those times, though personally, I felt saddened. Not only did Scheuer's fall from intellectual grandeur strike me as a tragic waste, but I envied him.

Scheuer had known Julie as a peer, and even though his words didn't echo hers, he spoke in the same confident way, with a solid understanding of political cause and effect. I found myself longing for that kind of clarity, that kind of certainty. I didn't want to remain a simple foot soldier of the revolution forever. I wanted history to know me for my commitment to ideals, not how many acres I'd decorated with tombstones. Scheuer, even in the depths of filthy exile, retained that knowledge and commitment.

Scheuer would go down in history as a thinker. If I didn't change, history would only know me as a temporary record holder for killing police.

I consoled myself with a few factual crumbs. Scheuer had referred to himself as a security risk, and his overt hostility doubled that risk. From Lucky, I also found that Mitchell had referred to him as a traitor on at least one occasion. Those two facts, and a general sense that Scheuer had the wherewithal and quite probably the motivation to turn on us sufficed for explanation.

Whatever Scheuer did, for whatever reason Scheuer had to die, nothing remained to do except get onto the bike and find Scheuer's final contribution to the revolution, a biker named Whirly.

Most mainstream traffic used the imperial freeways further south, which meant the bikers preferred Highway Two and biker bars appeared along the side of the highway roughly every hundred miles or hundred and sixty kilometers depending on which road signs you watched. Being way out in the sticks, Highway Two and the local residents had never been fully converted to metric, so a lot of the old signs using miles still stood.

Instead of heading straight up to Highway Two, we headed south to the imperial freeway and headed west, then north to spend the night in Spokane. Then, a giant loop complete, we headed back towards Helena on Highway Two. We didn't know how Whirly might react to the death of Larry Scheuer. He might prove willing to chalk up the murder and our

41

simultaneous appearance as pure coincidence, but if not, we wanted to approach from a different direction.

Lucky and I agreed on a few basics. She would keep the name Lucky. I would go by Geo. We'd just come from Seattle and what we did there would be no one's business but our own. If pressed, we would say we'd worked on the cruise ships. I'd never been to Seattle, but Lucky had, so she gave me some juicy details to make any stories more convincing. Whirly was a friend of a friend.

The biker bars had a naming convention that revolved around motorcycles. We saw The Swivel Hips, The Psst in Rod, and The Tread Mark. We ignored all those and concentrated on the ones with incomprehensible names, especially the ones that used some form of 99 or 1 in their name, the outlaw bars.

We ignored the Over 99 when we saw the parking lot populated by Brigands, rivals to the Mongols. The last thing we wanted to do was end up in the middle of a biker feud. I would end up calling myself Black and Lucky would end up calling herself Blue.

We tried our luck in a dive called One In A Hundred. Only a few of the patrons of the seedy country bar wore Mongol colors so we didn't feel too badly out of place. Still, not knowing much about biker etiquette, I decided to try the bartender rather than the clientele, half of whom played eight ball and half of whom hunched over the pine bar with cigarettes and glasses of thin-looking beer. None of the shaggy, leather and denim clad beasts seemed drunk or under twice my body weight. Every one of them looked Lucky up and down without too much concern about what I might think. That came as no surprise given their reputation as a whole and the fact that Lucky had tied a green t-shirt under her breasts, leaving her enticingly slim abdomen bare. To make herself more eye-catching, she left enough sag in her jeans to accentuate the flare of her hips and make her look like the wildest ride of a biker's life.

Ignoring the ogling bikers, I ordered a beer and lit a smoke. Lucky, after a moment, ordered a glass of red wine, which arrived cold and frosty but she didn't seem to care and might not have known better.

"Thanks," I told the bartender, keeping Lucky between me and the rest of the patrons and assuming a hunch over the bar, then added, almost as an afterthought, "I don't suppose you know if a guy named Whirly ever drops in here?"

I tried to make the question casual, and the bartender, a polar bear sized bald guy with a compass tattooed on his scalp and a titanium bead necklace around his neck, kept his reply casual.

"Nope," he answered wiping down the bar with a towel, barely looking up before going back to the other tasks of the bar.

"Well, ummm if you do," I added, taking a sip from the cheap beer, "Could you tell him Geo is looking for him?"

"OK" replied the overweight giant as if he could agree and then forget. The bikers went back to looking at their beers, but the room seemed quieter, more suitable to eavesdropping. Lucky looked in the mirror and primped, wrinkling her nose.

"I got some news for him." I said, trying to evoke at least some interest, spark some kind of conversation.

"Oh," said the bartender in a retard's voice. Half a dozen invisible chuckles ran through the room.

So much for that strategy. For the next twenty minutes I made small talk with Lucky, sprinkling our conversation with references to Seattle and another town called Chelan.

"Anyway," I said, finally killing the trivial conversation, "You ready to head out?"

She set her hand on my thigh and squeezed, grinning. "I'm always ready, you know that."

I grinned. She giggled, then added, "Just let me fix my shoe."

We stood and Lucky bent over to fiddle with her shoe, which gave the bikers a good view of what she might look like on her hands and knees. I had to wince, remembering what Scheuer had done.

Once outside and on the bike, Lucky rubbed my clavicle and whispered in my ear.

"Perfect. You looked just like someone who doesn't know a thing about bikers."

The following news article ran in Cheyenne's Morning Herald and was picked up that same afternoon by syndicated news networks throughout the Empire.

Ceasefire Breaks Again?
Buonsanto Field Office Torched

Authorities in the small town of Templeton awoke to a surprise this morning when they found a sales and service office of Buonsanto had been razed by fire with the emblem of the September Alliance, the raised fist, prominently displayed to identify the culprits.

According to a dominion police report, the perpetrators of the arson attack lowered the imperial flag and raised a homemade flag with the raised fist and the letters B-G-F. Employees of the field office, numbering twelve altogether, expressed shock and dismay.

One company official expressed "outrage" and proceeded to launch into a heated defense of Bovine Growth Formula, a veterinary additive to cattle feed. The formula has long been seen as a potential September Alliance attention-getter due to rumors that milk from treated cows causes girls as young as nine to enter puberty prematurely. Buonsanto has so far successfully thwarted media coverage of BGF with the threat of lawsuits, but such tactics don't deter the September Alliance.

"You read about these guys all the time," said Police Chief William Lauber, whose jurisdiction includes Templeton (pop. 453) and nearby communities, "But you know, we never figured they'd try and hit us out here. It just goes to show you. You never can tell."

Less tempting targets might be hard to find, but the attack fits into a string small in scale but large in shock to the rural, virtually crime free communities of the Rocky Mountain and Great Plains Dominions. Residents of the sparsely populated territories have long been accustomed to reading about terrorism in the newspapers, but viewed from the vast rural hinterland, terrorism always seemed remote and far away. The fact that the September Alliance or some copycat organization has chosen to bring its campaign to the wide open spaces and endless prairies has changed the way many residents now view terrorist threats.

"I don't care what they got to do," explained Harvey Supple, a *lifelong resident of Templeton and retired rancher, "They need to stop them terrorist attacks. Those commies will be burning down schools and churches next."*

Biker bars and highways had one thing in common, both look a lot alike after a few days. We visited fourteen bars over a highway stretching a thousand kilometers asking after Whirly at random. We would have had more success playing biker 'duck duck goose', simply ask every biker we met if they were Whirly and see who jumped up and growled.

"What do you want with a guy who ain't even been properly potty trained?" snarled a hairy biker that looked no different than any other except for smelling even worse. Everything else about him seemed the same. Earrings in both ears, heavy chain around the neck, short scraggy beard, long hair, plus the Mongol uniform, leather jacket with denim trousers and vest with wind-worn colors sewn on the back.

I shook my head. "That's between him and me," I answered, sliding my butt up onto a torn up barstool. The bikers' response to my inquiries had consistently been either sarcasm or the biting silence we'd encountered back at the One In A Hundred. It seemed this overgrown pile of leather and denim would opt for the former.

"You sure it ain't got something to do with that girl behind you?" he asked, unexpectedly targeting Lucky with a gesture of his pool cue. "She looks to be able to get that sorry mongrel's attention, even if it's for all the wrong reasons."

"Just some news from the coast," I threw out for good measure as he lined up another shot. "Got some mutual friends and they said to look him up."

"Fella like that doesn't have friends," scoffed the biker, possibly correctly. "He's a no good, lying, womanizing, cheating son of a bitch." Then, after half a second, he tacked on almost like an afterthought, "Dashingly handsome though."

"I'll keep that in mind," I answered, turning back to the bar to debate my next move. This biker seemed to know Whirly, a good sign, even if he found my plight amusing.

"He is handsome," quipped Lucky, taking me by surprise. "But I hear he has a tiny dick and can't use it worth a shit." I almost choked on my beer as half the twenty bikers in the bar started to laugh. "One squaw gave him the clap on purpose. Said it was on account of the cheating."

The laughter in the room turned to hoots, and one or two muffled suggestions as to how the scruffy biker should respond. He didn't smile.

"She with you?" the wookie asked directly and none too happily. He scowled, and looked more than half ready to fight *me* for what *she* said. That seemed a rather unappetizing prospect given the fact that he stood several inches taller and approached twice my weight with muscles I didn't even know existed. Still, if I didn't lay claim to Lucky, he would see me as a pushover.

Carefully leveling my words, I responded, "If I answer yes are you going to fight me on behalf of a guy who ain't even properly potty trained?"

That pushed him into a verbal corner, so he threw in the towel and came right out, tight-lipped, setting the word game aside and assuming his true identity. Lucky had sharp eyes and ears.

"You two been running up and down this road from Spokane to Helena and back looking for me. People don't do that if they ain't got a reason." He glared a moment. "And any news from the coast ain't likely to interest me much."

"Shame to hear I wasted my time then," I replied, gambling he would be hooked enough to follow us out. We did want something from him, but couldn't ask in a bar full of bikers, no matter how far outside the law.

I used both hands to push off the cracked naugahyde barstool and land lightly on my feet. I nodded to Lucky. "Let's roll, woman. He doesn't want to hear it and I'm hungry. Spotted a drive-in burger and shakes place in that last wide spot in the road and I'm thinking it might hit the spot."

Lucky used my forearm as a brace to drop off her own barstool. Baiting Whirly even more, she paused at the door and looked at him over her shoulder. He knew where to find us if he wanted, but if he didn't, we would need to find some other way of penetrating the Mongols. Baiting a biker was risky, but potentially worth it.

As it turned out, no sooner did we have our plastic trays of food, burger and fries on mine, chicken sandwich no mayo on Lucky's, than we heard a bike roar in from the east. I smiled and put my tray down on our overhang sheltered picnic table.

The top half of Lucky's bun went into the trash in compliance with her low carb wishes just as Whirly stomped up to our table. We set our food aside as the shaggy biker stood there a second, studying us with hands in his pockets and a scowl that broadcast his unhappiness loud and clear.

Leaning down over our picnic table, Whirly ignored Lucky and the kids working inside the tiny, whitewashed cinderblock building. He came up so close I could smell old leather and oil. Fortunately, we had the patio area all to ourselves, otherwise Whirly's belligerent stance would have prompted calls to the cops.

"What's to stop me from just beating the shit out of you?" he asked menacingly.

"The gun that I'll use to shoot you?" I answered with a trace of a smile.

Admitting to a gun got his attention. Firearms were strictly regulated on all imperial territory including the boonies. From what I understood, the bikers dealt in contraband pistols, along with contraband anything else, but they didn't carry firearms unless they had a specific purpose, which meant Whirly probably wasn't armed.

Getting caught with a pistol meant a minimum sentence of fifteen years, and having gang affiliation, I'm sure Whirly would get at least twice that, if not more. The Mongols only carried weapons when absolutely necessary so a single police stop, very frequent when you openly sport gang colors, didn't turn into an unwitting life sentence.

"You bullshittin` me?" he asked, obviously sizing me up, eyes squinting slightly over his wrinkled nose.

In answer, I held out my arms, letting him see the covered bulge in my waistband. Whirly grunted.

"All right then, let's try this. Why are two strangers toting thirty years apiece wandering around the woods looking for me? I'm not selling, I'm not buying, I'm not running, and I'm not scared. So what gives?"

Whirly's face didn't look the slightest bit scared, but he didn't exactly look on firm ground either. Everything about Whirly, from his wild looks to his sheer bulk, reminded me that bikers didn't need to carry guns. They weeded out people who couldn't rely on their fists. With a nod of my head, I indicated he should take a seat.

Whatever his reasoning, Whirly took the offered seat without removing the scowl.

"You ain't got no news from the coast do you?" he challenged rather than stated.

"Nope," I shook my head, ignoring the brightly wrapped burger and fries. Only Anglos could look at a cheeseburger with relish. I liked a good burger from time to time, but I couldn't live on them. In the Mountain Dominion, hamburger shacks outnumbered people two to one.

A long silence followed. Never before had I approached someone from outside the revolution. Knowing what to say didn't come easy. The wheels turned in my head, but nothing clicked. After a minute, Whirly got irritated.

"You gonna tell me what you want or what?" he demanded rightfully while I searched for words like a chicken pecking feed in barnyard dirt. I took a deep breath, then took the plunge.

"We're friends of Larry Scheuer," I started, stretching the truth just a little. "Or I should say, we're friends of Larry's friends."

Whirly's face went grim. He held his hands up to interrupt.

"Larry's dead," he informed us somberly. "They found him yesterday, in his house. Someone killed him. The dominions think someone offed him for his stash about a week ago."

Lucky and I looked at each other like that was news to us before I turned back to Whirly.

"You know that's not true, don't you," I said, playing him along. Something about the way Whirly broke the news of Larry's unsolved murder made me think of the big biker as a great drinking buddy, easy to get along with, someone who always had your back. "Larry's stash had nothing to do with his murder."

Whirly grunted, a tad quieter than before. "It's really about the blog on the internet, right? That's why he got iced?"

Lucky shook her head. "It's about the bombings out here."

Whirly looked confused. "You mean the ones the September Alliance been doing?"

We let a moment of silence fall, letting Whirly know we debated how much to tell him, playing the 'let him come to us' game for as long as it would last.

"Larry found out those bombings weren't done by the September Alliance." I said, rather plainly.

"Well if they didn't, then who did?" huffed the hairy giant with a slap on his thigh. Behind him, a squirrel twittered and inspected a garbage can, as unconcerned with our affairs as we were about his.

"That's what we're here to find out," I told him quietly, then leaned back into the breeze to watch the gears churn. Even assuming Whirly didn't watch much news it stood to figure that he would guess who we represented. Why else would mysterious strangers come to town? Once certain the gears clicked, but before he could respond, I added, "We also wanted to arrange some protection for Larry, through you, but from what you just said, we're too late."

"A lot too late," corrected the biker with what could have been a sad grimace. "He's been dead for a couple days already, just no one found the body until now."

Lucky pressed her palms to her eyes like she lamented Scheuer's passing, made a sympathetic sound in her throat, then shook her head. She turned to me, keeping quiet, but obviously trying to convey something with her eyes.

"Will you help us find out who did Larry Scheuer?" I asked. "Chances are, they're the same people doing the bombings."

"Well, I would," chuckled Whirly, "But who's to say I could? I mean if I could find that out I'd do it myself. Never mind the rest of it, Lar' was my friend."

That didn't bode well for the future, but I faked agreement, and concentrated on our mission. "Larry seemed to think you might help," I told him, not having to lie on that account. I leaned forwards confidentially. "That's what he told our superiors. We know that whoever did those bombings used military grade explosives and that their chemical signature means they purchased the stuff locally. That means local connections, and local connections means the Mongols, either acting on their own, or turning a blind eye." I gave Whirly a moment to digest that, then finished, "So now you see where Larry thought you might fit in?"

"Yeah," answered Whirly, eyes downcast in thought. His barrel chest expanded to give him breath to speak at length as he lifted his eyes.

"But it ain't that simple. I don't really know who runs military explosives. A couple people come to mind but I'm not exactly close to any of them. They're not the same kind of biker if you know what I mean. The money means more to them than it does to most. I suppose I could make an introduction, but that could get traced back to me, and I'm not sure I want anything you people do getting traced to me. Not if you are who I think you are."

"We'll keep you out as best we can," I promised, wholeheartedly in fact. The closer Whirly got, the more he might add up Scheuer's demise and decide on a little payback. Dumping Whirly as quickly as possible made more sense than keeping him close.

"Ain't good enough," countered the biker. "I need some kind of guarantee."

"There aren't any guarantees," I told him, speaking the truth. "But we'll protect you like one of our own if something goes wrong." I lied again. "Besides, we only need your help getting into position." That might or might not be true. "Once we know who to contact, we'll come up with some way to approach, probably get their attention and let them to come to us."

"You sure you can do that?" answered Whirly, balancing his own interests against a desire to help.

"Are we sure?" pitched in Lucky as I pondered how to respond. "You should know."

Whirly looked over at Lucky, bit back whatever he'd intended to say, and then started to chuckle as he realized we'd landed him on the patio of a burger joint with the same tactic.

With a tilt of his head, Whirly gave a huge laugh, then slapped his palms on dirty-denim thighs.

"OK, you're on," he said at length. "Give me a couple days to socialize and I'll be in touch. You know where to find me..." He let the sentence linger in an unspoken question.

"Geo," I answered, then indicated Lucky with an elbow, "And my girl is Lucky."

"I ain't so sure about that," answered the biker in a jovial tone, standing and preparing to leave. "But she sure is a cutie. Sharp, too."

He held out his hand and we shook, a real bone crushing shake, before he strutted back the way he'd come and left us to our lunches.

"You sure were quiet," I told Lucky around the first bite of my cooling burger. It's amazing how five minutes can turn a burger from a sizzling feast into a congealed lump of fat.

"I knew bikers back in San Jose," shrugged Lucky, not even feigning interest in her lunch. "They're a pretty macho group. If I'd butted in, he'd have lost respect for you, like you couldn't control your woman. We couldn't have that."

"I doubt it," I answered, taking another bite, then nodded to her. "You did good with that 'You should know' comment. That was perfect."

"Thanks," smiled Lucky looking confident but seldom on the receiving end of heartfelt praise. "But don't."

"Don't what?"

"Don't doubt what I said about the bikers."

Outlaw Bikers Terrorize Colvin

Last weekend, the outlaw motorcycle gang referred to as the Demon Eights, an offshoot of the much larger Mongol gang, descended on and seized the town of Colvin in the Mountain Dominion.

The population of Colvin, estimated at 320, found themselves terrorized by the gang of approximately 80 individuals.

One of the first things the gang did, according to witnesses, was to destroy the automated telephone exchange and the equipment on each of the two cellular phone towers nearby, effectively cutting the town's communications with the outside world.

In the course of the twenty-hour occupation there were numerous reports of criminal activity, including looting, several assaults, one stabbing, one arson attack, and four rapes.

Dominion police promise to track down and identify the members of the gang whom they believe responsible, but as any resident of a small Mountain Dominion town will tell you, outlaw bikers are likely to remain a threat in the near future.

I felt so alone in the revolution. For the first time since I'd joined on that autumn day two years ago, I felt well and truly alone.

Lucky couldn't replace Julie or Cat. She didn't have it in her to be what either one. Lucky wasn't an uncaring person or bitter or angry or anything, yet something coarse made her different.

Lucky had no trouble sleeping nude, which was fine, but her casual attitude extended deeper than that simple habit. You could see it in other ways, like how she walked around our motel rooms nude without thinking about it and didn't close the bathroom door all the way. On the few occasions we'd had sex, it felt like Lucky went through the motions automatically, making all the right noises, responding in all the right ways, saying all the right things, showing enthusiasm as I changed the script, but emotionally distant. I couldn't handle that, so we ceased having sex. Lucky feigned hurt.

Deep inside, Lucky had little self-esteem, and unless I could influence her, Lucky would remain a wild card, for this mission and beyond. She had smarts, and I had a feeling she'd chewed the same sour dirt of childhood unpopularity that I had, so I sympathized. I just didn't know what to do.

We waited for Whirly in a lakeside cabin. To kill time and get away from Lucky, who spent her time sunbathing in the nude, in autumn, I drove into a small town called Benson and made use of their public library.

For the first time, I applied myself in earnest to learning about the cause to which I had pledged my life. I started with Mercantilism, which was the socio-economic system based on sovereign nation states which molded their economic, diplomatic, and military interests into one unit and used it as aggressively as possible, mostly in the pursuit of gold. No one wrote too much about it because it had long since become obsolete, but I found it in the introductions of books on Economics and Economic History.

Mercantilism, I knew from my sketchy attendance and even sketchier attention to my elective classes in college, had been the root of Market Capitalism, which tried to grow two ugly heads, National Socialism, kind of a cross between Market Capitalism and Mercantilism, and Communism. Both heads died, the former first and the latter much later, but not before violently branding their legacy on the world.

Market Capitalism did grow two heads, namely Social Democracy and Corporate Capitalism. The first seemed like a fusion of Market Capitalism and the more intelligent breeds of Communism. I had no trouble with Social Democracy. I was at war with Corporate Capitalism, where corporations blossomed at society's expense.

Over five days, I filled a lot of ashtrays and did a lot of good general reading, but before I managed to delve into the fundamentals of Corporate Capitalism, Whirly returned.

"Heya," I greeted him from the cabin's front porch with my thumbs in my belt loops.

Whirly killed the engine and rested the bike back onto the stand, then slung off and stretched like he'd been in the saddle a long time.

"Heya back," he grinned as he unstrapped a twelve pack of cheap beer, then strode up the steps. "Thought I'd bring a little something since it seems we have something to talk about. Might make us thirsty."

By chance, Lucky wasn't sunbathing in the hammock, the fluffy white things I'd pointed out and referred to as clouds had ruined her plans. She'd gone for a lakeside swim a mile up the road instead, where they had a sand beach and dredged the weeds out of the lake bottom. Whirly and I could talk uninterrupted.

"Thanks," I oofed as the twelve pack landed in my gut like a football.

"Think nothing of it," quipped Whirly, who then asked to use the can to take a shit.

Whatever hope I'd had that Whirly and I could drink white wine instead of beer went out the window with that question.

"So whadidya find out?" I asked as soon as he returned and we sat down on the porch with open beers.

Whirly knocked half a can back, then lifted his eyebrows like I would enjoy what came next.

"Exactly what you wanted to know," he proclaimed like saving grace. "And I also found out where they'll be."

"Cool!" I exclaimed, already planning on calling Mitchell to let her know we'd gotten a lead. "Got any details?"

"Sure, gottem all," he replied, lifting his beer can and eyebrows in unison. "There's gonna be a Gathering on Friday. Everyone's coming, including those that are on the fringe, like this little group I'm about to tell you about. Missing a Gathering would be heap bad karma and a serious loss of prestige, not to mention politicking opportunities."

I grinned and took a swig of cheap, foamy beer. "We're not going to forget this," I smiled, knowing he would imagine 'we' meant the highest levels of the September Alliance, the supremos. "Can you tell me anything about these guys?"

"Well," started Whirly, "There's three of them most of the time. Others hang around, kinda come and go, but mostly there's three of them. Leader is named Bull. Petey and Smog are the other two. Like I said, these ain't regular Mongols. They're a lot heavier into the contraband trade and not just drugs, but I guess you already know that."

I nodded as blackflies and crickets buzzed in the background. Whirly continued.

"They come to all the functions, and they always pull their weight, but for most of us, these guys are almost non-members of the club yanno. They never go out riding, never see them at the cookouts, never drop by to get high or nothing."

"Then why have them in the gang?" I asked, feeling more than a bit naïve.

"Because they pay their dues," Whirly answered. It clicked then. The Mongols had a chain like the mob back home. You paid half of your take up the chain and in return you got the sanction to do business, the protection of the gang as a whole, and backing against any potential competitors. The mafia provided some amount of legal protection that I doubted the bikers could match, but the game stayed the same.

"I see that look of understanding dawning across your face," laughed Whirly, who crumpled his already empty aluminum can, tossed it onto the picnic table and reached for another. "Guess folks in your line don't really worry too much about money."

"Wrong," I answered, dead serious. "Money is always a big issue." I stopped myself before I could continue. The less I discussed the revolution and its issues with Whirly the better for both of us. For his part, Whirly just grunted.

We drank more beer as Whirly briefed me on the Gathering, which sounded more like an extended networking session in the guise of a huge party than it did any kind of parliamentary assembly. He also confirmed what Lucky had said about the role of women in the gang. They definitely played a secondary role and had no real membership at all. All rights stemmed from their relationship with a male gang member.

In my experience, women made the most effective revolutionaries. I'd served beside women in and out of combat, and the idea of having them take a back seat didn't sit well. Besides, equality between the sexes was a longstanding tenet of the revolution. Those ideals wouldn't help me amongst the Mongols, but I could try and shield Lucky from the worst of it.

Whirly paused and stared at me a long moment, like a question burned inside.

"You're the real thing, aren't you?" he asked, half like he couldn't believe it.

I nodded. He swallowed.

"I'm going to be honest with you," I told him straightly. "Larry Scheuer identified you as a sympathizer to the cause. He found your ideas similar to ours." That was all true. "He didn't think you would want to join our movement, but he did think you might provide some basic help." That was mostly speculation.

"He sure got that wrong," Whirly muttered over his third beer. "I don't really want no part of you, but I do want to do right by Larry, and I do agree with a lot of what you say in your manifesto. From what you say, finding out who did the bombings is pretty straightforward."

I needed to get around to reading the manifesto, but for the moment, it was better to sit there and continue to lie.

"Of course you do, it all makes sense," I agreed. "Like making sure we only identify ourselves to one person." He would get the implications of that. If he ratted us out, the revolution would know, and he would die in retaliation. Maybe. I would certainly kill him for it, but I really didn't know what Mitchell would or wouldn't do.

By the time Lucky got back, both of us were drunk, but we had a plan in place.

The following is an excerpt taken from an e-mail message addressed to Senior Chief Special Agent Truman Hess of the Imperial Ministry of Special Investigations.

...And as to Papadopoulos, we still don't know even his general whereabouts. The leads in New Orleans, Saint Louis, Sarasota, and Morgantown all either dried up or proved to be false, and the sightings in Australia were a wild goose chase to begin with.

It is possible that Papadopoulos remains in California, but that seems unlikely for the simple reason that none of the chatter we are picking up seems to indicate SA activity in that region, meaning there would be little reason for him to remain. I should add here that chatter in general is at a very low level, probably due to the unilateral cease-fire.

The two SA members arrested this last month proved not to know anything of his whereabouts. As those interrogations have proceeded, it has become clear that they were engaged in activities unlikely to have justified that kind of knowledge.

Truman, I need to be clear with you here. Two of my subordinates are solidly of the opinion that the most likely place to find Papadopoulos is in the Mountain or Great Plains Dominions simply because we are continuing to see terrorist activity in those regions. I don't want to sound like I'm beating a dead horse, but I think we need to deploy at least some resources in that area despite the objections you raised.

Beyond that line of reasoning, we have picked up a few more vague sightings, one in Shreveport and one in Charlotte. Neither of these sightings are going to turn out to be true I'm sure, but enough sightings have been in Dixie that we might consider concentrating our efforts there. Outside of the Mountain Dominion, it seems to be our best hope.

Moving on to the situation on Cuba...

The special agent who wrote the above e-mail had no way of knowing that Hess had been ready to commit additional resources to the Mountain Dominion but had received assurances from his superiors in London that such investigations would be fruitless. When he insisted, he received blanket orders not to pursue any investigations in either the Mountain or Great Plains Dominions. He found that suspicious.

The Gathering turned out to be largely as I'd imagined, even if the reception proved less than pleasant. It should have occurred to me that bikers would take their bikes seriously, and treat their machines like cherished possessions rather than functional tools of transportation.

My bike had no decorations, no elaborate detailing, nothing to indicate that I loved it, so when I pulled in beside Whirly, I got a chuckle from half a dozen wooly bikers. Any hopes of impersonating a fringe biker went out the window right there, so instead of blending in we found ourselves guided by Whirly, wandering from bonfire to bonfire, being introduced to at least a hundred people who offered hands to shake, beer to drink, marijuana to smoke, and stories to swap. They didn't, however, show any sign of trusting me or welcoming me into their number. Outsiders needed to earn that kind of respect.

"Don't sweat it," whispered Whirly with an arm around my shoulder. "There's going to be over four thousand people including girlfriends and guests like yourself. The more of them that knows you the better off you'll be, so we keep making the rounds."

"How long do you think that will take?" I asked.

"Just until we can get near them," he answered, nodding to a quiet pack gathered around a bonfire on the fringe of the Gathering. Unlike the other knots of people, which seemed to generate random whoops and heavy laughs, this one seemed almost a little spooky. If their eyes had started to glow like a pack of werewolves it wouldn't have surprised me.

A bald hulk passed before the fire and reached down to pull a blonde, overweight looking woman to her feet from where she'd previously been hidden from view. He stood easily six foot six and biceps bulged out of his vest like ripe grapes overflowing leather baskets. He took a kiss from the woman, spun her around and gave her a pat on the fanny, keeping calm the whole time.

"That's Petey," Whirly told me under his breath, then nodded to a darker, dragon-faced guy with smooth black hair to his shoulders that sat calmly smoking and observing the Gathering. "And that's Smog." He paused a moment. "They work for Bull, who is there."

Whirly indicated another giant of a man that looked every bit the image of his name. With a V shaped head that boasted a crewcut on the thickest skull in the ten dominions and shoulders made for juggling trucks, he didn't even need the tattoos that he sported in spades and displayed with the help of a sleeveless t-shirt with extra rips. His golden earrings didn't look at all feminine and contributed to the overall image of... a bull. Give him a couple of horns and hooves, and you'd have a minotaur wearing leather.

Beside Bull, lounging on her back across his bike with one ankle crossed over one raised knee, rested a dark haired woman I couldn't quite make out, but had to be Bull's girl.

"So how do we get close to them?" I asked Whirly, whose face looked a bit redder before, no doubt from the half dozen beers he'd packed away.

"I'm trying to figure that out right now," he confided, sounding more than a little unsure. "For now we keep circulating and hope an opportunity knocks."

I didn't like the sound of that, but before I could say something, Lucky chimed in with a question of her own.

"Who are the girls?" she asked, not letting her eyes stray.

"Don't know the blonde," Whirly admitted with a shrug, "But the brunette is named Debs. Pretty gal that one. She's been Bull's old lady for about four years now."

"Does she do shots?" Lucky asked like it actually mattered.

"Uh, yeah," grunted Whirly. "Saw her do some before, but only with Bull around."

"She ever dance the pole?" Where and why did Lucky get these questions?

"Yeah," nodded Whirly with a little more enthusiasm. Did it up in Lethbridge. That's how Bull found her you know. The story goes that she…"

"Any idea how long?" quizzed Lucky without letting him finish.

"I reckon about a year or two, maybe more?" shrugged Whirly, wonder over Lucky's line of questioning squeezing through the suds.

"Why do you want to know?" he asked, finally.

"No reason," Lucky answered, then turned up to me. "I'll be back in a bit. If you hear me yell your names you come running, OK?"

"Uh sure," I answered, no doubt with a dumb look on my face.

Lucky winked and slid around my side and out into the Gathering like a minx into water, without leaving a ripple.

"What was that about?" asked Whirly, looking to me for an explanation.

"Damned if I know," I replied truthfully, more than a little relieved to get some room to maneuver. Without having to look after Lucky, things might flow a little smoother.

With Whirly at my side, I made introductions faster than I imagined possible, and with a level of friendliness that I found both surprising and proportional to the amount of alcohol consumed. Still, I felt a very definite sense of clannish standoffishness at not being part of the gang, even if arms did go around my shoulder as a band began to play a rhythmic, easygoing tune.

Not knowing any better, I'd expected the bikers to prefer loud, angry music, but that turned out not to be the case, even if the tempo did turn up after a few songs.

A hairy biker with buck teeth and a third eye tattooed on his forehead explained the music as a part of the nomadic, laid back life that characterized the biker lifestyle more than the fistfights and drag races people like me imagined. Before we could exchange names, a meaty hand clapped down on my shoulder.

"Look," Whirly grunted in my ear, and I looked up at the stage of leather and chaps clad singers. "No," he insisted, using his hand to turn my shoulder towards another bonfire. "Over there."

I stared a moment, seeing half a dozen couples swaying to the music, arms around waists or squeezing butts. I almost shrugged because I didn't see anything, then one couple caught my eye, if only because they were a lot smaller than the others. A dark haired woman ground against a smaller blonde with short hair, and when she turned, I could make out the blonde's features.

Lucky.

"Is that brunette who I think it is?" I asked Whirly, wanting to shake my head, already knowing he would tell me that Lucky danced with Debs.

"If you mean the girl Lucky is with, that's Debs," he confirmed, taking another large swallow of beer. "They sure are a sight, aren't they?"

"Yeah," I responded glumly, wondering what we'd just been pulled into as Lucky, her arms around the other woman's neck, kept her eyes focused on the taller woman's and then licked her lips. The sapphic undertones weren't even undertones, more like lighthouses on a calm night, strong and clear.

Lucky and Debs had an appreciative audience. As the pair kissed, more than one howl of encouragement poured out of the biker throng, from men and women alike. The pair seemed to ignore it. I just watched, since the two didn't seem to break any biker rules or draw the wrong kind of attention. It actually drew the right kind of attention.

Over the flames of a bonfire, I spied Bull, with Smog at his side. I had their attention, and even over the distance I could see they conversed in low voices. As my eyes turned towards them, Bull's eyes moved away like he'd only given me a passing glance. Without looking back, he whispered something to Smog, who disappeared into the shadows.

"I gotta go talk to someone," Whirly told me quickly, then moved off without another word, leaving me to drain the last of my sour beer and toss the can into the fire. I watched Lucky and Debs alternately smooch and grind, even after the rest of the bikers found something more interesting to focus on.

Silhouetted by the fire, the two women danced with a life of their own, and had a hypnotic effect, like what I was seeing couldn't be real, yet was. I found the feeling surreal.

Someone passed me a joint but I shook my head and waved the hand away without looking, watching Lucky and her... prey? The joint didn't move as I watched Lucky slide a hand up Debs' stomach and toy with her denim-clad vest. When the joint still didn't move, I turned to see who held it, and found Smog.

"That your girl?" he croaked, looking sooty from the bonfires and living up to his name with the cigarette hoarsened voice of a true chain smoker.

"Yeah," I responded, pretending I didn't know or care about Smog.

"She's pretty hot," he rasped after just a moment while Lucky and Debs parted arms, brightly smiling and whispering something to each other, hands still tightly clasped.

"Got that right," I told him, turning to smile. "Name's Geo," I told him.

"Smog," he replied like he'd been baptized with it. "Friend of Whirly's are ya?"

"Yeah, sort of," I answered. "More like friend of a friend, but we were in the area and looked him up."

Smog seemed to like that answer, because he grinned like a chimney sweep with a mediocre dentist, all yellow teeth and the white eyes. "Any friend of Whirly's is a friend of mine," he coughed, then turned to go without so much as a nice to meet you just before Lucky skipped back.

She threw her arms around my neck and bounced to her tiptoes, pressing close and whispering in my ear. "Got her hooked."

"Her and half the rest of the team," I answered sourly, liking the result too much to disagree with her method. She tensed in my arms and I felt her fingernails dig into the back of my neck.

"What the fuck is that supposed to mean?" she hissed.

"Nothing," I yiked, caught by surprise.

"Don't give me 'nothing'." Lucky's tone had changed. She sounded disappointed and angry. "I want to know what that means."

"Later, OK?" I managed.

Lucky made a non-committal sound, then turned her head before whispering back. "You better smile right now, cowboy."

Following her gaze, I saw Bull and Debs approach, Debs in the lead. She embraced Lucky with enthusiasm and the two whispered to each other under their breaths. Bull nodded with his arms crossed. I saw for the first time that he sported a thick golden nosering through the cartilage linking the nostrils, just like a bull.

Debs smiled warmly as Bull rumbled in a low voice, "We were thinking of heading out to a campsite not too far from here for a little…" he paused, "entertainment." His thick, crew cut head moved, cocked just a fraction, making it something of a question. "We thought you two might like to join us and make things a little more interesting."

I let my eyes linger on the smiling Debs, playing the game right beside Lucky. She looked nervous and happy, but not as comfortable. I thought of Cat for a moment, and knew she would understand if we went off to have a foursome if it done in the name of the revolution, which it would be, but the sight of Debs made Naughty Nicky rise.

Debs stood an inch or so taller than Lucky, and her thick, almost jet black hair framed a really lovely face made all the more so by feathered earrings. They almost pointed to a sensuous mouth, and from what I could tell, she had a soft round body that curved in all the right places. Her denim vest didn't hide her more than ample cleavage and I could tell by the shape of her arms and legs that she wouldn't be plump under her clothes. In some ways she looked the opposite of lithe, cat-like Lucky. Naughty Nicky jumped as I leered, the expected reaction.

"Sounds fun," I finally said, taken completely by surprise by Lucky's resourcefulness.

Everyone grinned.

The following letter was written by one of the seven members of the September Alliance Supreme Revolutionary Command Council, referred to by other members of the September Alliance as 'The Supremos'. Couriers hand-delivered copies to the other six members of the council.

Comrades:

In our last meeting we discussed the possibility of a permanent or semi-permanent ceasefire and the formation of a political party. Because of the deep division of opinion, we never discussed another matter we felt pressing, and that is the purpose of this letter.

Because I am geographically far removed, and have a theatre of operations quite different from yourst, I have found the time and talent to investigate the likely effects of PATSI on any future operations we might undertake. With due respect to those dismissive of the point being raised,

I have to say that the investigation has proven that we have cause for concern, though perhaps not as much as originally feared.

To provide you with the positive side of things first, it seems that PATSI will not seriously harm our communications. You hold proof in your hands that we do not require the use of the telephone system the Specials so wish to access and record. Wireless transmissions are

70

currently open but encrypted. E-mail communications are euphemistic, with substitution and vagaries easily able to offset the capabilities of any kind of software parsing the Specials employ. If our operatives follow procedure, telephone conversations are protected in the same way. Our code is, as far as Cypher can tell, unbreakable.

In short, PATSI does nothing, and I stress the word, nothing, to curtail our ability to communicate. The other provisions seem equally unlikely to have major effect on our operations.

Warrantless detention is a red herring for public consumption. In the seven years of our operations we have seen nine of our comrades successfully resist or evade arrest and two escape after capture. In none of those eleven cases did the time obtaining a warrant allow one of our soldiers a window of opportunity. The same holds true for "no knock" and warrantless searches.

Trial in absentiae and removal of the right to legal counsel for those arrested may cause us some problems but are not battlefield issues. These provisions refer to comrades already under arrest or those easily convicted anyway. Military tribunals in the colonies or places abroad are for the most part irrelevant.

In short, comrades, PATSI does nothing to harm us. Our fears will remain the same with or without PATSI: infiltration, treason, rogue operations, forensic investigation, betrayal by associates.

The negative side of the equation is this. We do not know why the corporations have instructed their front men to put this legislation forward, for while it makes no headway against us operationally, it most certainly increases the overall level of government surveillance and undermines the core beliefs enshrined in the Eternal Charter.

I have to admit that I am still studying this aspect of PATSI. At the moment, it appears that the real goal of PATSI is to obtain legal tools for later use, perhaps against environmental or human rights activists. It could be that the incubi of the boardrooms are using this legislation to turn public opinion against us, using the argument that we play the spoiler by making this necessary. Indeed, one pillar of their argument is that if this legislation is not adopted, eventually our attacks will become larger and more indiscriminate. Additionally, it is not outside the realm of possibility that the corporations actually believe these measures might be effective, no matter the denial from law enforcement.

My greatest fear is that corporate and government interests are beginning to merge. We all knew that this was possible in theory, that hypothetically, corporations will devour everything, including government and society. If PATSI marks the beginning of the phase where corporations ally to divide government from society as a prelude to the conquest of both, this would be news of the worst sort. We are neither equipped nor organized to effect an overthrow of imperial government.

Time will tell about PATSI, but for the moment, we need remain vigilant. The amount of money invested in this initiative means that whatever their reasoning, the corporations are quite serious about seeing this initiative succeed.

Australia

Once we got to the campsite, a creekside hole in the wilderness about thirty meters across, Bull turned out to be a pretty decent guy. But then again, maybe all guys are pretty decent when they get to drink beer and watch two girls have sex in front of a campfire. Bull didn't make small talk, but while watching a private lesbian love show, neither did I.

"That's the best I've seen in a loooong time," rumbled Bull, eyelids cloaking his pupils. "You ever seen anything that good?"

"Never," I shook my head, not adding that it was also the first time I'd witnessed two girls do it at all. I had to admit that business aside, I found the sight and experience crudely fascinating, intriguing even. My eyes still stayed glued on the girls. As if to keep a boner strong, they knelt facing each other, pelvis to pelvis and breasts to breasts, locked so in a French kiss deeper than the Paris catacombs.

Bull chuckled. "First time, Geo?"

Busted.

I shrugged. "First time for everything." Then it occurred to me I could use the ten or more years age difference between us to my advantage. "How old were you the first time you saw two chicks make it, or uh," I struggled for the right words.

"You mean do the salamander?" He laughed, which earned him sidelong looks from the campfire. "I'd say seventeen or eighteen. Went with some friends down to Veracruz in the Kingdom of Mex and saw ourselves some live shows." He indicated the girls by the fire with a hand that made its enclosed beer can look small. "This kind of setup is a whole lot better though. Open night. Open skies, cold suds, beautiful girls, what else could you want?"

"Money?" I chipped in, making my play. I'd decided to try and get closer to Bull by pretending to be broke and in need of quick dough. With luck, he would consider hiring me.

"Bah," he scoffed like I should know better. "Money's good for some things, but not for this. This..." he winked at the girls, "is way better than money." That earned him a pair of blushes.

"So you want Debs tonight?" offered Bull in a deep rumble, rising to his feet and kicking his foot in the dirt to get the blood flowing. It was almost three in the morning, and time to roll into the sleeping bags.

He wanted to swap girls. I'd seen enough, indeed all, of Debs, to definitely want her for the night. Still, I had to think of Lucky, because if Bull handed over Debs, he would want Lucky in return. I didn't want to do that to her. She'd already done enough that she shouldn't have to have Bull inside her as well.

"Nah," I said. "I want Lucky."

"Then Lucky you shall have," conceded Bull without argument. He ran his fingers through his hair before making a gesture for Debs to jump into his makeshift bed. She squealed happily and all but shot over like a bolt of lightning.

"C'mon, princess," I urged Lucky, rising myself as she scooped up the sleeping bag. "Over here looks like a good place."

In a minute, we'd said good nights and rolled out a little bit away from Bull and Debs. I'd stripped down to shorts but Lucky insisted on removing them and we slid into the sleeping bag together.

As soon as we'd arranged ourselves, I winced as Lucky pinched me on the ass. She whispered fiercely into my ear, her free hand cupped to contain her voice. "Are you stupid?"

"Huh?" I yipped in genuine surprise.

"You're an idiot!" she hissed again, one hand cupped over my ear to avoid being overheard. "How do you think we're supposed to get close to them?"

"I was hoping he would hire me," I whispered back, her nude body a distraction to me, my nude body no distraction for her.

"Why?" she insisted. "Why would he do that? Why should we play that angle when we had a perfectly good way of getting close to him through me?"

"Lucky," I consoled softly, "I don't want you to have to do that. You did...Ouch!"

She pinched me harder.

"Do you think I really give as rat's ass who fucks me? You or him? Now you listen up and you listen good." Lucky definitely stood on her home turf with this subject. "You're going to fuck me now. You're going to fuck me so hard I'm going to beg for mercy, because if you don't..." She pinched my ass even harder and held it to make her point. "He's going to know something isn't right, and he probably already suspected when you rejected Debs, who, by the way, is a better fuck than you'll ever be. Now stop acting like a choirboy with the cardinal and do what needs to be done."

"Awright!" I groaned, the pain modest but highly noticeable. Her words stung a lot more.

"Good," she finished in that fierce whisper, the scent of Debs' sex still hot on her breath. "You better make me scream because they'll certainly be listening."

Lucky stopped, and together, we listened to the insects in the forest. A moment later, a soft sound from Debs joined the natural symphony. I looked down at Lucky, who looked stern and far from pretty, then took a deep breath.

The following news article appeared on the Imperial Broadcasting Company's web page available worldwide and in 128 languages.

Denials Flow Like Smoke

The September Alliance broke its silence for the second time since its cease fire yesterday, again to issue a denial of responsibility to an attack on a company. The spokespeople, using code words commonly ascribed to verify true communications from the terrorist organization, emphatically denied any connection between their forces and the attack on International Corn Products.

Some experts argue that leaflets attacking the manufacturer of high fructose corn syrup are genuine while others argue that the emergence of a splinter cell was inevitable, that radical political groups invariably lead to schism.

The fact that the Mountain and Great Plains dominions, which have only seen two attacks since the September Alliance (SA) emerged, are suddenly active centers of terrorism remains a mystery to experts, law enforcement and the September Alliance alike. Wording in the latest terrorist communiqué seems to indicate that not only is the SA not responsible for the attacks, but is actively searching for copycats.

Not many people seem to believe that the SA is being scapegoated. More seem to think that the organization is using its denials to mask a limited vendetta against corporate wrongdoers, this time aimed at large agricultural companies. Such a move was widely predicted following the brutal campaign against Val-Mart, where the SA began to target one specific company. Such a move heralded a more focused sector by sector strategy, where instead of attacking across the board, the terrorists could focus on achieving more limited goals in specific areas.

Morning came with a whimper. Even waking up to warm sunlight in tight proximity to a naked woman didn't make it feel good. I felt humiliated, and that had kept me up late. Sleep hadn't banished those feelings.

I unzipped the bag and slipped out, leaving Lucky to sleep, then drew on my pants. The cold morning air had me shivering, but I fished a smoke from my jacket pocket before throwing it over my bare shoulders.

"Catch," I heard and turned just in time to see Bull heave me a beer with an underhand toss. His chest, like mine, was bare, though much larger. It had to be, to hold the tattoos.

"Breakfast," he grunted as I caught the beer and popped it open to a spray of foam. This was turning out to be a long assignment. I didn't even like beer, let alone warm beer that foamed in your stomach and made you feel bloated. Nevertheless, when in Rome, you do as the Romans, so I tilted the can up, my head back, bit the bullet and had... breakfast.

I sat down on a log, directly across from Bull, separated by the ashes of the prior night's bonfire. The massive biker had apparently worn Debs out pretty well because except for her hair, she didn't emerge from their sleeping bag any more than a groundhog on Christmas.

"What a blast," I grinned, setting the beer down beside me and putting my hair into a loose pony tail.

"Had a good time did you?"

"Like you didn't?" I replied, which earned a broad if emotionally flat smile.

Bull shrugged and drained the rest of his beer without seeming to notice. With a powerful hand, he crushed the fragile aluminum shell and gave it an effortless toss into the campfire ashes.

"Hey look," I said, playing my hand. "I need to make some cash, quick cash. You know anyone looking for help?"

"Can't say I do," lolled Bull, obviously not interested in my financial situation. "There's a recession I hear. Work is probably hard to find."

"Who's talking about work?" I echoed before his voice faded. He'd seen the pistol, he should know what I meant. "I'd like to find something steady, but broke as I am, I'll take anything that makes a fast buck. If I don't find something within the next day or two, I'm going to have to do something on my own." I paused for effect and took another drag on the cigarette, then finished with, "Unless you know something?"

Bull shook his head. "Sorry man," he told me in a tone as solid as his skull.

I let my face fall like a rejected schoolboy's, but nodded my head. In a whispered conversation, Lucky and I had given that line only a thirty percent chance of working, at best. We'd hoped it would work, but we had another plan waiting in the wings, one that Bull would find irresistible.

Bull had no reason, absolutely no reason to trust me just because we'd watched our girls… The phrase 'do the salamander' echoed in my head. Maybe in time, I could build that kind of trust, but I didn't want to spend weeks with the bikers. Who knew what kind of tattoo I could wake up with?

"Mind if I ask a different kind of favor then?" I asked, sounding hopeful as I reached down for my shirt and pistol, making no effort to hide the fact that I had a pistol.

"You can ask," Bull replied, "But I ain't sure I'm gonna say yes."

I wondered if Bull had the brains to form sentences or just watched his words around strangers. The Devil only knew, but he led a small gang of his own so he had to have at least some smarts. Lucky would find out soon. Bull would get very comfortable with Lucky.

"Watch Lucky for me, just for a few days while I go scare up some purchasing power?"

Bull's nosering glittered in the dawn light. He looked at me a long moment, then asked. "You ain't afraid of getting her back with fingerprints?"

"Fingerprint her all you want," I half smiled, and had to force it. Even if Lucky didn't mind, my becoming her pimp sucked. Without letting my inner reservations show on my face, I shrugged. "Lucky's a big girl, can take care of herself, and besides…" My fake smile turned up a notch. "I'll be back." I nodded to the sleeping Debs. "And I hope your offer will still stand for at least one night."

"We'll see when the time comes," offered Bull, maybe a little bit grudgingly, but obviously liking the deal. After all, what I said had to sound pretty believable, and pretty desirable. We'd planned on it sounding irresistible.

Within an hour, both girls woke up and shared some animal crackers to go with beers of their own. Debs squealed in delight when she found out she would be 'sharing the back of the bike' with Lucky after I went through the motions of breaking the news that Lucky and I would be apart for a few days. Lucky feigned unhappiness all too well.

With everything going according to plan, I made up some sweet nothings for Lucky and headed out on the bike with a sigh of relief. God definitely hadn't cut me out for a biker's life.

Lucky could take care of herself with the bikers. She'd proven that, and shamed me in the process, but I still felt responsible for her. Underneath that nonchalant sexuality and sandpapery immorality hid a sweet woman. I could feel it, and I would bring it out one way or another, but for the moment, by mutual agreement, she was on her own.

We didn't know how long Lucky needed to discover who bought explosives from Bull, but I bet at least a few days. Bull certainly wouldn't tell her straight up, but Lucky had her ways. I could only wait.

As the highway once again stretched out and the bike devoured yellow stripe after yellow stripe, I text messaged Mitchell with a simple update.

so far so good

One day before this tale began, Konstantin Arazov received and read the following e-mail from his superiors in the revolution, written in Romanized Russian. Both users used generic Powermail accounts.

Hello my friend,

> *A friend of ours will be traveling in your area and I told him that he could look you up for a little vodka and hospitality. His name is Nikolai Popolov and I would appreciate it if you would help him out with anything he might need.*

M

North of Medicine Hat, on the southern edge of the Great American Shield lived a comrade named Red, born Konstantin Arazov. He lived alone in a cabin out in the middle of nowhere. The Mountain Dominion had a lot of middle of nowhere, but his cabin sat deeper in nowhere than most. Riding north out of Medicine Hat, it really felt like I'd left civilization far far behind and even the asphalt seemed to thin. I couldn't picture spending a winter there.

Red greeted me from the front porch of what was a real honest to goodness log cabin. He even had furs drying on some kind of rack and wood smoke came from the metal chimney. One look at the place and I knew a hot shower ranked next to impossible. One look at Red and I knew he liked it that way.

Clad in thick wool pants with suspenders slung loosely over a long sleeved undershirt, wearing heavy boots and a peaked cap that screamed East Bloc, he stared sullenly from beneath wispy grey hair.

"Comrade Nicky Pops," he said, though the Russian accent made it sound more like "Nyicky Popes". The accent fit him. He had one of those big wide faces and shining blue eyes that a lot of Russians had, plus that kind of stout, peasant build that could work all day and all night without tiring.

"That's me," I smiled, hoping to charm him. It didn't work.

"They tell me that you maybe needing something," he replied with a dour face.

"As of right now," I explained with a tired flourish, "all I need is a place to hang my hat and wait for the word."

Red took a drink from a steaming mug and invited me inside. True to form, the cabin boasted a single room, with two beds, a table, two chairs and a washbasin, all made of wood. The fireplace even had a pot hanging over the fire, though the pot-bellied stove in one corner offered an alternative.

"You want tea?" he asked, indicating a samovar, the first working samovar I'd ever seen. It actually had a candle under the reservoir that kept the tea warm all day long. The flame and the fact that no one had ever decorated the exterior made the poor thing look purely functional, but also alien, like it came from the Empire of Immigrants. For a moment I wondered if other people reacted the same way when my grandmother wore her *mandili*.

"Sure," I replied, not allowing my thoughts to dwell. With a groan, I slung the duffel bag off my back and onto the floor, tired from the seven hour ride. "I appreciate it, too," I added. "as well as the hospitality."

"Pah," he replied with an unconcerned wave of his hand, passing me a mug. "I was just to hope that I help you. It been much too long since I fought for the right."

I grinned, one revolutionary to another. "Don't count yourself out yet." Red was a known good. It was altogether conceivable that I might use him in one way or another, but I needed to know his skills. At the moment, I didn't have any use for extra firepower, but you never knew how things might turn out.

"So you a shooter or do you do support or what?" I asked.

Red set his mug of tea down and ran his palm over one shadowed cheek.

"I am more than shooter," he replied in his thick Russian accent, his words carefully enunciated. "I am best shooter you meet." The slow words didn't hide his pride. He jerked a thumb towards his chest and nodded with a face solemn enough to impress a surgeon.

"I am deeply humiliated that you were not told who I am. I am not just shooter. I am maybe best shooter alive today."

I lifted an eyebrow. "That so?"

"You may ask that of the eighty soldiers of the Chinese army I kill, or seven more of these corporate devils we both fight. Pah!" He rose from the table with the grace of a shambling bear and shuffled to the mantle on his fireplace, then took down a cigar box and returned.

"Here," he said, shaking the contents with a clatter out onto the table. Bright ribbon and polished metal gleamed on the coarse pine tabletop. Military medals. I picked one up and looked, trying to sound out the Cyrillic writing from my patchy knowledge of Greek.

"That one is for me wounded," Red admitted, taking it gingerly back from my fingers. He returned the piece to the pile and picked up another. "This is for defending motherland. When I shot and killed my fiftieth Chinese they gave me this."

"You served in the Sino-Soviet War in the nineties then?" I asked, noting his English improved as he kept speaking.

"*Da da,*" he nodded, plucking up another medal. "And served very well. Little *uzkoglazye** paid for what they took from *rodina*. Took our Siberia to plunder for their factories to sell cheap shit to empire. But..." he clapped a hand on his broad chest, "First they need to pay. I killed eighty of them, more than half officers and those just confirmed kills. I had more not confirmed." He set the medal down and pulled out a folded newspaper clipping, carefully unfolded it and spread it on the table.

Rupert Shaw Assassinated read the headline. I remembered reading about his death, at our hands, just before I joined the September Alliance. He'd been hired as one of the original workforce consultants in the auto industry, had invented the idea of sweeping layoffs as a psychological tool to win union concessions. He'd been shot by a sniper.

"And this one," Red added, placing another clipping before me and holding it with a thumb on one corner while smoothing it down with the palm of his hand like a sheet on a bed. "Bernadette Pierson." Her

---

* uzkoglazye - is a Russian slang term approximating "slanteyes"

name rang a bell, but nothing clear. She'd been some kind of lobbyist if I recalled, but if I also recalled, she too had been shot by a sniper.

"You're quite a marksman," I smiled.

"*Da*! The best!"

Putting two and two together, I added, "Trained by the Red Army before the collapse of communism then. What brought you to us? Did they just let you immigrate?"

"I live in Siberia," he replied with a shrug, "But my address it in Kaliningrad, now New King's City." He shrugged again.

That made sense. Kaliningrad had been ceded to the empire in the aftermath of the Sino-Soviet War that precipitated the Soviet collapse. They gave it up in return for writing down the debt to the imperial banks. Compared to losing Eastern Siberia to the Chinese and watching their union fragment into its constituent republics, Kaliningrad, renamed New King's City, had been a footnote. With half a million inhabitants, under imperial rule it had become the eighth "dagger" in Europe, and as such, its inhabitants had immediately received citizenship of the Empire equal to mine or anyone else's.

The daggers served an important part in the European alliance in that they give the Empire leverage against all the substantial European powers and some of the middleweights. Bornholm, New King's City, Bremerhaven, Gibraltar, Crimea, Sicily, Corfu, and Cyprus made up the eight daggers, each of which contained a military base that could ensure a quick and rapid military thrust into any European country that might misbehave. Julie had explained the logic to me.

Only the European countries, acting in unison, could challenge the Empire for dominance. Simply put, they had the manpower, technology and money to form armies and navies, challenge imperial companies for contracts and compete for economic resources. Prior to the Sino-Soviet War, Russia had been another challenger, but the daggers kept the European Union secure in its uncomfortable marriage to the empire.

To avoid problems in the daggers, the empire gave their residents full citizenship, which in turn gave them the right to settle anywhere in the empire for any reason. That, in addition to allowing them close ties with their compatriots in their respective European countries, allowed them to have much greater economic and social opportunities than they might otherwise have. In that way, stability was retained, and the daggers kept in place to threaten Germany, Italy, Spain, Poland, Sweden, Ukraine, Denmark, Greece, and Turkey. Only France and Romania didn't stand at the point of a dagger.

The strategic arrangement had served as a conduit for a dedicated communist and professional sniper named Konstantin Arazov to enter the Mountain Dominion without lifting an eyebrow in London. Eventually he contacted and joined the September Alliance. Who knew how many more like him might join once the Pacific Rus acceded as a full dominion.

When I asked to see his weapons, Red stood and went to a section of the floor, reached down and slipped his finger into a knot hole in the pine, lifted, and revealed his hidden arsenal. Six rifles lay carefully stowed in a rack, four with telescopic sights and two with laser sights. I whistled softly.

"Very nice," I said, eyeing the pieces with envy, noting the perfection with which each he lovingly maintained and stowed each weapon. The distinct odor of gun oil piqued my nostrils. The idea occurred that with several days to kill in the middle of nowhere, learning how to shoot one of these babies would fill the time well.

"Can you teach me to use these?" I asked, not sure if he would share his special skill.

"When I heard Nicky Pops come see me," the dour Russian replied, "I hoped very much that he ask me to teach him how to shoot. I will very happy teach you. Only seeing fat company *golobois* dead on front of newspaper give me more pleasure."

I looked into his beady eyes and smiled, not having the slightest idea what I would one day do with this skill.

The following news article appeared in syndicated news outlets in the empire and in most major dailies throughout the world.

Anti-Terror Initiative Gains 2, Loses 1

Backers of the Patriotic Anti-Terrorism and Sedition Initiative, dubbed PATSI, received a little bit of good and bad news this week as the first round of dominion level ratification began.

As was widely expected, the New England Dominion failed to ratify the initiative by a wide margin. With a vote of 75 for and 121 against, largely along party lines with smaller parties and independents generally favoring the nays, the initiative definitively failed its first test.

Later the same day, the vote was much closer in the Texas Dominion, where a strong history of individualism collided with a deep sense of propriety. The vote in Austin came down to 109 for and 85 against amidst heavy lobbying on behalf of the ayes, primarily from technology companies that would stand to gain from government contracts.

The same pattern held true in Eastern Australia where a surprising number of abstentions tilted what might have been a very close vote in favor of the nays. There, the vote came in at 101 for the ayes, 79 for the nays.

These results come just two days after representatives of the future Rus Pacifica Dominion, due to accede to the Empire next year, were handed a judicial verdict confirming that the ratification process will not reflect any vote they might take before accession, and will be considered only in an advisory capacity. In the event that the Pacific Rus accede and the ratification process is still in progress, a vote there would still not be considered binding because the process began prior to accession.

Neither side can claim a lead at this point, as none of the three votes were deemed competitive. Whatever the final fate of the initiative, today's voting marked only the opening salvo of the battle still to come.

R ed knew his stuff. Within two hours out in the rough, I'd learned more about sniping than I'd ever realized needed to be learned. He taught me that simple gravity makes a bullet drop just over an inch every one hundred meters and more as the bullet loses velocity, and he taught me how to judge wind speed by watching the leaves rustle on the ground. He intentionally skipped some lessons for the sake of time, like observation techniques. Other lessons he hammered on like the fiddler on the roof, like how to scout a position, and how from that location you spot a fallback position.

Red also taught me about pepper vodka, a hideously strong brew that agreed with neither my head nor my stomach, though Red swore the stuff would stiffen a man's constitution. After one night of that bitter potion, I had to pass.

"So why did you join the Alliance?" I asked as we took a break to eat trout Red had smoked himself. Red had a silent, solid manner that made me curious. He obviously hadn't emigrated for social or financial reasons and a woman seemed implausible.

Red shrugged like it should be obvious. "I like to live in wilderness, together with nature," he replied. "Kaliningrad was city like others in Europe, only more dirtier. When the army first sent me to Siberia, I know that where I want to live, under stars with wind in hair and meat that I hunt, living like a man. If Chinese devils not invaded, I still live there."

"Sounds like the reason you came here, but not the reason you joined the revolution," I stated flatly, picking up the powerful tripod rangefinder and staring at the bullet peppered plastic buckets and milk bottles we'd used as targets. We'd set them up a full kilometer away. Without the telescopic sights, I could barely see them. The fact that my hands had made those shots seemed almost unbelievable.

"I joined this revolution when I joined Red Army," Red replied, pulling pieces of fish off the bone with greasy fingers. "I would not serve in this army of this Russian Federation, serving *nuvorischky* while pensioners starve and skinheads drink whole night in streets. Not me. I come here to continue fight the enemy, the capitalism of your country. There is root of evil. Chinese slaves of corporations and government, like Europeans and Brazil. Only Russia had different way, and now Russia defeated, so I come here."

Red looked me square in the eye, sitting cross-legged with his rifle across his lap, the same as any Scythian warrior of a thousand years ago, as convinced of his words as he was that the sky is blue. I envied his simplicity.

"Russia defeated, yes," he continued, "But the fight now falls to Russian spirit, in me and in true Russians." He smiled broadly "And many Greek!" He slapped his thigh like a newly cured ham.

"And you?" he asked unexpectedly. "Why you fight?"

The question took me off guard. Only Julie had ever asked me to think about why I fought for the revolution, and she was dead. I'd only recently begun asking myself the same question, and had more recently admitted I fought for far different reasons than I'd joined. I'd joined up for Julie. I'd stayed in for Cat. That answer wasn't good enough, buy I certainly couldn't tell that to Red, so I said something else.

"I was born to fight," I told him, hoping my words didn't warp and twist in the air like the lies they were. "I believe there is a giant evil in this world, and I want to fight it. Same as you from what you say. There must be meaning in this world , and that meaning can't come from consuming material goods. It has to come from all of us together, not in competition, but in harmony."

"*Da!*" exclaimed the Russian with more enthusiasm than I deserved. He reached over and clapped my shoulder. "A hero! Like me!"

I thought he would break out the pepper vodka and drink a toast right there. Instead, he set aside his rifle and hefted mine. With deft flicks of his thick peasant fingers, he detached the sights and handed them back.

"New lesson, how to make sights to zero."

I took a look at the weapon and ran my fingers over the deadly oiled barrel and smooth wooden stock, wondering if I could use it to kill before I had the right answer to the troubling question Red had just raised. Why did I fight?

The following is one half of a telephone conversation between Virgil Kuhlmeier, aka "Bull", in Wenatchee, and an unknown person. Lucy Keyes, a.k.a "Lucky", overheard and partially memorized his words.

Yo. <six seconds of silence> Picked it up today. <eight seconds of silence> That depends. You got what I want? <twelve seconds of silence> Don't gimme that. That shit might go down back east but it doesn't go down here. My name ain't Jeeves and I don't come running at your beck and call. <six seconds of silence> Oh I'm scared. <two seconds of silence> You want to argue about it or do you want to do a deal? <twenty seconds of silence> No way. You're in my territory. We do things my way <five seconds of silence> The alternative is the high way. [sound of laughter] <six seconds of silence> Why not sooner? <eight seconds of silence> No I don't got a problem with meeting you half way. <thirty-five seconds of silence> I know a place near there. <nine seconds of silence> Unless you know a better one.

<ten seconds of silence> In the Badlands. There's a town called Stanton. You can find it on any map. Follow Knife River Road west out of town for about thirty miles. <four seconds of silence> Knife like the tool, river like the thing that has water in it. You'll see an old billboard for a restaurant called Betty's Home Kitchen. Just past that sign is a dirt road. Go north. <twelve seconds of silence> Whaddya mean which way is north going to be? Tell you what, you figure it out and when you do, go north about three miles and you'll find an abandoned campground. I'll meet you there on Tuesday, four o'clock sharp. <eight seconds of silence> You too buddy. <three seconds of silence> Leave your doors open and I don't want you to bring more than four guys. <ten seconds of silence> However many I think I need. See you there. [sound of phone being hung up]

66 "In the Badlands?" I asked Lucky over the telephone. "Who wants to have a reunion all the way over there?"

"How should I know, Nicky?" she crackled over the mediocre connection. Cell phone service in the sticks was chancy, but even worse with both of us in the boonies.

Doing a deal in the Badlands made me scratch my head. The Badlands lay pretty far east of Bull's usual stomping grounds. I could see a lot of incentives for doing the deal in such a remote and unsettled area, but not much sense in making the two and a half day ride out there from Wenatchee.

92

"Hmmmm," I moaned into the mouthpiece. "We'll talk it through when we get together. You got a fix on where exactly? And can you slip away from work?"

"*I think they're kind of keen to get rid of me already,*" she admitted with more dejection than I expected. "*But yeah, I got the same directions as...*" Static filled the air, but then her voice come through clearly enough that I could hear her gum crack as she chewed. "*You there, Nicky?*"

"I'm here," I answered. "Can you meet me in...?" I shuffled the map across my lap and found what looked to be the biggest town near the Badlands, "In Bismarck?" The town at least had a freeway running through it.

"*Sure,*" she answered without a care, "*I already checked the bus schedules and they run every two hours. One leaves in less than an hour, so I could go tell them I heard from you and say my goodbyes. Away I go, ready to blow.*"

Red shuffled in the background, listening carefully to my half of our conversation, waiting with the patience of a Buddhist monk. When we speak over the phone the subject of conversation is always, and I mean *always* kept vague, especially over a cell phone. I could tell Red wanted a piece of the action, and thought I might oblige.

"Sounds good," I replied, trying to think what came next. Red's cabin was a lot closer to the Badlands than Bull in Wenatchee. Doing some calculations, I figured we could make it in eight or nine hours as opposed to eighteen or nineteen for Lucky. "Call me when you're three hours away. I'll pick you up outside the depot."

93

"*OK, give mom my love,*" she finished, just in case someone listened.

"Will do, see you in Bismarck."

We disconnected and I hung up and filled Red in on what we knew.

"What you want to do," he asked, thumbs hooked into his suspenders, giving visual to the sliding Slavic vowels.

"Ideally I would like to be down there with them when they meet, but that's really not likely," I mused, clenching my hand into a fist to help me think. "If I showed up and asked to join Bull he'd mark me as a cop and whack me first chance he got."

"Lucky?" came the one word question.

"Nope," I answered. "I doubt the bikers would bring a woman with them on a deal. They're a pretty chauvinistic bunch. I think our best bet is to watch from a distance, take down license plates and see who shows up."

Red nodded.

"I'm hoping," I added truthfully, "this finish the mission, but we need to be prepared just in case. We'll need that spotter's scope." I referred to a short but stout telescope with range finding abilities. As an optical device, the thing blew the sniper scope away. Snipers used it when they worked in teams. "We'll bring the rifles as an insurance policy."

Red nodded again. "We leave tomorrow. That give one full day to observe area."

"Can't," I grunted. "Lucky didn't tell me the exact location in case someone might listen in." I debated calling her back and having her ring me from a landline, but rejected the idea as inconvenient. Deep inside, I still hoped to encounter some overly enthusiastic fans of the Alliance, students maybe, out to do their part and prove their worth. The coincidences didn't seem to favor that scenario, but I still hoped.

As we left the next morning, I felt tension rise in my gut. Bad winds blew, and it didn't take a weatherman to sense the coming storm.

Bismarck called itself a city but looked like a town. Downtown didn't get above four floors, and even four seemed the exception. Most buildings sported three or less. The extra wide streets, designed wide for piling snow, had an empty, forlorn feel. They looked like small town Main Street, but the number of buildings and a single, ugly, skyscraper gave it a more permanent feel. Someone had hammered the neighborhoods together from used chain link, clapboard, and two by fours, or that's how it looked. A shudder went up my spine at the idea of growing up in Bismarck.

Red had driven down from Medicine Hat in his slower, beaten up, borderline antique pickup truck, so I waited and tooled around the city for an hour, noticing not just the lack of traffic, but the lack of parked cars, pedestrians and open stores. Then it dawned on me, it was Sunday! I had to laugh. Like a small town, Bismarck closed on Sunday. I shook my head and smiled before locating the bus depot and then a restaurant. Two hours and a plate of the worst fettuccine alfredo I'd ever eaten later, Lucky called.

"*I'm almost there,*" she said, "*I overslept though. I'm only an hour away, not three.*"

"Great!" I told her, not feigning enthusiasm. I itched to find out the details so Red and I could finalize a plan. I would get some OJT on Red's latest lesson, "site preparation". The sooner we could prepare our observation site, the better.

"*Did you get a place to stay?*" she asked. "*I need some sleep. These busses aren't very comfortable.*"

"No," I told her, "But I will."

"*Make sure it has a comfortable bed. All that time on sleeping bags left me sore.*"

No doubt she had a lot of sore spots. I wondered what twist of personality Lucky had that made her able to so some of the things she did. She'd proven herself clever enough. Why hadn't she developed a different set of skills? I supposed that question brought us back to the self-esteem issue. I would address that with her, gingerly, but not before she got some rest.

"Will do," I promised, looking around the street to make good as quickly as possible. I figured I would gather up a bottle of sweet white wine and something else she might like. We didn't have a phenomenal amount of cash, but we had the brick of grass we could sell, and she deserved something for what she'd done. "Can I getcha anything else? Cheese? Crackers? Food?"

There was a long pause on the phone. Then, like she needed to think about it, she said, "*A cantaloupe would be good.*"

"A cantaloupe it shall be then," I told her, and hung up after saying good bye.

Ninety minutes later, room booked, wine and cantaloupe in hand, along with some ham I bought in lieu of prosciutto, I picked Lucky up from the depot. She looked a little worse for wear, with a huge hickey on her neck and clothes rumpled past the laundry point, but she threw her bag onto the back of the bike and slung herself up without a complaint.

"I never thought I would be glad to see you again," she sighed. That didn't exactly make me feel good, but then again, she could have said worse. Misreading girls is a lifelong hobby of mine and I'd racked up another collectible with Lucky. First I'd managed to disappoint back at the Gathering and then again at the campfire. Fortunately, she seemed ready to overlook my mistakes.

"Just glad to have you back," I grinned over my shoulder and kick started the bike. I lied, of course. Or did I?

"Really?" she asked, in typical Lucky fashion. Assurances that she'd been missed only seemed to make her suspicious.

With Lucky in the bathtub of the B&B, a luxury that had taken a little extra cash, I wasted no time getting on the phone to Red to let him know where he should meet me. Bismarck had a movie theatre named The Pinnacle. It seemed an ideal place. He could rendezvous in fifteen minutes.

Before leaving, I pounded on the bathroom door with the butt of my fist and told Lucky I would return shortly, then double-stepped down the steps two at a time. Minutes later, I rounded the corner to the movie theatre and nearly ran headfirst into Red. He gave a little flick of his hand to dismiss the collision.

"What you find out?" he asked under the bright streetlight. He wore a dusty wool blazer and peaked cap that looked like something out of a Cold War spy novel. With the wool pants and suspenders he looked the part of a KGB thug to the T. I felt like a renegade from a cheap spy movie.

"I found out Bull's gang picked up their payload in the mountains east of Seattle," I told him, relaying what Lucky's information. "They're meeting their customer thirty miles west of a town called Stanton. You take Knife River Road to a gravel road just past a billboard for Betty's Home Cooking. Go north about three miles and look for a deserted campground," I started. "I'll try and meet you there at eight tomorrow morning. If I can't, find a place without me, somewhere in the trees for more cover. We'll hook up at noon."

Red gave a slow shrug and gestured with his hands. "They say that in Badlands a beautiful woman behind every tree. You know why so, Nicky?'

I stopped planning and looked back into his beady blue eyes. Why *did* he say that?

"Um, no," I answered truthfully, a bit perplexed at the interruption.

"Because there are no trees." He smiled slowly, waiting for me to get it. When the humor hit me, I had to grin in part because of the source. His smile faded.

"I will find a place. Do not worry, Nicky." Again, the way he said my name sounded like Nyicky.

"Feel like seeing a movie?" I asked.

"More money for a stupid Hollywood people," he scoffed. "Back in USSR we never waste so much while people hungry. They not get one red penny from me."

I resisted the urge to say the Soviets built enough nuclear warheads to destroy the world eight times over while people went hungry and just said goodbye. Minutes later, I unlocked the door to the B&B and slipped back inside.

Lucky looked up from the bed with a wet towel folded neatly over her eyes and the comforter tucked under her chin. Like the rest of the furnishings in the room, the bedspread had been done in elaborate patterns that I associated with the turn of the last century. The room looked good, with period furniture and enough shiny knickknacks to make a robber baron smile.

"How'd you like the wine?" I asked as I opened up the window and knelt down beside it to smoke, using an empty can of Dundalo Orange Soda as an ashtray.

"It was good," Lucky replied with her eyes closed, though half a glass still sat alongside the rinds of what must have been half the cantaloupe and a plastic fork. My open, sticky Swiss army knife sat off to one side, leaving no mystery as to how Lucky had cut her melon.

"Cool," I said, exhaling through the screen. The temperature was dropping outside. In a week, we would have winter weather.

"I liked the ham with the melon, too. Did you learn that working in the Italian restaurant?"

"Yeah," I grinned, "It's underrated, as a profession, but I highly recommend everyone work in a *cucina* sometime."

A silence fell over the room, like we'd run out of small talk and had little to say to each other on a personal level. I wished there was some way I could begin to reach Lucky. She would be worth the effort, if only I could find the way.

"You want to come scope the position tomorrow?" I asked, sticking to business for the moment.

"Why?" she sighed, obviously wanting to sleep, obviously struggling with something inside that she didn't want to discuss. "I'm no good crawling through the bushes. I can't shoot and I'm a lousy driver, so unless you want a blowjob out there I don't see what use I'm going..."

"Enough, Lucky," I snapped, my goodwill taxed. I didn't want my temper to flare, so I stood, dropped my butt into the can and walked past her towards the knee high fridge. Getting another Dundalo sounded like a fine idea.

"Well it's true," she almost blubbered, pulling the pillow over her eyes.

"It doesn't have to stay true." The ease which the thought formed in my head surprised even myself.

I spun and walked out the door. She'd think on those words. Anyone would, because no matter her background, at heart, Lucky was a student. The 'students' of Larry Scheuer's understanding often lacked confidence in their ability to carry out acts of terrorism. Therefore, they tended to serve in auxiliary functions. Five names ran through my head in quick succession: Cat, Freddie, Maya, Boomer, and Di. Not one had proven incapable in the end, but each had had to free their mind, banish their internal limits. If Lucky, who held a natural tenaciousness and cold-bloodedness could do the same, she could rise. That thought made rousting her out of bed the next morning much more fun.

"Get up," I ordered, already showered and dressed. I'd decided to take the noon option meeting up with Red. While a grousing Lucky took her turn in the shower, I laid out the firepower we had at our disposal, displaying each weapon side by side on the bed, unloaded, the clip for each neatly arrayed next to the breach.

The deadliest weapon we had was the Brazilian *Pica-Pau*, a streetsweeper, fully automatic with a barrel only three inches long and a total weapon length shorter than my forearm. Despite its small size, the thing spat out bullets at the rate of 30 per second. The weapon did away with the concept of actually aiming at what you wanted to hit in favor of simply waving the barrel in the target's general direction and letting the sheer mass of flying lead take care of the rest.

Next came the DR-16, this one with the stock sawed off. A standard military issue assault rifle, it too had full auto capacity, but was most effective when used in semi-automatic mode. That way, it would fire as fast as you could pull the trigger, and its longer barrel gave it a higher rate of accuracy and longer range than the *Pica-Pau*. The heavier bullet also packed a lot more punch. In a shootout, it was my weapon of choice and the revolution went through DR-16s like water.

Laid out neatly beside the heavy artillery lay the pistols, arranged by caliber, starting with the large .45, then the nine millimeter with the highly illegal silencer, and last the .22, also with a silencer. None of these required any kind of special skill for general use, just aim and press, but hitting your target took practice.

Lucky emerged from the bathroom stark naked, actively toweling her hair dry. The scars criss-crossing her otherwise perfect body stood out in sharp relief against the all over tan she cultivated by whatever means necessary.

"What are you doing?" she asked, seeing the weapons laid out.

"Getting ready to teach you how to shoot," I calmly explained. Lucky lacked self-esteem and confidence so we would start building confidence and self-esteem. We would start with a close target and work up to a longer distance. Like gears meshing in a well-oiled machine, the process would begin from there.

"Pfah," Lucky scoffed, letting the towel fall but holding onto one corner as she peered curiously at the collection of hardware, utterly oblivious to her nakedness. "I can't hit the broad side of a barn."

"Just for that," I replied, looking into her eyes for the first time. "Your first target is going to be the broad side of a barn."

She looked at me like I couldn't be serious.

Four months before this tale began, Tadeo Hamanashi, intelligence liaison with the office of the Japanese Consul in Xiamen, prepared the following coded report for his superiors in Tokyo.

Humble Greetings to My Esteemed Superiors from the Imperial Consular Office in Xiamen, China:

It is with shame that I must report to you the failures of this office in regards to the pressing issue you presented in September, specifically the Shark Tooth criminal syndicate and the theft of anthrax from the Chinese military base in Shen-hu.

Our office has diligently worked at the task assigned, and will continue to do so until you in your much deeper wisdom should deem our efforts futile and direct us to other tasks.

Despite the most strident efforts of your less than perfect servants here in Xiamen, we have been unable to discover the reason for the theft beyond the scope of simple monetary gain for the thieves. All four soldiers involved in the plot, as well as their captain, have been executed by the Chinese Army, which has also closed the case. Our source inside the base believes that the final, secret report of the investigating officers concluded no others were involved.

Our agent in Shanghai independently contradicted the official findings, that the anthrax remains somewhere in southern China. He cites testimony from two members of the Shark Tooth criminal gang that claimed to have knowledge of a meeting in Shen-hu between members of their gang and soldiers from the army base. He verified their stories through another contact, a Shanghai prostitute known to service members of the gang. He further collaborated both stories by finding and interrogating a party official in charge of overseeing outbound cargo on the waterfront by helping him imbibe a large quantity of beer and imported whiskey.

Our failure to determine who wanted this anthrax and what they wished to do with it failed utterly, but we have managed to discover other, less important facts that bear reporting by your chosen retainers.

The anthrax was transferred onto the small, Ecuadorian registered trading vessel Cachalote I *in Shanghai, which set sail ostensibly for Honolulu, yet did not dock in that city. Instead, the ship appears to have called in the city of Seattle. No further information is available from this office and if it were not certain that your much greater wisdom had already referred the matter to our more capable*

103

colleagues in San Francisco, we would recommend at this time that it be done.

The greatest fear of yours and ours seems to have been averted. This deadly cargo is not destined for our beloved home islands, but for North America or beyond. Given the deadly nature of weapons grade anthrax spores, this comes as a welcome relief to us as well as to yourselves since a simple 100 grams of this deadly substance could effectively contaminate entire shipyards, factory complexes or, may the Emperor forbid such horror, university campuses. The Chinese believe the the thieves took a full kilogram.

The decision to share this information with our counterparts in imperial territory is much too great a burden for this lowly office and that decision has been left to your much more enlightened and capable hands.

With the highest esteem and respect of your humble servants in Xiamen,

Tadeo Hamanashi, Station Chief, Xiamen
<his chop>

Tadeo's superiors elected not to share their field agent's findings with the Imperial Intelligence Service as part of an intelligence spat regarding unreciprocated sharing of Japanese intelligence data on the Chinese submarine fleet, then under construction.

One thing you could say about the Badlands, it had plenty of open space. Finding a place to do some target practice didn't take long at all, and I doubted the dominion police ever wandered too far off of Knife River Road. Finding an abandoned barn didn't take much, and before Lucky knew it, she not only understood how a pistol worked, but knew how to load, when and how to engage the safeties, and how to assume a firing stance. She then discovered how easily one could hit the broad side of a barn. After a single shot, I'd taken a piece of chalk and drawn a three meter by three meter box. She hit that, too. Then she hit another box that was two meters by two meters.

"Damn," she cursed after I drew an awkward silhouette of a man, slightly larger than life but very recognizable. Without hesitating, she lifted the pistol into the two-handed firing stance and took three shots one after the other, feet perfectly positioned in the thick grass. Splinters flew away from the grey, weather-worn timber in fist-sized chunks. The first shot went wide, the second came close, and the third would have clipped an ear ona flesh and blood man.

"Not bad," I complimented honestly. It didn't take a genius to work a pistol, but Lucky seemed to relate to the piece. I could tell that somehow, when she held that pistol in her hand, a part of her she might not have known existed swam to the surface. Her eyes focused like a shooter's, and no amount of makeup could conceal the spark of malice glinting in her eye. When you hold a pistol, you have power.

"Thanks, Nicky," she said, then lifted the gun again, unbidden, and fired once more, this time one handed. She hit the silhouette in the foot. Ignoring me, Lucky squinted intently, assumed the two handed stance, fired, and hit the target in the hip.

"You're getting better," I told her, then checked my watch. "We need to get going. Red's waiting for us."

"K," she replied distractedly, lifting the pistol in a motion smoother than I expected and steadier than I would have thought her capable an hour before. She fired twice in quick succession, this time punching holes in the target's makeshift shoulder and chest. Lucky smiled in grim satisfaction. "I could get to like this."

"You already have," I told her plainly, then reminded her to reset the safeties and unload before showing her how to repack the clip with fresh ammo. Moments later, we hit the road.

Red had been right about his pretty woman behind every tree, or at least the part about there being no trees. As far as the eye could see, I saw low lying shrubs punctuated by tough stands of grass and larger clumps of thorn brush. The Badlands deserved its name.

Red had parked his truck a hundred meters off the main road and sat perched on the rear bumper, smoking a cigarette pinched between thumb and forefinger. As we approached, he spat loose tobacco from between his lips and rose.

"I found good place," he told me as soon as the bike's engine died and he'd met Lucky, whom he studiously ignored after a brief introduction. Maybe Russian girls didn't flaunt their stuff back in Russia and went straight from little girls to *babushkas* in the blink of the eye, but Lucky could melt Red's awkward ice if and when she chose.

Red drew what looked like a sewn together pile of rags from the bed of his pickup and slung them over his shoulder.

"There are not trees," he told me, stating the obvious. "So we have ghillie suit. We work with this land, not against." He held up the ghillie suits, long cloaks sewn with strips of burlap and cloth. This help us hide when we watch."

My eyes scanned the horizon while my brain searched for words to describe the landscape. Being a city dweller, I didn't have the vocabulary for blasted heath, rough hills, tough tundra or any of those things. After an hour creeping between thorn bushes and shielding my face from stinging blackflies and branches that moved in time with our passing, I had a lot of words for the Badlands, none of them pleasant.

Lucky had no such predisposition to silence. "Ouch!" she cried time and time again like it was my fault she'd chosen to wear short shorts. "Watch where you're going, Nicky!" After the thirteenth or fourteenth such outburst, Red finally turned back and fixed his merciless, beady gaze on her. She blanched and shut up, either intimidated or afraid of abandonment.

It didn't matter to me what Lucky thought. If she wanted to do more than spread her legs for the revolution, she would have to take the bad with the good, and that meant-- I swatted another stinging insect from my ear with an audible slap-- crawling through the overgrowth of the Badlands. I groaned.

"Here," announced Red an hour later as he slung the ghillie suits off his shoulder and hung them on the thicker branches of a dead bush. He'd chosen a spot a little below the crest of a low hill, in an area where the bushes didn't grow as thick and the ground fell off a little steeper. You had to hand it to Red, he knew his trade. The position he'd scouted gave us a great view of the abandoned campground.

I peered through the scope of a rifle, sweeping the crosshairs across the entire site. Some kind of a lodge had burned down, collapsing on itself into a pile of cinders and fallen timber. The dozen cabins that once peppered the yard had suffered a variety of fates, making the site look like a miniature ghost town, an impression made all the more vivid by the way the wind had stripped away the paint. Only a tennis court had withstood the elements, and even that had started to crumble at the edges.

"This should do," I nodded, eager to get back to Bismarck and out of the wilderness. I passed the rifle to Lucky, whose awestruck eyes looked from the gun to me then back to the gun before gingerly accepting the gift and lifting it into firing position. Wordlessly, she stared down the barrel.

"This the best," Red assured me. "Six locations to watch. Two there," he gestured to the north. "Three there," he gestured to the east. "And this. I, how you say, visit all this morning and this one the best."

It was my turn to look in awe. "You covered all that ground?" I asked, not sure whether to believe him or not. He must have covered six kilometers. Red was tough, but not young."

"I start early," he explained, but when we continued to stare he made a circular motion with his hand, "and not have you two..." he paused searching for words. "City slickers to slow me down." He grinned, obviously relishing the looks on our faces.

I looked at Lucky and shrugged helplessly. She wrinkled her nose in return.

The next morning, Red wasn't grinning, I wasn't shrugging, and Lucky wasn't wrinkling her nose. We were all business, dressed in Red's ghillie suit. He took camouflage seriously, and refused to allow me to bring a bottle of orange soda to the observation point for fear anyone who looked closely enough would spot the bright color.

I doubted we had anything to worry about. Bull's customers were probably just some college kids playing terrorist. We would spot their plates, locate them on the outside, and then approach with a demand that they observe our ceasefire and join the cause in proper fashion. Hopefully, they would fall into line and that would be the end.

"Movement," Lucky said, squinting into the spotter's scope. "I have an SUV entering the compound."

I glanced at my watch and felt my eyebrows wrinkle as I read only a quarter to one.

"They're not due until four o'clock," I sighed, then nudged Lucky to let me look. I hoped some interlopers wouldn't spoil the meeting. Lucky moved out of the way just enough to let me slide in and look down the scope but not far enough away that I couldn't smell her soap and hear her chew her gum. Red silently observed through the rifle scope.

Closing one eye, I peered through the spotter's scope. A black SUV had peeled into the old campground, raising a cloud of dust in its wake. Something seemed out of place, and then it struck me that the thin film of dust on the vehicle couldn't hide the vehicle's shiny new black paint. Amateur terrorists couldn't lay out fifty thousand pounds for that kind of ride.

"Red flag," I muttered under my breath as the vehicle came to a halt towards the clearing's edge.

"What?" asked Lucky.

"Something isn't right." I told her, not taking my eyes from the vehicle below. "Vehicle is too expensive, too new." I stared, then told her, "Grab the notebook, I want the plate numbers."

Slowly turning the delicate ridged knob, I dialed the sight in and focused on the plates, then read off the numbers for Lucky to copy, along with a bigger surprise. The SUV had plates from the Great Lakes Dominion, my home, but a long way away.

Red interrupted. "This important. Dial out if dialed in."

Without hesitating, I reversed direction on the knob to take in the whole scene. Three men had gotten out of the SUV, each in army fatigues, each armed with an assault rifle. One wore yellow shooter's glasses, another wore blackface.

"Professional mercenaries," I said to no one in particular, then rolled away to let Lucky peer through the scope

"No," grunted Red, his own attention fixed below. "These men not experienced in forest but they handle guns like soldiers. I think these men come from city."

Why do you say that?" I asked, interested in anything that might tell me more about our mysterious consumers of military explosives.

"Yellow glasses one thing. Boots only this high," he touched his ankle without taking his eyes from the scene below, "and green uniform no good for brown season."

"They're rolling," quipped Lucky beside me. "And the make of the vehicle is a Tundra Rover. Those just rolled off the production line six months ago."

"What about the guys in fatigues?" I asked, beginning to put the picture together. Even without a scope I could make out their figures from the observation place.

"They stayed. It looks like they're talking something over," mused Lucky, concentration evident on her face. "One of them is

110

pointing at the brush and talking, the other two are listening." As she spoke, the scar on her face elongated and contracted, going from a lazy S to a compressed S with each consonant in a motion that threatened to take my attention from the task at hand.

"They look for firing position," Red filled in. "And not best ones."

Lucky scooted out of the way so I could peer into the spotter's scope while Red supported his argument by pointing out better firing positions. When the scope focused again, I understood his point, even if he had a far superior eye for the technical aspects. I saw two guys struggling through the vegetation and a third one, the one with the shooter's glasses, talking into a cell phone. At least he tried to talk into a cell phone. We'd already discovered we'd left the service area. He only frustrated himself and eventually snapped the phone closed, then stalked after his comrades.

We spent the next hour speculating on the new arrivals. Lucky thought them run of the mill bodyguards, ex-police or military still making their living by way of the gun. She'd seen a lot of people like that working in Las Vegas, and to her, they had the same feel. Red disagreed, doubting their professionalism. He thought they might be ex or current cops, but nixed the idea of ex-military. As evidence, he pointed out each of their 'concealed' positions.

"A good soldier," he said in that limping, lisping Russian accent, "not take easy way. He not know where his enemy come from. Look," he gestured. "These men all point where gate was. All three fire there, but if people they want shoot go another place, only two can shoot. Some places, only one."

I stared at the scene below, he was right. Whoever these guys were, they weren't professional soldiers.

"Think they might be Specials?" asked Lucky, pushing back the headpiece of her ill-fitting ghillie suit. Red needed practice tailoring camouflage to a woman's size.

Red shrugged like they could be anyone, including Specials.

"No," I said this time, having the most experience with the Specials. "The Specials are professionals of a different sort. If they wanted to observe the transaction they would have Imperial Rangers or some other kind of specialized help. Or," the idea dawned on me, "They could have a nest like this picked out."

That thought got Red back to scanning the brush through the scope mounted on his rifle while Lucky and I took turns watching for movement down in the campground. We waited a long time, almost three hours.

"Here they come again," piped Lucky as she peered intently into the scope, forcing me to gobble up the last bit of a turkey sandwich. No pun intended.

Lucky purred softly but seriously. "Three more SUVs, all like the last one, brand new Tundra Rovers, two men per vehicle."

"Dial in and read me the plates first chance you get," I ordered.

Lucky nodded and purred something accommodating, then paused, her body stock still as the vehicles down below rolled back towards the gate and parked next to each other, one two three. Antlike figures emerged from the distant SUVs.

"OK first one," whispered Lucky, her small fingers finely tuning the dials. C as in cheese. H as in hair, I as in India…"

I scratched down the numbers as Lucky read them off easily, as if two kilometers were two meters.

"My turn," I told Lucky, and again she rolled out of the way to let me roll in behind her. Thanks to a bush, we practically spooned, but once peering into the spotter's scope, I almost jumped.

"I know that guy!" I exclaimed. Six men in suits milled about, stretching their legs. One in particular I knew. In fact, I still had nightmares about him. The cruel face below didn't belong to a *guy*, but a *wiseguy*.

"That's Donny Paglia," I gaped. "He's a mobster from River Valley. What the fuck is *he* doing *here*?" My eyes did not mistake me. Donny Paglia, mid level gangster and servant of Big John Longanza, murderer of my friend and mentor, Sam Stompanato, aka Turk, strutted in the campground. His other credits included one time torturer and would be murderer of your humble narrator, along with a laundry list of other crimes too numerous to mention.

"You know him?" asked Lucky.

"Yeah," I replied, getting control of myself. "We used to buy explosives from his mafia family back east. He tried to kill me, did kill one of our comrades, and convinced another to turn on us."

"Do you think this is where the mafia buys their explosives?" speculated Lucky, nicely ignoring the part about Donny trying to kill me.

Donny in a suit looked like Satan with a halo. I once thought of him as a yuppie with a mean streak. He had a casual saunter that said he could take on the world and sported a joking manner when he really didn't joke at all. The carefully combed hair and well trimmed mustache and beard gave the casual onlooker an image of a lawyer more than a mobster, but don't argue with Donny. You might win, and lose your life.

"Hard to say," I gritted. "From what you said, the Mongols picked up a load of explosives out west. Let's see what they do."

Different possibilities went through my mind. Donny's supply of C6 had evaporated back in River Valley and he needed to buy from Bull? The imposters hadn't really been using locally procured C5 to begin with? Bull had gotten his wires crossed? Nothing really made sense.

We didn't wait long to watch events unfurl. Even from a distance, we heard the sound of approaching motorcycles, engines echoing through the hills. In a few minutes, the Mongols entered the campground, circled through the overgrown gravel, and raised a cloud of dust.

Through the whirling dust I could make eight bikers who roared into the campground like a hungry pack of leather and denim hyenas. Like predators, they circled the SUVs three times before ripping off reassemble and approach like a barbarian skirmish line on wheels.

In the nest, our trio fell silent and watched as the bikers lined up opposite the suits. Exhaust and dust blew away with each gust of wind. I couldn't picture more stellar opposites, neat and clean with a cutting edge versus wild and ragged with iron spikes. Substitute some black hats and white hats, and you had the makings of a great cowboy showdown.

Bull swung one leg off his bike, sunglasses and jewelry glinting in the sun. The other bikers followed suit in unison. I only recognized Petey and Smog, but the others looked just as tough, openly armed with a motley array of shotguns at the half ready and pistols worn poised for quick draws. They looked more like modern day Huns than citizens of the largest, richest and most sophisticated empire ever to exist.

The suits, all dark and most with sunglasses, looked more like Specials than muscle. They didn't look like mobsters from Donny's gang who favored lots of jewelry, black t-shirts and leather coats. These guys were a whole different breed of thug. Donny's crew had been one hundred percent Italian, but I doubted any of these new guys were even half Italian. They looked more like Irish and Germans or Scandinavians and Anglos.

Donny approached the bikers with a swagger in his step, confident as always. Through the scope I could see his mouth moving and I could almost feel humorous patter raining down on the Badlands, but if Donny said something funny, Bull didn't laugh. Instead, Bull stood straight and still while Donny slung a stylish black rucksack off his shoulder, opened the flap, and drew out a wad of bills. He broke the paper wrap from the stack, threw it to the wind and then, one by one, he peeled bills off with his thumb, stopping at some point to show Bull what he had counted. When he reached the end of the stack, he drew out another wad, gestured, then patted the satchel like a pretty girl's fanny.

Bull tilted forwards and advanced on the smaller criminal with easy grace. One sledgehammer of a hand opened the top of Donny's satchel and he looked inside. Looking satisfied, Bull called something over his shoulder. Smog and another biker I hadn't met turned and unlatched a canvas covered crate. With deft hands, they unbuckled and unwrapped it, each taking one handle. Gentle as grannies, they gingerly plodded towards Bull and Donny.

With the spotter scope, I zeroed in on the case markings. The wooden crate had what looked like Chinese or Japanese writing. I couldn't tell which. No doubt the markings meant C6, the most powerful explosive in mankind's possession but perfectly stable to transport. Smog and his cohort could have played basketball with the case if they chose, but they either didn't know or wanted to put on a show.

"Looks like they're selling C6," I grunted to Lucky, impressed that the bikers had the connections to get the stuff to begin with. C6 is not easy to find, though as people gradually used up supplies of C5 and C4 it would become more prevalent. By my estimate, the bikers had about six kilos, enough for forty days and forty nights of bombs.

With delicate care, they lowered the box to the ground like it held fragile babies, then stepped away. Smog passed Bull what appeared to be a small, hand held crowbar, and the larger man bent over the case to pry the lid off.

Whatever Donny saw inside the case must have made him happy, because he made an arrogant gesture with his head that only he would make, then offered Bull the rucksack. The pair conversed briefly, Bull looking contemptuous and Donny looking like a charm school dropout. Donny made a gesture with his hand that I took to mean he might like to buy more explosives in the future, but Bull only shrugged disdainfully.

Mutual dislike obvious, the pair walked away from each other, leaving me to ponder what in the world could have Donny Paglia buying C6 in the middle of the Badlands. No sooner had the question tugged at my mind than I saw Donny pull a colorful silk handkerchief from his pocket and move to tie it at the nape of his neck.

"Oh shit!" I exclaimed, recognizing a signal if ever I saw one.

As if on cue, puffs of smoke appeared from the brush and the bikers on each flank tumbled from their bikes to kick on the ground. The suits moved almost as one, weapons appearing in their hands faster than the startled bikers could react. In a moment, with machine-like efficiency, the space in front of the SUVs belched a solid wall of gunsmoke.

Bull, to his credit, took at least three bullets, but stayed on his feet. One biker managed to fire from the ground, joined a moment later by Smog, but Petey and the rest lay still and dead within seconds.

For a moment, I thought the remaining bikers might manage to escape, but a stitch of semi-automatic rifle fire caught the biker near Smog. Bull lurched at least four times, bloody roses appearing on his torso before he too cartwheeled backwards to land on his back. Alone and outgunned nine to one, Smog never stood a chance, but he managed to dive behind a bike and go down fighting.

As the shooting stopped, I surveyed the passionless suits. They looked like they'd just submitted a timeline for a construction project instead of ambushing and murdering a tough kernel of proud bikers.

Donny stepped forward and stood over Bull, a pistol in his hand. He said something lost to all but Bull and the wind, then calmly shot the big biker in the head. The battle was over, but Donny did something odd. He reached down and took each of Bull's hands, laying them out like the big man had been crucified on the ground.

My brow furrowed as I watched Donny lift the pistol again, then calmly shot the dead biker through the palm of each hand. In my mind, I heard Donny humming a Dean Martin song.

What did Donny's gesture mean? I'd once killed a living man by the name of Hubert Braun by shooting him as he begged. I shot him once through each palm and then through the head. A few comrades had copycatted the move, but no one outside the revolution. The answer exploded in my mind. Donny was blaming the murders on the September Alliance!

I looked down at the scene one last time, seeing the shooters emerge from the trees, then rolled over and let Lucky use the spotter's scope.

"Oh myyyyyy God," she murmured, seeing the carnage more clearly than she had up to that point. "They're all dead."

'Thank you Lucky', I thought, seeing Red calmly gazing through the scope of his sniper rifle.

Mitchell had sent us to find whoever carried out terrorist attacks in our name. She wouldn't like the answer.

The following newspaper article appeared on page two of The Los Angeles Voice

New Party Proposes Clemency for Terrorists

The newly founded People's Progressive Party has announced that it will propose a blanket amnesty for all members of the September Alliance not directly guilty of murder once they obtain an elected platform.

This move comes as no surprise to those who have thus far chosen to portray the Progressive Party as the political wing of the September Alliance. The new party, which has a manifesto very similar to that of the terrorist organization, has denied any linkage between the two organizations and makes it a point to condemn terrorist activity while at the same time expressing understanding as to why some would resort to terrorism out of frustration.

Even if the Progressive Party should gain elected representation in one or more dominion parliaments, it seems unlikely they would garner enough support to see their initiatives through. In the imperial parliamentary system, third parties rarely hold the key to governments.

Coalitions are rare, and are usually the monopoly of the two largest parties.

Despite the odds, observers of the September Alliance are now feeling emboldened enough to link the formation of the Progressive Party with the terrorist ceasefire, though there appears to be at least one recalcitrant splinter group in the Rocky Mountain Dominion. These experts say that the September Alliance is trying to join the mainstream political process and should be encouraged rather than investigated. Law enforcement officials hasten to say that corrupt or criminal politicians are investigated and arrested as a matter of routine, and that the exceptions for crimes of a political nature are unheard of.

After a long nighttime ride to Calgary, lucky and I slept late the next morning and woke with an incredible appetite for hot breakfast and hotter coffee. Mitchell had ordered us to the pleasant city with orders to await contact. Red returned to his cabin.

After showering and waiting through Lucky's ruthlessly thorough makeup session, we wandered into a pancake house called *Barrett's*, which could have been anywhere in the empire, but seemed a little cleaner than most, and catered to a clientele that seemed a little lazier than most. Checker-shirted men lounged on the stuffed orange counter stools and sipped coffee from mass produced ceramic cups meant to withstand the worst of nuclear blasts and clumsy waitresses.

"You must have fought hard," I told Lucky, motioning to the spiderweb of scars on her forearms as I chewed a mouthful of plump sausage and pancakes with maple pecan syrup. I brought up the scars like casual small talk, but really meant it as a stepping stone to a more meaningful conversation about Lucky herself.

"Huh?" asked Lucky, apparently not following my train of thought.

"The scars on your arms," I clarified with a nod of my head. "You have a lot of them there, but not so many on other parts. That means you had to have been actively defending yourself."

A trace of fear flitted across Lucky's face as my chosen topic sank in. She seemed to shrink back into the wood and naugahyde seat like my words had pierced some kind of imaginary balloon she used to shield herself from the reality of her body. The clink of plates and silverware echoed behind her as a telltale swallow in her throat betrayed the depth of the chord I'd struck.

Lucky shrugged her shoulders, making her braless breasts bounce in the same tight, heavy metal t-shirt she'd worn the day she'd come to Reno. She lowered her head and shook it back and forth, staring down on the rind of her salted honeydew melon.

"Doesn't matter Nicky," she whispered softly, then speared a crescent of sweet melon with her fork. "It happened a while ago."

Whatever the nonchalance in her words, Lucky couldn't mask how deeply her fork sank into the melon, nor how quickly the melon disappeared into her mouth, or how hard she chewed.

"I don't know," I pushed, dabbing a sausage into syrup. "I think it speaks pretty well of you. It means you have guts, and you're willing to fight, not just…"

"Fuck for the revolution," she whispered fiercely, supplying words I wouldn't have chosen, but not meeting my eyes. She swallowed. "But I guess we can't all be you, Nicky, can we? Some of us need to use other talents."

"All your talents," I lectured without a clue as to how she would respond. "A lot of the girls in the revolution…"

"I know," she cut me off, sharp eyes shooting up defensively. "I know about Julie because I talked to Cat. Julie fucked inside the revolution. She didn't go outside. Cat did, but Julie didn't." Lucky brandished her fork balanced between two fingers, then lectured *me.* "Cat and Julie might have done some whoring for the revolution, Nicky. But they were never the whores *of* the revolution. I am. It's something I'm good at. It's how I make a difference. I'm fine with it and I don't care what you or anyone else thinks." She moved her head to wipe one eye on the tight sleeve of her bicep, smudging her eyeliner.

I stared at Lucky, plainly having hurt her more than I intended. My question had been to get her to open up, not diminish her even further in her own eyes.

"I'm sorry, Lucky," I told her, knowing I'd gone too far. I wished I could take the words back.

"Don't worry about it, Nicky," she responded bitterly. "I've got a thick skin, as you can tell."

Her attempt at humor didn't make either of us laugh.

Suddenly not hungry, I pushed my plate of food away and reached into my pocket for a cigarette. We had a late morning, hot coffee, and as far as I was concerned, all the time in the world.

"If you want to tell me what happened, you can," I told her, looking away but hoping she heard the sound of honest friendship and sympathy in my voice. "I'll listen, and that's a promise." I tapped the butt of the smoke on the formica tabletop and nodded for emphasis.

Lucky looked up with sad eyes. They say that a girl's appearance is the most important thing to her and she won't talk about its defects with just anyone. I wished I knew more about girls.

Lucky didn't say anything for a few seconds, and I wondered what went through her mind. Your personal ghosts and demons never leave, you just forget about them for a while and then, when you least expect it, they're back.

"OK," Lucky responded after a fairly long pause that ended with a deep and uneven breath. "But what I tell you stays between us, OK?" Her eyes looked up at my face, as if gauging whether or not she could trust me to keep her secret, no doubt figuring in my depressingly short but professionally expected lifespan.

Off in one corner of the restaurant, a table full of suburbanites burst into laughter, totally oblivious to the serious nature of our conversation. "Wait wait wait! There's more," joked a beefy guy in a white silk shirt with a black t-shirt beneath, his hands thrown up like a king throwing coins to a crowd.

Lucky and I let our eyes stray to the happy group of friends, and for a moment, I found myself wondering what it would be like to have such a happy, carefree existence. It seemed a good life, with girlfriends who hadn't made up but still looked pretty, telling tales of pleasure and pun. Did the life I'd chosen really offer more reward? I fought for a better world, but their world looked pretty good.

"I was born in a suburb outside of Phoenix," whispered Lucky after we stopped staring. "We weren't rich or anything, but not poor either. We lived in one of those clapboard houses with air conditioning and a driveway. My dad traveled a lot, was in sales, until he died in a plane crash when I was nine. My mom worked at a car repair shop, calling around to find the cheapest parts for the customers. She came home tired all the time so we didn't interact a lot."

Lucky paused and set aside her fork, intentionally avoiding my eyes as she took up her spoon and recaptured her bowl of cottage cheese. Her voice sounded distant, and more than a little sad.

"I went to high school, became a cheerleader without really distinguishing myself, but I found that if you had looks, the boys would follow. There's a certain way to advertise yourself and I managed to master it. La de da da, I get to community college like most of the rest of my graduating class and I find out there are a lot more pretty girls than I dreamed existed, and they're all competing for the same handful of alpha husbands. I really didn't want marriage, nor could I figure out what to major in, so I decided to take a year off to work, kinda figure out what to do.

"I got a job as a waitress," she jerked her head towards the older woman with cigarette stained fingers and coffee stained blouse who served our breakfast. "I didn't see much future in that. The work was too hard, the pay too little, so I looked around for other options, and found pretty much the same situation no matter what field I looked at. So long as you didn't have a degree, you got stuck in the underclass, so I decided to use my looks.

"I answered an ad in a local paper looking for attractive girls to work in Las Vegas. It promised good money without a major time commitment. Essentially, when I got through the process, the agency did two things. First, they auditioned you for the shows. If you could sing and dance at least a little, that's where you went, into the chorus line. If not, you went to the strip joints. Everyone wanted the former, but the latter paid a lot better."

Lucky rolled her finger in the air as if illustrating how easily I should be able to follow the flow of her logic.

"I got 'lucky' and managed to squeak into the chorus line at the Palazzo," she shrugged, naming one of the better hotel casinos on the strip. "We practiced, we danced, I made enough to support myself and do a little socializing. Mostly we danced in feather boas or skimpy costumes but a few were topless. No big deal to go topless since you were just one set of tits among thirty, right?"

124

I nodded.

"Wrong," she said, knowing she would take me by surprise as surely as she did. "That kind of money doesn't cut it in Vegas. Maybe it's enough for a country girl, but not for someone who has just enough sophistication to want more, but not enough to know how to play the game to her advantage."

"You see, Vegas makes you dream. It makes you think you can get lucky. You can win without doing anything. All you need to do is play long enough at the right table and eventually you win some kind of glamorous life full of glitter and champagne. The people who run Vegas understand that dream, and they know how to play it to their advantage."

"When I got to the Palazzo, real pros still ran it. I mean former gangsters. A lot of people liked the gangsters running Vegas. They thought mob casinos were more fun than corporate casinos. Corporations apply a principle called segmentation, where every part of the casino is supposed to make money. The casino, the restaurant, the manicurist, la de da de da. Everything is supposed to make money independently. The gangsters only wanted the gambling to make money and didn't care about the rest."

"The gangsters turned managers knew how to watch for girls like me, pretty girls with big dreams and not enough brains to make it come together. They look, and they wait, and they make you a proposition. At first, they suggest you go to dinner with their lawyer. The guy is nice, a family man. He's from out of town. He just wants company for dinner and you get a nice tip from Benny."

"Benny was the name of the guy who got you into hooking?" I asked.

Lucky nodded.

"That's where the story goes, but the first guy Benny set me up with, the lawyer, was to break the ice, get me used to pleasing men for money. The lawyer didn't ask me to his room. He didn't ask for my phone number. Benny explained it simply enough. All you need to do is laugh at his jokes, smile, and tell him you had a wonderful time. The next favor looks just as good, only it involves a different man and a little bit more, like drinks alone in his room. You fuck the fifth one, but it still doesn't feel like prostitution. After all, you're just doing Benny a favor and it's all a win-win game. Entertaining is part of casino life, and that's what you're doing, entertaining. Money doesn't even enter the equation at first. Benny just gives you a night off with some vouchers for free drinks on the VIP floor so you can dress up and try to catch the eye of the high rollers, hoping to land a sugar daddy. It never worked for me, but it did for other girls."

Lucky stopped to let her thoughts catch up with her words. A tear had formed at the corner of her eye and she used the heel of her palm to wipe it away.

"La de da de da. Before you knew it I'd entertained men for over a year. Big time gamblers who won, or lost, a lot at the casino, famous people, corporate hotshots that viewed me like the cream and sugar next to their coffee, a complementary service. Assholes! Every one of them! The gangsters were no better, but they at least talked to you like a person because they had no illusions about moral superiority."

I finally lit the cigarette I'd been holding, my eyes fixed on Lucky and her sad story. Like a creepy TV show, you could feel the horror coming a step closer every time she rolled her finger to indicate time went by. Lucky swallowed before she could bring herself to tell the next part.

"So anyway, I'm sitting there wasting my life, hoping to get lucky without any kind of clue that I'm doing things all wrong, but that's OK with Benny, at least until the day I start to lose my looks. In the meantime, he talks to me like a friend, makes me feel like a part of the casino, introduces me to various men that might be of interest." Smoke curled from my cigarette as another roll of the hand meant Lucky's story would speed up.

"Benny introduces me to this guy named Pierre Dellier, the bigshot CEO of some French tire manufacturer. For a minute or two I think its all the same game, but then another girl named Tina pulls me aside and tells me that this guy beat up another girl during sex, hurt her really bad. And then she goes on to tell me that *she* had a run-in with him that was just plain scary, like the guy ripped her dress half off and shoved her cheek into the brick wall down in the parking garage, and then tried to grind her face into the brick. She said that if two drunk guys hadn't stumbled across them she didn't know what might have happened and I could see she's scared to even tell me the story, and not just scared of this Pierre guy. She says she told Benny about what happened and Benny said he didn't believe her even though she knew he *did* believe her.

"That warning was enough," Lucky continued under her breath, eyes looking up and away at some object that made it easier to tell her story. "You hear stories about it happening all the time. You think it can never happen to you. Then one day you find yourself looking into the eyes of the fact that it can, so you shy away and find another man to talk to and hope it just goes away. That didn't happen. Pierre Comeaux took a liking to me, or maybe it was some kind of hate he harbored against all women. He went to Benny and asked him to oil the way but it was a no go. I knew trouble when I saw it.

"Benny didn't understand why I wouldn't go near his 'friend' when I'd been so easygoing all along." She paused, then spat, "Yeah, easy. Like a fool." Lucky shook her head in disgusted hindsight. "He turned the pressure on, first at the cocktail party where he introduced us, then afterwards one on one. He told me showgirls could be replaced, reminded me that he controlled my access to high rollers and could keep me on the dance floor Fridays and Saturdays if he liked. Benny scared me, but nowhere near as bad as Pierre, not in that intense physical fight or flight way."

"I didn't know Pierre detested rejection. I probably could have guessed, but even if I had, I still would have been caught between the Devil and the deep blue sea. He tried to buy me from Benny, but Benny already knew I wouldn't play ball. He sent me flowers. He sent me cards, and he even sent me a necklace but no way Jose. I was way too scared. Then, as suddenly as it all began, it stopped. I thought he'd gone away."

Lucky reached over and plucked my cigarette from between my fingers, twirled it as easily and as agilely as a baton and took a drag, her face looking like she thought I may as well know the rest.

"He caught me in one of the dressing rooms. Benny had asked me to wait for him after the show to discuss a couple of the new girls. He did stuff like that sometimes, but deep in my heart, I think Pierre asked him to place me in a vulnerable position. Most likely, Benny didn't know exactly what Pierre had in mind, but he cooperated. Why? Because that was his job!

"I knew the moment the dressing room door opened that Pierre wanted to rape me and that I couldn't stop him so..."

Lucky shrugged helplessly, her voice breaking. "You know what they say, Nicky, when rape is inevitable..."

She sighed like she would rather cry, had cried, and cried many times.

"Not that I could have enjoyed it, but I thought I could at least..." Lucky took a deep breath and visibly held back tears by closing her eyes until they passed. "I thought at least," she continued, the pain evident in her voice. "I though at least I could avoid getting hurt."

A distant bus boy set down a tub of dirty dishes with a clatter. A whole diner talked and ate and joked without sensing the tragedy my comrade relived in their midst.

"I didn't start screaming until the knife came out," she half said and half whimpered. "But by then, my strength was almost gone. Putting my arms up was all I could do, even knowing they could be hurt, that I needed them, it was better than having that awful sliver of cold metal inside me. I put my arms up and screamed as loud as I could, and then, just when I heard running footsteps, just when I thought help had arrived, he forced my hands down and slowly, carefully, carved the scars on my face."

"'That's for robbing me of my fun,'" he said, meaning that because I hadn't fought or tried to struggle, he hadn't been satisfied. "Oh God, if I knew he thought that way I would have fought like a tiger, but how does anyone know what a crazy person thinks?"

With one hand I reached across the table and touched Lucky's arm, hoping the simple gesture would steady her. To her credit, she didn't flinch.

"Security heard the screaming and came running, but too late. Pierre struggled with a big guy named Dan that always joked around with the girls. We never paid him any attention because he wasn't rich and he wasn't handsome, but I tell you he was brave. Even unarmed he took Pierre down knife and all without flinching, even when Pierre tried to stab him. They hauled the bastard away and called an ambulance and they called Benny and Benny saw me to the hospital with this pained look on his face. He told me everything would be fine, that Pierre would be punished, but you know what?"

"What?" I echoed, sensing the worst.

"After I got out of the hospital, I went back to the casino to get my things. I couldn't dance any more. I couldn't turn Benny's tricks any more. I had nothing, but Dan escorted me back to get my stuff and say my good byes. As I was leaving, we went through the main entrance and you know what I saw?"

I shook my head no.

"I saw Pierre arriving in his stretch limo, and as he got out, Benny met him. The bastard leaned down and kissed Pierre's hand. He kissed the hand of the man who ruined my face and body and the only livelihood I ever knew. Then, when I confronted him, he had Dan remove *me* from the premises for acting like a petulant child. Pierre just laughed."

"Christ almighty," I groaned in awe and sympathy. Lucky's story touched me, made me feel like the sensitive kid I'd been in high school instead of the terrorist I'd become. I wanted to hug her and hold her and make everything all better, but of course that wasn't possible. Not only did Cat figure into the equation, but Lucky lived well beyond the hugs and kisses stage of feeling better.

"It gets better," she grimaced, wrapping both hands around her brown coffee cup, metallic blue nails bright and out of place. "The casino, or really the parent company, Worldwide Entertainment, wouldn't give me a severance package unless I signed a waiver. I had to sign away my right to sue for the right to support myself for a few more miserable weeks until I could find another job. Eventually I got a waitress job at an S&M club. They liked the scars, and as they healed, I eventually ended up shaking it on their stage for the not so discerning side of Las Vegas."

Lucky lifted a finger knowingly. "That's how I knew Debs would go for another girl. After a year or so stripping..." She left the rest unsaid, and I didn't question her about her own preferences or lack of them. She'd gone through the sexual wringer enough times.

Sitting across from Lucky, I couldn't help but think she wouldn't be bisexual or heterosexual, but asexual. She'd burnt out on sex, and it left her hollow and empty enough that when she did it, with me or with anyone else, it was a job, labor. She used her body the way I used guns, as a tool, and loved it about as much as anyone loved an inanimate object.

Lucky didn't have to finish the rest of her story. I could fill in the blanks, but I sat quietly as she finished telling about how the casino covered up Pierre Dellier's crime. In some cities, that wouldn't have been possible, but like everyone knows, in Vegas, anything is possible.

Money means influence and influence means immunity. Vegas is big business and big business means big money.

As her tale came to an end, I felt how the hurt given Lucky purpose, turned a shy suburban blonde girl named Lucy Keyes into the vengeful, willing Lucky, tenacious whore of the revolution.

I wished I had the same sense of purpose.

The following news article appeared in syndicated news outlets throughout the Empire and in most major dailies throughout the world.

One Up One Down for PATSI

The Patriotic Anti-Terrorism and Sedition Initiative, widely known as PATSI, received a thumbs up and a thumbs down today as the Parliament of the New Zealand Dominion said 'aye' and the Quebec Dominion said 'nay'.

Both results came as no surprise to watchers of the controversial surveillance act, designed to strike hard at the September Alliance and any other would be revolutionaries. Both parliaments voted largely along party lines with limited numbers of defectors. Declared votes left little doubt as to the outcome in either dominion.

Yesterday's votes brought the total number of dominions voting in favor of the act to three and those against to two, with voting yet to be called in fifteen dominions. The English Dominion and Dixie Dominion both vote tomorrow and the initiative is considered a foregone conclusion in both parliaments, with ratification expected by landslide margins.

Two days after my heart to heart with Lucky, I got a text message from an unknown sender. WEST RIVER RUN DRIVE IN C YA 3:00

"Great," I bitched to the hapless Lucky. "Mitchell wants to meet at a drive in when we're driving a motorcycle.

Lucky wrinkled her nose. "Let's go half an hour early and wait outside," she suggested. "It beats trying to steal a car."

Her idea did beat stealing a car because I'd never learned how to steal a car. In River Valley, we'd had a guy who worked in repair shops duplicate keys and steal the cars months later. In California, we'd had a semi-professional thief do the trick. For all my other talents, I couldn't steal a car if my life depended on it.

I looked up at the sky full of boiling thunderclouds, thinking we might end up watching the movie in the rain. As it turned out, the weather obliged. We waited for Mitchell in sheets of wind and rain that slashed across the pavement like a giant squeegee. Even though we sheltered under an overhang, by the time a white sedan pulled over to let us in, we were both sopped to the skin.

Blissful calm followed the thunk of the car doors after we piled into the back seat. With one hand, I snatched the cheap ball cap off my head and let my hair shake out, not caring how much water poured off my riding jacket. Beside me, Lucky tossed her hair, expertly caught it as only a girl can, and tied it into a loose ponytail.

"You two look like you need to go through the wringer," rolled the flat, emotionless tone of Mitchell's voice from the front seat. She didn't turn around. Nor did the driver, who had short brown hair neatly parted with the precision of an accountant's sharpest pencil.

"We've already been through the wringer," I scoffed, knowing full well that Mitchell lacked a sense of humor.

"Not the worst wringer you've been through," she retorted without an inch of pity or honoring me with the stern fix of attention. She seemed calm and composed, even attractive in a natural way, her face set off by a dress that fit tight around her neck with embroidered flower attention-getters that formed a perfect arrow on the collar. The design reminded me of the dresses women wear in karate films. White trim set off her dusky skin and the embroidery highlighted her face.

"How about you, Lucky?" Mitchell quizzed in the same calm voice but even less personal attention.

"I'm OK," started Lucky. "For a few days I was stuck in Biker Hell but…"

"You survived I see," interrupted Mitchell without turning around. Lucky's face fell ever so slightly.

"Sure I survived," she rushed, "and I found out what we needed to know. You'd be surprised how many guys think you can't listen to a conversation if you have a vagina and don't…"

"Nicky told me," interrupted Mitchell again, still distracted by the windshield wipers. "Good job."

That flip remark irked me. Lucky had given her all for that mission, and she'd done a spectacular job in my opinion. Yes, she did sleep with Bull and Debs to learn what she needed to learn, but she'd done it without blinking an eye and returned safely with accurate information in record time. She deserved more than 'good job'.

"Here we are," grunted the guy driving the car, his voice tight with a Boston accent, making 'are' sound like 'ah'. He drove the car to the ticket office and rolled the window partway down to manage the ticket purchase. The roof of the car blocked my view of the girl's face, but I caught sight of a pale arm with plastic jewelry and unpainted nails making change. The driver nodded, thanked her, then piloted the car into one of several hundred open spots, away from the dozen or so other patrons who braved the weather.

"She said they'll start the film as soon as they get a break in the weather," the driver said, pulling the keys from the ignition and turning halfway around so I could get a good look at his prep school face. "Call me, Doctor Fish," he said, offering his hand in a calculated manner. "Sorry I can't tell you my real name."

"Zorba," I answered reaching up to shake. "I understand, but you can call me Nicky."

"I've been looking forward to meeting you, Nicky," Doctor Fish said as we shook. His handshake felt strong and confident, not what you expect from a preppie. Strong and sure of himself, decisiveness glinted in his eye.

Mitchell interrupted before Doctor Fish had a chance to introduce himself to Lucky, not that he showed any sign of doing so, which I found rude, again.

"Doctor Fish is being introduced to you," Mitchell began, "in case something should ever happen to me. He and I work as a team in

135

North America. Since you've become quite a valuable asset, I want to make sure we preserve you under all possible circumstances."

"Sounds good," I answered, ego smiling happily under her praise. I nodded to Doctor Fish and tucked my thumbs into my pants pockets, then reclined. "I just hope we won't be seeing each other." I smiled.

"I hope so as well," clucked Mitchell softly, "but this is a dangerous business as you know, and we can't assume. In our line of work, moles burrow up, not down."

"Yeah, enemies never sleep," I agreed, never having seen a mole.

"Dangerous enemies," added Doctor Fish. "Dangerous enemies with a lot of resources."

"Nicky doesn't need to be reminded of that," stated Mitchell dryly. "He's survived more shootouts with the police than anyone I've known." She paused. "Which reminds me, I have some bad news."

My heart gave a 'please don't let it be someone I'm close to' lurch, which could apply to one and only one person, Cat. With the exception of Cat, I existed in a world with no friends, no family, and few acquaintances. The last I'd heard, Cat was doing well, so I summoned the courage to ask.

"Who is it?" I croaked, feeling helpless.

"Gonzo," she answered without a trace of pity. "We thought he would pull through, but things didn't go well. He had an infection. Doc tried to save him but without the resources of a hospital he could only do so much."

"Oh man," I groaned. I hadn't known the Gonz long, but I'd liked him. He'd been recruited to the cause in prison while serving a stint for grand theft auto, a skill he'd put to use for the revolution after his release. A quiet, chubby, man with a ready laugh, he'd been the backbone of the Three Saints squad.

Gonzo had been gut shot in a firefight right in front of my eyes. We successfully got him away from the scene and kept him alive until the only doctor in the revolution could arrive. Like everyone else, I assumed he would pull through. Like everyone else, I'd been wrong. Score one for the bad guys.

"I'm sorry," added Mitchell without sounding sorry at all. She could have said, 'I'll see that and raise you two,' or 'Too bad the dice didn't turn up a seven.' She was that cold. Lucky, who shivered from the drenching and had her hands tucked up under her armpits, looked a lot warmer.

Gonzo and I just hadn't known each other long enough or well enough for me to truly and deeply mourn his passing. When you're a terrorist, you have to expect that you're going to lose comrades from time to time, and in victory or grief, the show goes on.

"I just hope he died in his sleep," I said, giving my head a shake. "And there's worse ways to go than dying in battle. Cancer would have taken a lot longer."

While technically true, cancer would not have been likely to manifest itself in Gonzo before another ten prime years had passed and dying of cancer isn't dying for a greater good. Life isn't clear cut.

I added on for good measure, "He was a really valuable resource." That sounded hollow, even to me, but what more could I say?

He'd impressed me as a terrorist, but I'd never really gotten to know him, so I didn't fake it.

"Speaking of resources," Mitchell spoke up, obviously not wanting to dwell on departed comrades, "How are yours holding up?" She meant our finances.

"We've got about four hundred and change," I informed her, "Enough to live on for another week if we're careful."

Mitchell passed me an envelope. "Here's two-fifty more. That's all I can spare. Do you still have the marijuana we used to bait Scheuer?"

I nodded.

"You should be able to get a couple of thousand if you can find a buyer."

I took the money Mitchell offered. Never pass up free cash. Alliance operatives are supposed to be self-financing, and she'd given what she'd given only because I operated out of my area and mobile over a wide area. Still, two fifty didn't amount to a fortune. I didn't have any local contacts besides Whirly and Red wouldn't know who dealt drugs. The few bikers I'd met for more than a minute were pushing up daisies out in the Badlands. Not that Mitchell would concern herself with such petty problems, but unloading a brick of reefer wouldn't necessarily be a piece of cake.

Outside, the rain started to slow as Doctor Fish looked over the front seat.

"Take a look at this," he suggested, then leaned back over the seat and passed me a rolled up magazine. "You need to be careful. This just came out today. Keep a low profile."

I wrinkled my forehead and unrolled the magazine, then let out a "Wow" of surprise. There, on the cover of *Imperial News Weekly*, in the lower right hand corner and partially obscured by type, was my picture. I'd made the cover of the most widely circulated news magazine in the empire, and not in a good way.

'*Is Peace in Their Hands?*' read the cover, and I looked down at the photo again. One of four, mine had a grainy, seedy appearance in keeping with the general theme of savagery and mystery. Each photo bore a mock mug shot placard on the bottom. Mine read, not surprisingly, '*Papadopoulos, Nicholas T., aka Nicky Pops*'.

Lucky peeked timidly over to look at the magazine, her eyes registering a visible tang of surprise. I could only shake my head and skim the supporting text that questioned whether or not peace could be made with the September Alliance when such dangerous people walked the streets.

"Shit," I groaned, half to myself and half to my comrades. "It's going to be two weeks before that damned rag comes off the shelves and a year before it leaves the dental offices."

"Just be glad it isn't a better photo," answered Mitchell without a whole lot of concern in her voice. "You've dealt with worse. You'll manage."

While technically true, that didn't figure the role of sheer luck into the equation. I'd slipped through dragnets, evaded manhunts, shot my way through cordons of cops, been posted on a hundred APBs and never been caught. People won at roulette, but that didn't necessarily mean they possessed skill at manipulating the fall of the ball.

"I'll read it later," I sighed, and passed the magazine to Lucky, who promptly flipped it open to the relevant article. Whether she did that to symbolically hide from the conversation or out of genuine interest I had no way of knowing, but she folded it out on her sticky bare legs and bent her head like an A student with a math book.

"Just as well," concluded Mitchell, who then waited a long two minutes for an unusually loud drumbeat of rain and hail to pass.

The noise had an effect like silence, making me focus on Mitchell with my eyes alone, to take in her piercing green eyes. Intelligent and cunning, they focused beyond you and onto the revolutionary goals to a degree that made you dread being a pawn on her side of the chessboard. She was pretty in an untouchable way, with a hint of natural color to her skin and lush brown hair that framed rounded features, but little femininity lay beneath the skin.

In the noise that interrupted the conversation, I started to wonder for the first time how I might go about leaving the revolution. My level of commitment had sunk to an all time low, and without Julie or Cat I had no personal anchor. Maybe the time had come?

When the rain subsided, Mitchell turned the subject to the mission at hand.

"We ran the plates for those gas guzzlers," she opened in a tone that meant she'd discovered something interesting.

"Whadidja come up with?" I babbled, my poor grammar making me feel like a teenaged buffoon.

"They're all registered to the same place. A legal firm called Fester, Fowler, Fagan, and Finch. They're based out of New York, but these vehicles are registered to their office in Winnipeg, opened only four months ago, the vehicles purchased a week thereafter."

"That's right before the fake bombings started," chimed Lucky in a shy voice.

Doctor Fish nodded. "Exactly."

"That ain't coincidence," I added. "Not after what we saw in the Badlands."

"No, it's not," agreed Mitchell. "We realized that when we first made the connection so we did more research. She passed a stack of printed web pages over the seat with a read it yourself shrug. "We found out this firm plays a quiet brand of politics. They lobby in different dominions and in London, usually for Big Agra but they're not fussy. They've funneled funds through the Bay Street Project and thus have had a major say in drafting new legislation in various committees. They're willing to write that legislation on behalf of their corporate clients, for a fee."

Mitchell passed me a manila folder. "They're what we would call bad apples."

"And you want them gone," I finished for her, knowing where the train stopped.

"Not yet," she replied, a bit to my surprise. "Remember, we have a ceasefire to uphold. What you're doing out here is top secret and very much behind the scenes. No one can get wind of it."

"It's about the new political party isn't it," asked Lucky from my side, catching all of us by surprise as she clapped the magazine closed "Same reason this magazine is wondering if you guys will turn in Nicky and the others on the most wanted list."

Rain or no rain, you could have heard a pin drop as Mitchell slowly turned to Lucky.

"It is because of the new political party," Mitchell confirmed too quietly, fixing her gaze on the hapless Lucky, who visibly cringed.

In a soft whisper that rippled like a menacing growl, Mitchell leveled her words like a double barreled shotgun. "Don't think for a second we would turn on Nicky to get that party going, or anyone else who served the revolution. The people who founded this revolution did so for principles." She paused, then added, "And morals."

Lucky's face fell as she registered the insult but didn't respond. She obviously didn't deal well with authority. On that day, in that car, she didn't need to, because I'd just heard enough. Not only was I far from certain the revolution wouldn't trade my life, or at least my freedom, for two seats in a dominion parliament, but I didn't need to hear my superior turn on a loyal comrade. Mitchell had literally ordered me to take the lives of hundreds of men and women. Lucky didn't deserve punching bag status because she happened to have *fucked* a few grown men. And women.

"Ease off," I told Mitchell, catching her by surprise. "She's only saying what I'm thinking and she did a damned fine job back in the sticks. Give her some credit and if you don't like her methods, give her some more credit because she doesn't like them either, but she uses them anyway and they got the job done."

Doctor Fish turned towards the windshield. Lucky turned away towards the rain pelting on her passenger window, symbolically leaving the fight.

Mitchell turned back over the seat and we glared at each other for half a minute. We'd never been close, even if we worked together, yet we'd never been openly hostile before. I'd disobeyed orders and skirted orders I didn't like. She'd never taken me to task for those breaches because somehow or other, I'd always managed to tie a pretzel and make everything come out right in the end. That could change in an instant.

"You don't lead this revolution Zorba, you serve it," she said, coolly responding to the challenge. "I suggest you remember that."

I leaned my wet head back onto the warm upholstery and gave a distasteful scoff, just to show how little I cared, then countered. "And I suggest you remember that without people serving the revolution, you don't have a revolution." I kept my voice in control, not mocking her, not calling her names, but standing my ground. "Remember that Katrina Kreider lady, the informant that took down the Texas Company?"

Mitchell had to remember Katrina Kreider. The whole world knew about Katrina Kreider. She'd become famous not for having penetrated our network, but for turning in her badge and going on television saying the people in the Texas Company were a lot nicer than the Specials, and she regretted her choice.

Mitchell gave me a get on with it shrug.

"The Specials lost Katrina Kreider because they were a bunch of pricks, not because of some twist of fate. If Hess treated her with dignity she would still be on our asses and there's no telling how many good people we would have lost." I jerked a thumb towards Lucky. "Don't piss away your best people."

"You're walking on dangerous ground, Zorba." Mitchell had the air that one day she wouldn't need to listen. For all I knew, she saw me as much a liability as an asset and would indeed trade me for those two parliamentary seats, assuming I lived long enough to be traded, a tentative bet. High profile terrorists have notoriously short life expectancies.

Doctor Fish turned to watch, silently observing the tension, missing nothing. If the Specials ever got hold of Mitchell, he would need to know how I operated, how to use me effectively.

After a long moment, Mitchell told me in a voice cool as any I'd ever heard. "Be glad you're not expendable yet. I need you for this mission and I need you after, so let's keep our minds on current events."

That sounded like a good idea.

"Where do you want to go with Fagan Feeney firm?" I asked to the accompaniment of the steady fall of rain, glad that the argument had passed, but seeing no sense beating around the bush or making small talk with the mood soured. At best, someone could describe my relations with the higher ups as 'awkward'.

"Go to Winnipeg, find out what this guy Donny is doing. Find out what this law firm has been contracted to do. Find out, and tell me. We'll decide what to do from there."

"Can I kill Donny?" I asked, bluntly. I had a score to settle. He'd killed a man I'd admired.

"Sure," she responded, not caring much. "Just make sure it can't be traced to our organization." She paused. "And make sure killing Donny doesn't put the lawyers on their guard. If we need to move against them, we mustn't to lose the element of surprise."

I had to agree. Why harden a soft target?

"I'll be in touch as soon as I know something," I promised with every intention of keeping that promise.

Without a word, Mitchell passed me a folded piece of plain white paper. With a grunt I leaned forwards and accepted. It would contain specific information on how to contact her in the near future.

"Make sure you destroy this after you commit it to memory," she half ordered and half suggested, unnecessarily either way. I knew the drill.

"Will do," I assured her, business as usual. "Anything else?" I asked as I passed the square to Lucky, who plucked it from my hand and slipped it between the pages of the magazine.

Mitchell's eyes sparked.

"Lucky doesn't need to see that," she said, sounding slightly annoyed.

"Well if someone decides to pop me, how is she supposed to contact you?" I asked the obvious question.

"She'll be in contact every day. You're the one who will be in the field. I'm taking Lucky back with us." She talked to me like the class dunce. "What were you planning on using her for, Nicky? Scheuer is dead and lawyers aren't like bikers. Her..." Mitchell paused to choose her words. "Her talents won't help you with lawyers."

Lucky snorted, undoubtedly understanding what Mitchell didn't, that her talents helped with any man. I played it a different way.

"I want backup," I told Mitchell. "You don't know Donny. I do. He's tough, he's smart, and he chooses his people carefully." In fact, before he'd known my true calling, Donny tried to recruit me. "I want backup."

Doctor Fish shook his head disbelievingly, but once again Mitchell answered, slipping back into her habit of ignoring Lucky.

"Just how is she going to back you up? If she tried to fire a gun she'd shoot herself in her foot."

I opened my mouth to speak, to tell Mitchell that firing a gun wasn't rocket science. You aim, press, and stick your tongue out like a dog, but Lucky beat me to the punch.

"Not any more," she said, leaning forwards in the grey light of rain so that the white scar on her right cheek stood out like gold embroidery on a general's epaulets. "Nicky taught me how to shoot."

The car went quiet and even the rain let up enough that we could see the big screen through the haze. A dozen cars occupied the space meant for hundreds. Maybe the drive-in's traditional place in society had been usurped by movies?

"It seemed like the smart thing to do," I explained. "We had the time, she lacked the skills, we had the ammunition, so we spent some time practicing. If I get more time, I'll show her how to make a gift." By 'gift' I meant a bomb. Somehow or other, the two words had become synonymous in September Alliance slang.

Mitchell shook her head, obviously not attaching any weight to the subject. Most September Alliance operatives held day jobs, and with the cease-fire in place, it seemed doubtful that another mission awaited Lucky's under appreciated talents. The patrons of the Hellfire Club might miss Lucky, but serving the revolution probably lay several months in her future.

"OK," Mitchell agreed with a sigh, like the last thing that mattered to the revolution was Lucky. "Keep her on if you want. Teach her as many new tricks as you can. Contact me when you have something solid."

"Right," I agreed, wanting to leave while the rain paused. "Anything else I need to know?"

Mitchell dug her hand into her jacket pocket and drew out a rumpled but otherwise common white envelope and passed it back over her shoulder as she turned back to face the screen.

"From Cat," she said, her voice again devoid of emotion.

My heart leapt, and I had to stop myself from snatching the letter out of her hand and accept it like a grown up. That didn't stop me from gripping it in my fist like a tightwad with a tenner.

"Thanks," I quipped. "Did she give it to you personally?"

Mitchell nodded without turning around. "She's doing good, expect to see her after your mission is finished."

Funny about how we'd all worried Cat would die and assumed Gonzo would live. You never knew what life had in store for you. Good news from Cat would warm my belly.

"Ready, Lucky?" I asked.

"You guys aren't going to stay and watch the movie?" asked Doctor Fish.

"What's playin'?"

"The Trailblazers. It's a Western. A shoot 'em up."

"No thanks," I told him, opening the door and sliding one foot onto the wet pavement. "I've seen enough of those."

Catherine "Cat" Weatherington wrote the following letter in assumed confidence while she recuperated from gunshot wounds in the September Alliance's Flagstaff safehouse. Mitchell opened, read, and resealed the letter while in her possession. Nicholas Papadopoulos opened the letter, read its contents several times, and finally burned it in the ashtray of his hotel room. He did not see, and thus did not suspect, any sign of tampering.

My Dearest Nicky,

I love you so much. I want to come out and say that right away. The pain of the wounds is nothing compared to the pain of not having you here beside me, but I tell myself every day I recover is one less day I need to wait before seeing you again. Oh Nicky how I miss you.

I'm doing well, or so the doctor says, and he is a real doctor. He tells me I'm lucky to be alive, and that the doctor who did the surgery must have been 'one hell of a doctor'. I heard you took her hostage when you broke me out of the hospital. Damn it you shouldn't have taken such a risk. If you weren't such an evil genius I would be furious with you, but I am happy to be alive and kicking without help from the hangman's noose. Thank you **XOXOXOXOXO**

Mitchell tells me she's sent you on a mission out in the Mountain Dominion and that is why you can't be here. Please don't do anything reckless while I am gone. I know you, and I know how impetuous you can be. Just remember you're not alone. You have me waiting for you, and I want you to come back safe and sound.

Nicky, something is troubling me. I've overheard things here in the safehouse. A lot of the time they forget I'm here, or think I'm asleep. The Supreme Command is very serious about making the political party a legitimate and legal *affair, but it is also generally known that it is the political wing of the September Alliance, and the government is holding the political party hostage. So long as there are no terror attacks, the party can function, but there is also a steady ratcheting up of government demands to turn in some of the worst killers. They mean us. So far, the supremos aren't budging because they need us for leverage, but they are starting to talk of compromises, like exile in Brazil. I don't like the sound of it and I want you to be careful around our own people. The Specials are notorious for accepting dead bodies when they deal.*

When we finally see each other again, I will tell you more. The safehouse (I can't tell you where it is) has seen a number of VIPs in recent days, and I think I have decided which ones can be approached. Mitchell is not a supremo, but she has enormous influence. She and three others are the generals. If anyone gets turned over to the Specials it should be them. They plan the campaigns while we just fight the battles.

Take good care of yourself, watch your back, and remember that when I thought I would die, my last words were..

I love you Nicky,

Cat **xoxoxoxoxoxo X!**

Lucky started calling me Saint Nicholas on account of how I stood up for her, reinforced by the approaching holiday season. That somehow morphed into Saint Nick, and on the third day, through a cloud of never before heard giggles, I became Saint Nicky. She thought it was cute.

We wanted to head for Winnipeg straightaway, but had to sell the brick of weed. Selling to strangers posed too many risks so we wanted to try Whirly. That meant a five hundred mile ride on a bike back the way we had come, preferable to armed robbery but a far cry from convenient. Necessity dictated and so we rode.

The pavement slipped away under our wheels as we covered mile after repetitive highway mile. The scenery, which at first I had found magnificent, became dull and bland, and the distances, which had seemed fascinating, became a frustrating impediment to finishing our mission and getting back to Cat.

Cat's letter put me into overdrive. It felt good to be alive again, even if the revolution seemed more checkered than ever. Staring out over the road, thinking of Cat made me feel like the good guy in a movie. It took a look at the speedometer, which had somehow inched up from ninety to a hundred and five, to snap me out of my daydream and back to reality.

We'd met Whirly in a bar called 'No 2 99', a pretty clear one percent reference. Whirly had been well known in the bar, which his gang frequented. Since the jolly wookie apparently didn't like answering his phone or checking messages, his favorite dive seemed the logical place to start looking. We figured a guy like Whirly could unload a brick of marijuana with ease and might even buy it outright.

The swinging doors of No 2 99 parted like the saloon of a modern day western movie. Substitute slotted wood for rubber and aluminum and you got the same effect. Substitute hairy cowboys smelling of horse for hairy bikers smelling of motor oil and you got the same crowd. Substitute a lone gunslinger for a terrorist and you got my predicament. Bikers lounged over tables, around pool tables, and at the bar. Mongol colors were the rule, not the exception. Lacking those colors marked me as a stranger, almost.

"Heya, Geo," greeted one biker who looked vaguely familiar. He had a round face with long red hair that he tied back with a black bandana. I'd met him at the Gathering, but couldn't remember his nickname.

"How are ya?" I asked, as cool as possible, feeling more comfortable now that I had a known face and nickname. I didn't feel quite at home in the shabby bar with its cracked mirror and single shelf of spirits in gallon bottles, but it didn't seem the alien moonscape like the first time. I slid onto the stool next to the vaguely familiar biker and hunched over on my elbows, signaling the bulldog of a bartender, whose belt, bracelets and necklace were all made of welded bike chain, that I would like a beer.

"Not so bad," answered the biker. "Joker said you might come around ag'in, lookin' for Whirly maybe?"

The name Joker jogged my memory and I pictured a tall biker in dirty white pants with a long face and a mustache neater than most. He held some kind of middle rank in the gang, like a pack leader or something similar. I cursed myself for not having brought Lucky. She would have remembered.

A glass of thin beer slid down the bar and stopped perfectly positioned for my right hand, an impressive pass for a bulldog with fingers fat as sausages and stubby as machine bolts.

"Yeah," I told the red-haired biker as I took a sip of beer. He hefted his own glass and I got lucky, spotting the letters R-O-S-S tattooed across the knuckles. His name was Ross. No. It was close to

Ross. Rossi? Boss? Roscoe! His name was Roscoe, but a nickname as much as a name. "You know where I can find him?"

"I can find out if you got a little time." Roscoe's head bobbed up and down, his voice sounding a little bit sneaky. He also didn't look me in the eye. Our conversation had the feel of a drug deal about to go bad, but I didn't see a way out.

When I didn't answer straight away, Ross rubbernecked to look me in the eye. "You got the time?" He asked seriously, "And a coupla coins for the payphone?"

"Yeah," I told him, leaning up on the barstool to jingle the coins in my pocket. I drew the whole handful, several days worth, and dropped it as a bunch on the counter "Take all ya need," I told him with a nod. With my doubts banished, things seemed normal again, and if a little chunk change would speed things along I would be all the happier.

"Gotcha," Roscoe said, and smiled with what looked like genuine goodwill. He stood up, tucking his thumbs into the pockets of his dirty jeans, "Just gimme a chance to make some calls."

With that, Roscoe sauntered off towards the door even though the bar had a pay phone mounted behind the pool tables. I figured he didn't want to contact other gang members from a known gang hangout.

With Roscoe gone, I turned my attention back to sipping beer and smoking cigarettes. After a glance at my watch, I looked up into the cracked mirror and saw a biker drop some coins into an antique looking jukebox. With an audible shudder, the device turned on with a hum, scratched at the air, then started the slow ballad of the biker favorite, *Number's Up,* basically the funeral dirge of a heroic biker of yesteryear as he revved his engine and headed towards cloud nine. I wondered what

Heaven might look like to a biker. Somehow angels singing hymns and playing harps didn't fit the picture.

I took a look at the bikers in the bar, and found them, without exception, looking back at me en masse. We both found other things to look at in an instant. Cigarettes, beers, pool tables, anything to avoid the pitfall of being caught staring. Bikers didn't trust outsiders.

Six cigarettes, three beers, and nine lonesome ballads later, Roscoe returned, slapping my back with a wide palm.

"You got yourself a damn sight o' luck there, Geo," Roscoe half confessed with envy. "Debs says she'd like to see you ag'in, and I think she meant it."

More than likely, Debs wanted to see Lucky, since she and I sadly hadn't had two sentences of meaningful conversation. I'd skirted her company for fear of offending Bull and endangering both my mission and my life.

"You mean Lucky," I said, not seeing any harm in him hearing my thoughts. His brow wrinkled.

"The little blonde?" he asked, looking puzzled.

"Yeah," I answered.

"Should gather her up and bring her up wit' ya. She's a looker," he grinned. "Even with all that extra work, she's got a tight little body. I loved lookin' at that ass."

He didn't know the half of it, nor did he seem to realize he was talking about someone's daughter, but what could you say? The bikers have their own ways. I could only worry about myself.

I chuckled like he and I shared a joke, though I'd begun to think of him as a moron. Then again, the stupid facade could mask a Roscoe smarter than he looked.

"Hey Roscoe," I grinned. "When you said I should bring Lucky 'up' with me, what were you talking about?"

"Oops," he gaped, looking even dumber than he had a moment ago. I determined right then and there that no one with bright green teeth would ever fight in the revolution.

"You ever hear of a town called Powell?" asked Roscoe. Without waiting for me to admit I didn't, he went on, "Towards Coeur d'Alene, about four hours northwest." Elaborate directions followed.

"Thanks," I said and clapped him on the shoulder. "I owe you one, hope I can repay you sometime."

Roscoe laughed. "I don't think you need to worry 'bout that."

As I left, it seemed every head in the bar turned to follow. I felt the hairs on the back of my neck stand up for no reason. I would be glad to see the end of the bikers. They made me paranoid.

The following dispatch originated in the Imperial Embassy in Kiev and referred to fugitive September Alliance operative Spencer "Cobra" Jakoniuk, widely believed to be hiding in Ukraine after fleeing imperial territory. The author of the letter, Virgil Tross, worked for the Imperial Intelligence Service and was a former acquaintance of the recipient, Truman Hess.

Hello Truman and God bless you,

It's good to know you're still alive and kicking. Back in Antioch I would have laid down money that either the Devil or the drink would have gotten you by now, but I see neither was the case and you prosper more every day.

I've sired two beautiful daughters, and Moira and I are thinking to adopt a boy. Mostly the orphans here are soiled from the Chernobyl disaster or vodka or gypsy parents, but we're hoping to find one that can benefit from being raised in a Christian home.

I also thought I would let you know, in confidence of course and only because you and I go back a long way, that one of my subordinates, a Reports Officer, has had some contact with your Cobra fugitive from the September Alliance. The agent managed to confirm his identity and establish his whereabouts. We did some digging and it seems your man is the nephew of a VIP in Lvov, where he's living under an alias. We've studied it up down and sideways and it really doesn't look like we can smoke him out. We could resort to extra-judicial tactics, but we're being told not to engage in that kind of thing in Ukraine, at least for the moment. Without the extraordinary rendition option, I went digging through your man's file.

Cobra used to live in Atlantic City and has two married cousins still living there. At one time, he stood as godfather to his female cousin's boy, now seven years old, by the name of Alex Darfield. I think we can use this boy to lure Cobra back to Atlantic City.

Cobra took the godfather obligation very seriously and likely still does. Any way we ask the question, the psychiatrists say we can use this kid to lure Cobra back onto imperial territory. What I recommend is a little trick out of the former KGB playbook.

If we eliminate the boy's parents, maybe have their car get hit by a train, it would place Alex in a vulnerable position. We could intervene to prevent him from going to the home of one of his relatives and instead direct him into foster care. That should get Cobra concerned enough to risk a covert reentry where you can nab him. If he doesn't, you can always have the boy infected with a disease to up the ante.

I'd also like to let you know that Moira and I will be in London for six weeks starting mid February. I know you are there frequently and if you would like to get together, maybe for church and brunch, it would be a pleasure to see you again. I know you're busy and wouldn't want to take much of your time.

May God's blessings be on you and your family as we go about the Lord's work, each in our own way,

Virgil

Truman Hess read the dispatch from Virgil Tross five times.

Puttering into Powell with Lucky on the pad and our duffel bag strapped onto the carrier made me feel like a biker. Of course the leather gloves, sunglasses, and wind in my hair helped. I could understand the attraction of the lifestyle. Vast expanses of wilderness, the freedom of the wild, the ability to set your own rules and live as you wished were all powerful forces.

I wondered, when the revolution finished with me or I finished with the revolution, if Cat might like to spend time in the Mountain Dominion. After the last few years, spend some time away would suit me fine, in a cabin far from people, or on the road seeing the dominions one by one. Then again, I would miss my own food. Bikers ate cowboy food, meat and beans and sometimes greens.

I spotted the town of Powell at the exact moment the tang of burning charcoal touched my nostrils, and had no doubt I would find bikers clustered around a grill drinking beer and rubbing their girlfriends' bottoms to the apprehension of churchy townfolk. Until we drove past the welcome sign, it never even crossed my mind that Powell might be a ghost town.

"Powell – Pop. 104" read the sign as we drew close enough to see the unmistakable signs of mass abandonment. A cinderblock gas station, looking naked without its windows, interrupted a picket line of houses with peeling paint and collapsed porches. Judging by the price of fuel still displayed in fading red, Powell had been abandoned thirty years ago. I'd heard the west had lots of ghost towns, but had never seen one.

I felt Lucky squirming to see over my shoulder, her arms wrapped tight around my waist.

"I don't like it," she announced over the putter of the motor. I didn't answer because the pavement took a turn for the long neglected worse and I had to cut our speed even more. I struggled to keep a grip on the handlebars while the bike vibrated hard.

With a shake of my head towards a thin grey column of smoke rising over the rooftops, I grunted my agreement, but we needed to unload the brick of marijuana and refresh our finances soon or resort to even riskier methods out of desperation.

I leaned my head back far enough that Lucky could hear me, far enough that the slipstream tossed my hair. "I hear ya. Let's find Whirly and do our deal then get gone."

The smoke led us to the front lawn of a once a prim and proper little white church with a steeple and wide front doors. It had withstood the test of time better than most buildings in Powell. Even the flagstones and low stone steps leading to the boarded up entry were in pretty good shape. No doubt it had once been the pride of the town. The bikers used it for a picnic.

Spread across the front yard, a dozen or so bikers sat eating the remains of their meal, grilled steaks and potato chips. Their makeshift grill had the size and shape of a cattle trough with a real barbecue's grill thrown over the top.

The bikers themselves lounged around the front yard of the church, including what used to be a park bench. They'd obviously raided deserted homes for doors and leftover furniture that they'd then assembled into crude tables. Some of them had lounge chairs, but I had their attention.

I recognized two of the bikers, one of which was Joker. Even if I'd missed him he would stand out because of his top hat with the jokers of a deck of cards tucked into its ribbon. With his unshaven face, grey eyes and one hand tucked into his belt, he looked more like a gambler from a cowboy movie.

The other biker I recognized didn't look quite so eccentric. He had a ponytail down to his belt, but wore more of the standard biker attire, a heavy denim jacket with a thick leather vest and black leather gloves that had had the fingers cut away. Only a thick gold chain set him apart from the rest because from it hung a palm-sized imitation gold hawk, and Hawk was, of course, his nickname.

Idling up on the bike, I lifted one hand in greeting like an Indian saying 'Hao'.

Something felt odd about the way they watched me. I didn't expect to be welcomed with open arms after having just met them, but something distinctly unfriendly shone in their eyes. If I'd known I would meet such hostile looks, I might not have come, but it was too late to backtrack

"Heya, Hawk," I greeted like I hadn't sensed anything at all. "Nice to see ya again." I smiled over to Joker and greeted him as well. Neither smiled.

"Geo, ain't it?" asked Hawk in a bad way, like he had to half spit my name to say it.

"Yeah," I responded over the purr of the idling motor. "Whirly's friend if ya remember."

"Friend of Whirly's," mused Joker without so much as a tilt of his lips. None of the assembled bikers seemed to want to participate in our little exchange.

"Seen him around?" I asked, feeling more nervous by the second.

"Sure have," answered Hawk, rising from his lawn chair and giving his paper plate a toss onto the door cum tabletop.

"Great," I replied. "Any idea where he is?"

"Sure we know where he is," answered Joker, still without a smile. "We ate `im." With one hand, he half extended a greasy, half folded over paper plate with a partially eaten t-bone in my general direction.

"Want some?"

The pack of bikers shifted, not reacting to the humor. Something was in the air. I hoped Whirly would emerge from behind the chapel. Adrenaline started pounding in my veins as Hawk cleared his throat.

"Aww," he started, talking to Joker without taking his eyes off me. "He don't want none. Him and Whirly are *good friends*." That didn't sound friendly, and neither did what came next. "Bet him and Bull are *good friends* too."

Bull's name caught me by surprise and I had to wrack my brain for an answer. Should I play surprised? Should I play dumb? Should I play it cool?

"Betcha him and Dogman Scheuer is *good friends*, too, ain't they."

"Makes me sick," added another biker.

"He wantsta make lotsa people sick," added another.

Lucky's hands gripped my shoulders before I could answer as she breathed into my ear, her voice so urgent it bordered on panic.

"There's no women. They didn't bring their women. They didn't come to camp out! If they did they would have brought their wo..."

Just as Lucky whispered in my ear, three things happened at once. One of the bikers took a sidestep to swing a hidden shotgun up to fire, kind of pushed his right leg back and pivoted his left as his hands moved like a baton twirler's. At the exact same moment, Joker and Hawk opened their coats and reached towards for pistols while I instinctively gunned the engine on the bike as hard as I could.

The bike rammed the makeshift table Hawk and Joker had thrown their plates onto, striking just under the headlight. The engine packed enough power to push the door forwards into both men, plus two more bikers and the tire of a bike, and bowled them over like ninepins. The door flipped as gravity took one corner into the ground before velocity could relinquish its grip. Hawk screamed for a reason I couldn't see as the front wheel of the motorcycle rode right over the makeshift table, breaking it into splinters.

My hands seemed locked onto the grips. I'd hit the gas instinctively, without really knowing what I was doing, or thinking of the consequences. Before I could back off, the front tire wheelied up into the air. The church steps seemed to rush forwards and I saw the boarded doors far too late to stop. Ducking my head before impact, the back tire hit the bottom step and brought us back down with a jolt. The bike bounced up the steps. I struggled to keep right side up, Lucky clinging for dear life as the bike bounded over the last step and into the door. Just before we crashed through, a shotgun blast blew a hole right over our heads. The echo of the blast blended with the crash of metal and wood as we smashed through the double entry and into the church.

Instinct forced my hands off the controls as my arms shielded my face from the impact of bike and rider on wood, but only the front tire impacted the weak, poorly boarded doors. Like a battering ram giving its final blow to castle gates, the bike smashed through, stuttered and staggered forwards to wobble, momentum spent, right up the center aisle of the dark interior before the front tire caught on a pew and brought the bike, and us, down.

Behind me, Lucky finally lost her battle to stay on the pad as my hands groped for the controls and caught only the left with one finger. The world spun as the bike twisted and I shoved with my calves to sprawl face first down the aisle.

The bike crashed and the biker's shotgun fired again, the blast going well over my head.

"Lucky!" I shouted, rising to my feet and yanking the pistol from its holster. My eyes struggled to adjust to the dim light, but I made out running figures approaching the door.

"I'm OK!" Lucky replied, visibly shaken and struggling to sit up from a distinctly non-sensual sprawl.

"Good," I shouted, crouching and moving away from the open center aisle, aiming the pistol towards the door. "Get some…" I fired at the first silhouette that appeared in the door, the muzzle flash lighting the once sanctified interior. "Cover!"

My feet danced left as the shadow jumped back behind the wall, then reappeared one arm and a pistol extended blindly towards where I'd just been. I fired again, missing, a bright chink of light appeared in the wall next to the shadow as two muzzle flashes responded, the shots wide. The biker couldn't see me because his eyes hadn't adjusted to the dark.

My third shot at the biker brought a cry of pain and he whirled out of the shadow back into the sunlight, howling to his friends that he'd been hit. An arm appeared around the door. I ducked behind a pew. Shots rang out. I rose, catching the biker just as he tried to muscle his way through the front doors and into the blue and grey cloud of exhaust and gunsmoke. I shot him once through the shoulder, and when he didn't go down, once more through the chest. Without a sound, he sagged silently to the floor like Goliath struck by David's sling.

I had five shots left, so my free hand worked towards the extra clip in my pocket. I could make out the sounds of Lucky doing something by the bike, could hear her grunt with exertion.

"Get some cover," I hissed into the dark church, afraid to shout. Lucky, in the open by the bike, was vulnerable. Any biker that entered would have a clear view, and a clear shot.

"In a second," her quiet, urgent whisper replied, but I couldn't respond.

A biker danced directly across the threshold, from one side of the door to the other, much too fast to get a bead on him. I would have done the same thing, try and get a brief look at what lay inside the church before rushing in head first. To one side, I heard hammering at a boarded up window. Once they worked that board loose, they would have me in a cross-fire.

A head poked around the door and I yanked my arm up to fire, but it ducked back. Quickly, I moved, not towards the back of the church, but towards the center, towards Lucky, away from where they would expect me to move.

Shots rang out as a pistol and hand reached around the corner and shot blindly into the church. They didn't hit anything, but a moment later, half a torso emerged, the barrel of a shotgun swiveling not towards me, but towards uncovered Lucky.

Faster than I thought possible, I jerked the pistol up and snapped a shot at the shadow. The shot didn't connect, but it came close enough to force the owner of the shotgun to jerk back before he could fire.

Lucky, or at least the top of her head, scrambled past the open end of the pew, dragging our duffle bag behind her. We were still trapped, but at least she'd gotten some cover.

A crash and a splinter of light made me aim towards the boarded window and put a warning shot right through. Another pinprick of autumn sunlight poked through the dark interior of the church like the eye in the sky, searching for me. The sounds stopped. The shadows didn't appear at the door, and I found myself in the silence of wood dust and gunpowder drifting through still air, both hands on the pistol, waiting as the bikers planned their next move.

"Got it," Lucky exclaimed from somewhere between the altar and the pews behind me. She had to be talking about the *Pica-Pau*. If we could get the streetsweeper out we would have a chance. If not, we had less than a minute before the bikers stormed the building.

One biker lay in the entry, presumably dead, and I'd wounded at least one more, but that left roughly a dozen or more to cause problems. What had gone wrong here? Why had the bikers decided to kill us?

I tried to think things through as I guarded the door. They didn't know we had drugs so their motive couldn't be robbery. Where was Whirly? How did they know about Scheuer? How did they tie *us* to Bull and his crew?

Another shadow darted across the door as I grasped for answers and only came up with more questions. Gripping the pistol in both hands, I stayed in a firing stance, aiming towards the door, moving back towards the shadows on careful feet. I heard a metallic clack as Lucky got her mitts on the automatic.

A bang from the window caused me to aim that direction, only to stop midway as a bang from another window made me swivel again, but in the opposite direction. Their distraction worked, they had the timing down pat, because no sooner did I focus on the new window than someone ducked right through the door and into the space between the outermost row of pews and the outer wall.

I cursed to myself even as the guy popped up just quickly enough to snap a shot in my direction. I fired back and then swung towards the door just as another biker tried to duck through. I fired just before he would have gone into a crouch, catching him in the right shoulder. He sank down with a cry that turned into a moan, but I had to fire back at the one hiding behind the pews as he peered above the wood. I missed, turned to the door, pulled the trigger…

And clicked empty.

I cursed and vaulted back over two rows of pews, only one row from the dais. Shots rang out over my head, pinging off the stone altar and smacking into the wood paneling at the rear as I landed on my back. With a press of my thumb, the empty clip sprang loose and fell to the floor. My free hand jammed the full clip in as quickly as humanly possible, but I heard heavy, running footsteps and the victory cries of bikers as I struggled to my butt with a sit-up that would have done my gym teacher proud.

Coming to my knees, I had the advantage of defending a fortified position, but they had the momentum as I had to put *my* head over the protective wood of the pews. No sooner did I do so than the crack of pistol fire and the boom of a shotgun forced me to duck down and turned the world into a whirl of splinters and smoke.

With a lunge, I belly crawled towards the center aisle, hoping to appear where they wouldn't expect, but ended up firing almost simultaneously when a hulking leather shadow appeared, brandishing a pistol like an usher extending a deadly collection basket. We fired almost simultaneously, but I was just a little faster, and he fell, clutching his chest as his pistol clattered to the floor.

I could sense them massing for the charge, just for a second, because then the floor vibrated with their feet and I felt them take a collective breath, even over the moan of their injured. Criminal gangs could sometimes show a surprising level of discipline. I knew in my mind's eye that they signaled to each other wordlessly, coordinating their actions like professionals. Any moment, and they would storm forwards and kill me.

They'd forgotten about Lucky.

The *Pica-Pau* chattered for more than a moment, and I heard bikers cry out in fear and shock as the chatter of machine gun fire rattled through the chapel. I got my head over the edge of the pew just in time to see the stream of Lucky's badly contained fire popping holes of light in the wooden church walls faster than a pepper shaker on egg white. Sunlight danced through the seven-millimeter openings like a serpentine game of tic-tac-toe on a board fifty across. Lucky visibly struggled to control the weapon's recoil. I could see her fighting with it out of one eye, face minted in determination and arms toned with exertion as she strove to keep the barrel down towards the scattering bikers.

By some miracle, Lucky didn't hit anything human, but out they went, back through the doors on their hands and knees to escape the massive hail of lead. She paused to get a better grip on the gun, then fired over their heads like a teacher emphasizing her point. After only a few seconds, the chatter of ammunition turned into the clatter of metal on metal. She'd run out of ammunition.

Steadily, I rose and sidewalked out of the pew, pathetic pistol held at the ready in both hands, just like a cop.

"Yeow!!" Lucky yelped from behind, and I glanced over my shoulder long enough to see her shaking her hand in the air. She must have touched the hot barrel. After burning through a whole clip, she could thank her lucky stars it didn't glow red.

"You OK?" I asked, edging towards the doors. In the still of the church, I could make out the voices if not the words of the bikers outside.

"Yeah," she answered in a voice tougher than I'd heard in a while. "I burned my hand on the barrel when I went to change clips." She hissed through her teeth as she looked down at her palm, winced, and shook her head. "Stupid. I should have known better."

"We'll get some salve for it back on the road," I told her, jumping over the dead biker and our prone bike in turn. "But if you hadn't gotten that thing out when you did, we'd both be dead."

"Really?" she asked.

"Oh yeah," I assured her truthfully, very glad I'd taught her how to load and fire.

I motioned for Lucky to hold back, then carefully approached the shot up double entry. I risked a peek outside through one of the larger bulletholes, didn't see anyone, then leaned out the door for a longer look.

The roar of motorcycle engines ripped through the air and I saw them circle out as quickly as they could. Three of the decorated iron steeds still stood in place, waiting for riders who would never return. Without the victory cries, yips, or rebel yells I'd heard at the Gathering, the bikers fled the scene.

"Do you think they made us?" asked Lucky quietly by my side. "I mean as terrorists?"

I shrugged. There was no telling what they'd thought. I didn't even know why the Mongols would care if we whacked Scheuer. He might have had some minor value to them as a customer, but big deal. Bull, I could see, but somehow or other, the Mongols had tied us to both Bull and Scheuer, and the only link between the two was Whirly.

Judging from the hard faces of the bikers, whatever fate Whirly suffered, I was glad not to share.

The news article below was typical of those seen throughout the empire.

Clean Sweep for PATSI, Violence Follows

PATSI ratification swept across the globe yesterday, as four dominions gave their blessing to the controversial initiative.

Parliamentarians in the Welsh, West Australian and South African Dominions, defying sit ins, street protests, scattered violence and peaceful demonstrations, approved the Patriotic Anti-Terrorism and Sedition Initiative while police in three Great Lakes Dominion cities clashed head on with enraged, organized protesters.

In Pittsburgh, where the Imperial Civil Liberties Union had concentrated its staff, the largest protest proceeded quietly, but in Milwaukee, with fewer organizers to control the crowd, police donned riot gear when confronted with semi-organized battalions of protesters armed with a variety of improvised weaponry intent on storming the Imperial Building.

Rocks, missiles, and Molotov cocktails answered police water cannon in Flint, as opponents of the initiative, which critics say curtails basic democratic and human rights, found themselves taken by surprise when police sought to preempt a possible repeat of events in Milwaukee. Meanwhile in River Valley, student radicals and other youth raised their fists and chanted the name "Nicky, Nicky" as they approached police picket lines, invoking the name of homegrown September Alliance terrorist Nicholas Papadopoulos to voice their rage and raise the spectre of violence directed against the police.

Police in Cape Town, Chicago, Cincinnati, Perth, Pretoria, and Youngstown all faced similar, though smaller demonstrations.

Adam Mueller, spokesman for the Imperial Civil Liberties Union, hurried to deny any affiliation between his organization and the September Alliance, referring to scattered instances of graffiti and pro-terrorist chants as proof that the best of trees produce a few bad apples, and highlighting the radically different agendas and approaches of the two organizations.

Opposition to the Patriotic Anti-Terrorism and Sedition Initiative has grown in recent weeks as more and more of the pending legislation has come under public scrutiny and the full weight of its measures becomes more clearly understood by the public at large.

To counter the negative press, the legislation's sponsors have paid out over seven million pounds in an attempt to steer public opinion in their direction. Over half of that sum has gone to a single image consulting corporation, Clear Skies Inc. and their law firm, Fester, Fowler, Fagan, and Finch.

Despite growing opposition, PATSI appears set for ratification. With approval sealed in nine dominions and rejected in only two, it seems certain that the initiative will succeed in at least five out of the remaining nine dominions.

What the newspaper did not say, because its journalists had no way of knowing, was that the private backers of the initiative, from a range of seventeen industries, had quietly decided to quintuple their already large political action funds.

S topping in a pair of tiny towns called Carmichael and Tompkins gave us a chance to visit a few cowboy bars and offload some of the weed to shady locals. We'd gotten a few hundred off the dead bikers but to operate in Winnipeg we needed more. Neither of the two deadbeat hicks we found could lay their hands on more than five hundred, which was the going rate for a half pound. That gave us with an extra thousand in cash, still toting a pound and a half of sellable dope that would get me a year or more if I got caught dealing under my George Stanakis identity.

I itched for a contact in Winnipeg. Not only did I need to sell the grass, but I also needed someone with knowledge of the terrain. We would need things like surveillance equipment that came neither cheap nor easy. You didn't just walk into a city the size of Winnipeg and start shopping for the tools of spycraft without drawing attention. Even with Lucky buying some of the stuff it would be better to go through a third person.

At the moment, I didn't want to bring another person on. I had Red in reserve if I needed a shooter, but I preferred to leave him in reserve. I wanted someone we could lean on, but not have to trust completely. I wanted a sympathizer.

We looked for a cybercafé in a town called Webb, didn't find one, so kept moving up the road even though the temperature plummeted. We mercifully stopped in a larger burg called Swift Current and Lucky headed out in search of a second hand store for scarves and heavier gloves while I searched out an internet connection. I found one in a cybercafé adjacent to a bowling alley.

"Tree minnits upahnd ," bleated the woolly cave dweller clad in faded green checkered flannel over a black t-shirt and grey sweat pants with dirty thighs. I translated that to mean, "Three minutes per pound," and anted up without question. The rate was good even if the connection turned out to be slow. Nevertheless, I soon had www.hot4U.com up and signed in with the pre-created ID Mitchell had me memorize. The site was a free personals service with a home page that flashed pictures of happy men and women framed with valentines.

GyroScoope I typed in quickly after clicking past a series of advertisements and choosing *Member Login* from the list of options, then added *b00mb00m* for the password. That brought up my site homepage, which had all sorts of random information about 'me' and a picture that some unfortunate soul had placed on the internet for public use. I chose *Find a Date!*

As the computer took its time drawing a black and white form full of drop down menus and radial buttons I took a swig of orange soda, not my preferred brand. It had a funny, almost sickly sweet aftertaste. I wrinkled my nose, lit up a smoke, and filled out the fields.

I selected *above average* for height, *below average* for weight, *blonde* for hair color, and *blue* for eyes. I said yes to pets, no to smoking, yes to drinking, no to willing to travel, then answered as I had memorized, yes yes yes like an orgasming woman, then no no no for don't stop, then yes yes yes again, simple but effective. A click on *search* brought up four potential matches. One of them used the screen name *ColdDeadBunny*, just as I'd memorized. Another click brought up a profile with a stranger's face and generic words of encouragement to the males of empire. I ignored all that and simply chose the option to send mail.

After a popup that proclaimed my response to be the twenty-first sent to *ColdDeadBunny*. I typed a quick message.

Hi. I'm nu in town & looking 4 sum1 2 sympathize with. I like casual conversation and shopping, exploring the city and people watching. Serious relationships r not 4 me and I can understand if that isn't 4U2 then maybe you know sum1 that might work well 4 me. Ur fon # is best.

When finished, I stabbed out the smoke and went to find Lucky. We bought dinner from the lunch counter of a grocery store and headed back onto the road. With stops, Winnipeg still lay a dozen hours to the east and we needed to make some headway.

Freezing, our bodies humming with the vibration of motor and pavement, we pulled into Moose Jaw just before six and after dark, then got a room for the night. Moose turned out to be another wind-blasted speck on the map of the Great Plains Dominion. It looked a lot like Bismarck, which is to say Hell, but the motel had a free internet connection.

At four thirty in the morning, I dressed and made my way back to the lobby where a tired and bored looking clerk told me to help myself to the computer and also pointed out the free coffee. Helping myself to a cup of cream and sugar with a little coffee flavoring, I settled in before the screen and checked for a response on Hot 4 U. To my surprise, I had one.

"I'm not interested," read the response, *"but I do have a friend who might be right for you. 9398-1086-2722. For you, she'll answer to the name Peanut, but just this once. She's not exactly an open person and she's a trifle scared to be in the company of active men like you, so please, be careful of her feelings. She'll be expecting your call. Take good care of her."*

I spent the rest of the time waiting for Lucky and browsing the Girls Seeking Girls section.

Local police in the Rocky Mountain Dominion have positive evidence that Nicholas Papadopoulos is in that dominion and presumably active in some way shape or form. Officers investigating the shooting deaths of multiple Mongols motorcycle gang members have positively identified the fingerprints of Nicholas Papadopoulos and other known felons in the deserted town of Powell, near Post Falls. Unknown fingerprints were also taken from the murder scene, where it appears a fierce firefight took place between Papadopoulos, his currently unknown associates, and members of the Mongols gang. Papadopoulos appears to have survived the encounter and though his present whereabouts are unknown, he is presumed to remain in the area. Dominion police are searching temporary lodgings of all types and have begun inspecting isolated country residences. Mountain Dominion Police Commander Vernon McAlpin has taken personal charge of the case. He can be reached at 4352-3348-6082. Identification of Papadopoulos is absolutely positive through fingerprints, DNA, and reliable witness identification. There is no mistake.

Within minutes of reading the above communication, Truman Hess disobeyed his superiors and ordered over two hundred of his men to Spokane where they were to establish a base of investigations and carry out one single order: "Capture or kill Nicky Pops". By that time, Nicky had arrived in Winnipeg.

P eanut turned out to be far less than I had hoped for, but I still had hope. Over the telephone, she gave us an address and told us to meet her there, but as if to prove her inexperience, that address turned out to be her apartment. Standing at the front door in the hallway, smelling her neighbor's dinner and listening to their children through the walls, Lucky and I had to look at each other and shake our heads.

"Hi," Peanut greeted us in a bright and sunny voice, as if we were friends coming to dinner instead of revolutionaries committed to the violent overthrow of the current socio-economic system. Her smile, framed in a pudgy face wrapped in a homemade but decorative headscarf, was equally bright and clueless but avoided the homely category.

"Peanut?" I asked, not quite sure what to say.

"That's me," she gestured with a drama school wave of her hand. "Did you guys have a nice trip?"

Of all the things she could have asked…

"Just fine," answered Lucky before I could think up something sarcastic.

"Can we come in?"

"Oh sure!" Peanut exclaimed with another dramatic wave of her arm. The gesture made her scarf look like a turban and I half expected to be called *saheeb* as we entered. Her headware would have looked more natural if she would have let at least one hair show, but as it stood, she looked half like an overweight cancer patient and half like an Indian elephant handler.

Peanut made and wore her own clothes, and made a lot of other people's clothes as well. Multi-hued cloth draped every vertical edge and stacks of folded cloth lay on all the horizontal surfaces. Three well-oiled sewing machines, and you could tell they were well-oiled by the smell of new machine oil, crowded the walls. Spools of thread, all colors of the rainbow, hung on brackets where most people would have hung pictures.

"Do you want some tea?" asked our plump hostess.

"Sounds good," I told her, pulling off my gloves and shoving them into my pocket. One week from December you expected cold, but the motorcycle heater sucked.

"How do you want it?" she called over her shoulder as her round little body bounced energetically into the kitchen. Over her shoulder, swathed in black cloth sewn with thick golden thread at the seams, I got a look at a teapot decorated like a smiling bumblebee.

"Cream and sugar," I replied in a voice loud enough to make it into the kitchen.

"If she asks us what we do for a living, I'm going to cry," whispered Lucky, whose face hadn't warmed and still glowed like my favorite reindeer's nose. The look of semi-amused distress on her face was almost comical.

I chuckled. "Take a look out the window, just to be on the safe side," I whispered back as the faint aroma of tea hit my nostrils. A few clinks and tinks later, Peanut bubbled over the threshold. In her hands, she held a tray with two cups of tea, which she set down on a folding

176

card table that had a free rectangle of about the same size as the tray and lay suspiciously within arms reach of the largest sewing machine.

"So you sew for a living?" I asked as an opener.

"Uh huh," she answered with a squint, then plucked a pair of granny glasses from the working area of the sewing machine. "It's not much of a career, but I make a living."

"Everyone needs to make a living," I coaxed. Sewing seemed more like a pseudo-career than a real living, but a lot of sympathizers didn't fit the workplace mold.

An awkward silence filled the room when Peanut didn't respond. Not sure what to say, I sipped tea with my fingers on the rim of the flowered cup to avoid burning my fingertips.
When I sat the cup down, I found Peanut squinting up like I was a book on the library shelf.

"It's really you, isn't it," she half asked and half gaped.

"If not, I'm a damn good imposter and you're in a lot of trouble," I joked back in return.

"I haven't done anything."

"Yet," I corrected. Lucky chuckled and stepped away from the window, giving me a small wink to let me know the coast was clear.

Peanut's face came very close to going pale but she had just enough olive pigmentation in her skin to prevent that. Still, you could see the blood drain from her face, and I had to remind myself for the first time that Peanut was not a seasoned soldier, nor a soldier at all. The fact that we stood in her apartment attested to the fact that she knew absolutely nothing about subterfuge or the brand of spycraft routinely practiced by Alliance operatives. She was a civilian with just enough commitment to be of assistance but not enough skill to make the team.

I set a hand on Peanut's surprisingly soft, rounded shoulder, then whispered reassuringly, "You're not going to be asked to do anything that would get you in serious trouble," I told her, though technically she'd opened the door to serious trouble the moment she agreed to aid and abet a fugitive. The fact that that fugitive had his picture on magazine covers and the ten most wanted wouldn't help.

A look of relief crossed Peanut's face and she seemed to calm down enough that I almost didn't notice her hands shook when she put her glasses on.

"What do I need to do then?" she asked, before getting flustered and gesturing like a frustrated wedding planner. "And do please sit down. Make yourselves at home."

After arranging ourselves on chairs that had fabric, clothes, halfway sewn clothes and clothes that had been finished then ripped apart, we continued.

"We need someone who can give us advice about where we can buy certain types of equipment," I told her, then continued on in order to explain what types of equipment we would need and what types of establishments would sell them. From there I explained why we couldn't just pick up a lot of telephone and other listening devices that the television shows commonly call "bugs" and walk out the door without attracting attention.

"That sounds easy enough," she admitted. "Anything else?"

"Do you know anyone who deals pot?" I asked hopefully, watching her face.

Peanut's face fell. "Yeah," she admitted, sounding more like *ja.* "My brother does. He's not big time though."

Not only did Peanut not know she shouldn't invite wanted fugitives into her home, she also didn't know not to involve family members.

I shook my head with vigor. "No family members," I stated flatly and emphatically enough that comprehension dawned in her eyes. The scope of what could happen in her life and the lives of those she loved flashed in her eyes, along with horror at what she might have done.

"Maybe your brother has a friend?" coached Lucky from her perch on a faded sewing stool, the older kind that have flip up seats so inside you can store buttons, needles and thread and anything else they use for sewing. Lucky herself looked more than a little tired. Black circles rimmed her eyes from the long hours on the road without enough hot coffee and food.

Peanut paused at Lucky's suggestion, then brightened. "Oh I think so! Not a friend of my brother's but a guy I used to work with at Medina. He sold sewing machines with me, or at least he tried. He got fired for not selling any." She giggled. "He says I took all his customers but it wasn't my fault he didn't know how to sew."

"You sure you're on good terms then?" I asked, just to be sure.

"Oh sure we are," she answered dismissively enough that I believed her. "I buy from him sometimes." Her eyes narrowed like she didn't understand. "You came to Win to buy pot?"

"No," I answered, not bothering to elaborate on how drug use was *verboten* among active members of the revolution. "I want to sell some that I have."

"Hmmmm," grunted Peanut, and the conversation drifted into how soon she could put us in contact with this dealer and if she knew him well enough to handle the transaction herself. The fewer lowlifes that saw my face the better. I didn't need a former sewing machine salesman getting busted with a dime bag and trying to cop a deal by describing the guy he bought from. We decided to leave the grass in Peanut's care and let her do the deal.

"Which brings us to the matter of a car," I explained when we finished. The motorcycle had done its job and we hoped to sell it for some quick cash, but I doubted it would go for all that much. The engine hadn't sounded good on the road, and with the weather turning cold, the bike was no longer practical. We also had good reason to distance ourselves from anything that smacked of biker.

With short but to the point words, I outlined our need to buy a car, sell a bike and get some new threads. Peanut took it all in.

"Well none of that sounds bad at all," she commented when I'd finished. "I thought you guys would have wanted something a lot more illegal than that.

"That means you can get me a car legally?" I asked hopefully.

"I think so," she answered truthfully. "Or at least semi-legally. Dusty, the guy who I'm going to try and get to buy your marijuana does a lot of deals like that. He might even take his payment in dope. That would make it nearly untraceable."

Heaven smiled. Problems were solving themselves left and right. Finding a sympathizer had been the right move. Without local knowledge, we could flounder for weeks just trying to get the necessities together.

With a dig into my jacket pocket I got out a cigarette, stuck it in my mouth, then searched for a light.

"Oh no," piped up Peanut. "Not in here you don't."

I must have looked surprised, because Peanut shook her head. "First, I don't like the smell. Second, I can't sell clothes that smell like someone's dirty ashtray, and third, it's against the terms of my lease. If you need to smoke, you can go outside."

I chuckled and put the cigarette away, tamping it down for good measure.

"No problem," I told her. "We were about to hit the road anyway. Sleep and a warm bed will feel really good tonight." Wasn't that the truth? My bones ached from the cold and wind.

"You mean you're not staying here?" asked Peanut, again looking puzzled and betraying her naivety for the third time that night. She didn't know the minimum penalty for knowingly harboring terrorists exceeded the maximum possible lifespan of a human female by about fifty years. Even so, Peanut could end up as a liability. She could prove more eager to help than we knew, and pose a danger of a different sort. She could also get cold feet or turn us in for any number of reasons.

Lucky didn't stand.

"I'm staying here." She grinned. "Its warm and cozy and I'm not wanted for anything. Any cop that walks through that door and asks my real name would smile and wish me a nice day when I gave it to him. And besides…" Lucky ran her fingers through her already tousled hair. "I'm tired and so far only one motel we've stayed at had a bath."

I laughed softly and smiled. "No problem." Lucky had thought things through, and there wasn't any reason she couldn't stay with

181

Peanut. In fact, it might even be better. If the Specials came looking for us they would come looking for a pair. If the pair weren't paired up, we might avoid unwanted eyes.

"You got it," I grinned, and playfully shot her with my thumb and index finger. With few words of farewell, I slipped back out into the night in search of a motel or room over a bar.

100,000 respondents answered the questionnaire below on the politically neutral website www.politicaljunkie.org.

Since the ceasefire, are you more or less sympathetic with the goals and objectives of the group known as the September Alliance and its political party, the People's Progressive Party?

- o *More sympathetic*
- o *Less sympathetic*
- o *No Opinion*

Do you believe that the September Alliance and the People's Progressive Party's agenda is a good or bad thing?

- o *Good*
- o *Bad*
- o *No Opinion*

If the September Alliance maintains its ceasefire will you be more or less willing to support the party in the upcoming general elections

- o *More willing*
- o *Less willing*
- o *No Opinion*

Would you consider switching your party affiliation to the People's Progressive Party if the cessation of violence continues?

- o   *No, would definitely not switch*
- o   *Possibly could switch*
- o   *Probably would switch*
- o   *Yes, would definitely switch*

Your current party affiliation

- o   *Conservative*
- o   *Labour*
- o   *Liberal*
- o   *Regional, single issue or smaller parties*
- o   *Independent*

The results showed by an overwhelming majority that people identifying with all political parties had become more sympathetic to the goals of the September Alliance since the ceasefire and that many self-identified Liberals or people identifying with minor or smaller parties would consider switching party allegiance. Political commentators used the poll as supporting evidence to highlight the growth of support for the goals of the September Alliance.

The following day, I headed out to sell the bike while Peanut took care of the grass and Lucky went in search of maps, phone books and ever-useful second hand stores. No one ever noticed anyone who shopped in a second hand store or paid any attention to what they bought. They assumed the places were chock full of junk and the clientele the human junk equivalent. When you're keeping a low profile, they're ideal. You don't get the same anonymity with used motorcycle dealers.

"So where you in from?" asked the grizzled, grey haired and bearded biker who had obviously spent more than one summer on the road. His disheveled dealership office showed every sign that he belonged in the biker lifestyle, smelling more of motor oil than carbon paper and with concrete floors exposed under the furniture. The attached machine shop overflowed with tools and bikes not one of the leather wearing employees seemed in a hurry to work on, and only a huge imperial flag draped over the double doorway divided the shop from the office.

"Chicago," I lied without caring or expecting him to take an interest.

"You rode this baby up from Chicagger in November didja?" asked the biker, following up with another question whose answer wasn't his business.

"The exact reason I want a car for the ride back," I replied, trying to keep him on track. "This bike did good coming up, but don't want to freeze on the way back."

"Up nort for a while then?" he followed up. Why did he even care?

"Just visiting a girl," I told him, lying again.

"Oh jaaaa," he hawed and winked like no one ever visited women in Winnipeg. "They make them nice and soft up here, plenty good at keeping you warm at night."

"Ummmm." I started with a glance at my watch, "Do you think we could agree on a price? I really would like to get back to her."

I could tell by the look on the biker's face he got the unspoken intent of my words. 'Don't pry into my business.' Being an old biker, he could live with that. Being a human being, he would remember the face of a man who didn't want to discuss his business. He gave me a fair price and, as I left through two rows of bikes for sale in the front lot, he watched me through the front window. I could see his face set seriously and still between the faded posters featuring bikes with blonde bikini models. With worn leather and a black bandana he looked like an ugly doll on the toy store shelf.

I told myself he would forget me as soon as his next customer came through the door. In my profession, and especially with my face plastered over the front page of *Imperial News Weekly*, the key to survival lay in remaining normal and forgettable. That was why I hated taking a cab to meet up with Lucky. As luck would have it, I had to have face time with a cab driver straight off the boat from Latvia because Winnipeg fit into a neat groove, big enough not to be able to walk but too small for a public transportation system.

The cab driver acted like a lot of immigrants, way too smart to be doing the job he did. You could tell that after the first few broken sentences, the neatly combed hair and how he kept his radio tuned to a classical music station. Back in Latvia he could have been a professor, a doctor, who could tell? I just hoped he didn't read newspapers because a guy like that might just pick my face out of a lineup. To avoid any more interaction than absolutely necessary I pretended to read the ad section of a newspaper and paid without waiting for the change.

Lucky and I had agreed to meet in Winnipeg's downtown library because we could find it easily. The building dwarfed everything in the vicinity, even office buildings. It struck me as odd that a city a quarter the size of River Valley had a library four times larger. Then again, if River Valley had a winter that required mummification and monster snow throwers it might have a greater demand for books.

With the onset of cold weather, I expected to find the library a busy place, and have to find a quiet corner to talk to Lucky. However, Winnipeg would teach me that cold weather is a subjective term. I might find it cold, but in the last week of November your typical resident of Winnipeg still barbecued on weekends, so when I walked through the heavy brass doors and into the marble foyer, I found the place almost empty.

Lucky sat reading a newspaper with one leg crossed over the other, the way you would expect a businessman to read only Lucky chewed gum. She also wore blue jeans and a red t-shirt so tight a snake would have trouble shedding if it were skin. An advertisement for a perfume called BANG striped across her braless chest in big white letters no matter that men might view it as an invitation.

When Lucky saw me, she set the paper aside and gave a ditzy shake of her head that made her earrings glitter.

"What's new in the world?" I asked in a voice instinctively smothered for a library.

"Nothing you'd like to read about," smiled Lucky in the same whisper. "But I have lots of other stuff you'll love." She gestured with her head towards a sixty-something man who half dozed behind a wooden counter laden with lamps and computer terminals. "The librarian said I could take any one of the study cubes or meeting rooms. They're all free until four."

Privacy. Who could live without it? Somewhere in the back of my mind I remembered reading that libraries were a no-go zone for surveillance of all sorts. That made it even better.

Within moments, Lucky and I seated ourselves in a small, second floor room with a pine table and a large window facing the handrail over the open lobby. I doubted anyone would snoop but closed the plastic curtain anyway. Without waiting, Lucky laid out her haul.

"Maps," she stated, throwing a stack of folded maps down onto the table with a smack that pushed perfumed air up into my nostrils. "Phone book," she added throwing it down with a thump. "Digital camera," she added, setting a small silver camera down on the table. Ignoring the latter two items, she unfolded the map and pointed to an area marked with yellow highlighter.

"This is the building where Fester, Fowler, Fagan, and Finch have their office," she began. "It isn't far from here, so I strolled past on the way over. The building is seven stories, about average for downtown Win if you discount the twenty or so skyscrapers. Our guys are on the third floor."

"You went inside?" I asked.

Lucky nodded. "No sweat. There's a security desk, unmanned when I entered but a guard came back after about three minutes. I only saw the one, and he was unarmed. I doubt there's another. There's a small convenience store in the lobby, which gave me an excuse to go in and flip through some of the fashion mags on the rack, but other than the teenager behind the register, I didn't see a soul. The building is half empty."

That would make sense given Win's, and I'd already started to think of Winnipeg as 'Win', rank in economic importance. Being the only city in the region would only let it sink so low in the rankings, but the region itself specialized in laying barren. Whatever wealth it possessed lay in its farms and that cash wouldn't come in until next summer.

Win's obscurity didn't bother me. No one would look for me in Winnipeg. After all, what would Winnipeg have that would interest a terrorist? *Why would a law firm of lobbyists be interested in Winnipeg, unless they, like me, wanted to operate out of sight?*

I shook my head and turned to Lucky, whose serious face held a touch of pride at the thoroughness of her work.

"Good job," I told her, "but why the fuck is a law firm in Winnipeg hiring gangsters and buying C6?" I couldn't for the life of me figure out how blaming bombs on the September Alliance benefited anyone.

"It doesn't make sense to me, either," Lucky admitted. "I didn't talk to anyone on my first recon. I can try again, see who tells me something."

I shook my head again, but not in confusion. "We need to get inside and investigate. We can speculate all day and worry about the fringes, but until we know for sure what they're up to, we're burning time."

"Getting into their office is easier said than done," Lucky replied, then added with a humble but clearly forced grin, "My secretarial skills are pretty bad if the boss actually wants me to take shorthand or type a memo."

I gave Lucky a wry grin, but inside I wished she would stop subtly putting herself down. She'd impressed me, but she still needed to impress someone harder to convince. Herself. There is a time and place for intimate talk and the study room of Winnipeg's public library wasn't it, so I filed the idea for later.

"Leave getting inside to me," I told her. "Just leave that to me."

Jonas Abernathy was a member of the Mongol motorcycle gang and a confidential informant for the Ministry of Special Investigations Organized Crime Division. As part of the investigation into the shootout between Nicholas Papadopoulos and members of the Mongols, Jonas made this audio statement to the Drummer Boys in the company of his handler, Special Agent Anthony Lespertini.

Abernathy: This is no shit. I know exactly what went down between Pops and the Mongols, but I want more than my usual salary for telling. I got that cleared with Tony here and you guys ain't gonna go back on that agreement. <Sounds of agreement from attending officers. Sound of cash being counted> Right then. The Mongols pegged Pops after someone saw his picture on a magazine cover. After that, a few questions got asked and they realized he'd kinda zeroed in on Bull and his crew then dropped out of sight. By the time Debs calls back to the gang and tells them Bull ain't come back from a business meeting they put it all together. Bull was into something heavy duty. No one but the Joker knows what for sure, but they know it was heavy, and it had to have been

189

for Pops and his boys. You know the rest of that story already or at least as much as I know. Maybe more.

Can I have one of those doughnuts? <pause> Thank you. Maybe some coffee, too? <pause> Thank you.

The Mongols tried to ambush Pops, or Geo as they knew him, in Powell. You know how that turned out, but the Mongols still ain't gonna let things slide. They're hotter for him now than ever before and let me tell ya, they don't shrink from a fight. Every Mongol on every road is asking just where they can find Nicky Pops and they'll get him, too. They know he passed through a town called Tompkins, got the lowdown from a two-bit dealer named Billy Morgan. Billy says your bird was heading east so there's only three towns he might head for, Regina, Winnipeg and Thunder Bay. Any other place he had in mind he woulda picked a different road. That's where the Mongols are gonna look for him, and that's where you should look, too.

Privately, the Drummer Boys concluded that Nicky headed for Toronto by a roundabout way in order to circumvent detection by the police since there was nothing in Regina, Winnipeg, or Thunder Bay that would interest the September Alliance. By coincidence, a bomb exploded in a Timmins trailer park. Although later determined to be organized crystal methamphetamine producers settling scores, the Drummer Boys at first viewed it as further evidence Nicky had proceeded east.

We couldn't just walk into the offices of Fester, Fowler, Fagan, and Finch, so we tried a different approach. We bought bugging equipment at a pretty penny. The actual bugs didn't cost much, but a laptop and wireless recorder-receiver came at a stiff price. It took almost all our funds to get the equipment, to the point where if I didn't come up with cash soon, I would be homeless. I might be able to con my way through a day or two in the bare bones room I'd taken above a bar, but that prospect didn't appeal because it might not work and would also draw unwanted attention.

Laying out that much cash hurt, but it could have been worse. Lucky charmed the proprietor of an electronics shop with a fictitious sob story about an abusive husband. He fell for it hook, line and sinker, and made sure she got the best buy for her money, then gave her a discount on the recorder and transmitters, four acoustic units for oral conversation in the office and one or the telephone. Peanut purchased another unit for the phone, fudging something about a writer's circle, and she persuaded a gullible friend to buy another. When I purchased one more bug with the laptop, we had the necessary equipment.

Before dropping out, I'd majored in electronics and so did most of the technical work, not difficult once you figured out the settings. Using the software to keep track of the source of each recording proved trickier, but a daylong session of trial and error eventually ended in a late night success.

Another problem presented itself with the transmitter ranges. The range of the acoustic units only gave us five hundred meters, which sounds like a lot, but really isn't when you figure in the fact that the space between needs to be fairly free of obstruction. When we analyzed the terrain, we came up with a hemisphere with three usable arcs, two of good size but at an angle, and one narrow but almost dead on.

Since Peanut's plan for a car had come through, we decided on one of the angular arcs because it fed right to a parking garage that would cost us fifteen quid per day, and only a fiver on weekends. With that in mind, Lucky parked the car with the grille facing towards the building Fester, Fowler, Fagan, and Finch had chosen. An hour later, I entered, set up the rabbit ears for the receiver behind the grille and attached the wires I'd prepared, running them through the car's ventilation ducts and into the cabin. From there, they plugged into an adapter, which in turn fed the recorder under the passenger seat, itself linked to the laptop hidden beneath the driver's seat.

With all the components in place, we just needed to plant the bugs. To do that, we had to rely on our brains and the skills we had each developed as active members of the September Alliance.

Security at the office building proved pretty typical for office buildings. It had a front desk with a guard, another guard roaming the halls and spending half his time either lounging at the front desk with his colleague or spelling that colleague for lunch, cigarettes and bathroom breaks. Embedded in the front desk sat a passkey recognition system that I would bet quid to quotations brought up a picture ID on the guard's monitor.

To get around security, we paid a quick trip to the second hand store, purchasing a cheap but passable business skirt with matching blazer for Lucky. To complete the picture, we also got her a new blouse and briefcase which we stuffed with manila, red and green folders, then devised a strategy.

The law firm's classic building was one of the oldest in the city, having had its façade done in carefully carved stone with a clearly chiseled '1903' set in the corner foundation. By the looks of it, the building had been rehabbed several times, but subtly sagged in a way that spoke of age and faded glory. When the building had first opened it must have been the pride of a booming city coming of age, but now, it seemed a relic of a bygone era, a building made of stone in an age of steel and glass. I hoped I wouldn't have to blow it up. Something about the faded majesty appealed to me, even as I sat and smoked outside its antique brass entrance, bundled in a heavy wool coat and thick scarf.

Lucky and I had rehearsed her lines to get a sense of the timing. We also rehearsed how long it took to walk across the lobby floor. Timing was everything. If we could plant the bugs without being challenged or observed we would be home free, but if the slightest thing went wrong, it could alert the Four F crew that something had gone amiss. They would take countermeasures.

The whole operation felt good from the start. Lucky proved sharp as a tack and I barely took three drags off my smoke before I looked up to find her approaching with a decidedly no nonsense look on her face, heels clicking professionally across the cold cement sidewalk. She'd pulled her hair into a bun and done her makeup in the serious but light fashion of an earthbound yuppie female. Without missing a beat, she strode past without a second look, pushed through the ornate revolving doors and disappeared into the warmth of the lobby.

I counted to ten, took a drag from the cigarette, counted to ten again, then took another drag. I felt the tingle of excitement run through my shoulder blades as the Eye of God looked down from on high. By success or failure I would shape the future of the world. The power ran through my veins like so much rich red blood.

I took a drag. I counted to ten.

Whatever the Four F lawyers had going on, I would know soon, because everything would go perfectly smoothe, clockwork perfect, like a well oiled machine. I counted to ten. No one would get shot, no one would get killed, because the drum of good luck beat in time with my heart. I counted to ten.

I took a drag. I counted to ten, and when I finished, I tossed the cigarette and pushed through the same revolving door that had swallowed Lucky. Like exiting a spaceship onto an alien planet, I entered the faded grandeur of the empty lobby, noting *The Willoughby* gracefully etched into the awn of a cherub decorated arch that had seen one too many paint jobs and one too few coats of paint removed.

With careless grace, I crossed the lobby, feet moving across the fake marble floor that had three footpaths worn into its surface. Lucky had the full and undivided attention of a twenty-something guard whose face screamed *hee-haw* despite the blazer and tie.

With an easy turn of my hand, I flipped open my cell phone and turned it on speaker, pretending to be preoccupied as a reason to keep my head down. Between the gesture and the scarf, the security cameras would have difficulty seeing my features if and when they were ever reviewed. Out of the corner of my eye, I saw Lucky clutching a green folder in her hand. Red for no, green for go, just like always.

Ignoring Lucky and the guard, I approached the counter and spotted the pad for the passkeys just as the doors admitted another building patron.

"Did they by chance leave a forwarding address?" asked Lucky of the mesmerized guard.

"Yes Ma'am," he drawled as he drooled, either from lust or outright stupidity. "We got it here in the desk somewhere."

"Would you be so kind?" she asked back in crisp, formal tones.

With the kid's attention on Lucky, I passed the cell phone over the passkey reader and touched the number eight, which made a beep approximately the sound his computer made for a routine entry and, on speaker, loud enough for the guard to hear.

Without allowing myself the luxury of a second look, I pressed right on without breaking stride, like I had every right in the world to walk right past security and did so every day of the week. Despite the hitch in my breath, it must have looked perfect, because the guard never looked twice.

Lucky would hold the guard's attention until I entered the elevator, then depart with the forwarding address of a former tenant, but neither she nor I had foreseen what came next.

No sooner than I'd pressed the button on the lift than I turned to catch Lucky's eye, and saw a familiar face enter through the revolving doors.

I didn't have a name to match the face. I'd only seen the man once, back in River Valley. He'd been sitting across a small table from Donny Paglia on the day Turk introduced me to the mob. Even if I hadn't known the connection, I would have pegged him for wiseguy. His clothes all but screamed 'connected'. Despite the cold, the guy wore a blazer with a black shirt, yellow tie and three gold necklaces with cascading pendants accenting it all. He also had that tough, gum-chewing swagger to go with his Italian good looks and the unmistakable body posture that said 'I'm carrying a gun' in any language. He didn't so much enter through the revolving door as shove his way through.

I glanced up at the elevator, seeing it light the number six. Just my luck the thing had been on the top floor when I called. I undid the top button of my coat and felt for the reassuring weight of my pistol.

"Yo, G-man!" the mobster called out to the guard, who waved back and, even though I couldn't see, probably gaped like a fool. Lucky turned to glance at the mob guy, registering disdain. Of course she didn't recognize him. She'd never visited River Valley let alone recognize its low level gangsters.

I wished I'd brought a newspaper or something, anything to shield my features.

The elevator dinged on the third floor as I waited, feeling the adrenaline start to flow as my fingers undid the second and third buttons of my coat, just in case. Just as I'd only seen Donny's henchman once, he'd only seen me once, and I'd since changed appearance more times than a fashion model. He might very well not recognize me given that I'd been in and out of hair colors, hairstyles, clothing styles, worn glasses, worn colored contact lenses and more. I didn't even have the same hair color I'd had in River Valley. Back then, it had been my natural black, but now a close but distinct chocolate brown in a shorter style, though not really short and growing out at its usual fast pace. He could just walk right on by. If he did recognize me, one of us would die.

The lift dinged on the lobby floor just as "Vinnie" stepped into the elevator parlor. Instinctively, I turned so he would only see my profile and lifted the cell phone to my ear like I was listening to a voice mail. My heart hammered in my chest and my hand itched like it needed the rough pistol grip to be soothed.

With an impatient growl, Vinnie brushed past me with a polite "You gonna go or what?" and stalked into the elevator like he dared me to say something back. With a deep breath, I stepped into the elevator and clicked the phone closed.

I waited for Donny's man to press his button, the third floor, then pressed the fourth for myself. At least we had a short ride.

Heart pounding, I snuck a sidelong glance through the reflection on the polished metal doors, resisting the urge to draw my piece and just start blazing away, heart racing so fast he must have heard it. The fragrant smell of marinara that hadn't simmered long enough wafted up from the brown bag in his hand but even that couldn't dispel the dryness in my throat.

I glanced at him again in the mirrored surface of the elevator doors, only to find him looking back. His head turned and I could make out the smell of too much peppery cologne as his eyes locked on mine.

"What the fuck're you lookin' at?" he grunted, mouth half open.

"Sorry," I apologized, feeling hair stand on end as the elevator stopped.   "Your necklaces caught my eye."

"Yeah," he snarled, then spit his gum onto the floor as the doors whooshed open. "Take that and go buy yourself some."

Without another word, the tough stalked out of the elevator as I brushed back, looking and feeling intimidated but also happy not to be directly in the line of sight if Donny himself waited in the elevator lobby. Fortune smiled and the doors closed, leaving me to resume my ride with only an adrenaline rush and the tangy fragrance of marinara and cologne to remind me of the close call.

I stepped out onto the fourth floor. Outside the building, a red and white sign displayed in huge letters that the building had the entire fourth floor for rent, and sure enough, I found glass doors to either side open and waiting with only a few paint cans and brown walkway paper to witness.

Whoever had vacated the offices left most of their cubicles behind, though they'd been stripped of desks and chairs. My watch read 5:15, so I had at least three hours to kill before planting the bugs. With a little looking around, I found a former manager's office that still had a sofa and an artificial palm tree. Both looked weirdly out of place with only carpet indentations where the rest of the furniture once stood.

I took a look out the window and spotted a couple of guys hanging Christmas lights at the building across the street, then sighed. Another Christmas without Julie came in five weeks. She'd hung herself on Christmas Day, and left a void neither the revolution nor Cat could fill. With Julie had died my innocence, my happiness, and my belief in true love. It all seemed tragic, sitting there in an empty office, still about the business of revolution, but without Julie. I'd dreamed differently, and grandly, of glory and love.

We were going to live and love and change the world and emerge as heroes, or so I'd thought. Instead, she'd died and I grieved, the world hadn't changed and I lived the life of a fugitive. I wished everything could have been different.

I felt most sorry for Cat. Cat loved me, truly loved me, yet I couldn't love Cat back, not the way she loved me. My ability to love with purity of heart and open-armed trust fled when Julie died. The same held true for the revolution. I could and did serve the revolution, and believed in its cause, yet I couldn't believe in it with the same selfless dedication Julie had inspired.

I sighed once more before I lay down on the couch and put my feet up, feeling like a patient in the shrink's office. From my pocket, I removed a peanut butter sandwich, unwrapped it, and took a bite, taking solace in the sweet taste of marmalade. How else does a terrorist handle depression?

Wolfgang Diebenblatz, owner and operator of Outland Motors in Winnipeg spoke with Jeremy "Flash" Farrow, member of the Mongols motorcycle gang. Flash promptly relayed the conversation to his leaders and received one ounce of crystal methamphetamine in exchange for the information.

Diebenblatz:	*That's him arrighty.*
Farrow:	*You sure? I give Joker a bum lead and he's gonna take it outta both ahr hides*
Diebenblatz:	*Knew there was somethin' weird abaht `im.*
Farrow:	*Why's that?*
Diebenblatz:	*Came innere and sold me a bike, said `e rode it up from Chicagger.*
Farrow:	*So?*
Diebenblatz:	*Fuckin' thing had California plates.*
Farrow:	*Any idea where `e is now?*

Diebenblatz:	*Not a fuckin' clue, but I betcha `e's still in the city somewhere.*
Farrow:	*Whyddja say that?*
Diebenblatz:	*He didn't ask where he could buy a car.*
Farrow:	*Joker says he's workin' with some blondie got a lotta scars. Seen her?*
Diebenblatz:	*Nah. `E was alone when I sah `im.*
Farrow:	*Arright. Thanks, man.*
Diebenblatz:	*You gonna put in a good word for me?*
Farrow:	*Course. But you see him again you lemme know.*
Diebenblatz:	*You betcha.*

Roughly thirty members of the Mongols lived in the Winnipeg area. Approximately eighty other associate and aspiring members also lived there. After Flash contacted Joker, the Mongols ordered forty additional members of their gang to the city.

B y nine o'clock I felt pretty safe in thinking everyone had gone home for the day so I broke from my hiding place, careful to take the remains of my peanut butter and jelly sandwich. Shoving the plastic wrap into my jacket pocket and coming down through the stairwell, I entered the elevator lobby of the third floor, peeking out cautiously to see that someone had locked the glass doors. Unless they'd locked a guard in for the night, I could assume the office was empty. That left the major barrier between myself and the law

200

offices of Fester, Fowler, Fagan, and Fuck... err... Finch, an alarm that would sound if the door opened.

I slipped across the carpeted foyer and examined the lock and alarm. Both seemed good quality, but nothing that couldn't be dealt with using techniques I'd learned back in River Valley.

First, I disabled the alarm. It consisted of a closed circuit. If you broke the flow of power, the alarm sounded. The doorjamb held the passkey reader and power supply, plus a magnet that ensured the alarm wouldn't go off every time the building trembled. A steel plate gave the magnet something to grab. You couldn't open the reader from the outside without destroying or ripping it off the wall, but the weakness of this system lay in the door.

The people who installed the alarm hadn't accounted for the people who mounted the door. I had at least half an inch of play to work a screwdriver into the gap and keep the magnet and plate connected. With that in place, I worked a folded section of a steel from a tin of Danish butter cookies that the magnet grabbed as soon as it entered the gap. Easing off on the door, I freed my hands and attached an alligator clip to the piece of metal. I then pulled a refrigerator magnet from my pocket and wedged it into the same gap, where it clapped itself to the metal plate of the reader. By attaching a second alligator clip and then running two feet of wire between, I convinced the alarm that the door remained shut.

The lock itself was easy for anyone who has ever been shown how to pick one. You didn't need to be a locksmith, just generally know how a lock worked. You needed four things, a fishing hook with a tight rubber band to lift the hood that shielded the tumblers; an hex wrench that had been filed thin on the business end that the locksmiths called a tension wrench; and a long needle fitted into a wooden handle that had its tip bent to an eighty degree angle.

To start, you hooked the rubber band through the eye of the fishhook, something I'd done at Peanut's house, which is also where I'd gathered the things I needed. You then use the fishhook to lift the tumbler hood and loop the rubber band over the handle until it pulls tight enough to hold the hood up. Watch your eyes if you try this at home, but that gives you access to the tumblers.

Next, you work the needle, the sturdier the better, into the slot and angle it towards the tumblers. Then, you ease the flattened hex wrench into the bottom of the slot and apply pressure with the side or palm of your hand, like someone is trying to open the knob by holding the key. Keep the pressure steady and work the tumblers one by one. As you find and depress each tumbler, the hex wrench gives just a little. Once you've depressed all the tumblers, the knob turns and you're in.

In my case, this whole process took just over seven minutes, eight if you count taking off my coat and laying out the tools. That doesn't mean I'm a master thief in the making. I can't rob jewels out of secure cases or make off with the Hope diamond after dangling from the ceiling on a wire, but I can make my way past most simple locks and alarms.

Once inside, I took a brief survey of the office suite. The largest office boasted oak shelves full of imposing, austere law books. The top of each bookshelf displayed trophies related to golf. I found one which had a wooden base and three golf balls that had been decorated with drunken smiley faces positioned to look like they were rolling out of a shot glass turned on its side. A red beer glass lay sideways on a plastic lawn, mouth towards the balls as if to catch them. On the base, a strip of brass had been etched with the words "Congratulations from your friends at the Nineteenth Hole."

I figured the biggest office would be home to the biggest fish, and so set the first bug, one of the acoustic units designed for recording conversations in a room, inside the beer glass, exactly the kind of place called for in the directions. From there, I quietly padded across the room to the desk and turned on the low reading lamp. Carefully, I unscrewed the mouthpiece of the telephone handset and pulled the guts out of the casing, tugged on the fine wires that split the line and wired in the second bug. Before reassembling the phone, I took my private cell phone from my pocket and set up the hands free. With my thumb, I punched Lucky's number. She answered on the first ring.

"I'm here," she breathed lowly into the phone without making me identify. I could picture her in position, inside the car in the parking garage.

"OK, then," I half whispered under my breath. "I'm ready with…" I checked the identifiers. "One and five."

"Standing by," she answered professionally, and somehow through the tone of her voice I could see the screen of the laptop light up her scarred but pretty face.

"Testing, testing," I whispered.

There was a long pause, followed by, *"I'm recording on one. Go ahead on five."*

I cleared my throat and used a mechanical pencil with the lead withdrawn to tick over the activation switch on the second bug, the one

I'd wired into the phone. The line didn't need to be live to activate the bug, but I replaced the voice piece and screwed the cover back on finger tight.

"Testing. Testing." I said, then heard the recorder answer through Lucky's phone, sounding distant.

"Testing. Testing." My own voice, faint and mechanical but my own, sounded higher in pitch than I expected. It sounded like a boy's voice, and for an instant, I had to pause, biting my lip. I'd killed nearly three hundred people, a whole lot of them armed and dangerous, almost half of them cops. How could my voice sound like a teenager's? No wonder I'd never done well with girls. They liked deep voices and …

I shook my head to snap out of it as Lucky's calmly spoke into the phone. *"We're good on five."*

"Gotcha," I told her without elaborating. "I'll be in touch."

Whatever nastiness Fester and company were up to, Donny Paglia would be square in the middle. Why else would they hire him? To get the dirt and get it quick required getting to Donny.

Leaving the big office, I took a look around. I counted seven offices and twenty cubicles. Although half the cubes lay empty or were used for storage, all the offices had been taken. With quick but calm steps, I snooped through the first three, deciding from family pictures or knickknacks that Donny hadn't taken any of them.

The moment I tried to enter the fourth office I knew I'd found Donny's. It boasted a pair of brand new and high quality locks. I didn't know the guy inside and out, but I knew Donny well enough to know why John Longanza had chosen him as chief enforcer. Donny Paglia paid attention to details. He was an astute, cunning and ruthless man. He probably asked himself what he would do if he wanted to spy on himself. He probably didn't trust the law firm. For that matter, Donny probably didn't trust his own mother. It took me almost two hours of careful lock picking to get his door open.

Donny's office personified Spartan. Unlike the others I'd already reconned, his had no photos, no trophies, no art, no decorations. The room had a desk and on the desk lay a dusty computer and a cell phone charger. A single pen sat in the built in cup. The office belonged to a man who gave away nothing of himself, who shared nothing of his thoughts or feelings. Only an ambitious, cold-blooded, hard-nosed, efficient killing machine would have an office like this.

Taking the penlight from my pocket, I slid into the seat and held the light between my teeth while I worked his phone apart and wired the bug in like I'd done before. Feeling more confident, I reassembled the phone and searched for a place to plant the second acoustic device. I ended up using a tube of Peanut's super glue to fasten the tiny device upside down underneath his desk, close to the floor.

I called Lucky, the screen from my cell phone throwing odd shapes and shadows in the darkened office. Her voice came in crystal clear.

"Took you long enough."

"I found an immovable object, had to use my irresistible force."

Lucky chuckled.

"I'm ready on two and six," I told her over the airwaves where any pig could listen in, also the reason we wanted to keep our conversation short and vague.

"Standing by," she replied in a professional voice, not wanting to be triangulated any more than I did.

We ran through the tests once again, but this time static made me take the phone apart and tighten everything up. That cleared up most of the problem. We would have to hope for the best.

I took care to put everything back exactly as I'd found it. We couldn't predict what Donny might or might not notice and I'd just as soon he notice nothing at all.

The names on the plaques all meant nothing to me, so determining who else might be important turned out to be more vexing than I thought. In the end, that made me decide on the receptionist's phone, which would reveal who called in. I couldn't decide on another phone or where to put the last acoustic unit, and half wished we'd saved the money as I exited and disassembled the alarm bypass. When I closed the door, the lawyers would never suspect my visit, let alone imagine the reason why.

By the time I took the stairs up to the vacant office to wait for daylight, my mind had already turned to our financial situation. I had a hundred pounder and change, nowhere near enough.

The newspaper article below appeared in the Winnipeg Daily News. With the exception of the local slant, it was typical of many which appeared in newspapers empire-wide.

Two Close Calls for PATSI

Great Plains Edges Towards Uncertainty

The Patriotic Anti-Terrorism and Sedition Initiative passed the parliaments of two dominions this week, but by closer margins than predicted. The results, although positive for backers of the initiative, are worrying insofar as they represent a further tightening of public opinion as more and more of the provisions have become public.

Citizens have become uneasy about key elements of PATSI, in particular the warrantless wiretaps. The public seems to widely accept the increased use of surveillance, but doesn't seem to understand why court oversight should be eliminated. Revelations that law enforcement has already used these provisions in more mundane criminal cases hasn't gone over well in the public sphere.

The results in the Island Dominion, which comfortably passed the initiative 98-84, were much closer than the predicted majority of over one hundred and ten ayes while the Scottish results, at 105-90, set off alarm bells in the pro-initiative camp and don't bode well for the results in the Irish Dominion next week or in California just days after that. Experts watching the polls say that if current trends continue, the initiative will go down to defeat.

Nowhere is the race tighter than here in the Great Plains Dominion, never known for electoral volatility. New poll results show a three-percentage point swing to the nays, reducing the overall majority in favor to fifty-two percent.

Political pundits are now far from certain that PATSI will pass, and indeed, its fate may be decided here in Winnipeg and the other cities of the Great Plains Dominion. With our largest cities, Omaha and Des Moines on opposite ends of opinion and the rural population split evenly down the middle, delegates from Winnipeg may have the rare opportunity to decide the PATSI issue throughout the entire empire.

Franklin Kann, a resident of suburban North Point, expressed his opinion outside city hall yesterday, saying that...

Crime finances September Alliance operations. Ideally, a squad would have a steady stream of income through some kind of ongoing criminal enterprise, but robbery works just as well, especially when you just need one shot of cash. Drug dealers are the victims of choice because they have a lot of cash and can't call the cops. However, they also tend to be dangerous, having a tendency to surround themselves with bodyguards and toughs of all sorts.

As much as I preferred targeting drug dealers, I had to settle for another option, not only because of the danger of taking a gang on single-handed, but for the very practical reason that I didn't know where to find the dealers. Winnipeg wasn't California, where they have an endless supply of good weather and you find kids selling dime bags in every park. Wherever they sold drugs in Winnipeg, it wasn't outdoors, at least not at the onset of winter. I decided to try a bookie instead.

Believe it or not, it turned out to be a lot easier to find out where you could place a bet than where to buy drugs.

"Oh sure, you betcha," laughed Brad, the owner and operator of the bar where I rented my room, a big burly guy who looked born to dance with bears, tend bar and break up fights. "I just put down some on the Wings myself," he laughed again, referring to the local hockey team. "In fact, if'n ya wish, there's a feller name'o Branco'll be coming around

208

tonight. He likes giving odds, does it most every night all through the season."

"Think you can point him out?" I asked, feeling like maybe I shouldn't. The bar owner might not be aware that 'Branco' was the local numbers runner rather than just another customer that liked to wager, but it felt like I was fishing too close to home, however temporary. Still, with ninety quid in my pockets, I couldn't waste time figuring the best angle. I needed cash and needed it soon.

"Thanks," I told him, then fished for more information, playing on the bookie's name. "Ain't Bronco a little horsey for a name?"

"He's from Serbia," replied the bartender without looking up. "But dontcha worry, he speaks really good English, better'n you or me."

"What in the world brings a Serb to Win-ny?" I asked, having to pause before tacking on the 'ny'.

"What makes anyone go anywhere?" countered Brad with a shrug that jiggled his belly. "Winny's a nice enough place. Probably a lot of people in Serbia want to come nort'."

With a practiced hand, Brad skimmed foam off the beer with a flat card and set the half golden and half white glass down to settle before resuming his pour.

"You're not from Winny yourself, George," he added, using the alias I'd provided at booking. "What brought you here?"

"A girl." I told him, since he'd never seen Lucky. It seemed best to stick with the same story I'd told the bearded motorcycle dealer. He'd swallowed that line without blinking, though something about that encounter still niggled at the back of my mind. I couldn't put my finger on what bothered me, but every time I pictured that dealership I felt my shoulder blades tighten like someone stalked me from a distance.

"A girl?" grinned the heavy bartender. "If that's the case, you best saddle up your horse and ride off the way you came afore you end up with a mountain of trouble." He smirked in a good humored way and held up his left hand to show me a gold band adorning his ring finger.

"Look what happened to me." He winked.

I laughed like we'd just become friends and he went back to work. After a few minutes, I drank back the last of my beer, then placed both hands palm down on the bar to push off the stool.

"I'll keep the dangers of Winnipeg women in mind," I grinned as my host looked up, "and I won't tell the missus, either."

The jovial barman winked and tossed a towel over his shoulder.

"Ja betcha it's already too late," he mock scoffed. "Feller drops everything and rides to Winny to meet himself a lady is already hooked and hooked bad."

With a genuine smile, I waved farewell, then headed out the door to find Lucky. I would need her help.

Three hours later, just before four, I returned, finding the bar filling with stuffed chambray and flannel shirts and cowboy hats adorning every other head. Not a table stood empty and I was lucky to find a place near the big screen, which had a couple of talking heads giving pre-game predictions for the Winnipeg Wings as they prepared to take on the New York Skaters. The Wings had a shot at the playoffs. People would gather to watch.

Parting with another fiver bought me a pint of lager, which seemed to be the drink of choice for Wings fans and I didn't want to stand out. With my change came the promise that Brad the Bartender would point out Branco when he arrived.

"Sure, he always comes afore the game," Brad promised, and sure enough, an hour and a half before face-off, hunched over the bar, I felt a tap on my shoulder.

"Got a light?" asked a clean cut, lean young man about my age who gestured towards the plastic lighter resting on top of my near empty pack.

"Help yourself," I told him, passing him the lighter. Before I could get my elbow up, he leaned forwards whispering in my ear in a voice low enough to drift on the scent of his double-breasted leather jacket.

"Bradley says you would like to bet on the Wings." The faintest trace of a Slavic accent tickled his words.

I smiled, not because I liked him, but because I needed him. Branco had a shifty, beady blue-eyed way of looking at me that instantly blossomed into distrust. He might have been taking bets, but he looked like a guy that could sell angel dust to seven year olds.

"Just a small one," I told him. "Was thinking about a fifty. What's the spread?"

"Skaters by one," he mouthed around the butt of his cigarette, my lighter flaming as he lit the cig.

"Really," I asked, trying to sound gullible. "I was thinking Skaters by two."

"You want it, you got it," he told me with a shrug, exhaling smoke that joined the aquamarine haze over the bar.

"Uh," I said, cementing the impression of a minnow in the carp pond. "how about even up."

"Even up goes to the house," he told me, shrugging again. "Vegas rules. I only wager for fun, but that's the way I do it." His attitude told me he'd heard the arguments against that rule a hundred times and more.

"Uh," I said again, like I chewed it over.

"Your name is George, right?" he asked, seeing my certainty slip away.

"Yeah."

"Tell you what George, I'll give you one better than the Vegas odds, just for the sake of one betting man to another."

I spent the next ten minutes fending off various deals that Branco would make to get my bet, but made like the henhouse and chickened out. To recruit another potential regular, Branco would likely have given very good odds, made me a winner the first time around and paid up with a smile. The odds would tighten as the payouts set the hook, and he would receive a stream of money over time to compensate for his original investment. The only hitch to his plan, was that even if the odds favored me, I didn't intend to be around to collect whenever he got around to paying, and if I lost, I didn't want to fork over a fifty when he came collecting.

So close to face-off, Branco couldn't spend much time baiting new business, so he excused himself, slithered away, and pressed palms with more loyal customers. As I sensed he got ready to leave, I pulled my coat on, told Brad the Bartender that I needed fresh air, and stepped out.

Less than a minute of shivering later, Branco emerged like a sinister demon from a raucous pit.

"Hey Branco," I greeted him, shoving forwards off the brick wall by my shoulders with an unlit cigarette clutched between my fingers. "Can I get a light from you this time?"

Branco grunted with something akin to disgust, but reached into his pocket to produce his lighter, offering it like he didn't have time to waste on such a low and indecisive creature as a Papadopoulos.

"Thanks," I told him again, pausing to lower my head over the flame. Out of the corner of my eye, I saw the lights of Lucky's car turn on. It seemed odd to have darkness at five, but Peanut had already explained the effect of latitude on daylight hours.

Across the way, Lucky had seen me light up, the sign that the person I spoke to was indeed whom she needed to follow. To our thinking, Branco simply wasn't important enough watch for a tail, and even if he discovered a woman following him, he wouldn't exactly hit the panic button.

I passed the lighter back to Branco. "Thanks man," I told him, earning a careless nod as he grunted something inaudible and marched off on bookie business. The clock ticked towards faceoff, and I imagined he would have one or two more stops to make before he either watched the game or headed back to his superiors.

As luck would have it, he watched the game in a place called Slapsticks, a sports bar near the stadium. I kept in touch with Lucky the entire time, and she parked, entered, and kept an eye on him as he took bets until the middle of the second period. Following that, he made a few phone calls, made some notations in a little black book, went to the bathroom, came out with his hair freshly combed, bought two girls at the bar a drink, patted their fannies, then headed out.

"It looks like he's going to dinner," Lucky told me over the phone, a trace of boredom in her voice. *"Name of the place is Scar..."* she paused. *"Scar dale eddja or something like that. S-K-A-R-D-A-L-I-J-A,"* she spelled. *"Not that easy to pronounce."*

"I think it's pronounced 'scar-dahlia'," I told her over the phone only to be interrupted a moment later when the Wings scored, causing the bar to explode into an uproar.

"Whatever," Lucky concluded in typical fashion. *"Ready for the address or do you think he'll move on?"*

"Come get me," I told her. Chances were good that the restaurant housed Branco's boss. Criminal enterprises tended to be ethnically based, and I found the connection a bit too much for coincidence. Of course, I didn't tell Lucky until we met face to face.

"Heya," Lucky greeted as I slid into the passenger seat. The dashboard lights lit her face, and she wore a white winter coat that bulged with stuffing and had white artificial fur trim on the hood and cuffs. She'd also come up with a pink hat and matching mittens that went well with the coat and didn't bother her driving. Of course, the glowing dashboard lights made her look like a miniature astronaut in profile, but when it came to cold, Phoenix-born Lucky didn't play games.

On the ten minute ride to the restaurant, I told Lucky I thought the business a front for the bookies or a convenient and complementary place to do illegal business. It wasn't until I stepped inside that I knew it was the former.

If the flower pots sprouting cigarette butts didn't provide a clue, the fact that eight of the twelve tables in the dining area had the chairs turned up with their legs in the air gave it away. Not many people came to eat at the Skardalija.

We hadn't seen Branco's car in the rear parking lot so we figured he had moved on. However, two of his clones lounged at one of the remaining tables with their backs to the wall, sharing a heavy warped glass ashtray with a golden hue. Each man boasted a leather jacket over dress shirt and screamed 'hoodlum' with his eyes. Each had a teacup filled with what could be anything. No sooner did I walk through the door than their eyes snapped to follow my every move.

Besides the hoods, two more men sat at the bar facing a third, whose tuxedo shirt and vest proclaimed him the bartender, although his curly salt and pepper curly and wire-rimmed glasses made him look more like a school teacher. Of the two men seated at the bar, one seemed cut from the same cloth, though less formal, and smaller in stature. The last and fattest man looked like a local, even wearing a big, white, felt cowboy hat with a colored band and a checkered shirt. His cowboy boots cocked comfortably onto the bottom rungs of the bar stool. His right hand boasted six sausage-like fingers, one a cigar that stained the air like fresh blood in clear water.

"Howdy," I said, approaching the bar. None of the trio greeted me in return, so I continued, "Pretty cold out ain't it?"

The bartender nodded, his beady eyes not the slightest bit interested in my weather report.

My chances of robbing this place didn't look good. I had five alert men in the front room, three almost certainly armed. I saw no sign of where they kept their cash. They didn't care for strangers. Not wanting to give up easily, I kept talking.

"Thought I would come in for some of that Serbian brandy you guys make, you know the ones from pears and apricots and stuff, thought it might chase the chill."

I knew the drink but had forgotten the name. Back in Greektown we'd had a lot of Bulgarians move into the neighborhood back in the nineties when communism collapsed. River Valley never had a Bulgarian neighborhood, so they settled in with us Greeks, mostly on account of the fact that they could attend our churches rather than from any kind of cultural affinity. In fact, we seemed culturally about as far apart as two neighbors could possibly get, but Pop liked to drink their fruit brandies. He said they had a cleaner taste than ouzo and not as sticky as whiskey.

I also knew that while Bulgarians had next to nothing in common with Greeks, they had a lot in common with Serbs, so if the Bulgarians had fruit brandies, the Serbs would too.

"*Palinka,*" filled in the bartender with a thick accent. He gave a Balkan shrug, a shrug that said I could order *palinka* or I could step into a food processor and turn it on. He didn't care which.

"Yeah, that's it," I answered. "You got any of the pear flavored one? Pear had been Pops' favorite.

"Of course," he answered as the other two stared. With a practiced hand he tipped a brandy snifter off the rack and caught it in the palm of his hand, turned it right side up and reached for the bottle.

Beside me, the guy with the lesser formal wear said something in Serbian, and the bartender shrugged again, then set up the glass. He made a dismissive gesture with his hand and poured a thin stream of pale yellow liquid into the glass, then answered in the same language.

Presumably, they said something about me, but I pretended ignorance, studying the layout of the restaurant. If anyone worked in the kitchen, there was no sign and the feeble light showing through the windows on the swinging kitchen doors meant only one or two lights were on..

The two guys sitting at the table with teacups made sense. They were sentries, plain and simple. Their table sat next to a corridor formed half by a wall and half by the service entrance to the bar. Whatever cash the bookies had lay beyond those two Serbs.

The bartender stopped pouring and made a gesture that asked if he'd poured enough and if not, what more could I possibly want?

"Thanks," I told him, then tipped the glass to my lips. The term 'firewater' didn't do the stuff justice. I didn't know how my old man could possibly enjoy the harsh taste. It might have been pear flavored, but they'd forgotten the pear and instead poured in an extra measure of gasoline. I had to force myself not to hack and cough but my eyes watered. They chuckled even though I kept a straight face.

"You wants anything else, you ask," the bartender told me with yet another wave of his hand, only to be interrupted by another well dressed, salt and pepper haired man who'd chosen a black shirt with tiny black and silver buttons and a crease so sharp you could use it to open the mail.

"Goran," the guy started, which could either have been the bartender's name or something the guy wanted. A whole river of Serbian poured out after that word. Goran, if that was his name, listened carefully

and nodded, so I assumed the newcomer had some authority. He glance at me over a long nose then spoke to the bartender. Even though I could only make out the word *palinka,* I knew he'd pegged me as out of place.

Goran gave another shrug as if to tell his boss the world was a crazy place and that if he had a Serbian bar and restaurant, eventually some weird people would walk through the door and order Serbian food and drink.

"You like the *palinka*?" asked the man in the strongest Serb accent I'd heard so far, his cold attention turning to me.

I nodded.

"Strong," he said with a thump to his chest. "For a man, and good for the winter."

Paying no more heed to me, he set his hand on the shoulder of the big man in the cowboy hat.

"You are ready?" he asked by way of a statement. "The others want that we start."

"Yup," answered the fat local as he shifted his weight off the stool. "Feel me an ace-high straight all ready to pop out like a calf from a cow."

The fat man couldn't see the scowl on the face of his host, or the look of concern that crossed Goran's. Both of them snuck looks at me out of the corner of their eyes, studying my reaction.

They not only took bets, they hosted an illegal card game, perhaps a high stake card game.

Figuring any cop would try and look like he hadn't noticed, I smiled. "The only kind of straight I ever draw is an inside straight, which usually proves too tempting to resist, so I resist the whole game." That got a wry smile and they relaxed enough for Goran to walk back into the kitchen.

I took a sip of pear brandy and watched as the local quenched his cigar in a whiskey and water colored glass then followed the other two, presumably the restaurant owner and hired dealer.

I stared down into the pale yellow liquor, which didn't taste as awful as it had before. Without hurrying, and ignoring the two Serbs guarding the corridor, I calculated what to do next.

The Skardalija had proven more formidable than I'd thought. No doubt they had a bookmaking business going, but the card game proved more tempting. Like any game, it would have winners and losers, presumably big winners and big losers. If I could pick out the winners, I could take them down outside.

With that thought in mind, I downed the last of the firewater, which had the honor of being the first and last *palinka* I would ever swallow, and set the glass down. With the warmth of the liquor swelling in my belly, I stopped Goran, who emerged from the kitchen with two platters of cold cuts decorated with colorful but unknown pastes and jellies wedged between. Crackers ringed the outer rim.

"Where's the john?" I asked, standing.

He indicated the hallway with a nod of his head. "On your right," he answered with a pause, then seemed to pluck the correct word from the air. "The second door."

With a quick step, Goran stepped into the hall himself, bringing his tray of snacks. I followed quickly on his heels, not so quickly that he would notice, but fast enough to peek into the back room when he went through the door, which turned out to be a curtain. As Goran swept it open, his body blocked ninety percent of the view and I only saw the owner and one player, an old man in a yellow shirt with a glass of red wine and poker chips arrayed in his corner of the table.

Mindful of the eyes of the Serbs guarding the game, I didn't pause to look, but went into the bathroom, did my business, then stepped into the stall and pulled a few squares of toilet paper off the roll. They kept the bathroom surprisingly clean. Whether or not he ever intended the place as a restaurant, the owner had laid out serious cash, even to having black granite and classy fixtures for the stall and sink.

I pulled the door open and blew my nose, seeing one of the Serbs' heads pop around the corner. Pretending to be careless, I dropped the toilet paper, then bent over at the waist to pick it up. From that angle I couldn't see much of the card room, but could count feet. I counted six pairs, one of which stood and one of which belonged to the dealer. Two other pairs wore cowboy boots and two wore loafers.

I made all that out in the split second I had before I needed to stand back up and head towards the bar like I hadn't seen anything at all. Goran again stood behind his bar, but when I asked how much I owed, he just waved his hand dismissively.

"No money," he told me. "You just come back and drink more *palinka.*"

I smiled, thanked him, closed up my coat, pulled on my gloves and headed out the door. Passing the cigarette filled flowerpots, I quickly walked to the side street, trying to beat the cold.

No sooner did I open the car door than Lucky tried to put the engine into gear and haul ass.

"Easy, easy," I coaxed.

"You didn't get it?" she asked, looking amazed.

"We will," I assured her, then went on to tell her what I'd seen.

"So," I finished, "all we need to do now is try and distinguish the winners from the losers, then take down the winner."

"Are you serious?" came Lucky's response. She looked at me like I was stupid.

"Of course I'm serious," I told her, not getting why she would look at me like a fool.

"You never played cards, did you?"

I admitted I hadn't.

Lucky sighed and held up her mitten hands, then explained. "The way these games are run in Vegas, they start the game and they don't stop until it's over. Food and drinks are brought to the table." Lucky smiled sweetly. "And waitress gets a nice shiny chip for a tip."

I chuckled as I watched Lucky's breath fog the car as she spoke.

"The players drop out one by one as they go broke until there's only two left. They play until the last one is out of money or they drop from fatigue, but until then they play and play and play. You said you counted how many there were, right?"

I nodded, never having known how enlightening waitressing in Vegas could be.

"I counted six pair of feet, one was probably the dealer and one was probably the host's. There are at least four players and I guess I counted about half of them, so there's probably seven or eight players."

"Not if they play by Vegas rules," smiled Lucky. "They'll have six players. It has to do with the logic of a fifty-two card deck. Five cards per player are dealt, and everyone can ask for three more cards, so forty-eight cards, seven players would make fifty-six cards, too many unless they did double deck. If they double up the cards it tends to scare off less experienced players, the ones who feed the others. That's common in Vegas, but in a game like this one I doubt they would want to do that, so there's going to be six players. They might play with five, but the more players, the more the house makes, so they do everything in their power to get the maximum number."

I bit my lower lip and remembered the granite counters and stalls in the bathroom. The guy who ran this place liked to think he had class. He probably *did* have class, and not a small dollop of pride. He would run his table by the highest standards, and that meant Vegas rules.

"So all we need to do is wait for the players to file out," I mused, and then take down the last one or two. I guess we'll need to identify which one won and which one lost by the way they act."

Lucky nodded. "We should be able to figure it out."

She put the car in drive and started to twist the wheel.

"Where are we going?" I asked, confused.

"Anywhere," she replied without so much as a whiff of concern. "The first ones won't lose their shirts for at least five hours."

We dined on tuna sandwiches and caught a movie, then headed back to the Skardalija, arriving just before two in the morning. Since only a rumor of tight parking ever occurred in Winnipeg, we had no trouble lining up a spot with a clear view of the carpark, a view we enhanced with the sights from the sniper rifle.

We took turns keeping an eye on the exit, and sure enough, by two o'clock, the first of the losers emerged. Although not the same guy I'd seen smoking the cigar, it could have been his brother. They looked

222

and dressed practically alike, right down to the band on their cowboy hats. This one didn't light a cigar when he left, however, but instead sadly shook his head and bobbled his shoulders, then unscrewed the lid of a hip flask and took a long drink before climbing into his pickup truck.

"I'd say that was a loser," I grinned.

"In more ways than one," agreed Lucky, who looked tired. She'd rubbed her eyes more than once. I'd toyed with the idea of letting her sleep in the back seat until the winners emerged, but decided we needed her awake and alert.

By the time three more obvious losers, including the cigar smoker, made the sad and solitary journey from exit to vehicle, Lucky and I had each stepped out of the car for fresh air twice. I'd also smoked four cigarettes at the crack of the window, a police car had made us duck down in the seats, and the clock on the dashboard clicked past five o'clock. It had been a long night.

"You really think there's six players?" I asked, hoping we hadn't let the winner slip by.

"Maybe that's him," answered Lucky, changing the topic as another figure emerged from the restaurant door, scented the air and then trudged towards a compact car, key in hand.

Raising the scope let me catch the departing figure in the crosshairs.

"Goran," I informed Lucky, still not certain if that was his name but figuring it would do as well as any other.

"That's a good sign," Lucky yawned. "Means they're wrapping up if they let the bartender go."

I agreed with a yawn of my own and didn't respond. We'd long since fallen silent, fatigue having exhausted our array of small talk. After what seemed like an extension of eternity, the door opened again, and the last two players emerged, along with one of the Serbs who had been guarding the game. His duties, however, didn't seem to extend into the carpark because he kept right on walking while the players stopped to chat.

"Which one do you think it is?" I asked Lucky, whose lips pursed as she squinted into the rifle sight.

I chose a middle aged guy with slicked back hair, a thin mustache and a patent leather jacket. He had a sleazy look that reminded me of a former and unfortunate comrade named Zero. He wore dishonesty like an angel wears a halo, but also had some of the most intelligent eyes I'd ever seen. You can always count on a guy like that to find a way to win. He'll have some kind of scam going.

The other finalist was the little old man who had had a glass of red wine at the table. He had a sad, expressionless face and hair that looked like once combed wire. Of course he'd put a hat on, one of those old time fedoras that clashed with his orange windbreaker, which in turn clashed with his green polyester floods and white socks. Despite his light clothing, he seemed immune from the cold, and his face held no expression as he listened to the other player talk and smile.

"The short one," said Lucky, certainty ringing in her voice.

"What makes you think that?" I asked in return, seeing no reason in body language or facial expression to think he might have won, or lost, or even played. "That guy looks like he's come from a funeral, not a card game."

"What do you think makes a good poker player?" came Lucky's retort, not lowering the slender telescope. "And besides, it isn't him that makes me certain. It's the other one."

"Why's that?"

"Because there's only one reason he would talk to the short guy. The poor man has his money. He's fishing for an angle to get it back, or how to make losing it worth his while, maybe seeing if the winner can be played. What else would they talk about? Chasing girls? Crooners from the fifties? A bunch of dead people?"

That did make sense, though I had to admit I liked the idea of robbing the greaseball better than robbing a sad-eyed old man. I pictured him a widower, likely living alone and with one joy in his life, poker. It felt like taking candy from a baby in the moral sense. I had to tell myself that a good poker player would always be able to find someone to stake him for a game. I'd seen something on cable where a gambler talked about the horror she felt when she lost her first million, and how quickly she felt better when she won two million the next. Gamblers lived by boom and bust.

The old man drove the oldest car on the lot, naturally. It looked like one of those giant gas guzzlers from the sixties. Of course, it probably consumed less gas than a modern SUV, but that didn't concern me. The sprinkling of cars starting to appear on the roads concerned me. With darkness running out and the world waking up, we would run out of empty streets.

When the old clunker, far too old for me to recognize the make or model, turned into the street after a fifteen minute warmup, Lucky turned in behind.

From the get go, isolating his car proved tough. We couldn't take him near the restaurant, and he turned out onto Queen Anne's Way, which had way too much traffic to pull off a carjacking, even at dawn on Sunday. We also had to turn off the street a few times to avoid rousing suspicion because the old man drove so slowly that no one in their right mind would refrain from passing. We pulled over every time we saw a letterbox, just for pretense.

We nailed him on a side street, probably two or three blocks from his home.

"There's our opening!" I cried to Lucky as the old man neared a traffic circle, one of the ones designed to keep drug dealers from blitzing through neighborhoods like pit bulls on acid.

"Gotcha," Lucky replied with obvious tension in her voice. She didn't ask what to do, just followed her instincts as I drew my scarf across my face and clicked the safety off my pistol. A moment later, the old man's car eased right to meander past the concrete flowerbed with its yellow reflective CAUTION sign. No sooner had his tail cleared than Lucky gunned the engine and we jerked left so hard we swayed in our seats. With another harsh twist of the wheel and a squeal of tires we swayed right and made it around the circle to cut the old man's car off.

He didn't even look surprised, there in the driver's seat. He looked morosely from his window as if people cut him off all the time as his car came to a stop. That changed the moment I stepped out of the car and he saw the gun in my hand.

With hot breath dampening my scarf, I lifted the pistol as I saw his hand reach for the lever of the transmission.

"Don't even think it!" I shouted, then swiftly aimed to shoot out his front tire with a loud *bang* as I advanced towards the driver's door. The poor old guy froze for a moment, then pushed back into his passenger seat to get away. I opened his driver side door with a hard yank, knowing that with the pistol shot, the clock had started ticking. It might be Sunday morning, but gunshots wake people up. They would turn over in their beds and listen for five or ten seconds, then push back their covers and rise, then peek out their windows, so maybe forty seconds there, then they need five seconds to realize what was happening. Ten seconds after the shock registered, someone's fingers would jam 9-9-9 faster than a kid at his favorite video game. We needed to blitz through the robbery and fly down the road.

Without wasting a second, I reached into the car and grabbed the old man by the shoulder, waving the pistol under his nose so it would look as large and powerful as anything he had ever seen.

"Please don't kill me…" he pled in a frightened old man's voice. Terrified, he held up his grey hands while the radio played church music in the background and vied for audio supremacy with the heater fan.

"Your winnings!" I told him, half climbing in to frisk his windbreaker. The poor guy was too terrified to surrender what would save his life. After the second grope, I touched what felt like a pad of paper, so I yanked hard on his windbreaker, gripping and throwing the old man forwards and back like a rag doll until the zipper wrenched free.

"Give it up!" I ordered him, not waiting for him to obey but reaching inside his jacket and grasping for the thick wad, an envelope holding a sheaf of paper the size and shape of money.

"No! No!" The old man cried as I took the paper and tore a square off its corner with my teeth to see that it indeed held cash.

Without pausing, I pushed back out of the car and lunged the three steps back to Lucky, jumped in the passenger seat and we raced away in seconds.

I hated taking money from an old man, but the revolution needed the money far more than he did. I'd given him nightmares for the rest of his life, but compared to some of the things I'd done in the name of a greater good, it was a small thing.

"Holy shit," I breathed in awe once I had the envelope open. Neatly folded notes almost an inch thick filled the interior like a letter of good will from God himself.

"How much is it?" asked Lucky in response to the excitement in my voice.

"They're all hundred pounders," I told her, amazed that people could play cards with that kind of cash. "Except for a few miscellaneous notes. I'd have to say there's twenty grand here."

By damaging the psyche of one harmless old man, we'd solved our financial problems for the near future. I felt like a monster, but Donny and his lawyer friends would soon teach me the real meaning of the word.

The transcript below came from Breakfast in Blighty, *an early morning radio talk show broadcasting in Greater London, hosted by Reginald Balfor, known for his rapid fire delivery of rather non-politically correct news commentary and tongue in cheek weather forecasts.*

Rise and shine, Blighty! It is now seven o'clock and I'm Reggie Balfor come a calling, though I should begin the day with a fine Irish 'Top o' the morn' seeing as our friends across the Irish Sea have the lead in the news this morning. Seems they've been following their natural instincts and trying to sail south as the imperial navy tacks north. This time they've gone and upset PATSI, that fine piece of legislation that'll be protecting us all from the slavering terrorists for years to come. In typical Irish fashion they've split their vote down the middle, but as of this morning, it seems the nays have it by a margin of only ... get this... three votes. Oh now that doesn't bode well for PATSI where they're now predicting defeat in North America's remaining dominions. Now let's all have an introspective moment of silence for poor PATSI <four seconds of Reginald's trademark sound of tea being gulped from a cup> And now time for everyone's favorite moment, the weather. Surprise surprise it's cold and rainy, which should come as no surprise at all seeing as the boffins predict a full week of the same and have been for the...

We got the car back in the garage late on Sunday night, then activated our listening devices for Monday morning. After that, I called the Four Fucks Law Firm from the lobby of a diner. The call activated the bug on the switchboard and Lucky confirmed a clear signal. With all systems go, it left us with a lot of time to sit around and wait.

Monday morning's return trip to the library brought me face to face with Timothy Schramm's back breaking work on the imperial economy, *Applied Laws of Economic Dynamism within the Free Market Capitalist Structures of the Developed World.* The introduction was fairly straightforward, but it took me four hours to penetrate the first chapter and one further hour to comprehend that the book was way more complex than my education. The tome boasted charts with graphs and mathematical equations to manipulate them, something my education hadn't included. I didn't have the foundation to lay the groundwork to establish the base for comprehending what I needed to know.

If Julie were there, she might have guided me to another topic. I didn't need to devour Macroeconomics to understand the revolution. If there had been some impartial but learned bystander that I could discuss these things with, he or she might have recommended that I try something at a lower level than the post doctorate, but I didn't have Julie, and I didn't have a competent advisor. So, at that time, I set the books aside and walked away to find understanding elsewhere.

Sad steps took me from the warmth of the library, and the way the chill of the wind slipped into the small openings of my coat reminded me of the first day I'd become a fugitive. Dodging a police task force, I'd raced to the nearest phone to alert my comrades and follow our emergency protocol. I'd never felt so scared or alone in my life.

In one minute, I'd lost a family of seventy. I'd lost my first love, Julie. I'd lost my job, my few friends, my personal belongings and everything I hadn't stowed in my pockets or wallet. I had comrades at large, fleeing or fighting for their lives, but everything in my life except the revolution disappeared in an instant. In Winnipeg, I faced much the same feeling. I had no one to visit, no one to call, no hobbies to pursue. I just walked the streets, alone with my memories.

I spent each of the next three days wandering through downtown and uptown Winnipeg, ostensibly getting to know the layout of the city, but really killing time until each workday ended so we could harvest our day of eavesdropping.

"She's such an idiot," growled Lucky as she pulled her headset off. Beside her, on my unmade bed, lay a legal pad with thirty names listed all in a row. Lucky had started with the switchboard. As people called in and identified themselves, Lucky duly recorded their names and used stroke marks grouped in batches of five with a diagonal stroke to keep track of how many times they called. One caller had a question mark to identify him because he always tried to flirt with the receptionist, a girl named Shannon that Lucky considered an idiot.

"I like him," mimed Lucky in a half piggish and half girlish squeal. "He's so sweeeeeet." With a disgusted grimace, she rolled her eyes. "If I have to hear one more love squeal I'm going to scream. And she's so fucking horrible whenever she talks about another woman."

I grinned, the headphones around my head playing a babble of legalese from the head honcho's office. His name was Baxter. I couldn't make heads or tails of the details, but in general he spent his day on the phone giving orders to subordinates, following up on orders he'd already given, laying out his findings before clients and, as Pop would say... "Etcetera, etcetera, etcetera."

His most recent call concerned a clarification of current law regarding the finer points of drug patient testimonials, with a lengthy and long winded explanation as to when they could be used in advertising, under what circumstances, and for what purposes.

The aggravating thing about this mission wasn't the sheer amount of time consumed, but the boredom. My best hope, Donny Paglia's phone, flopped big time. Donny didn't use the office phone all that often. We'd recorded three of Donny's calls, one of which came from a colleague named Silvio, whom I bet was the receptionist's Romeo and my Vinnie from the elevator. He sounded like Donny's personal bodyguard, errand boy, and driver all rolled into one. The other two calls concerned Donny's advance lunch order and a call to the dry cleaners.

All said, nothing interesting happened on Donny's phone, or Baxter's phone. We couldn't identify anything suspicious from the receptionist's desk, and the other taps also flopped, consisting of a mix of routine legal matters and miscellaneous personal business.

The audio in Baxter's didn't tell us anything either, but in Donny's room, we at least got a nibble.

"How are preparations for that special assignment going?" asked Baxter in a distant, mechanical voice, like he'd literally held onto the doorjamb with both hands and stuck his head in the office before speaking.

"You leave that to me," replied a distracted sounding Donny.

"Come on, just let me know," answered Baxter's voice, half in a plea and half in a conspiratorial whisper. *"The big man might call me and ask."*

"Now what you don't know," answered Donny in a mock lecture but true disdain, *"can't hurt you."*

I could almost picture Donny dismissing the lawyer without a second thought. The gangster certainly didn't lack confidence and the dynamics of the conversation registered instantly. Whatever Baxter and his legal people did in Winnipeg, it fronted what *Donny* did in Winnipeg. Baxter might be the boss, but Donny didn't take his orders.

Donny must have read an expression on Baxter's face or a response to something unsaid.

"Let's just say that plans have been made for Edmonton, and we're planning for Minneapolis right now. If anyone asks, that's as much as you can tell them."

"That's great," came Baxter's suspiciously enthusiastic reply. *"Just let me know if you need anything."*

"Will do," assured Donny, who must have made some gesture, because an eager Baxter said, *"Oh yeah, uh, right!"*

Donny sat in silence for fifteen seconds before muttering under his breath. *"Fucking pencilneck."*

Other than a goodbye to an unknown person, we got nothing else from Donny. I checked and saw a ten thirty timestamp, which meant Donny had spent about an hour in the office that day, about average.

"So what do you think?" I asked Lucky as I drank some orange soda and lit a cigarette. With the window open just a crack, a draft slid into the room, but Lucky didn't complain.

"I think this sucks," she complained with her legs crossed and her notepad in her lap. "And it's going nowhere."

I had to agree. After seventy hours of recorded telephone conversation, we had barely a glimmer as to what Fester, Fowler, Fagan, and Finch had hired Donny to do. About the most interesting thing we'd learned was that Shannon was always horny. That didn't help since I didn't want to come any closer to their office and she preferred rich men.

233

"Let's give it a few more days," I grimaced. We'd gone through a lot of cash and a lot of effort to plant those bugs and suffered from a serious lack of alternatives. If we couldn't learn what we needed from eavesdropping, we might have to do something desperate, like kidnapping Silvio or Baxter. Since the implications of that idea also included torture, I couldn't bear to even think of it.

"If you say so," surrendered Lucky with something less than confidence. Judging by the look in her eye, I would have to say she was far less impressed with Nicky Pops than she'd anticipated. That thought didn't please me, but I couldn't let my ego get in the way of better judgment.

Thursday night found us in my room again, with a more expansive collection of recordings and notes, but no more knowledgeable than before.

"This isn't working," I told Lucky, not bothering to turn off the player. Baxter's voice could prattle on into infinity for all I cared. Why did anyone become a lawyer? How did law become so complex? From all those calls I learned one thing, laws covered anything and everything people did.

"Well, we did learn one interesting thing," hummed a distracted Lucky.

"What's that?" I asked, not having anything come to mind. After eight full days of eavesdropping, we'd learned next to nothing. We'd learned Donny had another guy named Sim, and that they didn't like to talk about their plans. Other than that, we'd gotten some slim insights into their personal habits, but nothing worthwhile.

"We learned Donny's gonna visit The Cookie Cutter's Lounge tomorrow night."

That didn't help. If Donny got so much as a glimpse of me, he would shoot on sight. I couldn't go anywhere near him. Knowing Donny's Friday night whereabouts would only let me sneak around somewhere else. I said as much to Lucky.

"He doesn't know me," came her solemn reply. "I know how to play gangsters the way some girls play the flute.

Lucky's serious face left no room for doubt. Her eyes watched me like a prizefighter waiting for an opening, and the softer side I'd gotten to know disappeared. Almost as if to emphasize the point, Lucky reached over and pulled one of my cigarettes from the open pack on the bed, then lit up as like she smoked every day.

Lucky had come a long way since we'd started to work together, and I'd come to care for her like a sister. If my senses served me right, she'd come to respect herself a lot more since that day in Reno. I didn't want her backsliding.

"Nah," I shook my head. "He's too smart." It wouldn't do to tell her my real thoughts, but as luck would have it, they were written on my face.

"I know how to handle men like Donny," explained Lucky. "They're about power, and feeling powerful. I can get him. I can hook him. I can find out what we need to know, and I don't mind doing what's necessary along the way." She paused. "He's really pretty handsome, you know."

Forget about thinking the last thing I wanted to see was Lucky backsliding. The absolutely positively last thing I wanted to hear about was a handsome Donny.

"No. No." I told her, already smelling a useless gesture. Her solution was too perfect, really. Lucky knew how to hook a man like Donny. Only brutal and extremely uncertain options remained. We both knew Lucky proposed the best, quickest, cleanest way.

"Its nothing I haven't done before, Nicky," Lucky assured me as she blew a trail of smoke out the window. Even though she only wore a t-shirt, she ignored the cold, and it occurred to me that maybe Lucky's body had numbed with her decision, that subconsciously, she began to fortify herself against the prostitution to come.

"You don't need to do that," I replied softly, musing alternative strategies. "You're a lot more talented on your feet than you are on your back." I paused for emphasis.

Lucky laughed softly, but not softly enough to disguise a submerged and hardened scowl, "That doesn't mean I'm not talented on my back. Honestly Nicky, you're a terrorist, not my mother. You don't need to bother yourself about my chastity. One thing I've learned since being with you is that you appreciate my talents. Let me use *all* my talents."

"Lucky, you're not the whore of the revolution," I told her, only to make her laugh.

"You mean I'm not *just* the whore of the revolution." She took a drag on her cigarette. "No. Thanks to you, Nicky, I'm not just the whore of the revolution. You've taught me a lot, more than you probably know. I have a lot to thank you for."

Lucky used her cigarette to point at my chest. "With you, I've survived my first firefight and made a difference in its outcome. I've learned about surveillance and how to pull off a resource raid. You've made a big difference in how I think and how I fit into this revolution, Nicky, but we need to succeed, and the best way to do that..." She pointed to herself with the butt of her cigarette, "is for me to seduce Donny and find out whatever I can."

"Donny may not be the pushover you think," I objected, defeated.

Lucky smiled with a confidence I'd never seen and said, "There's not a man on this planet I can't handle, Nicky."

Jonas Abernathy accidentally left the following voice mail on the voice mailbox of a secret telephone number belonging to his handler, Special Agent Anthony Lespertini. The pair normally used the mailbox for messages they wished to hide from Anthony's superiors

"Yo, Dickwad. <four seconds of silence> If you're there pick up the phone. <three seconds of silence> I guess you're not there. <two seconds of silence> Anyways, I'm just calling to letcha know that your boy Nicky Pops has been sighted over in Winnipeg or at least that's the word around the campfire. Speaking of campfires, I'm heading out on the road with Horse and his guys. We'll see if those fags have the connections they say they do but I'll be incommunicado for a few days at least. <two seconds of silence> I just thought I'd letcha know your boy's

237

in Winnipeg. Nothing is solid and I ain't got no address or nothing, but he was seen in the city. Better catch him before the Mongols do. Later.

Special Agent Anthony Lespertini lay at home with a cold, but acted on the information as soon as he heard Jonas' message, three days later.

To my surprise, Lucky didn't dress up, she dressed down to look like a poor girl passing herself off as a debutante.

"It's about power," she told me, deliberately dabbing into place one more layer of eyeliner more than necessary. She'd chosen cheap shoes and a high-hemmed dress cut in a classy style but from inferior cloth. The lavender color looked a little too faded to fit, but not so faded that the dress looked old. She'd also donned an imitation pearl necklace and dimestore bracelets. If she intended to look like a minx on the prowl, she succeeded.

"Mobsters always want to feel they're in control and calling all the shots," Lucky explained. "When they look for a woman, they look for one they think they can control. They want someone who needs them, depends on them, because that's the only way they feel secure. It frees them up to be assholes later on."

You had to hand it to the girl, Lucky knew her trade.

"Oh," she added. "And you know what they say about winning a man's affection through his ego?"

"I've heard of it," I shrugged, having suffered bitterly in learning the technique's effectiveness when wielded by a professional named Julie.

"Well," she finished, hitching her dress up an inch. "That goes double for gangsters." She turned and smiled, a lipsticked Mata Hari serving the revolution and proud of it.

At that moment, seeing her in the doorway of Peanut's bathroom, I had nothing but admiration for Lucky. Her inner strength had ballooned. She didn't compromise herself at all, a far cry from the young woman I'd met in Reno that lacked confidence, self-respect, and talent beyond the bedroom.

I'd compromised myself in the name of revolution, but Lucky beat me hands down. At its core, sleeping with someone after kissing their ass and whatever else it took to play a particular ego was a very personal thing. For a woman to surrender herself like that took courage and strength, all the more when her comrades didn't respect the act. I'd already seen first hand evidence of how Mitchell viewed Lucky, yet Lucky stayed strong.

I reached out and touched my comrade's soft shoulder with my fingertips. There in the lines of her eyes, I saw the hurt from the past, and the toughness that let her spring back, and a hint of the ability, an almost wondrous ability, to love.

"Sis, you don't need too do this," I told her softly. "We can find another way.

Lucky whispered gently, "If you only knew what a kind man you are, Nicky." Then, to my surprise, she poked me in the stomach. "Now let's go win this war."

Charles Tuffy submitted a paper to his Political Science professor wherein he challenged conventional thinking in regards to extremist groups and the political process. The paper received the highest grade possible, though it never left the Miami University campus.

Extremism vs. Populism

Conventional thought states that extremist groups should be brought into the political dialogue where their ideas can be challenged, and thus wither. The purpose of this paper is to argue that the September Alliance is an exemption from this rule for, though their methods have been extreme, their rationale represents a form of populism rather than extremism. At its conclusion the paper will recommend that the People's Progressive Party should be banned from political activities until the September Alliance verifiably disarms and responsible parties are held accountable.

In the body of this paper I will introduce evidence that shows that the September Alliance differs from traditional extremist movements in three ways. First, most extreme political groupings do not seek to enter the mainstream dialogue, fearing the attacks from moderates and opposite extremists alike. The September Alliance [SA] behaves to the contrary, making every possible attempt to enter the political process. Second, the manifesto of the SA is, line by line, capable of garnering large amounts of public support, more so than the programs of the three main parties. No fringe party or grouping known to me is able to claim the same. What arouses public horror and fear is their methods, not their manifesto. Last, The September Alliance is organized around a set of principles that are currently in place in countries with which the empire has warm and close relations, such as the Scandinavian nations. These countries are admired throughout the empire and the world.

By the time this report is concluded, the reader will have come to the correct conclusion that I do not support the entry of the People's Progressive Party [PPP] into the political process, and that I would deny them electoral participation, fundraising, media access and more...

I'd forgotten the Mongols. The Mongols, like a bad credit report, hadn't forgotten me. I'm not sure where they spotted me, but they laid an ambush I failed to spot. About an hour after Lucky went off in search of Donny I wandered into a shack serving the saltiest Polish sausage I'd ever eaten. When I emerged, I walked up the street and rounded a corner by a parked van, only to almost collide with its rear door opening in my face.

At first, I stepped back, startled but not alarmed, thinking the near collision one of life's little accidents. I felt safe on a cold, quiet street in a small city where no one knew me.

Boots landed on pavement, sounding crisp and sharp like a quickly struck drumbeat, and a moment later, a biker rounded the door with trouble on his face. Unlike most of the bikers, who sported woolly heads, this one had long straight hair, almost like a prim high school girl's, but he didn't look girlish in the slightest. He looked tough, and as his hands reached to seize the front of my coat, I felt raw strength enhanced by prison weightlifting and mad hatred of anything weak.

"Get him into the van," another voice urged as another set of heavy boots hit the pavement. I'd started to struggle with the first attacker and couldn't make out the features of the second, but had few doubts he was even bigger, meaner, and uglier.

I cried out as the biker swung me around like fifth grade bullies with the teacher's back turned. He intended to throw me into the arms of his henchman, but a lucky twist of my foot changed the direction I spun, away and towards a parked car. Instinctively, my right hand went to my belt, but instead of closing on the warm metal pistol grip, met the tightly sealed wool of my buttoned coat.

Without a fraction of a second to spare, I had to shove back and roll over the hood and off one shoulder onto the ground to avoid having the bikers snatch me again. Their hands barely missed, thumping onto the cold metal as I rolled away. One hand caught my coattail but couldn't hang on.

"Fuck," shouted the first biker, and I could see the silhouette of a third against the lights of the van's cargo compartment. I'd been kidnapped by criminals twice before, and both times had been lucky to survive. I had no wish to trust my luck to a third shake of the dice.

I made it to my feet just in time to duck under a tackle from the second biker, who got enough of a grip to take us both down in a sprawl. Instinctively, I rolled left, clawing halfway to my feet and taking a boot to my backside. Whatever the attacker's intent, the kick propelled me a few staggering steps forwards.

Struggling to my feet with a grunt, I hefted my coat like a girl hikes her dress to show her panties, getting one hand on the gun in my waistband and drawing as I heard someone behind me say "Fuck it, gimme a clear shot!"

With one hand, I seized the post of a parking meter and spun. I whirled like a Debs on her shiny chrome pole, spinning out and low as a single gunshot came from the van. It missed, but as I spun, I raised my gun and fired three times. Shooting from a pole dance disallowed any chance of a hit, but sent the bikers scrambling for cover calling, "Gun!"

Not pausing, I continued the spin. I couldn't win against three men in the open any more than I could duke it out with one of them in a fair fight. Knowing that, as I swung around the meter's pole, I ended in a sprint to the nearest shop door.

Lights still shown in windows, one with a glowing neon OPEN sign. I yanked the door open with a jangle of bells, half registering a cleaner's setting as a bullet punched the store window, punching a neat hole with a perfect spiderweb.

The woman behind the counter screamed as I plowed through the door. Two hands flew up to cover her terrified fifty plus year old face, grey hair in a bun. She had the face of a hard working woman, the kind of woman the revolution wanted to help, but I didn't have time to sympathize.

With a leap I somersaulted up and over the counter, scattering yellow carbon copies as the smell of steam and solvents filled my nostrils. I jumped through racks of plastic wrapped clothes, pushing and shoving my way headlong for the back door. An old man emerged, his mouth a giant O of surprise as I roughly shouldered him out of the way and plunged ahead. Behind me, the Mongols shouted loud and clear. The older woman screamed again as they roughly ordered her out of the way.

I hit the back door at a run, palms, cheek and chest colliding with the door before my left hand grasped the knob, jiggled, shoved, and finally pushed out into the alley. It was still early, about eight o'clock, so plenty of light shone from various windows. The opposite side of the alley consisted of a long row of self-standing garages with garbage cans neatly arrayed to the left of each door.

With my breath a frosty cloud, I looked both ways, saw no difference, and ran to the right as fast as my legs could carry me. The sound of the laundry door behind me cued me to jump into the gap between two garages and I folded over the gate of a chain link fence like a gut shot soldier into a foxhole, then rolled and dashed forwards like a desperate dash across no man's land. The flicker of someone's telly lit a typical bungalow's backyard as I raced towards the front.

Disaster struck as I reached the gate to the front yard. I tried the catch and shoved hard but it only gave an inch. I tried again, harder, but it still wouldn't open. My eyes searched and found a bicycle cable looped around the post, the kind they coat with all sorts of colored plastic. By the time I gave the freezing gate a confirmation shake, I realized it was no use and jumped over. As I landed, I saw the bikers by the side of the garage.

"There he is!" shouted one.

My heart leapt, and I half ran and half turned, firing blindly as I did. Mongol bullets whizzed by my head and shoulders as I flew around the corner. By some miracle, I wasn't hit. As I rounded the corner, I felt the first true heave of exertion expand my lungs, sprinted across the street towards a yard that didn't have a fence, vaulted over a cement saint feeding cement animals and leapt over another fence. Within moments I lost myself in the maze of bungalows.

Neither the Mongols nor I could afford a running gun battle to draw the cops, so after a few quick looks at my trail, I made tracks as quickly as possible, then found a doghouse in the back yard of a vacant house for sale. I crawled in to catch my breath. The door offered just enough view that I soon spotted police cruisers coasting up the street as they searched for the source of gunshots.

Not much later, the bark of dogs on a scent got me moving. It didn't take a genius to figure out the cops put a canine unit into play. Desperately, I made my way as quickly as possible up the street, keeping to cover in case I spotted more cruisers.

Three streets from the doghouse refuge, the barking of a neighborhood dog sparked an idea that I'd picked up from a movie. Momentarily shedding my coat, I tore my shirt off my back, got my coat back on, and approached the dog behind the fence.

Tentatively reaching out, I found a beagle, a loud but not vicious breed, so I leaned over the fence and petted its fur a moment before insistently tying the sleeve of the shirt through its collar and cinching it tight. The dog whined and squirmed but happily endured the indignity for a striped peppermint candy.

With the shirt looped through its collar, I opened the gate, let the dog sniff more candy, then threw them as far as I could. The dog took off at a run, trailing my shirt, and my scent, in its wake. The louder, more focused barking of police dogs helped me choose another direction, almost blundering into a squad car minutes later. If the police hadn't been intent on questioning a couple of teenagers bent over the hood, I might have been spotted, but luck held long enough for me to get back to the main street, where I took the chance of hailing a cab, directing it south. I shot pool with a few of the locals to kill time while the heat died down, blending in but not drinking.

I'd survived another encounter with the Mongols. I hoped it would be my last.

This post appeared in the open forum on www.politicaljunkie.org

Everyone is talking about how PATSI is suddenly in trouble but I don't think so. PATSI seems likely to be approved if you ask me but everyone is suddenly measuring it against "Predicted". If Predicted were an alternative piece of legislation that might be relevant, but suddenly everyone is doubting that PATSI is going to be approved because the Argentine Dominion gave it 68%, far less than "Predicted" even if 68% on anything is practically unheard of. Same thing with the Cascades Dominion... They rejected it by more than "Predicted" and now everyone thinks the initiative is in trouble despite knowing from the outset that the Cascades would vote nay. PATSI needs all three of the remaining dominions in order to pass and I bet it gets through as long as it doesn't have to compete against "Predicted".

Sleep abruptly ended with the vibration of my cell phone. The encounter with the Mongols had shaken my nerves. On the way back to the bar, signs of massive police activity lingered well into the night. Helicopters stabbed bright searchlights down onto the streets and squad cars with their cherries going cruised up and down, loudspeakers warning residents to stay in their homes. I'd thought that kind of response beyond Win, but they'd surprised me. I'd taken a cab back, and that alone saved me from questioning.

With a flick of my thumb, I opened up the display on the phone, seeing Lucky's number on the caller ID and eight minutes after four in the morning on the clock.

"Hey," I answered, pressing the blood warm phone to my ear.

"He's hooked," boasted Lucky's voice, squeaky with excitement. *"I told you the way to a man's heart is through his ego. I've got him thinking he's some kind of Casanova demigod. Where are you at?"*

"Nowhere you'd like to be," I told her in return. "Can you meet me at the car?"

"Sure," she promised in a voice with even more confidence than before. *"Just let me call a cab."*

Lucky made it to the car before I did, and she could count her blessed stars that she didn't get raped on the way up. The garage stairwells not only lacked any kind of glass for passersby to see inside, but the dim lighting would have let an elephant hide in the shadows. They also didn't have night staff, something well documented on the sign with the fees. If that weren't enough, the doors of solid steel sealed the entry and came with a money back guarantee that not a sound would escape, like a woman screaming for help.

"He's hooked," greeted Lucky before I slid fully into the driver's seat. She didn't look up from the laptop screen, which cast gold and blue flickering light across her face and throughout the interior. Then she added, "And we've got twenty-one hours of conversation to listen to." She paused. "No matter. We won't need it."

Lucky must have hooked Donny good. I smiled to myself. She didn't look rumpled, worn or used in the slightest. A few stray wisps of blonde aside, she looked exactly like the moment she'd walked out the door of Peanut's apartment. Donny must have comported himself like a perfect gentleman.

Lucky had an excellent plan of attack. She'd complimented Donny's silk shirt and diamond pip pin as well as his jacket, told him he stood out from the rough men in Winny and generally played to Donny's sense of panache. I could see how that would work. Donny would be vain in just that way, pretending to be a stylish gentleman no matter how uncouth his background.

"So are you going to see him again?" I asked, after Lucky's more extended recap.

"Tomorrow," she grinned, snapping the laptop closed. "He's cooking me dinner in fact."

I lifted both eyebrows in amazement.

"He made a big deal about how Italian men always know how to cook, so I wiggled my way into an invitation." She almost giggled as she smiled. "I'm bringing a salad."

"You're bringing more than a salad," I breathed, amazed at how well she'd done with such a dangerous target. "You need to plant that last acoustic bug. Donny may not work from the office, but we'll sure as shit glean something from his home."

Lucky's eyes narrowed. "I'm not so sure he won't do business from home. He went to some lengths to tell me that his employer furnished the house. He's only there temporarily. He's subtle, but he likes to brag."

Lucky shifted in her seat, then piped up, "Oh!" like she'd forgotten something. "Those other two guys, Silvio, his last name is Trocci and the other one they called Sim, his real name is Szymanski. I saw a note and Sim was spelled with a 'y'. Donny bragged about having employees, not roommates. I have to hand it to him, the man knows the art of conversation. If I weren't so tuned in I would never have figured him for a braggart, just thought he promoted machismo."

I chuckled.

"Can we go?" Lucky asked, "I'm hungry."

"Sure," I said with a start, then shifted into reverse. "But I want to recon his place as soon as you leave tomorrow. I'll stay close all night in case something goes wrong."

"Circling like a hawk," she smiled, looking pleased. "Honestly though, don't worry, I'm on really solid footing. I'm smarter than him."

We didn't yet know that being smarter wouldn't be good enough. Fate had surprises in store.

Media throughout the empire interrupted their regularly scheduled programming to broadcast this breaking news from New York City. Nicky and Lucky heard a similar version on their car radio.

...We are interrupting our regular programming to bring you this breaking news.

A group claiming to be the True September Alliance has broken the terrorist ceasefire and triggered multiple explosions in New York City. The situation remains muddled, but at least ten and as many as fifteen explosions have ripped through the city less than fifteen minutes apart. No one knows if more bombs are set to explode or if the terrorists have spent their bolt.

Emergency crews are arriving on numerous scenes but as of this moment we still have no reports of casualties. We do have confirmation that over a dozen hospitals in the city have been told to expect heavy casualties, as have the morgues.

New York City Police Spokesman Norman Zeeman confirmed that they did receive a call from a group purporting to call itself the True September Alliance and authenticated it as genuine. The caller correctly predicted the location of the first bomb. Little more was said other than that the police were cooperating with Fire Department personnel to evacuate other high-risk locations.

To summarize the situation as it stands now, New York has been struck by multiple and powerful bomb blasts. A group which appears to be a splinter cell of the September Alliance has claimed responsibility and there are casualties. We will be updating this bulletin as more news becomes available.

We now return to our regularly scheduled programming...

Lucky drew on my experience as a restaurant cook in order to make her salad, something I ribbed her about. You've really got to be bad in the kitchen if you can't make a salad. I recommended a salad of romaine lettuce, thin sliced red onion, bacon, avocado, tomato, feta cheese and Italian dressing. How could my favorite be wrong?

We mulled the bad news from New York and decided to visit an internet café to see if we'd gotten word from the supremos.

As if to herald bad news to come, a steady snow began to fall. At first, only a few flakes drifted aimlessly across the blacktop, but soon became clear the snow would thicken and stick.

On the ride to the café it seemed Win had an abnormally large number of cops about, but I didn't pay much heed. I parked and entered the café, only to find the place sounded like a video arcade. The local teenagers had some kind of a mechanized video war going. They shouted and smoked and drank soda pop, each one dressed in a uniform flannel shirt worn over a black t-shirt and a coat of acne for a face. I paid them no mind. They could only draw any attention meant for me.

It took a few minutes to light a smoke, grab an orange soda and get settled into www.hot4U.com's login screens. Sure enough, I had mail from someone named BluBabyBlu that had a wonderful picture of a phenomenally pretty woman with green eyes and chocolate brown hair. With a rueful grimace that she couldn't be real, I kissed the tips of my fingers and pressed them to the screen to show my appreciation, then read the far less pleasant message.

Hi Baby,

I'm far better than who you are with in every way. You should dump who you're doing and come get together with me in New York City. I'm looking for wild boys that don't listen and need discipline. If they don't do what I say after one chance, I let you in on the game, like Carmine Squall. Don't let any kind of current relationships stop you. I'm way better.

Hurry, I'm waiting nearby the Abilene

Jessica

No one could mistake the meaning. "These orders supersede all others. Proceed to New York as quickly as possible and look for a flag and drop near something called Abilene. It will direct you to instructions you can use to make contact with C Squad. Give them one chance to rejoin the September Alliance. If they refuse, use all means necessary to prevent rogue operations."

That last line hung in my mind as I leaned back in the chair and took a drag from the smoke. I'd conducted rogue operations at one time, and I'd gotten an unspoken ultimatum to cease or die. I'd been ready to die. I'd tried a desperate gambit to force the Specials to free Julie and it failed. Out of ammunition, out of money, comrades dead or captured, nowhere to run with a dragnet tightening by the minute, death had seemed inevitable and glorious.

I wondered how Julie would react to these orders. I could easily picture her deciding she knew better than the supremos and going solo, but how would she react to receiving orders to kill fellow revolutionaries?

A trickle of smoke managed to get in my eye, and the subsequent tears must have made it look like I cried because I caught one of the teenagers staring. He gave me a wry smile and turned quietly back to his own business. The tear matched my fermented wretchedness. The fact that our mission had been going well and relatively bloodlessly hadn't forced me to face my doubts, but the new orders brought them up nose to nose. More than ever, I wanted Julie beside me. I needed her wisdom.

Not only did the thought of killing comrades sit poorly, but I wondered about the decision to yank me from our current mission. Sure, what C Squad did was serious, very serious, but hardly something that required me immediately. I took a sip of soda and pondered my options as half the teenagers yipped for joy and the other half groaned.

I could buy time and see what Lucky came up with. The dating site didn't have a way for one user to tell if another had read his or her mail, so as far as Mitchell and the supremos knew, I hadn't yet received their orders. Then again, who was Nicky Pops to second guess the supremos? Orders were orders, and these orders had come quickly. They sported a crisp confidence that smelled like Mitchell. I peered at the screen. The girl in the picture did share Mitchell's general appearance as far as skin, hair, and eye color went so Mitchell must have been the author.

Shaking my head, not wanting to disappoint Mitchell, wanting her to know I truly had learned to follow orders, I clicked on the reply button, then stopped. It wouldn't hurt to see what Lucky came back with in a few hours. I could make preparations to leave in the meantime and barely lose an hour or two.

Pointing the cursor at the 'X', I almost forgot to log out of the dating site but remembered just in time. For good measure, I hit the 'home' command for the browser, then stood, stretched and started to button my coat when something caught my eye.

Ignoring my coat, I slowly sat back down and peered at the list of local news items. There in the Winnipeg column, second from the top, read the caption *Winnipeg Hotbed of Terrorism?* Biting my tongue as the article opened, I felt hot flashes run up and down my back. They only got worse as my eyes scanned the article.

The Drummer Boys had arrived in Winnipeg in large numbers and, while no one really knew their mission, the Drummer Boys did one and one thing only, capture or kill terrorists. As the only known terrorist in the city, it stood to reason the Specials had my scent.

The journalist wrote in a vague fashion, like he didn't know all the facts but knew enough to form a partial picture. He quoted a low ranking policemen from the Winnipeg force that could neither confirm nor deny they sought a key terrorism suspect. I needed no more confirmation. New York sounded like a great idea.

Closing the browser, I stood and quickly walked back to the car. Fifteen minutes later, I'd stomped up the stairs at the bar, thrown my duffel bag onto the bed and shoved everything I owned into its mouth except a solitary t-shirt that I used to wipe away any fingerprints I might have left. For good measure, I tossed in the sheet and pillowcase in case the Specials ran a DNA check, though if they were that intent, no precaution I took could stop them. My best efforts would only slow them down.

With an 'oof', I threw the bag over my shoulder and skipped quickly down the steps to find Brad the Bartender. I paid cash at the bar, took my change, and smiled as I left.

"Got tired of the Winnasauruses ja did, eh," grinned Brad before he wished me luck. I chuckled for his benefit, even though my stomach felt like a bucketload of caterpillars had crawled in for brunch.

If the Specials had arrived in Winnipeg… No. Make that, *when* the Specials had arrived in Winnipeg, they would case any place offering temporary accommodation, starting with the hotels. Thank goodness I'd been poor when we arrived, or I might already be under arrest. Sooner or later, and probably sooner, they would check places like Brad's, and know exactly what questions to ask. I'd gotten lucky.

Not knowing where else to go, and not wanting to compromise Peanut, I pulled into a laundromat and killed time doing laundry. No one looked for terrorists in front of a dryer.

While the machines ran, I tried to think where I could stay. Sleeping in the car was a cop magnet. Peanut's place was out. Motels and hotels were out. Red was too far away. Looking for ever shadier accommodations only postponed the agony. Finally, I remembered the empty house where I'd taken shelter in the doghouse.

After folding the hot laundry, an act which made me miss home because it made me remember my mother's face and smell my grandmother's basement, I tossed the duffel bag into the trunk, slammed it shut, and searched out a hardware store.

Snow, true to the weatherman's predictions, had grown heavier, though for the moment it hadn't stuck. As I pulled into the hardware store's parking lot with the radio playing a worsening weather report, but bad weather worked to my advantage.

Inside, I purchased a crowbar from a bald guy who sported a nametag with the name 'Irwin' and a chimpanzee IQ. Still, I avoided eye contact, conversation, and questions, got back into my car as quickly as possible and hoped no one would ask questions.

With the heater going and the wipers dusting watery snow from the windshield, I thanked Heaven for the cover snow would provide, prayed for luck, and parked a block from the vacant house.

The snow didn't reduce visibility as much as I would have liked, but it gave some cover while I jangled through the chain link gate and forced open the back door. It would have been better to search under bricks and in nooks and crannies for a key, or pick the lock, but the longer I took to force an entry, the better my chances of being spotted, so instead of dilly dallying, I opened the screen door, stuck the tip of the crowbar into the gap between door and jamb and heaved. Wood splintered and metal creaked, but with four sharp two-handed tugs, the door gave way.

Shaking off the cold, I closed the door, and in the dim light found myself in someone's utility room. The quiet seemed total, the kind of quiet you only get in the absence of people in a place where people should live.

The crowbar barely made a sound as I set it on top of a deep well freezer and my footsteps creaked eerily as I paced into a suburban kitchen, then a family room, and finally a dining room. The heater ran and the house had one light burning in the living room, which still boasted its drapes and brown and beige wall-to-wall carpet. Not a stick of furniture remained in any of the rooms.

Once again a desperate fugitive, I stretched out on the floor and propped my head on a softer section of the duffel bag. I'd lost the right to sleep comfortably.

Bradley Foster, known to Nicky as Brad the Bartender, formally answered police questions four hours after he bid Nicky farewell. The stenographer transcribed his answers below.

Q: Mister Foster, has it been explained to you that these proceedings are court supervised and any false evidence you knowingly present is considered a criminal act subject to prosecution?

A: Yes.

Q: Do you have any questions?

A: No, I don't.

<Transcriber notes that Mr. Foster has now been presented numerous photos of Nicholas Papadopoulos in a variety of appearances>

Q: Does the man you saw resemble any of the men in these photos?

A: Like I said before. The one with the brown hair looks like him, but ummm, number six also looks like him.

Q: You say this man took a room at your inn?

A: Well I don't call it an inn, but yes, he stayed in one of our rooms.

Q: For how long did he stay?

A: Three whole weeks.

Q: Did you observe any unusual activity on his part during the duration of his stay?

A: None. Except for the night he wanted to place a wager on the Wings, he was a really quiet fellow. He didn't make any fuss and he didn't make any trouble, paid in cash when he left. He seemed like a normal, friendly guy.

Q: What name did he give when he checked in?

A: George Stanakis.

Q: Did he say where he was going when he left?

A: He just said he was leaving. I assumed he meant he was leaving Winny.

Q: And that was at approximately six o'clock, correct?

A: Yes.

Q: Did you observe in which direction?

A: Like I told the patrolman who first came, all I can tell you is he turned right onto Hanover Street. After that, I didn't pay any attention.

Bradley and his wife, Susan Foster, were released forty-eight hours after questioning. They received no compensation for lost business income due to their absence.

I didn't like leaving my heavy firepower, but decided I had a better chance of surviving a firefight with the Specials if I could avoid getting into the firefight in the first place. Even with a DR-16 and the *Pica-Pau,* if even one or two cops identified me, my chances of surviving the encounter were slim. They could call in nearby patrol cars, SWAT teams, even the Imperial Army. Who knew what the Specials had brought into the vicinity. They had their own stormtroopers. So, after careful consideration, I concealed a pistol, pocketed the silencer, and trusted my luck. With brown hair, I didn't stand out in a crowd.

Armed, shaved, and clean, I snuck out of the house just before five a.m., searching the nearby windows for any sign that the neighbors observed my departure. If I couldn't blow town soon, I would need a new refuge if for no other reason than the nature of the vacant house precluded my coming and going at any time other than deepest night.

Four inches of snow had fallen and been swept away by the city crews during the night so driving proved no problem as I angled the car out of the city and onto the main roads. I found a café, ordered a coffee, drenched it in cream and sugar, then settled down at a checkered table with the daily newspaper. Flipping through the articles, I found no mention of the Specials which meant they'd silenced the local media. Not good. They meant business.

I bit my lower lip as I weighed the risks and hoped Lucky would call soon. If possible, I wanted to bail out of Win within the hour.

When the phone finally rang, it didn't grant my wish..

"We need to talk right away," Lucky insisted, the moment I answered the phone. *"I'm in the grocery store right around the corner from where I'm staying. Silvio was supposed to take me home, but I told him to drop me off here instead. Can you come get me* right now?"

"On my way," I answered, keeping the conversation short. The less said, the better, so after tossing the environmentally unfriendly double styrofoam cup into the chrome trash bin, I swung into the car and headed back towards Peanut's place.

Lucky's face peered out of the store from between a 2% milk poster and an advertisement for carrots. Even inside, she bundled up tight. The mercury didn't need to fall far for someone from Phoenix to get the chills.

When she saw me, Lucky dashed out of the store and into the passenger seat, slamming the door behind her. Without so much as a greeting, she blurted out, "We've got big trouble."

"I know," I told her. "The Specials have arrived, and they know I'm here."

"Fuck the Specials," Lucky interrupted. "Donny's planning something big. Silvio came back late last night, after we finished. Donny has a hot tub by the way. He's really kind of a romantic I think. He used rose scented candles and..." Lucky shook her head to stay on subject, shivered at the memory or cold and continued. "Silvio came back late last night, after we'd fallen asleep. He knocked on the door and Donny got up. They went downstairs and I overheard them talking."

I listened, the safety of New York receding with every word Lucky uttered. My heart sank.

"They're planning another terrorist attack, two of them, and this time in crowded shopping malls. You know those big ones they have on the telly sometimes? Those two. One is in Edmonton and the other is in a Minneapolis suburb. I'm not sure what they're planning to do, but they're planning on killing a lot of people, thousands I think, maybe even tens of thousands."

"They've got the explosives to do that," I mused, remembering the wooden crate with Chinese characters. Properly set and timed, the case held enough C6 to take out not just the malls, but the parking lots and a few dozen football fields of anything standing beyond.

"Any idea why?" I asked Lucky, not sure what Donny would gain from mass murder. He was a gangster, not a psychopath. If it didn't involve money, he shouldn't be interested.

"Someone paid him," suggested Lucky unnecessarily, half shrugging and half holding her palms up in a 'who knows' gesture. The scars on her face seemed whiter than ever. "To make them think it's us."

I stared hard at the windshield. It didn't make sense. Why would anyone hire a gangster to carry out an act of mass terror in order to blame it on us? Who would want that? Who would benefit? The more I thought, the less sense it made.

"It has something to do with California," Lucky told me. "I can't be sure what. I was listening through the vent on the bathroom floor and the heat kicked on, but they mentioned California. I managed to make out the word 'Tuesday', but that was it."

I wondered if it could be something about the Val-Mart offensive, the only link between California and the revolution that I could think of. Before I'd arrived, California was a terrorism backwater with a dysfunctional squad paralyzed by betrayal that had only survived by sheer luck.

"Makes no sense," I told Lucky in a tone that sounded serious even to me. "I don't get it. Maybe someone upstairs has an idea." I felt my jaw clench. Something important was going on. I could feel it. I needed to do something. An ominous unease settled deep as the marrow in my bones. Agamemnon's premonitions about Iphegeneia couldn't have felt worse.

"Do this," I told Lucky, "Get in contact with Mitchell right away. Use your communications protocol and do it electronically. The less I'm seen in public, the better."

"Huh?" asked Lucky with a doubtful look on her face, which prompted me to brief her about the Specials.

"That's not good," she added after I filled her in.

"No, it's not," I told her, then spilled the beans about the orders to New York. "While you're at it, check your hot for you account. You might have received orders to accompany me."

Lucky's face fell slightly, and I knew she thought Mitchell had overlooked her altogether. Mitchell didn't value Lucky as an operative. That would change, but Lucky bucked up instead of letting it get to her. "Will do. Anything else?"

"Not necessarily," I replied. "I'm going to try and get the recorder in position for eavesdropping on Donny. If I need your help, I'll call. What room did you put it in?"

"The kitchen. It seems that's where he spends most of his time. They have an overhead pot rack with dangling brass pans. I put it in the smallest one."

"Here," Lucky said, and drew a small diagram of the house on the back of a receipt. An inked in cupid's arrow pointed to the left rear. For good measure, she wrote down the address and passed it briskly. "I'll do better next time. He's supposed to call me this afternoon."

"Right on," I told her, "Keep me posted. We stay split up until the heat blows over or we get orders to move.

"Gotcha," Lucky said, her hand lifting the door handle. "You'll know as soon as I know. She stepped out.

"Hey Lucky," I called after her. She bent down, the wind stirring wisps of blonde about her made up face, her expression blank but curious.

"You know, if anything happens to me, you need to accomplish this mission alone."

Lucky turned serious and etched into her pretty face was more than a hint of the fear and grief she would feel if I died. The way she held her chin straight made me remember how I mourned Julie, and think how deeply Lucky might mourn for me.

"I will," Lucky squeaked in a tight voice, and I believed her. I hadn't given an order. I hadn't told her as a reminder. I'd told her so that she would remember that she served the revolution, and played an important role. That said, I might very well be killed or captured in the next few days, and if that happened, she would need to fly solo.

The deathly serious look on Lucky's scarred face told me she understood the gravity of what I'd said, and realized that the responsibility could indeed fall to her, and she would carry it out to the death if necessary.

"Never worry, Nicky," she half whispered. "I'll do my duty."

As she turned to leave, I thought I spied a hint of a tear where her eye met smudged mascara.

Rachel Galloway, a real estate broker in Winnipeg, filled out the following statement at the police station on her way home from work.

While showing the empty property at 302 Camacho Lane, I observed a man's full duffel bag in the living room and signs of use in the bathroom. When I inspected the house, I found that the back door had been forced open. I also found jars of peanut butter and honey, as well as a loaf of bread, leading me to believe that a homeless person has not only entered the home, but is currently using it for shelter. I request that the authorities take action to apprehend the trespasser, not just send him along his way with a warning.

Winnipeg police sent two officers to investigate, not knowing that they would encounter not a homeless vagabond, but the killer of almost one hundred police and special agents, the notorious terrorist, Nicky Pops.

Donny's house lay so far on the outskirts of the suburbs that it deserved country manor status. He had a mansion of the sort developed over the last twenty years. They featured large, partly brick and partly glass and pressboard exteriors with more rooms than they could efficiently heat and more yard than they could use if they fielded a football team. It even had a driveway thirty meters long. Triple rows of planted trees bordered two sides of the property. Whoever set Donny up in those digs hadn't cut corners.

With Lucky's sketch of the layout in hand, I studied different approaches from the darkness of the cooling car, wearing a black sweatshirt under my dark brown coat. The well kept front yard made for scant cover, not enough shrubbery. Just beyond the trees to the mansion's left stood the eastern border of a gated community with a reinforced fence over three meters tall. It might be possible to approach along that side, but anyone looking out the window from one of the segregated homes would have a clear view of my activities and instantly call the police.

The rear of the house offered better opportunities, having a dry creek bed six meters across, neatly dividing Donny's house from his neighbor's. That gave me a total of twenty meters of decent cover, if I could get to it. In the end, I chose to approach from the right, simply because approaching from the rear would require me going that way anyhow. To the right, Donny's triple row of trees bordered a recently bulldozed open lot with only a chain link fence separating the two. In the open lot, three low crests made miniature ridges where the earth had been pushed around. Beyond the vacant lot stood a creaking convenience store with two antique gasoline pumps and veteran sign advertising kerosene.

Most likely, the convenience store would soon be bulldozed for new mansions and might have folded already. Not so much as a nightlight shone from inside, so if they still opened for business, they did so during the day.

Wrapping my scarf across my face, I exited the car and slung the recorder over my shoulder, now fairly accustomed to the cold. I walked to the back, opened the trunk and removed the plastic storage tub I'd purchased that afternoon. I pressed the lid into place and locked it down, then took one last look around before crossing the empty street.

Once across, I kicked quickly through the snow to gain the partial cover of the dirt mounds and hurried from sight. When I'd gone a suitable distance, I heaved the tub over the top of the fence, then hauled myself up and over, folding my abs painfully over the stiff wire and tearing my coat on the way down.

With a grimace, I ignored the damage and discomfort, brushed the snow off, and gathered my stuff. Without wasting time, I dodged through the row of trees near the back.

Donny's kitchen faced the rear of the house, the center of three rooms cornered by an enclosed, finished porch. According to the bug's spec sheet, drywall and appliances shouldn't interrupt the signal, but I wanted the clearest signal possible, and thus the least obstruction and best angle, so I chose the right rear corner.

Without wasting time and with one eye on the dark mansion, I set the lid of the tub on the ground, then broke the receiver/recorder out of its case and turned it on. A flashing red light proclaimed the battery at full power. Glancing at the house, I pressed down on the test button, watching a green light appear, which meant the unit searched for a signal. If Lucky had placed the bug properly, it would automatically activate when it detected sound above a significant level.

To protect the receiver, I placed it gingerly inside the plastic tub, locked the lid into place, then found a rock to weigh it down as a precaution against a wind strong enough to lift the weight of the receiver. In Winnipeg, that was a real possibility. They didn't call it a windy city for nothing even if Chicago snatched the title.

I checked my watch, seeing it was now three thirty in the morning. I needed to get back to the vacant house before people started waking up and made it impossible to sneak in.

With that thought in mind, I hustled back along the treeline and hopped the fence, cautiously but steadily approached the road, then waited to make certain the coast was clear before dashing back to the car. Moments later, I had my scarf down, the engine running and the empty house on my radar.

As usual, I parked two blocks from the vacant home and started back, staying on the plowed street instead of on the snowy sidewalks, only half of which had been shoveled.

Even though my mind dwelt on what we would learn from conversations in Donny Paglia's kitchen, an old habit kicked in, and probably saved my life.

Sometime after being outed and becoming a fugitive, I'd learned to subconsciously 'walk the line' pretty much anywhere I went. By walking the line, I mean scan parked vehicles for any sign of activity. You never knew who could be inside one of those cars, Latino street gang members, mafia toughs, undercover police, bikers, it could be anyone, so I'd unconsciously learned caution, and on that snowy night in Winnipeg, it paid off.

Walking the line in Winnipeg didn't involve a whole lot. Most homes had private driveways. The neighborhood I'd holed up in was no exception. Very few cars parked on the street. Even with my mind on Donny, when the interior of one car flickered electronic red, it not only caught my eye, but made me focus.

A plain looking two door sedan rested two houses from my sanctuary and twenty meters in front of me. If I kept walking, I would pass it, but I slowed, eyeing the car suspiciously. The interior flitted red again, and as I plodded forwards, I could make out the back of two heads silhouetted in the streetlight glare and moonlight reflecting off virgin snow. From the box shape of the car, to being parked on a residential street at four in the morning, to the flitter of electronic equipment, they could only be cops.

I had to assume the cops had come because I'd broken into the house. Some nosy neighbor or sharp-eyed wag must have seen me coming or going and notified the police.

There could be another explanation, but I couldn't think of one in the time it took to approach.

With confident hands, I drew the silencer from my pocket and pistol from my waistband and reached behind my back with both hands. I attached the heavy tube to the barrel with one click then reached into my coat and took out a cigarette.

Snow crunched under my boots as fading moonlight gleamed off cars and snow. I approached the police car, pistol hidden behind my right leg but ready for use, picturing what I would do, muttering what I would say. With one hand, I drew my scarf across my face.

Breath steamed through the wool scarf as I closed on the police. Only as I passed their salt streaked fender did I see one of the heads turn at my approaching shadow, but too late.

Keeping the pistol down, I tapped on the driver's window and held up the cigarette. The round faced cop behind the wheel, light haired, pushing fifty, wearing a heavy wool coat with earmuffs loosely wrapped around his neck, gave me a mean look through the glass.

Insistently, I made a flicking gesture with my thumb so he would get the drift. He just shook his head and made a clipped, angry gesture that I should move on, then looked away. I didn't blame him. No one is in a good mood at four a.m.

Acting the part of an idiot, I tapped on the glass and pointed to the vehicle's ashtray, where most cars had a cigarette lighter mounted. That got me another red faced scowl, but I made an impatient gesture of my own, silently urging him not to be an asshole.

The cop's angry face tightened and his shoulder lurched. The window began to lower, centimeter by centimeter. When he had it half way down, he growled.

"Take it somewhere else."

"Aw come on man," I urged in a pleading tone. "Just let me use the lighter."

"I said *no*," he snarled again, beady eyes fixed on mine. "Now go home."

To emphasize his point, one hand lifted and flipped open his badge.

"You a cop?" I asked, like the stupidest man on Earth.

269

"Yeah, I'm a cop," he sighed, "and if you don't want any trouble, I suggest you move along and go home."

"Awright, awright," I told him, took a step back and lifted the pistol. His eyes registered a moment of shock, but only for the single remaining heartbeat of his life.

I pulled the trigger and instantly, before the *pffsst* of the pistol could register, a red spot appeared just under his nose. I'd intended to shoot him between the eyes, but had somehow, even at point blank range, managed to miss. Still, he slumped back in his seat, and I ducked, sighted his partner in the passenger seat, and fired again.

My second shot also went low, catching the surprised policeman in the chin, which turned his head like he'd been brutally slapped by a giant. With a growl, I reached into the car and opened the door by the handle as the second cop weakly reached for his gun. Leaning into the car, I fired twice more, this time shooting him through the temple as I'd meant to do in the first place. For good measure, I shot the driver again, the muzzle flash lighting the vehicle interior in brief but sharp yellow light.

With one deft motion, I stood straight and closed the door, smoke still curling from the tip of the silencer. Eyes alert, I scanned the street left and right. Not a single window lit up. Not a car door opened.

I shoved the pistol into my coat pocket, ready to use again if needed, but quick-stepped to the vacant house. I needed to get my gear and flee the neighborhood. Killing the cops had been risky, but necessary. I couldn't, absolutely couldn't, lose the firepower I'd left wrapped inside that duffel bag. Furthermore, to complete the mission, I needed the laptop because it had the software necessary to upload the recordings.

Barging in through the back door, I noticed the crowbar missing from where I'd laid it on top of the freezer. I found it in the kitchen next to the chrome sink, but pushed on into the living room, traipsing water and snow with every squeaky step.

It took only a moment to grab my gear before I pounded back out the door, headed back up the street at a walk that bordered on a trot. Two minutes later, I slid into the car, jammed the key in the ignition, and took off as quickly as possible without raising suspicion, tires grinding on packed snow and fingers wrapped so tightly around the cold wheel that they hurt.

So much for my sanctuary.

Mitchell responded to Lucky's contact by using a generic, prearranged, account on a public use computer. Because Lucky would check her corresponding account from another open access computer and then discard it forever, Mitchell used unusually blunt language, eliminating or modifying only words known to attract government parsing software.

L,

We suspect that Fagan & Co are going to try and use these attacks to influence the outcome of the debate on PASTY. The initiative passed in California so it is still alive and needs both the Mountain and Great Plains to vote yes. By committing mass murder in our name, they hope to generate enough hysteria to guarantee passage.

Do not send N to NYC. Red has received orders to join you within two days. Additional reinforcements will also arrive though at the moment I cannot say when, how or who. You will be notified via your fifth communication protocol.

Use all means necessary to prevent these attacks. If N is eliminated you are to assume command. You have our confidence

Well done on both missions. It is good to know that N can be relied upon to obey orders. Our doubts regarding his commitment are laid to rest, though we caution you to beware. He can be stubborn and spontaneous, given to acting without thought or regard to the consequences, perhaps one day leading to his own demise.

Your worth in this field is, as always, highly valued. Proceed with N to NYC immediately after mission accomplished.

Gory to the Revelation!

Lucky had been secretly ordered to evaluate Nicky's fitness for duty and commitment to the revolution.

L ucky and I hooked up at the grocery store, where I gave her an emergency lesson in how to prepare a simple but tasty recipe for veal marsala. She'd sweet talked Donny into letting her cook that night, using the lure of her body in his hot tub. She needed to make good on her promise. For my part, I'd spent the early part of the day in the parking garage, sleeping in the back seat.

"That's all there is to it?" gaped Lucky after I walked her through the recipe. She seemed amazed that such an elaborate sounding dish could be prepared so simply. In its basic form, the recipe only called for breading veal cutlets and browning them in oil, then making a sauce from the pan drippings with broth, mushrooms and sweet marsala wine.

"Anyone can do it," I grinned, nodding to her basket, which already held the ingredients.

"Well I never would have known," she smiled as I guided her towards the books and magazines section of the store. "Where did you learn to do that?"

"The restaurant I worked in cut corners when they got behind," I confessed for the first time. "I learned a lot of quick and easy recipes. Veal marsala is one of my favorites."

"Well if it's good enough for you, it's good enough for me," shrugged Lucky, who then let her smile fade.

"Did you get a message off to Mitchell?" I asked in a quiet voice.

"At noon," she assured me, face serious.

"Good," I told her, then asked, "Are you sure you're up for another night of this?"

"Easy as pie," she grinned again. "Honestly Nicky, I'm starting to think of you as my surrogate father."

"Not since we slept together," I grinned back, referring to our few encounters back in Reno and on the road. It seemed like a long time ago, but only several weeks had gone by.

Lucky giggled, and, odd for a woman so free with her body, blushed.

We smiled in unison, an act which dragged out into an awkward silence. Maybe I didn't quite see Lucky as a lover, or quite as a simple friend or comrade, but I cared. Judging by the look on her face, the feeling was mutual. The tough little whore had given way to something softer and more human, and we both liked it.

"Anyway," I said, "There was news on the radio about the California Dominion, some kind of legislation being approved. They said the focus is now on the Rocky Mountain and Great Plains Dominion, and they vote over the next two weeks."

I paused, letting Lucky fit the three simple puzzle pieces together.

"The trigger for their attack?" Lucky whispered.

"I'm willing to bet money on it," I nodded, trying not to admire her face, perfectly framed by her fur lined hood. "That's why it's so important to have you in the house tonight. I'm willing to bet they have a little powwow about how to proceed."

For the first time, a touch of worry flittered over Lucky's face.

"Don't worry," I told her, "I'll be close by. The moment you need help, you call me."

Lucky nodded, then smiled again.

"I can't wait until this is all over," she breathed. "The stress is killing me."

"At least you don't have the Specials breathing down your neck," I told her. The Specials were still setting up shop and things were already hot. In another day or two they would really mean business.

"When is Silvio picking you up?" I asked.

Lucky pushed up her sleeve and looked at her watch, whose off-white band matched the scars on her forearm, part of the subtle way in which she'd dressed down for the sake of Donny's ego.

"'Bout fifteen minutes," she grimaced. "I hope he's not early. I'm not sure how I would explain things away if Silvio saw me talking with you and passed it on to his boss. Donny doesn't strike me as the type to buy the stranger in the store routine."

I had to agree with that. Donny could sniff bullshit like a bloodhound. I knew from painful experience how hard, and dangerous, it was to lie to Donny Paglia. He'd torn out one of my fingernails trying to scent the truth and hadn't even changed facial expression. Lucky had enough problems without coming face to face with that kind of ruthless determination.

"Yeah," I told her. "I better roll. Besides, I need to get a police scanner. The more I know about their movements the better."

Lucky agreed, and I shoved off to the local Air Wave shop, which not only got me off the street and away from prying eyes for two hours, but also let me handle the transaction with anonymity because the harassed looking clerk seemed never to ring anyone out. Instead, he waded his way through a Lake Discontent of customers returning defective merchandise. When he saw I wanted to make a simple purchase, he almost breathed in relief.

I installed the scanner in the car, running it right off the fuse box distributor using a kit that came with the scanner, then sat up in the seat and turned the set on. With a soft touch, my fingers edged the dialer through the channels, eyes fixed on the activity lights until at last I zeroed in on the correct frequency.

"Code ten-three at six oh nine Portage Avenue," hummed the unnaturally calm voice of the 999 operator. *"Probable jay one. Multiple callers identify the aggressor as male, standing one hundred eighty five*

centimeters and approximately one hundred forty kilograms wearing blue jeans, boots, and a denim jacket. Suspect has brown hair to his shoulders and is said to be unarmed."

I listened carefully. Experience had taught me that a J1 was shorthand for domestic violence, one of the most common dispatches after dark, but rare during the day. The first numbers, 10-3, meant they dispatched the call due to telephone reports. In moments, police units responded with their acknowledgements.

Police call codes had been standardized throughout the dominions back in the eighties and learning the most common had proven worth the time and effort many times over. The first code to learn had been the dreaded rapid mobilization, especially the unhyphenated Level Five, the city-wide emergency mobilization of all units and stations used to respond to riots, large scale gangland shootouts, and of course, terrorism. A Level Five emergency call directed all police, all auxiliaries, and all off duty police to take immediate action as prescribed in followup instructions. More than once, following successful terrorist attacks that had been close calls, Level Five mobilizations had gone out for me.

Cold dread follows a Level Five. Your heart hammers in your chest. Every face you see turns potentially deadly and you struggled with the urge to shoot anything that moves or makes eye contact. A Level Five makes you a marked man, fighting for your life. I hoped never to hear or be the subject of one again, which made finishing our business with Donny and the lawyers that much more important.

At the moment, only additional squad cars marked the uptick in police activity, bad news when coupled with the knowledge that places of use were being systematically swept. Soon, the Specials, experts in coordinating and reinforcing Level Five alerts, would begin tightening their hold on the city. They had the muscle and expertise to involve not just the police, but the army, the phone companies, retailers, ISPs, toll collectors, boy scouts and anyone else they thought useful. They'd just arrived and hadn't fully deployed, but that only bought so much breathing space. Things would get a lot tighter very quickly. I found out how much faster moments after I finished pumping gas and went to pay.

The gas station clerk, a Leb not much older than the gas he sold, stared wide-eyed as I placed my cash in the tray under the scratched bulletproof security glass. His face tightened slightly, his shoulders tensed, and his eyes looked to the left so inconspicuously that he could only be trying to hide their movement.

"Fourteen pounds, eighteen," he told me in an unnaturally constricted voice, taking the twenty from the tray with fingers that looked ready to shake. He hit the buttons on the register and the cash drawer opened. He started to fumble for change, and, as he did, I eyed the place he'd looked.

There, next to him, thumbtacked to a corkboard filled with bounced checks and receipts for who knew what, hung a copy of a composite sketch of myself. Judging from the caricature's appearance, they'd sketched me within the last day or two, which meant they'd gotten to Brad the Bartender. He would have given them information on my current hair color, hairstyle, recent clothing combinations, and a lot more.

"Thanks," I told the kid as he slid the change into the tray. "Have a good day."

With quick steps back to the car, I struggled to stay calm. I couldn't see what the kid did back inside, but even a shy kid would call the cops. In big numbers, the promised reward for information leading to my arrest had been posted under my picture. The staggering amount would decide for anyone. I didn't need to see him call the police to know he did.

In moments, the police would know not just my appearance, but the make and model of the car. If the gas station had a security camera, they would know the plates.

Without need for further inspiration, I headed the car right for the freeway, skipping free stoplights and making an illegal left turn to make time.

"All units, all stations, we have a Level Two alert in the vicinity of Trafalgar Park," started the scanner, cutting off a routine traffic stop in mid transmission. *"Be on the lookout for suspected September Alliance suspect Nicholas Papadopoulos fitting the description last issued. Suspect was seen four minutes ago at the Imperial Petroleum station on Douglas and Wood, seen driving north on Wood in a grey-green Cosmopolitan sedan ..."*

Just because they'd issued a Level Two alert didn't mean I was safe or even safer. A Level Two alert still summoned every available officer to be on the lookout for the object of the hunt. The Winnipeg police probably deferred calling a Level Five pending confirmation. The Specials wouldn't allow them to make that mistake twice.

With the clock racing faster than my engine, I drove up onto the freeway and busted twenty clicks over the limit as quickly as the gears could shift. The burst of speed allowed me to overtake other speeders about one every ten seconds, a quick pace, but not so quick as to risk a crash or guarantee any cop that had missed or dismissed the Level Two would come racing up to my bumper.

I licked my lips, letting the tires grind distance into safety, counting the kilometers in clicks of my tongue until I could get to Donny's exit. If I needed to ditch the car, so be it, but …

An idea formed in my head, and still with four clicks to go, I veered off the freeway and onto an exit, following it with deliberate care onto a main suburban road and then hooked onto another with a left turn. There at the crossroads stood a major strip mall, with two grocery stores, a massive clothing chain, and a wide selection of franchised stores of all descriptions. I took the third exit into the parking lot, rolled into a spot near the back and got out.

With the swift and certain movements only a matter of life and death can ensure, I popped the trunk, slung the laptop and its case over my shoulder, pulled out the duffel bag, and threw it into the passenger seat. I yanked the scanner from its mount, bent down and pulled the connections faster than I'd ever done anything in my life, then shoved it into my front pocket.

Now ready, I got back behind the wheel and cruised past the line of shops, each one of the hated corporate stripe. Pushing slowly behind an SUV, I waited for something to click, something that would work.

Like a magic number on the lottery ticket, a Silver Screen video store appeared near the end, close to the exit onto the thoroughfare leading back to the freeway entrance, one hundred meters away.

I swallowed, pulled into one line of parked cars and waited, heart beating, adrenaline coursing through my veins, one hand tight on the butt of my pistol. 'If Julie could see me now,' I thought. 'She would be proud.' I hoped. Somehow or other I still craved her approval, no matter time and events gone by.

My entire world whirlpooled into a tight focus on the parking lot as three teenagers pranced out of the video store, the oldest looking boy with bright red and white plastic movie cases in hand. Two boys and a redheaded girl, all looking as happy as happy could be, no clue what terror awaited.

I threw my scarf across my face and got out of the car the moment I saw the lead boy aim a remote door lock at a silver SUV. The backup lights lit briefly and the trio started towards their vehicle.

With quick steps, I approached just as the girl started towards the passenger side.

"You!" I growled at the kid with the keys, a tall kid with a striped shirt showing at the V of his winter coat.

Both boys turned as one, eyes puzzled and without the smarts of the city to tell them that no stranger has a good reason to approach you on the street except, maybe, to ask the time, and even then, it was a bad idea to let your guard down.

"What?" asked the kid, obviously bewildered.

I closed the gap and drew the gun.

"Oh my God, Travis! He's got a gun!" yelped the girl like the kid needed her to tell him.

I aimed the gun at the kid's chest. "Remember me, Travis?" I demanded as if he should, and should be afraid. The ploy might keep the cops from immediately associating the theft with their hunt for me. It wouldn't hold long but might buy an extra fifteen minutes.

"N... n... no," he stammered, his face registering shock he'd probably never felt before.

"Gimme the keys," I demanded in a tough growl. His face went blank, so I shoved his friend out of the way to a collective gasp from all three. "I said *give me the keys!*"

The poor kid got so scared he dropped the keys in the crushed snow. As he bent down to pick them up, I half lunged forward and shoved him by the top of his head, sending him staggering back with a look on his face that would put an abandoned puppy to shame.

"You tell anyone about this, Travis," I snarled over the barrel of the gun, "and I'm gonna be coming for you." I gestured at the girl, who had hidden her mouth behind her palms. "And her."

I scooped up the keys and wiped them on my coat.

"Who are you?" asked the agonized teen.

"You know," I spat. "And if you don't, ask your dad." That should cause him some agony before he called the police.

Fortunately, a million silver SUVs populated the road, and as I ripped out of the parking lot, the setting sun gave me some darkness for cover and extra traffic for camouflage.

Once on the freeway, I passed Donny's exit and took the next, which lay three clicks down the road. Where Donny's place had bordered the countryside, the place I exited really was the country, but developed enough to boast a Mexican restaurant where I sat in the bar nursing an orange soda for an hour and then ordered a dish of *pollo con salsa verde.* The spicy treat turned out to be a lot better than the burritos I'd eaten daily in California, and when I sat back from the table I felt warmed inside and out, even if the hot food didn't match the wintry weather. I wanted nothing more than to sleep away the stress and fatigue in a Mexican siesta. Of course the revolution had other ideas.

"Nicky," rushed Lucky's voice the moment I answered the phone. Her hushed and rushed whisper told me at once that she didn't call for nothing. We'd agreed that she would only call in an emergency, and the fact she used my real name meant she'd found a qualifying emergency.

"Yeah," I answered from the table, bending my head so customers in the booths to either side couldn't make out my words. "You okay?"

"Yeah," she whispered. *"I'm in the bathroom and I've only got a few minutes so listen close."* Without giving me so much as a second to acknowledge, she kept right on going. *"You were right about California being the trigger. Silvio and Sym are coming tonight and they're meeting with Donny. I think they're leaving tonight to carry out their attacks on the shopping malls. When he got off the phone, Donny came in and told me that he would be meeting with Silvio and Sym about something very important, and that I had to stay upstairs. When he went into the den I saw the wooden case from the Badlands."*

"Shit," I groused. "We've got even less time than I thought."

"You don't know the half of it," she cut in. *"Nicky, it's not C6 in that case."*

"What?" I asked, unprepared. What else would someone use to attack a target that big? You would need a couple truckloads of dynamite, and semtex or C5 made poor substitutes. Any professional would use C6 if they could get it, and Donny could get it.

Before Lucky could answer I heard a commotion on the other end of the line, followed by *"Just a minute!"* in a nice 'feel sorry for me' voice all women master. Lucky, sounding even more rushed whispered.

"I gotta go. I don't know the details and don't think I can get them."

"Can you get the bug into the den at least?" I asked.

"I think so," she hurried. *"I can try at least, but I gotta go."*

"OK," I surrendered, "just tell me what it is so I can come up with a plan."

"Anthrax."

Without so much as a goodbye, Lucky disconnected, leaving her parting word hanging ominously in muted mariachi music and cigarette smoke.

'Anthrax,' I thought, the word ten feet tall in my mind, dread and disbelief mingling in Lucky's terrible revelation. I didn't know much about anthrax, but did know it added new dimensions to deadly. Donny planned to use anthrax on the shopping malls and the world would believe it was *us*. The fallout would eclipse catastrophic. They'd need a new word to describe public horror.

We could deny involvement all day and even the splinter cell in New York would deny using Anthrax, but it fit too perfectly. No one would believe us. The shopping mall stood for everything the September Alliance hated and the Mall of the Americas and the Great Edmonton Mall were the two largest shopping malls on the continent, regularly making the newspapers as they dueled for the crown.

I had to stay calm. I had to stay professional. I had to weigh my options and choose the best course. Even if I called for help, no one could get to Win fast enough. I could try and crash into Donny's mansion and kill him and his men, but that went beyond risky and into foolhardy territory. They would kill me.

I threw a twenty pound note onto the table to cover my six pound meal, which would make my waitress happily recall my face for the police, but couldn't be helped. I needed to make tracks.

Out in the parking lot, I hastily wired the scanner into the SUV and turned it on. After a few minutes listening, I found a Level Five in effect, but they hadn't yet located the car I'd abandoned at the strip mall. They soon would, and that would tie me to the carjacked teens. The carjacked teens would tie me to the commonplace SUV right down to the correct plates, and I would be meat for the law enforcement grinder.

"Immediate use of deadly force is authorized," the dispatcher recited mechanically, *"for any officer or agent attempting to arrest Nicholas Papadopoulos. Papadopoulos has a previous history of violent resistance to arrest and should be considered armed and dangerous."*

The words amounted to a shoot to kill order, armed or not, even if I attempted to surrender. I needed to buy time.

Another silver SUV pulled into the lot, a replica of half the SUVs in suburbia as well as the one I drove. The thought crossed my mind to hijack that one too, but thought better of it. I didn't want to push my carjacking luck any further than I already had. Then, the light went on.

Pulling onto the road, I drove a short distance before finding a bowling alley whose parking lot fit my needs. I pulled into the lot, towards the rear where shadows provided some cover, away from the street and the Christmas decorated business entrance.

Taking the screwdriver, I sidled across the lot, and after checking to make sure no one could easily see, bent down at the rear license plate of a car parked between two much larger vehicles. Semi-sheltered from view, the screwdriver slid into the wedge of the screw, which held fast until I put my strength into it, then broke free with a snap and unscrewed easily. The second screw held out longer, but I got the unfortunate car's rear plate off. Doing the same on the front side was safer if not easier, because the car immediately facing provided near total cover.

Plates in hand, I walked back to the SUV, pulled its plates off, and put the stolen ones on as cold metal singed my fingers. Hopefully, by the time the owner of the victimized car realized what had happened and figured out what to do, I would be long gone. I didn't know how many people checked their license plates to find their car, but it would be a low percentage, especially after a night of drinking in the bowling alley.

Overconfidence, or maybe celebration at my own pseudo genius, proved my undoing. While I concentrated on the plates, I failed to spot someone watching. Whether that person observed from a parked car or from inside the bowling alley made no difference. Someone spotted me and realized I was up to no good.

"There he is, eh! I told ya so! He's breaking into cars!" someone shouted just as I finished putting on the front license plate. My head shot up so fast I banged my shin on the sharp bumper. A small cry leapt out of my throat from sudden pain and surprise as an army of flannel shirts and ball caps emerged from the bowling alley. Heavy boots pounded hard on the pavement, thundering my way like a redneck stampede.

The posse numbered at least thirty, more than I had bullets in my gun, and they wanted blood. Even if I had time to draw and shoot I couldn't, there were simply too many and opening fire would bring every cop in the north down on my head faster than a hammer drives a nail.

I barely had time to think as the mob closed the distance, awkwardly turning to my right to sidestep out of the gap between the parked cars and managing to cut my *other* leg, in the calf this time. The metal caught my pant leg and I had to yank hard to free it with a tear to clear the space just before the first set of hands tried to haul me down.

With a desperate lurch, I managed to dodge one lunging bowler, thankful the parked cars weren't spaced further apart so the pursuers had to press through the narrow gaps in single file. With the lead pursuer down, his cohorts had to stumble over his back, which bought me precious seconds to break out of the cars and into a sprint, limping slightly but moving faster than a racehorse out the gate.

Like drunken racecars, the horde of angry plainsmen pounded in my wake. Taking a chance, I crashed through a stand of trees hoping for cover, only to find a two meter chain link fence standing between me and an open field. I nearly ran headfirst into it in the dark, but came up short just in time, cut to my left and sprinted blindly, expecting to trip at any moment.

Behind me, the makeshift vigilantes called to each other as some fell behind and some got lost in the dark. I thanked fortune I'd worn dark clothes.

Abruptly, I spotted a section of fence that bent and sagged, like a giant stomped on it a decade ago and no one had bothered to fix it.

The sound of footsteps closing in gave me the guts to lunge through the gap, staggering as my boot jangled the links and my weight brought it further to ground than ever.

"Fuck!" shouted someone crashing towards me from behind, joined by another as I landed on the far side and pelted across a snowed over farm field. The fence jingled to a cry of pain as someone stumbled.

My bad luck held. Even though the bowling alley crew gave up the chase, by the time I got across the humongous field, clouds had covered the moon, leaving me lost and disoriented. Even when the clouds parted and moonlight lit the field, I couldn't tell which treeline masked the bowling alley.

I fought the urge to panic, and half expected to see police join the hunt but the rednecks must have figured chasing me off was enough because no cops appeared. Either that, or the police had more important people to look for than a car prowler. After all, they had a terrorist loose in the city.

With that thought in mind, I tried not to laugh as I tried, and failed, to retrace my steps. It took me two hours to find the right fence, and after recrossing, found myself disoriented enough to turn the wrong direction. It took another fifteen minutes to realize my mistake and double back.

Another fifteen minutes found me peering at the parking lot from the trees, out of sight and forgotten, but unable to return because of lingering bowlers. They eventually filtered off in small groups after a handful reenacted the chase from earlier, pride and bravado ringing in their beer sodden voices.

When the last pickup pulled away, I moved with numb feet and aching legs back to the stolen SUV and shook my head in appreciation of the whims of fate.

No one seemed to have noticed I switched plates.

The following transcript is from a phone call between Donny Paglia and Silvio Trocci.

Trocci:	*Yeah boss?*
Paglia:	*Get back here, right now. We got a problem, a big problem.*
Trocci:	*I'm tryin', but the cops have a roadblock set up and it's got everything backed up from here to Philadelphia.*
Paglia:	*A roadblock? What are they looking for? Drunks?*
Trocci:	*Doesn't look like it. Looks like they're searchin' for someone important.*
Paglia:	*You're clean. Get past it. Hurry up.*
Trocci:	*I'm tryin'. What's the problem?*
Paglia:	*You'll see when you get here. There's a mess to clean up.*

The scanner identified a roadblock between myself and Donny's place, and the SUV's stock issue GPS helped me get around it. Burning an extra half hour didn't seem so bad given how long I'd already taken. The dashboard clock showed just past midnight, three hours later than planned. Lucky said Donny planned to meet with his guys at ten and planned on restricting her to his room a little before that. It was nice to know he could dovetail business and pleasure so well.

Parking the SUV behind the convenience store, I envied Donny. He'd had a hot dinner of veal marsala, a warm woman named Lucky and no doubt an after dinner drink. The first two came courtesy of me, who had spent the night trying to evade police dragnets and kicking through a frozen field where icy wind instantly sliced away any warmth your body generated. Who was the good guy?

With a disgruntled shove, I opened the door and shouldered the laptop, then started to get out. Thinking better of it, I walked to the SUV's cargo hatch and broke the DR-16 out of the duffle bag. I gave a quick check to make sure the street was empty, then headed across the piles of rubble and dirt. I had to crouch once as a car passed, headlights cutting through the night. I didn't need more headaches and unforeseen events.

Landing on the far side of the fence made the earlier injury to my leg flare, and I quietly cursed under my breath as I shook it out, but didn't give the pain more than a thought. More important things occupied my mind.

Tossing the stone weight aside, I opened the storage tub, turned it upside down and set the computer on top. My hands worked the USB cable into the port before the cold could numb my fingers and make dealing with small objects difficult. Only then did I cover the screen with my hat and scarf and power up.

Shivering in the snow with my hands tucked into my armpits and breath steaming in the cold night, I waited for the computer to go through its startup screens and activated the software for the receiver/recorder. In a moment, I watched the screen click through the download status bars, one eye on the all but darkened house.

Downloading the recordings seemed to take forever, but really took less than five minutes before the computer finished and I could tuck it back in the bag. For good measure, I set up the receiver again, even though I didn't see the steady glow of the ready light detecting its transmitter.

That seemingly small fact didn't register.

With the laundry tub shielding the glow of the computer screen, I calculated five hours of conversation, far more than I had listening time if the California vote did indeed pull the trigger for staging the attacks.

I snapped the laptop closed, stood up and headed back to the SUV to listen in the warmth. My fingers ached to call Lucky on her phone, but we'd agreed, no incoming calls while she twiddled her thumbs with Donny. Phone calls from strangers, and male strangers at that, couldn't be risked.

I cracked the window and lit a smoke, then used the drop down menu to locate the menu options, my finger lightly running over the smoothe touch pad. I had three conversations to choose from, the first over an hour, the second only seven minutes, and the last three and a half hours.

Clenching the cigarette in my teeth and squinting to keep smoke from stinging my eyes, I pulled the headphones out and strapped them on, then clicked the first recording.

The software skipped twice, then brought up a window that looked like something from a recording studio, a black background with a golden grid and a line through the middle that wavered and rose as the audio stream played.

"So what are we having?" came Donny's voice, loud and clear with only a hint of echo.

"Veal marsala," squeaked Lucky in return, for all the world sounding like a woman excited to cook for such a great man, then a chance to please him in bed.

"Now just how did you know that's my favorite?" replied Donny in a voice I recognized as one he used to patronize and lie. In this case, he lied harmlessly, but not always.

"Mmmm," giggled Lucky. *"An angel told me."*

"And do you always associate with angels?"

"Only when I can't find the right devil."

I wanted to puke, and moved the mouse to the fast forward. With a click and hold, I advanced the conversation fifteen minutes. The sound of meat frying in oil filled the background.

"No, this way," Lucky giggled. *"You turn them over when they're brown."*

"And to think you…"

I skipped forward again, not needing to hear them cook dinner. I didn't feel completely comfortable listening to Lucky make lovebird talk with Donny. I felt something unpleasant. As I skipped forwards three minutes, I knew the feeling, jealousy. Cat would not be happy.

The next few sentences didn't reveal much more. In some places I only heard the sounds of running water or cooking. In most, the conversation centered on cooking dinner, but forty minutes into the recording, I caught something interesting.

"It's called gaglioppo," cooed Donny. *"It's made in Sicily, a very strong red. You can't usually find it outside of Italian neighborhoods, but it's my* favorito. *Try it, you'll like it."*

"Oh," squeaked my comrade. *"That's strong."* A sip-long pause followed. *"It is good though. How did you find out about it?"*

"Never mind," answered the gangster. *"There's something else I need to tell you."*

"Okay. What's that?"

"This project I'm workin' on with Sym and Silvio... You know, it's coming to a close you could say, and when it comes to a close, I was thinking to take a little trip down to the Island Dominion." Donny paused. *"I was thinking to spend a month or two on Martinique, and I was hoping you would join me. I know it's short notice, but whaddya say?"*

"Short notice?" asked Lucky. *"How short?"*

"I was thinking of going tomorrow, or even tonight."

"Tonight or tomorrow?" Lucky didn't fake surprise.

Donny told Lucky she could come in a few days, and money posed no obstacle. Lucky acted uncertain, and they agreed to let her think. Then the conversation drifted to setting the table. After they left the dining room, the recorder counted to sixty in the silence and clicked off.

The second conversation turned out to be more enlightening. I found myself listening to Donny speaking to Baxter.

"Yeah, it's me," he started, sounding relaxed. A pause just long enough to take a drag on a cigarette followed. *"I only have a few minutes here. I have some company that you could say is less than informed about our project."* Silence followed. *"I am keeping you informed. What else do you think this telephone call is about, my new veal marsala*

recipe?" Seconds ticked by as I listened, the laptop reflecting in the windshield.

"They're leaving tonight. All the plans are made." Donny's tone remained condescending even if his words stayed polite. *"That's right. I have one heading to Edmonton and one heading to Minneapolis. They both know exactly what to do and they have all the gear they need."* A long silence followed. *"We* are *leaving imperial territory. Martinique is still French. Guadaloupe is the one we took."* The gangster's voice held equal measure animosity and frustration, but after another short silence Donny chuckled and interrupted. *"Don't you worry, never fear,* bella fortuna *is drawing near."* Another silence followed. *"I said,* bella fortuna. *It means good fortune."*

Baxter must have had a lot to say, because Donny kept silent for a long time. The sound of liquid sloshing into a glass trickled in the background.

"No worries," interjected Donny again. *"I've always wanted to be rich."* I could picture Donny with his butt up against the counter and a drink in his hand. *"They'll be here at ten to get their final instructions. I expect to have them on the road before midnight if nothing goes wrong."* Another pause followed. *"Have you looked out the window? Something is going on. The cops are everywhere. It might delay our departure unless you can come up with some guarantees."*

The rest of Donny's conversation sounded a lot like the part I just recited, hopes for a successful conclusion, assurances that everything would go well, and solicitations of security from a legal aspect. They had it all down. Thousands would die, and Donny would get rich. What more could he ask?

A moment of panic filled me that Donny's and his men might already have departed. Only the fact that Lucky hadn't called up sounding the alarm calmed my nerves.

I lit another cigarette, then clicked on the third conversation.

"*Mmmmm, I love the feel of your chest, it's so* strong, *so* masculine,*"* purred Lucky's voice, husky even with the bad acoustics.

"*And I like the way you move,"* came the deeper voice of Donny. Somehow or other I could tell he had a hard on, just by the tone of his voice.

"*Like this?"* asked Lucky in a naughty pitch. I couldn't see what she did, but given her experience as a stripper and her natural ability to read a male, I bet it was good.

"*Oh do that again,"* hummed Donny, olive oil and arousal running richly through his voice. "*I like the way you move almost as much as I like the way you look."*

"*For a man like you, I can move like this."* Again, I couldn't tell what Lucky might have done, but the tone of her voice made me smile at my own reflection in the windshield.

"*Oh yeah!"* Donny's reaction confirmed my suspicions.

"*And like this?"*

"*Even better,"* answered Donny with an air of appreciation I doubted even he could fake.

Silence followed, or at least the silence of two people molesting each other followed. I tried not to picture Donny kissing Lucky. They say even prostitutes won't kiss, that it's too intimate and much more personal than intercourse. To try and block the image from my mind, I concentrated on blowing smoke out the crack of the window from the corner of my mouth.

The last time Lucky had done something like this, she'd asked for cantaloupe when she'd finished. I wondered what else I could get that would make a good treat. Even though she scoffed at such gestures, I felt like showing her that I appreciated her sacrifices.

Donny made a sound like he'd just been swallowed by a warm, comfortable cloud. I sighed. He'd been swallowed all right, and by something warm if not cloudy. He gasped. I groaned.

"You like?" purred Lucky's voice.

Donny said something in Italian, which made Lucky giggle, then coax him in a soft voice.

"Maybe we can continue in the hot tub?" she pled in a soft, enticing voice.

"A wonderful idea," answered Donny. *"We have just enough time."*

"You go run the water. I'll finish cleaning up."

"I like the way you think, like you read my mind." I could picture the smug smile on Donny's face, already basking in his conquest of Lucky. The well-kept, razor sharp beard and mustache, well remembered from the night he'd killed Turk, my friend and Donny's cousin, made him look satanic.

Kitchen sounds continued for just a moment, and I could sense Lucky's tension as she cleaned plates. Now was the time to move the bug. She'd skillfully maneuvered Donny into a few moments alone. As if to confirm my thoughts, I heard a huff, then a clatter of brass. Then it sounded like bare feet landing on kitchen tiles. The silence that followed told me that Lucky moved very silently, or very quickly.

Small sounds filled the background, letting me know that she'd made it to the den and started the search for a good hiding place. I could barely make out the sound of her breathing, but what I heard sounded alert and quick. Unfortunately for her, she wasn't quick enough.

"What the fuck are you doing in there?" Donny's voice demanded without a trace of romance but a double helping of murder.

"I came in to look for whiskey glasses," Lucky lied, well enough that I would have believed her, but I wasn't Donny.

"Bollocks!" thundered the gangster, a killing rage lining his voice. *"What's that in your hand?"*

"It ain't nothing', Donny," replied Lucky with a hint of real fear. My mouth went dry, and I glanced at the clock. The recorded events had taken place three hours ago, while I fled a crowd of redneck bowlers and kicked through the snow on a farm.

"Lemme see that."

"Ow! Donny!" Lucky's voice transformed a simple 'ow' into a gasp of real pain. I could feel the pain through her voice, just as I could sense the struggle she put up as Donny pried her fingers apart.

"I know what this is," Donny growled in a low, dangerous voice. *"It's a TKL listening device and transmitter."* An unpleasant pause followed. *"I know* exactly *what this is."*

Lucky cried out in time to the sound of flesh striking flesh, and then I heard the sound of a struggle, with Donny's guttural grunts a step ahead of Lucky's cries of desperation that so forcefully brought the scars on her forearms to mind, how she'd once desperately used her arms to shield her body from a blade.

"I've been hit harder by sick kids," scoffed the gangster, scarcely out of breath. *"Now I want you to tell me who sent you to plant this?"*

"I'm a cop," panted Lucky, out of breath from her losing struggle. The desperation in her voice made me want to rush in and save her, do whatever I needed to do to get her out of there, but caution made me stay and listen.

"You aren't a cop," scoffed Donny with an angry sneer to his voice. *"If you were a cop, you wouldn't be using a TKL. You'd be using an Inquisitive, and besides, if you were a cop, you would have been told not to come snooping around. Even if you were a Special, you would have been told not to bother us. There's not a cop in the empire that can touch us. Now, I'm asking you again, who sent you?"*

"I'm not telling you anything!" screeched Lucky in a voice laden with sudden fright. I could hear the terror in her voice, how it made the timbre of her answer waver just under her words.

"What the..." started Lucky, *"Where?"*

"Just back to the kitchen for a little more veal," explained Donny, dripping deadly sarcasm.

"Ah ah ah.... AAAHHH!" screamed Lucky, making me sit straight up in my seat and reach for my pistol. The sound of fear turned to terror, and adrenaline coursed hotly through my veins just at the sound.

"AAAAAHHHH!" she screamed again, and I could hear the unmistakable sound of feet striking a hollow kitchen appliance. What happened?

"You want me to do the other side?" threatened Donny, and it dawned on me what he'd done. He'd forced her face onto the burners of the stove.

Lucky sobbed in a way I have never heard a woman sob. Low and deep, like it pushed up from the bottom of her lungs.

"Your wish is my command," quipped Donny in a voice I recognized only all too well, his humor voice, only it held no humor. That voice made it sound like all the world was a big joke, including crimes against humanity. That voice belonged to a man that could drown babies, push old grandmothers down on the sidewalk and strangle a newborn puppy in one hand.

In the dark and cold of the car, with the air from the heater fan fluttering over my face, I held my breath as Lucky screamed again.

"If you kill her, Donny," I told myself. "I'm going to make sure you die the slowest, most agonizing death ever."

"Aww," joked Donny's voice in that deadly mock humor. *"Didn't like that one, did ya? Well, let's see if this makes you a bit more talkative. Now who sent you?"*

"Baxter!" Lucky cried.

"Try again," murmured Donny in a not to be lied to tone. Why didn't he believe that? Was he some kind of a human lie detector? His world must be full of double crossers. He should at least nibble.

298

Donny must have done something else, because Lucky whimpered loudly in pain, through clenched teeth, the same kind of primitive sound Donny had wrung from her a few minutes ago.

"Baxter," she whimpered softly after a moment, probably unable to think of another line.

"Tut tut little girl," answered Donny, his voice cold, determined, and ruthless.

And so it went. Donny tortured Lucky for forty minutes, until she broke.

"The September Alliance," she almost cried, sounding like a small schoolgirl asking for a cookie. *"Please stop."*

And Donny stopped.

For almost two minutes I listened to the sounds of heavy breathing, deep and full of exhaustion on Donny's part, soft and shallow with pain and shame on Lucky's.

Finally, after what seemed an eternity, Donny's voice, obviously speaking directly into the microphone judging by the volume, growled.

"Whoever's listening to this, you can tell your boss I have a message for them."

"No!" cried Lucky in a short, sharp cry of pain and terror, followed by an unmistakable groan of prolonged agony. I couldn't tell what Donny, but her gasp of agony lived long and loud enough to tell me it wasn't pleasant.

"N..." gasped Lucky in her final breath, but if it were to call my name or simply say 'no', one last time, I'll guess until the day I die.

Lucky's final death sounded like a hiccup followed by an orgasm. She gasped softly, then her breath shuddered. I sat in the stolen

SUV with my mouth open. Shocked beyond surprise, my cigarette had long since turned to ash. I twitched and it disintegrated onto the back of my hand.

My throat constricted as I heard Lucky's body fall to the floor, smacking the tile like a side of lifeless meat. With effort, I forced my mind not to relive the good times I'd had with Lucky, not think about her story, not think about the last time I'd seen her and how confident she'd sounded.

I kept my head clear and took a deep breath even as I numbly screwed the silencer onto the barrel of my pistol and jammed a full clip into the breach. Already, in my mind, I approached the house with murder in my eyes and rage in my heart. Donny Paglia would pay for what he'd just done, pay with his life.

Neither my prayer nor my plan got far, for no sooner did I open the door and set one foot on the ground than I got the shock of my life.

Donny Paglia stood twenty feet from the car, still as a statue, flecks of snow on his shoulders and hair, like he'd waited all night.

Mitchell left the following message in Lucky's voice mailbox. She placed the phone call from a public phone in Hartford, four days before she would disappear without a trace in New York.

Hey girl. It's me. I thought I would tell you your co-stars are on their way. Red's getting there first but Butterfly and Pyro are hot on his heels. Butterfly is flying in so she'll need a makeup kit when she arrives.

Hang in there and if anything happens to your leading man, remember, you're the star.

See you soon on the next stage…

"The problem with those TKLs is the limited transmission range," Donny explained over the barrel of a gun pointed directly at my chest. He looked more like Satan than ever with the beard, mustache and long black coat over black shirt and slacks. Only a hot pink tie broke his solid black outfit.

"That and…" he chuckled, "the simple fact that the receiver has a check error function that allows anyone with the right equipment to zero in on the recorder. "I knew it was you the moment I saw the back of your head in the car. Did you get my message?"

"It was garbled," I told him sarcastically as I peripherally eyed the DR-16 on the passenger seat, well out of reach. That left me with just the pistol, but at close range, it would do a fine job.

Donny didn't bother ordering me to drop my gun, which I gripped tightly in my hand. He knew better than to think I would.

The left half of my body felt warm where the heat from the SUV heater forced hot air into the night. My face and right side caught the chill of the night, but my weapon hand stayed warm. Rage gave way to adrenaline flavored calm

"Where's Lucky's body?" I demanded, fearful of showing hesitation before a man like Donny.

"Like I said, she's with my associates," shrugged Donny, "but I doubt she has anything else to say." He licked his lips. "I imagine the frozen ground is giving them all some trouble, Nick. Or was it 'Nicky'? Is that better? You know damned well she's not alive. You wouldn't have let her live either."

"I'm not like you," I spat, the truth no matter what someone might think. Donny and I were both killers, but no more alike than a killer whale and a lion. Both were mammals with teeth, but the similarities ended there.

"Come on, Nick," sighed Donny, the barrel of his pistol lit by the moon and snow. "You know the game, I know the game, she knew the game. For her, game's over. But you..."

There had to be a reason Donny hadn't killed me when I stepped out of the car. Donny didn't play fair, so he wanted something. By the same token, if he intended to let me live he would have ordered me to drop the gun, which meant that within the next few minutes, or possibly even seconds, he intended to shoot.

Donny had already summed up the score, and not a trace of fear shone on his face. He either wasn't afraid to die, or didn't think he would. Either way, he looked eerily calm.

Lucky's face swam before my eyes for just a moment, but I forced it away. Donny's "associates" were disposing of her body. I didn't envy them the task given the number of police and roadblocks.

We stared at each other a long moment before I realized that no matter what Donny wanted, I didn't want anything from Donny. I could shoot him dead, then stroll right into his house to finish my mission. Nothing stopped me except the gun in his hand. Donny on the other

302

hand, needed or wanted something from me, probably my help in his anthrax attack, and that gave me an inch of power, even if my pistol pointed at the ground while his pointed square at my chest. If I could spring a surprise, it might narrow the odds to where I stood a fighting chance.

"I have one question for you, Nick," continued Donny, his voice crisp in the cold air. "If you answer it honestly, we might be able to strike some kind of deal where you can live, if..." He let the word 'if' dangle like a worm on a hook. "If you can be smart this time. The last time I offered you a deal, you didn't live up to your end. I'm hoping you've grown up since then."

Of course, he referred to the time he offered to let me live if I brought him some of my comrades so he could turn them over to the Specials. I hadn't lived up to my end, hadn't even tried, just played for time until circumstances changed in my favor. It worked once. It might work again.

"Before you ask your question, I have one for you," I told him in a voice I hoped sounded full of despair.

"What's that?"

"Do you like cantaloupe?"

The unexpected question caught Donny off balance. His face went blank, his eyebrows narrowed, wondering what I meant.

I dove to my right, raising my pistol.

I had the element of surprise, but Donny had been ready. His pistol cracked and I felt the bullet's impact on my left shoulder, high, by the clavicle and collarbone. If I hadn't surprised him, he would have killed me, but I'd spoiled his aim with a simple question. His second

303

bullet passed between me and the ground as he overcompensated for my momentum.

I fired at Donny's silhouette just before my right shoulder impacted the snow, Donny took a step back but didn't fall, and our pistols aimed at each other once more.

We fired as one.

The Specials updated the Level Five alert in Winnipeg with this bulletin.

All units all stations participating in the search for Nicholas Papadopoulos, please be advised of the following update. Papadopoulos is now believed to be in possession of a stolen vehicle make Lowen, model Sequoia, license number golf papa seven, charlie whiskey six nine three. Suspect was last seen in this vehicle in the northern suburb of Lancaster and there is a strong possibility that Papadopoulos remains in the northern suburbs.

All personnel should remember that Papadopoulos is known to be armed at all times and has previously used deadly force to escape arrest. Those attempting to apprehend Papadopoulos have authorization to use deadly force at officer's discretion.

Repeat, all units, all stations participating in the search for Nicholas Papadopoulos, please be advised that…

Even if Nicky had been listening to his police scanner, he would not have heard the update. On orders from the Specials, police and associated units had switched to a frequency that commercial scanners could not, by law, be equipped to monitor. If he had listened, he would have noted that his ploy with the license plates remained undetected, but roads out of the Winnipeg metro area were being systematically blocked off.

G od decreed that I should live and Donny Paglia should die, but He did not decree that I should remain unscathed.

Donny's first bullet missed my head by inches and glanced off of my collarbone to tunnel through my clavicle and out through the back of my coat. For several stunned minutes, I lay face down in the snow in awe at the quiet of the night. I existed like a numb bubble of warmth in a sheet of ice, alone with my thoughts and afraid to move. With one eye, I watched falling snowflakes melt on the hot barrel of my pistol, leaving small, steaming droplets tinged by distant streetlight.

My fingers felt numb. I'd never been shot before, and only registered the impact and associated sensations of burn and bite, little by little.

I'd fired blindly at least four times from the ground, maybe six, trying to fill the air with so much lead one would have to hit. I don't know which bullet actually killed Donny, but the fact that I still lived made it likely that the first or second had done the deed.

Hot pain seeped into my consciousness like I'd placed a curling iron on my bare shoulder and turned it on, slowly at first, then hotter and hotter until it forced me to stir.

Slowly, painfully, I pushed myself up to sit cross-legged in the light snow. I pressed my free hand to my shoulder and it came away wet with warm blood.

Donny lay face down in the snow, like Lucifer freshly fallen to lie in the mud of Earth, unmoving, snowflakes collecting on his coat and hair.

'Cantaloupe,' I muttered to myself. 'I betcha he wondered what the fuck I was talking about even as he was floating above his body.'

I pushed myself to my feet, feeling the unnatural warmth of sticky blood spreading over my shoulder and chest. With a grimace, I pulled my coat away and saw the burned, puckered bullethole. I winced as I shrugged, and realized that I couldn't move my left arm all that freely. That made disposing of Donny impossible.

In the end, I simply dragged Donny away from the rear of the convenience store, not normally a great distance given the fact that we were pretty far out of sight, but with one and a quarter arms, it was murder.

With numb hands, I dug through Donny's pockets, taking his keys, wallet, cell phone and other items I thought useful. I left his watch, ring, pocketknife and items I didn't think I would need. It seemed an odd fate for a swanky gangster, to be shot and stripped of valuables, but this game had higher stakes than sentiments about dead greaseballs.

I pocketed everything on the way back to the SUV. I'd had the vehicle in one spot for a while, and the cops would be sure to start casing the area soon if they hadn't already. I couldn't leave it behind the store and couldn't dump it along the side of the road. Not to mention that I would need some way to get out of the area when I finished. My best bet was Donny's car, which he'd hopefully parked in his garage, the same garage that could make an excellent hiding spot for the SUV.

I couldn't leave the anthrax behind. If Donny worked for some secret government agency, they might reclaim it, use it later, and keep their plan right on track. I needed to get it, do something — anything — with it, and run for my life to New York.

As I pulled into Donny's drive, my phone vibrated, but I'd put it in my right coat pocket and couldn't take my hand off the steering wheel, so I ignored the call, parked in front of the three car garage, got out and fumbled with Donny's keys until I found the one that opened the front door.

The chirp of an alarm greeted me as I stepped into the warm house. Not surprisingly, Donny's place had an alarm system, and it chirped to let me know that I had two minutes to enter the correct sequence of numbers on the security pad or the alarm would call the police. If they had even a clue as to my whereabouts, they would respond in force to as much as a squirrel sighting.

Since guessing the right code, even with faded numbers and dirty smudges on the five, eight and seven keys, ranked next to impossible, I did the next best thing. I smashed it to pieces with the butt of my pistol before it could make its call.

With that problem solved, I went to the garage, opened the automatic door, and pulled the SUV inside, next to Donny's little Palmetto coupe. The last time I'd seen him, he'd driven a four door sedan, and the hand made Italian automobile with custom seats and an engine that could outrace a speeding bullet represented a step up in his world, not that it would bring him back to life.

I closed the garage door and verified the key on Donny's ring fit the ignition on the Palmetto, and only then did I check the caller ID on my phone. I didn't recognize the number, and no one had left a message, so I struggled with the impulse to ignore it and go find the anthrax. I decided to call the mystery caller back, in part because I felt the level of danger high enough that I needed every scrap of information I could get.

My worries didn't stop with the police. Two and possibly more of Donny's henchmen might come barging through the door at any minute. As far as I knew, only friendlies had my number. I could count them on one hand. Cat, Mitchell, Red, probably Doctor Fish, the now deceased Lucky, the probably equally deceased Whirly, and Deuce in California. It could always be a wrong number, but I hoped for an ally.

I chose the call back option off the menu and pressed the phone to my ear. With my eyes closed and suffering the hot throb of my shoulder, silence stretched, then clicked into a connection. Three times the phone rang on the other end before a familiar voice answered"

"Nicolai Popolov," gurgled Red's heavily accented voice with garbled music playing in the background, like he drove with the window open. *"I am two hours from you."*

"We don't have two hours," I answered. I wanted to blurt everything out, all at once. I wanted to tell him about Lucky, and about the anthrax, but on two cell phones in a Level Five sweep, that kind of a conversation was tantamount to suicide.

"Everyone in this country in such hurry," he slurred. *"Back in Si-beria we not always..."*

I cut Red off. I didn't have time for a lecture on how to be a better Siberian. Red certainly didn't know about Lucky's death, and might not know anything at all about what we were up against, let alone the fact that I'd been shot, the cops were closing in and I had no way out of Winnipeg.

"Just…" I winced in pain and frustration. "Can you make it any faster?"

"Where you at?"

As quickly as I could, I gave him my address, telling him to come loaded for bear, which was a mistake that cost me two minutes trying to explain what 'loaded for bear' meant, another minute saying that I doubted it had anything to do with the Russian bear, and two more minutes just trying to get him to drop the subject. When I finally hung up, I at least had the satisfaction of knowing help was on the way.

I struggled back into the house and searched out the bathrooms, looking for a first aid kit. The downstairs bathrooms were little more than toilets and sinks, but the upstairs had been stocked with, among many other things, a bottle of disinfectant.

Baring and disinfecting the wound proved painful and difficult, but I did it with gritted teeth and many a grimace in the bathroom mirror. Bandages from the first aid kit proved difficult to apply, but I got it on at least halfway straight. A bottle of aspirin provided some painkiller and I stuffed the bottle into my pants pockets. At the moment, I had a little pain. More was on its way.

I also came to the conclusion that my collarbone was at least cracked and possibly chipped, as was my shoulderblade. I had no way of dealing with that kind of an injury, and little idea what might happen if I didn't. Nor would I have known what to do in any case. Beyond band-aids and disinfectant, competent first aid remained firmly fixed in my future.

Warm and dry for the first time in a while, I set about looking for the anthrax. Donny's house was large, but pretty forward in its layout, especially the upstairs, which consisted of a stairwell at each end and a hallway connecting the two. Doors opened into rooms on either side. The eastern stairway opened into the master bedroom with its attached bathroom, a.k.a my battlefield dressing station.

While there, I searched Donny's room and walk-in closet. He had good taste in clothes, flamboyant, but tasteful. I doubted he'd decorated the room, which seemed too vanilla for his taste, just a four-poster king sized bed and some polished wood furniture.

Searching Donny's rooms didn't yield anything, not that I would have expected it to. I certainly wouldn't sleep in a room with anthrax. I would want it stored somewhere close, so I could keep an eye on it, but not that close. My best guess pointed to the den. From Lucky's comments, Donny 'worked' out of his den.

Trying not to sway, I headed back down the stairs and tried to put the pain and stiffness of the gunshot behind me. The first floor layout was more complex. I had a dozen rooms to pick through but found the door to the den wide open.

Donny's den looked like someone else had decorated. Brown wood paneling and walls lined with bookcases didn't strike me as Donny's style, especially not after having seen his office downtown. The desk looked fairly well used but boasted nothing of interest. A nicely done silver pen and pencil set had been left on the blotter along with a whiskey glass containing at least a finger of the amber liquid. I bitterly wondered if Donny had it in his hand when he surprised Lucky.

I stepped into the office, catching the faint scent of a good cigar, which added to the overall feel that I'd entered the office of one of my college history professors, all of whom instantly suffer heart attacks to see their worst student, me, making history.

That pleasant thought didn't slow me down any more than the throb in my shoulder. The den boasted a leather loveseat with matching a recliner and padded desk chair. On its seat rested a briefcase and two identical suitcases. It was to these that I turned my attention first.

Cracking the lid on the first, I spied what looked to be a lab tech's white coat. A quick look revealed not a standard lab coat, but a full body suit, with hood, reinforced feet and an attachment for an air supply and mask. I'd come across a chemical warfare suit. If I needed any further evidence, there two air bottles hid between the side of the couch and the coat rack. Each one bore clear markings that they were property of the imperial government and not for underwater use.

Slowly, I closed the lid. Donny had been serious. He intended to anthrax two entire malls. I shuddered. With a deep breath, my fingers latched the suitcases closed as my eyes scanned the room for the big tamale, the anthrax.

I searched the briefcase first. It held three million in cash, more money than most people make in a lifetime. Presumably, Donny had gotten part of his pay up front. The money made a great consolation prize, but I kept looking for the anthrax.

Only the term 'awe' can describe what I felt when I found the anthrax and held it in my hands. Packaged in foil and tightly sealed plastic, splattered with Chinese pictograms and numbers, I felt the Touch of God on my shoulder the moment I found it in the file cabinet. I'd held

C5, C6, semtex, detcord, and all manner of firearms, but nothing compared to the rush I got gazing on anthrax.

The fine white powder held the power to take thousands, if not tens of thousands of lives. With this, I could change the world. I could avenge Julie's death by wiping out entire office complexes of Specials and clean out boardrooms coast to coast. Not a single corporation would survive if and where I chose to deploy this weapon in New York, Boston, or London. With this powder, I could determine the fate of the empire and decide once and for all how the people of these lands would live.

The very thought set the Eye of God on me, and I bathed in His golden light. Nicholas Papadopoulos, Savior of the World. My eyes closed as I breathed. The stone that the builders rejected, got made into the corner stone. I could achieve what Julie and I dreamed. I could give her death meaning it never had, and in the same instant make myself more than a legend, I could shock...

The sound of the garage door opening snapped me out of my thoughts, and the Eye of God drew back to leave me in the brutal reality of Earth. Donny's minions had returned.

A swift push closed the file cabinet drawer. A swift tug freed the silenced pistol and only then did it come to mind that I'd left the *Pica-Pau* and DR-16 in the SUV. There was no way I should have made a mistake like that. I'd been distracted by the gunshot wound.

Knowing I wasn't functioning at one hundred percent didn't make me more confident. Neither did the knowledge that they would be alert. They'd no doubt seen the strange vehicle in their garage and knew company had arrived. Did they know Donny was dead? Did they even know he'd gone looking for me? I could only guess.

As quickly as I could, I tiptoed to the front room and stepped around the corner, waiting in ambush. If they entered through the garage door, they would come through the kitchen, into the dining room and then into the main room. I would be waiting. I drew up around the corner, where the hallway from the front door joined the main room, and clicked the safety off.

My back pressed against a polished wood bathroom door, and, on impulse, I opened the knob and stepped inside, leaving the light off and stepping back behind the door. The inner crack left me enough room to see into the main room, though the door hid me from sight on their most likely approach through the kitchen.

The sound of my heart beating eclipsed the burn in my shoulder and I struggled to contain my breathing, which is anything but easy when you're simultaneously in pain and experiencing an adrenaline rush.

Somewhere far away but in the vicinity of the garage door, I heard a sinister creak, eerie in its solitude. I closed my eyes, picturing them coming in, picturing them peering around the corner and into the house.

"Boss?" came a voice, almost timid but tough. In the movies, the criminals are always pushovers by the handsome skinny good guy, but in reality, they're usually big, mean, tough sons of bitches, and they're not afraid to hurt you.

Silence greeted Silvio's voice. My hand tightened on the grip of the pistol, and I felt the tickle of sweat on my shoulder blades. For some reason, my tongue couldn't get comfortable in my mouth. It rubbed up against my tooth and itched, forcing me to consciously ignore the irritation. The harder I tried to ignore it, the more insistent it became.

Beneath my feet, I felt an ever so slight change in the floorboards, as if someone tiptoed carefully in my direction. In my mind, Silvio and Sym advanced through the kitchen, one covering while one moved, like professionals. I took a breath, and saw them in my mind's eye again, Silvio signaling all clear as he assumed a firing stance and let Sym advance.

The seconds dragged on. How long they took, I couldn't say, but it felt like an eternity, the kind of eternity that keeps you on the balls of your feet and makes you wish you were already dead. A bead of sweat trickled down my temple but I didn't dare move to brush it back, just in case I accidentally touched something and gave my position away. I stayed stock still.

Through the crack in the door, I felt a slight change in the air just before my arrow slit of sight suddenly went black at eye level. One of them had approached the corner and leaned over as quickly as rain drops from the sky. Without a sound, the shadow moved back and away from the narrow slit of light. I could make out some kind of motion from the shadow of the man's arm, but couldn't hear so much as a breath. He'd checked the bathroom.

The barrel of my pistol tilted up, business end ready to fire through the door. A floorboard creaked. My tongue shifted in my mouth. I resisted the urge to swallow. The shadow moved again.

"No one's home," came a hushed whisper, followed by the sound of someone flapping an arm.

Through the rectangle I could see the back of a beefy man with grey hair that had solid shoulders and an impressive physique. He wore a grey turtleneck and black trousers, not flamboyant at all. My best guess told me I'd spotted Sym for the first time. One hand hefted a large pistol, the kind of magnum you usually only see in cop movies. His left hand held his right wrist to brace his arm.

A whisper came from the other end of the room in a voice so low I couldn't make heads or tails out of what he said. I licked my lips, hoping that they would drop their guard.

A small beep sounded in the room, then another. Sym seemed to be waiting for something. Seconds passed one by one.

Donny's cell phone seemed to scream into the silence as it chirped in my front pocket.

I didn't have time to curse my luck, or blame myself for not having turned it off. I whirled back away from the door, as stunned as the two men must have been that Donny's phone rang so close. One foot almost slipped on the tiles and my shoulder fired a painful warning shot as I brought the pistol up in both hands. Sym finished turning around, but the element of surprise was all mine.

Pfssst pfsst pfsstt sounded the silenced pistol in my hand, sounding more like a faded crack in the hollow indoor setting.

All three shots landed in the center of Sym's broad chest, and his grey eyes flew wide open in time to the black spots grouped around his heart.

Sym made a sound like he couldn't breathe -- he probably couldn't -- and slumped back against the wall, knees buckling, wide eyes already losing the light of life.

I stuck my head out the door as Sym collapsed into a sitting position that reminded me of the one Larry Scheuer had fallen into before Lucky pushed him over with her toe.

A bullet cracked into the wood just over my head, and I ducked back, then on instinct, ducked again. Silvio's pistol fired three more times, punching through the plasterboard where my head and shoulders had been only a moment before.

I collapsed to the floor like I'd been hit, making a sound as close to any man I'd ever heard shot, letting my lungs empty in a rattle. With one foot, I pushed back against the wall, using the pistol to cover the bathroom door as my shoulders slid involuntarily across the tiles. With eyes and gun focused, I waited for Silvio to appear and assess the damage.

Donny Paglia's phone chirped once more and then kicked over to voicemail.

I reckoned without Silvio's savvy in the way of the gun. Instead of peering around the door where I could put a bullet between his eyes, he thrust his pistol around the corner and fired blind and low. It took all my willpower to stay cool and quiet as the porcelain toilet exploded into fragments and water from the bowl rushed out onto the floor.

Another bullet passed right over my shoulder and thudded into the wall with another spray of plaster and a muted metallic ring from inside the wall. Scariest of all, the last bullet went right between my legs.

It shattered the tile and threw chips up onto my face, but didn't hit anything precious. Water from the broken toilet soaked my pants.

Silvio had burned his element of surprise, and luck favored me, I kept still and aimed once more towards the door, hoping he couldn't hear me breathing.

Donny's phone beeped in my pocket, reminding him that he had missed a call.

Silvio didn't take chances. Instead of taking a quick glance inside the door, he pushed the pistol around the corner again, ready to fire, but this time I was ready. At a distance of only six feet, I fired first, and hit.

Silvio's hand spun away like a billiard ball struck by a hard hit cue ball. The gun flew from his hand and he cried out in pain and surprise.

Without thinking, I pushed myself to my feet and scrambled after his retreating footsteps. Surprisingly, he didn't head for the garage door. He bolted for the den. I got off one quick shot that nicked him in the buttocks and made him jump as he disappeared through the doorway.

Assuming that Silvio had a gun hidden somewhere in the den, I charged after him, only to come up short as his unarmed but dangerously larger frame appeared in the doorway. I'd run into Silvio's ambush.

Stars flew as the hood's fist collided with my jaw, and knocked me back against the wall, barely managing to hold onto my gun. Silvio closed, one hand gripping my wrist, the other wrapping around my shoulders, using his upper body strength to push me down inch by inch. Not for the first time in my life I wished I was taller and stronger.

The irresistible strength of the goon had me gasping in exertion as I struggled to keep my footing, unable to bring the gun to bear, slowly losing the hand to hand struggle as we came face to face, only an inch away from each other, close enough to cut nose hairs and smell breakfast.

Silvio's face showed pure determination. Mine must have shown strain because he redoubled his efforts.

My free hand depended on my wounded shoulder, which cried out in pain every time I strained against the stronger man. Nevertheless, I desperately flailed at Silvio's face, trying to get a fingernail into his eye. He dodged, he shifted, he squinted and some of the pressure came off, but he kept the advantage.

Desperately, I leaned my head back and brought my forehead squarely down on the bridge of his nose.

Silvio cried out and stepped back in shock for a fraction of a second, but then blindly surged forwards, arms curled like a bear. I managed to get half a step to one side and shove the pistol into his rib cage. As I pulled the trigger, he arched his back and went stiff from head to toe, just like in the movies.

The square jaw of the man trembled as the strength seeped from his arms and he sagged, hands weakly clawing at my biceps for support. He sank to his knees, then slumped to one side. One the ceiling I could see the bullet's impact, a fine spray of red the size of a cantaloupe, looking like a scarlet still life drawing of a meteor.

Thankfully, I took long deep breaths, then slid down to rest on my wet butt. My hands shook uncontrollably, then my feet, then my legs, and I found myself shaking the fear, just like the old Spartans used to do after a battle.

Unlike when I'd first taken up this life, shaking the fear didn't last longer than a few moments. In the beginning, releasing the stress had brought tears to my eyes and even my jaw trembled as I shook, but as time went by, I seemed to be developing a tolerance for fear. Three or four minutes of shaking, mostly in my shoulders, but also my legs, and I found my breath slowing, my body relaxed, my eyes closed.

By the time Red stood on the porch with his hands in his pockets, an hour later, I'd done a lot. I'd made up my mind what to do with the anthrax and how I would let the world know what I'd done

I'd set up the laptop on the kitchen table and typed a note to Truman Hess, which I'd left up on the screen. I'd also typed up another letter, which I'd copied onto a CD from the den along with selected conversations we'd recorded in our eavesdropping, excluding Lucky's death. I needed time to swallow that bitter pill before sharing it with the world.

I photographed the anthrax packages and labels with Donny's digital camera, and added the files to the CD, then made multiple copies.

Last but not least, I suited up in the den and opened one bag of anthrax, carefully measuring a finger's worth into each of seven plastic baggies, then resealed the main supply and carefully stowed the unopened bag in one of the suitcases, using the lab suit to provide some padding. The individual baggies I triple bagged, wrapped and then rolled in tin foil until they looked like fat cigars.

"Don't touch anything," I cautioned Red as he stepped inside. "The cops are going to find this place soon and I don't want them to get your fingerprints.

Red nodded, stepping over Sym's body.

"You did this?" he asked, sounding impressed.

"Not without some effort," I replied, polishing off the last of a salami sandwich I'd helped myself to. I brushed crumbs from my coat, drained the last of a glass bottle of soda, and burped.

"We clean you fingerprints?" Red asked.

"Nope," I told him with a grin. "I want them to be sure it was me." I smiled, tugging the pistol and its attached silencer from my belt. "That's for their ballistics lab, just to make sure there's no mistake."

"Why you want this?" gaped Red with a look of pure confusion.

"So that they'll know we *didn't* use the anthrax, of course. Now, let's get out of here."

I hefted the suitcase containing the anthrax and we stashed it in the secret compartment under the front seat of Red's pickup, which was also where he kept his rifles. Fortunately, there would be plenty of room for me with a little squeeze.

"If we don't use the anthrax, and everyone knows we didn't use the anthrax but could have, we'll do more for our cause than we would if we used it or held it in reserve," I explained to Red as we got things arranged by the light of the rising sun.

As much as the deadly powder made me feel like a god, it couldn't be used, not by us. If we used anthrax, we would be stained beyond redemption forevermore. If we could get the truth out into the public light, then we had a better chance of making political gains. Sadly, they would be limited gains, but better limited than none at all.

"How police going to find this place?" asked Red with that sour expression on his face, like he kept thinking I would forget something. "Maybe one two three weeks before someone come here."

From my front pocket I took the last item I'd stolen from Donny's home, a can of spray paint. Just before I ducked into the cab, I turned to the white garage door. Using the can of spray paint, in large sweeping strokes, I spray painted the upraised fist, the sign of revolution past and present. I sprayed it large, thick, and easily visible from the street.

"They'll be here soon," I promised Red, clapping him on the shoulder. "Trust me."

And so I left Winterpeg, like a thief in the night. In my wake, I left little trail, save for the message to the Specials. For the typical citizen of Winnipeg, I left little more than a rumor that once tied up traffic. The few bodies would go to the morgue, the records would be updated, the Specials would give up, and the city would slowly return to normal. Brad the Bartender would spend the rest of his life behind his bar, telling and retelling the story of how he had once known the most notorious killer ever spawned by the September Alliance...

Nicky Pops.

Truman Hess read Nicky's note late on the evening Nicky departed Winnipeg, exactly twelve hours after Nicky wrote it.

Dear Truman,

I'm gambling that you are the one honest man in government. If I'm wrong, then things aren't worse than before, but if I'm right, you might be able to serve true justice instead of chasing me around the ten dominions. You'll never catch me anyway.

The three men I killed were former members of the Longanza crime family. They should have stayed in River Valley and run numbers or they would be alive today. Instead, they decided to get involved with some people who have a different agenda and wanted to nuke a couple of shopping malls and pin it on us and make us look like murderers. (We may be murderers, but we serve justice and don't do this kind of thing.)

I wasn't able to discover who Donny Paglia worked for. I'm leaving that up to you. Somehow or other they got ahold of Anthrax all the way from China and used the Mongols to deliver it. They wanted to use it on the people in the Mall of the Americas and Edmonton Mall. If you doubt me, you will find maps and ventilation engineering diagrams of both malls in the den. They have Donny's writing on them.

I've left you one of the two bags of Anthrax that I took from the guys. I took the other one because I don't know if we can trust the police or some of your specials so I thought I would play it safe. You'll find the other bag where only you and yours would visit. If you can't find it, take out a personal ad in Imperial News and I'll let you know some other way. Same as last time.

I can't investigate this any more. All my leads are dead ends, but you can. I've left you Donny's cell phone and you should be able to look at the call records, find out who payed for the house. He was also with a lawfirm called Fester, Fowler, Fagan, and Finch. Maybe there is a lead there. The bosses name is Baxter. Follow Baxter and you'll find the people who ordered this. I've left you the recordings I made of their phone calls, and his computer should have something too. Maybe his credit cards but you know how to do that better than me.

I should let you know that I have a little of the anthrax set aside, but I'm not going to use it. I'm sending seven samples to the editors of major media outlets with my real name but fake return addresses. They will also get copies of the recordings and all the evidence I can give them. The anthrax samples are proof and there is some other stuff as well. It isn't that I don't trust you. I don't trust the people above you and this is good for both our sakes.

Nicholas Papadopoulos

P.S. For what its worth, I'm sorry about your wife. I feel really bad about how she died. It wasn't me who pulled the trigger. It wasn't supposed to be that way. Remember I lost someone I loved too. If I could bring them back I would.

When he finished reading the note, Truman immediately called his three most trusted aides into his office and closed the door. The four men remained closeted inside the office for over six hours as they discussed the ramifications of Nicky's note and the evidence he had left. They also allowed the search for Nicky to continue in Winnipeg for two additional days, even though they had no hope of finding him.

I returned to River Valley with flowers and the business of revolution in a plastic bag under my arm, a pistol in my belt, and a wreath in my hand. My hometown boasted the honor of being the single most dangerous place I could visit, even with the disguise Butterfly had made in a Duluth hotel room.

Red and I met up with Pyro and Butterfly in a wind blighted frontier city called Fargo, just south of Winnipeg. Pyro was an old friend and comrade from Los Angeles and a former navy firefighter who had served beside me and impressed me with his pyrotechnic talents during the Val-Mart offensive. Butterfly, a new and incredibly beautiful face, had a career diplomat for a father and the pampered daughter of an Indian Raj for a mother. Where most of the women I'd met in the revolution had been good looking, sleek and sultry, Butterfly was the first to be out and out beautiful, and her experience with makeup and clothing went beyond the salons and into Hollywood territory. She was, in essence, a mistress of disguise.

We came from the four corners of empire, and four different walks of life, but we had one thing in common. We all had orders to proceed to New York. Along the way, the last chapter in the story of anthrax would be written in River Valley, where my war had begun.

I didn't expect Truman Hess to understand what I meant when I said I would leave the anthrax in a place where only he and his would find it. I knew little of his lifestyle or personal habits. He'd made it his business to know all of mine. It was his job to know that.

Truman had buried Kathy Hess in the southwest corner of Harvard Grove Cemetery, located on the southwest side of the city. Ironically, Julie's mother buried on the same grounds, but on the northern edge. I'd downloaded a map of the cemetery and marked both plots on the printout, easy enough to do since both Kathy and Julie qualified as 'persons of interest'.

Kathy had been interred in a medium sized family plot with knee high markers and well tended brown grass. Winter would soon arrive and cover it all with a pristine white blanket of snow, but for the moment, leafless trees and iron grey dawn made me feel like I truly walked in the land of the dead. Occasional ice cold rain droplets gave Kathy's headstone a bullet ridden appearance.

For a moment it seemed odd that a stone plaque should be all that remained of someone who had the energy to cheat on her husband, the fire of will to spit in our faces as we held her prisoner and the sheer guts to reach into her purse for a pistol against two men with pistols already drawn. I saw her again before my eyes, blonde, slim, eyes full of defiance. It almost felt wrong to have killed her, but I didn't dwell.

With the respect people instinctively show the dead, I bent down and planted the bag of anthrax at the foot of her headstone, along with the note flagging it to the Hess family's attention complete with appropriate names and phone numbers at the Ministry of Special Investigations anti-terrorism hotline. To give it some protection from the elements, I covered it with the wreath. One week before Christmas, I didn't think it would attract attention.

When I rose, I stared out at the sea of headstones, each of which marked not just a life, but a life story, however long or short.

With a lump in my throat, I passed though the land of the dead, finding Julie's tiny headstone in a sparsely populated section not far from the wrought iron cemetery fence. A cold wind blew through my padded disguise. Thanks to Butterfly, I currently resembled a greying middle-aged man with a thick gut, big nose and glasses. If Julie could see me, she would turn over in her grave.

Where Kathy Hess' headstone had been as normal as any other, Julie's had attracted more attention. The dead grass around the smaller stone still bore flecks of black paint and I could see how part of the polished stone had been scrubbed clean of cruel graffiti. The uppermost part of her headstone also bore the melted stubs of candles and dried flowers that had been left with respect.

I'm not sure what I'd expected Julie's final resting place to look like, but that cold morning, I felt that as insignificant as her burial place seemed, she had somehow left her imprint on the world. Why else would there be signs of love and hate where she rested?

On one knee, I set a gloved hand on top of Julie's stone. I wished, truly wished, that I knew what she thought just before she died. Did she die mocking me? Did she think of me as a fool? I knew she didn't love me, but there were far worse things to have been in her eyes and I prayed that none of them applied.

I could draw on Julie's spirit still. For the first time, I had command of a squad headed into dangerous territory and not all of them would survive. I hoped and prayed that I made a difference in the world, and that whatever I had foiled in Winnipeg would eventually come clear. If I thought that to justify my own actions, I didn't feel it inside.

The wind stirred the leafless trees, and I listened in case Julie spoke from beyond the grave, but of course, she didn't, so I recited everything that had happened over the last year. I told her of my desperate gambit to free her, and how we'd brought Val-Mart to its knees, and how we'd foiled the anthrax plan.

Once finished, I took seven steps with tears in my eyes before spun about and trotted back, gripping her tombstone tightly in both hands, this time with tears of real grief.

"It isn't fair that I loved you so much," I sobbed. "And it isn't fair that you aren't here to see what I've become. You always said never to surrender but I've done a lot more than that. I've taken command of a squad of my own and I've brought Val-Mart down and saved a few thousand people from being anthraxed to death. I'm fighting hard in the revolution and you're not here to see it."

With a deep breath that stuck in my ribs, I wiped the tears from my eyes with the sleeve of my winter coat.

"I just wish you could see it. We're going to win someday, I can feel it."

Only the emptiness of the winterscape answered.

"Goddamnit," I finally whispered, pounding my fist on her tombstone. "Why did you leave me? I still love you, Julie. I do. Think of me as a fool for loving you but I love you even now, revolution or not I loved you from the first moment I first saw you."

I closed my eyes and listened hard for some kind of an answer, some sign that my words had been heard. I listened in love and grief and rage so intently that I started to lose my balance and the cold ran up and down my sleeves and back and my feet started to feel numb.

Only silence replied.

The following news article appeared in the Winnipeg Daily News and in most syndicated newspapers throughout the empire.

PATSI Defeated for Good

The vaunted Patriotic Anti-Terrorism and Sedition Initiative died a final death in the parliaments of the Great Plains and Mountain Dominions yesterday. The double defeat by a slim margin in both bodies appears to have been the result of an abatement of terror attacks in recent months.

Desmond Redgrave, from the London based Center for Legal Studies, had this to say. "PATSI had a lot of provisions that didn't sit well with the public at large or with the tradition of freedom and political participation that we take for granted. So long as there were terrorist attacks, people were willing to make concessions in their personal freedoms. Without the terrorist attacks, they saw no reason to do so."

The close votes, 103-97 and 102-98, and lack of abstentions showed just how easily a major terrorist attack could have changed the face of empire. Prior to the attacks in New York City, many predicted even more serious defeats. The fact that the September Alliance quickly issued a disclaimer and issued promises that the newly formed splinter cell would be "dealt with", probably cost PATSI its ratification.

Truman Hess of the Drummer Boys also appeared in quotes today, saying that with or without PATSI, his office had more than enough authority to aggressively pursue terrorists under current law, and that the additional powers PATSI would have given his agents are actually available today, but with due process under court supervision. "All it means is that we need to get permission from a judge first," scoffed Hess.

Indeed, Hess' words seem to echo that of many lawmakers across the empire, where anti-PATSI feelings have grown and intensified under scrutiny. According to the most prominent nay voter from Winnipeg, Jasper Wright, as time went by, opposition to PATSI crescendoed into a rabid pitch.

"If our vote in parliament reflected public opinion, it would have been one fifty to fifty. I tell you, there was a lot of money behind this drive, and we all felt it, but still, without some kind of credible terrorist threat, in the end, we couldn't turn our traditions upside down because of something that might happen in the future. When they drafted the initiative, we had an active, dangerous terrorist network to worry about. Now we don't."

Later that day, Truman Hess denied rumors that the Drummer Boys had stopped a major terrorist attack against an unspecified shopping mall. "I can only tell you we did no such thing," he was quoted as saying.

For the first time since I'd joined the revolution, I felt the weight of leadership on my shoulders. As I slid into the back seat of the car, and I saw the three faces of *my* men and women turn to me for direction, I knew for the first time I could never walk away, never leave. Born into a terrorist's life, I would live it until death.

Their eyes turned as one, waiting, expecting. Right now, they were three, soon they would be five and perhaps six. Their lives rested in my hands. I was a long way from the college student Julie had recruited for his naiveté. In the last year, I'd grown up, and in the last hours, I knew I would never leave the revolution alive

There's a lot I can do right in this revolution, and a lot of good that can be done in this world. Just because the business of revolution is never clean doesn't mean that the business of revolution doesn't cleanse.

Purified by blood and fire, I have left one family and joined another. Cat, Freddie, Pyro, Deuce, Maya, Rico, and now Butterfly and Red, they are more than friends, they are comrades, and they need me. Fate links us together in life as it will in death and history. I need no more reason to do what I do than those who are at my side. I need no books. I need grasp no theories. I need faith in myself and in our cause and I need the trust of my comrades in arms.

"All for one," I said, as I laid my palm out in the center.

Three hands slapped down onto mine, uniting in one large fist from four.

"And all for one," they echoed.

I clapped my free hand down on top of the stack with a solid slap that echoed in the car. Through life and death we would stand together, bound by a sacred bond of blood. Students, professors and killers, we will change the world.

Brace yourself New York.

About the Author

David Landt lives and works in Chicago, Illinois with his beautiful wife and lovely daughter. He loves to travel and has a degree in International Studies. He does not support terrorism in any way, shape, or form.